MURDER
in the
French Quarter

Lee Frost

PublishAmerica
Baltimore

© 2004 by Lee Frost.
All rights reserved. No part of this book may be reproduced, stored in a retrieval system or transmitted in any form or by any means without the prior written permission of the publishers, except by a reviewer who may quote brief passages in a review to be printed in a newspaper, magazine or journal.

First printing

ISBN: 1-4137-3157-0
PUBLISHED BY PUBLISHAMERICA, LLLP
www.publishamerica.com
Baltimore

Printed in the United States of America

With immense admiration,
the author dedicates this book to his darling wife,

Phyllis

whose brilliance, tenacity and undying love
made this project possible.

Chapter 1

Day 1

IT WAS WEDNESDAY, March 1st, just after one in the morning. A light rain was falling in New Orleans. Eddie Marshall drove his white five year old Volvo station wagon down Canal Street, turned right onto Bourbon Street, and proceeded into the French Quarter. After driving one block, he crossed Bienville Street. This was now the start of the official nine block long area, which was where the action of the French Quarter really got its reputation.

Mardi Gras had ended only a week before, but the hangers-on were still there in mass, looking for one more big party. Eddie drove slowly down Bourbon Street, hitting his brakes as a group of drunks lumbered past the front of his car.

The Quarter had a life of its own. You could buy a drink here, twenty-four hours a day, three hundred sixty-five days a year. The area was full of bright lights and fast action. People danced in the street, moving from bar to bar, from girly shows to Dixieland joints. It was all there.

Eddie drove slowly for three more blocks and finally stopped just before he came to Toulouse Street. A large crowd had gathered at the corner. Some people had umbrellas, but most did not. Getting drenched did not bother this crowd. After all, they were in the Big Easy!

A young girl was perched on her boyfriend's shoulders, he was holding her by her ankles. What was happening here was a ritual of Mardi Gras, or the joy of the Quarter, or just for being in the Big Easy. Eddie sat in the car, waiting. He knew it would all be over in a few minutes. Eddie was in no hurry.

High above the young girl and her friend was another crowd of people on the balcony the Kit Kat Klub. They were all challenging the young girl to show them her breasts. Women and men all shouted in unison, "Show your tits! Show your tits!" As they continued their chant, others on the street below joined in. "Show your tits. Show your tits."

The girl who straddled her boyfriend's shoulders was named Cindy; his name was Chuck. She was a long-legged lovely young thing of nineteen, he was a football player type of twenty. She wore a pair of skin tight Levi's and a pair of Adidas tennies. She wore a light grey sleeveless cut-off jersey, which just covered her breasts. Chuck had seen her breasts before, even fondled them on occasion. Cindy knew she had a great set. They were perfect. Now came the challenge.

As Cindy sat on Chuck's shoulders, hearing the pleading from the crowed around her, she became more and more convinced, that showing her breasts was the right thing to do. She grabbed the jersey at the bottom and slowly pulled it upward. The screaming crowd went quiet, in anticipation of what was to be revealed. But Cindy was only teasing them. She released her hold on the shirt, and waived her hands high in the air. Then the cheers resumed. "Show your tits. Show your tits."

Once again, Cindy grabbed at the bottom of the shirt, and she pulled it up just below her neck, showing off the greatest set of mammary glands anyone could remember. The cheer from the crowd was deafening. Cameras started flashing, necklaces started sailing. A torrent of beads flew through the air. Cindy was smiling, enjoying the moment of gratification.

A car behind Eddie honked its horn. Eddie glanced back and then forward. He hit his horn twice, and the crowd to his front started to part. Eddie slowly pulled forward and moved on down Bourbon.

In the next block he passed the Dixieland Bar and Grill. Red Moon and his band were playing, 'When the Saints Go marching in'. Then in the seventh block things started to change. The street suddenly got quiet. Eddie had moved into the residential section of the quarter.

It was still raining. No one was there. It was almost like a scene in a science fiction movie. He drove a few more blocks to St. Ann Street, turned left, and parked just up the street.

Eddie was a large man, six feet two and about two hundred eighty pounds, in his early forties. He wore an LSU sweatshirt, with the sleeves cut off at the top. LSU stood for Louisiana State University. His light brown hair was cut short, almost considered a crew cut. Eddie may have been in his early forties, but his hair cut and sweatshirt might pass him for a man in his mid-thirties, even late twenties. He carried a plastic bag.

Eddie walked back to Bourbon Street, dodging the rain as it fell from the covered balconies up above, and quickly moved into the laundry facing on Bourbon. There, he was greeted by an African American woman, Lila Washington, the owner and operator of the "French Laundry, Fluff and Fold."

"What's goin' on here?" Lila asked. Lila was a large woman in her mid fifties, and she wore a light colored house dress that totally covered her girth. Eddie had been in this laundry three nights before and also on several other previous occasions. Lila had never noticed him. The last night he was there, three other patrons were also present, but Eddie did not wish to become involved with outsiders. Now he was pleasantly surprised that only Lila was there.

"I'm going to die on this one," Eddie answered. "I just stained the shirt I gotta wear tomorrow, to my wedding. I spilled some red wine on the sleeve." Eddie dropped down on one knee. "Please help me stay out of the hell for my sins of this night. I just had a bachelor party. How bad can it get?"

Lila started to laugh. "Okay, I'll fix it. Where you got the shirt?"

He opened his plastic bag and removed the shirt, handing it to Lila. She took it to the far back of the room and spread it on a table.

As soon as Lila got busy with her work, Eddie casually moved away from her, heading for the service counter area located in the front, on the left. What Eddie needed was to find the location of the overhead light switches.

When Eddie was here last Monday, he studied the wall, looking for a light switch, but was unable to find any. Then he noted that there were five half inch pipes, possibly electrical conduits, that ran thought the room, and concluded inside the under counter area. Since the place was always lit, the electrical installer simply ran the power directly to the switch box.

Eddie quietly moved in, opened a few of the cabinets, and finally found the circuit breaker box at the far left. He slowly pulled the door to the box open, revealing the operating panel which was labeled with plastic stick um, machine. The number one position was labeled "Lights left," and the number two position was labeled, "Lights right." Below that were five switches marked for electrical plugs throughout the room.

Lila mixed some white stuff, and spread in over the stained sleeve, then rinsed it off. It was perfect.

"There you go, honey," Lila offered. "You wanna wash an' press job on this?"

"No thank you ma'am. I got that covered. How much do I owe you?"

Lila suggested two-fifty for her expertise, Eddie gave her five. He then thanked her again and left.

He walked across the street, not looking back. He didn't want to look back. She might have been watching. He did not wish to act suspicious. Just leave the laundry and walk out of sight.

Eddie walked around the block. It took about eight minutes by his watch, and he wound up back on the corner of St. Ann and Bourbon. He walked into the market, located just across the street from the laundry and got a cup of coffee from the old guy in the back. He then walked to the front and paid the cashier fifty cents. She wore a red T-shirt and was doing a crossword puzzle, but she took a moment from her task to take his money.

Eddie sat down on a high stool over by the long tables, watching the movement from the laundry across street. From there he could easily see Lila inside. She would soon leave for a quick break, if she maintained her evening schedule. It was just a matter of when would she do it. He was patient.

The Quarter streets were narrow, most of them only 18 yards wide including the sidewalk. One could easily see across the street. Eddie sat with his hand covering his face, so as not to be recognized if spotted by Lila. At about 2:10 a.m., she took her break.

She left the deserted laundry wide open and walked up Bourbon Street toward Lafitte's Black Smith Shop. The fact was, the laundry was self managed. Every operation it the place was handled with coins. Two quarters operated the washing cycle, two more for the dryer, and one quarter for each, soap and bleach. So for two fifty you did a whole load of laundry. Nobody with a crowbar would ever try to rob this place. This was, after all, the "Big Easy."

When Eddie was there two weeks ago, there had been two others doing their wash and Lila did the same thing. Shortly after two in the morning, she announced she would be back in a few minutes and left. Now when Lila left, the place was empty. Eddie took total advantage of the situation.

He returned to his car and popped the trunk and withdrew a heavy laundry sack. It weighed about one hundred twenty-five pounds, more than a bag of clothing, but Eddie handled it as though it were a rag doll. With the laundry sack slung over his shoulder, he quickly walked back to the laundry, went inside and placed the bag on the floor.

Eddie was breathing heavily, not from the weight of the bag, but more from the anticipation of things to come. He looked out of the door to the front. All he could see was the lady in the red T-shirt doing her crossword puzzle. He moved in behind the counter, kneeled down and threw the two top circuit breakers off. The room went dark.

There were two street lamps outside. The first was placed at the corner of Bourbon and St. Ann, the second down the street on St. Ann. Some light streamed into the room, giving only partial glimpses of Eddie and what he was doing.

He moved back to his laundry bag, and opened it up, took out a pair of rubber gloves and placed them on his hands. Then he reached deep into the bag and withdrew a naked, dead woman. You could see her face and head first. It had been battered beyond belief. Her right eye was swollen shut, and the entire side of her face had been savagely beaten. Dried blood covered the side of her head and matted her light blond hair. She may have been a pretty girl, but nobody could attest to that now.

Eddie grabbed her by the armpits, glanced back to make sure he wasn't being watched, then picked the naked body up and forced it into the clothes dryer. As he did so, he noted that a piece of paper he had taped to the lower back of her body had rubbed against the side of the dryer and had come free. It was important for Eddie to display this message. He stuck his hand inside the dryer and felt around for his note, found it at the bottom of the dryer, pulled it up and reattached it to the lady's back.

The dead girl was a small woman, about five foot two. Her body was a tight fit in the confines of the dryer, but Eddie managed to make it. The last thing he did was to force her head inside, and carefully push the door closed, causing her face to be shoved against the glass opening. Her body presented a grotesque picture for the entire world to see.

He had been back in the laundry for almost three minutes. Any second, someone could have come in. Eddie was starting to breathe heavily. He glanced outside and saw that the lady in the red T-shirt, was now oblivious to her surroundings, searching her crossword dictionary for a word. Eddie stepped back and admired his work. It pleased him.

He walked back behind the front desk, snapped the top breaker back on, and slowly the fluorescent lights jumped back into life. Then Eddie casually moved off into the night, having done the best he could, and with no one knowing the consequence.

It was early Wednesday morning, a bright, lovely day, as Sam Pennington made his way from Barracks Street where his apartment was located and turned south onto Bourbon Street. Sam was enjoying one of the finest days New Orleans had to offer. The sun was shining, it was seventy degrees and a light breeze stirred the air.

Sam was in a relaxed mood, wearing one of his favorite outfits, charcoal gray slacks with a black dress shirt left open at the collar. He finished this off with his best black blazer. He also carried a black tie in his left hand jacket pocket, just in case a situation arose where he needed to dress up a bit. He was a rather good looking white American man, six feet tall, with dark brown hair and steel gray eyes.

This was Bourbon Street, notorious for wild music and wilder women. It was where it all happened. It was the place to party, known the world over. But that was the crazy part of Bourbon. That would happen five blocks down the street. This was the residential part of Bourbon, the lower Quarter, and the place where nice people lived. It was amazing how much difference five blocks could make. In this area, the houses were colorful and well appointed. Many of them were built in the 1800s and a few as early as the late 1700s, with lovely balconies and magnificent wrought iron railings – "lace" the locals called it.

Sam reached the St. Ann Market at Bourbon and St. Ann Street. It was an old, dilapidated place which had, in the mid 1800s, been a horse stable. He put fifty cents in the coin box outside and grabbed a newspaper. He pushed open the old green shuttered door to the market and entered.

The place smelled musty. Sam loved old and musty. The smell of the 1800s still saturated the area. The locals zipped in and out, gathering a few cans of foodstuff and maybe a six-pack of beer or some wine. But the real success of this market was in the back, where you could find a fairly good deli and a variety of food, ranging from oyster and shrimp and soft shell crab Po' Boys, to the famous café au lait and beignets.

Sam moved in, tossing his newspaper on the high table near the window. He pulled himself onto a stool and glanced toward the kitchen, immediately catching Phil's eye. Phil was a skinny guy about Sam's age. He owned the place and was among a long list of the true characters of the Quarter. Phil was balding and all the hair he had left was jet black and kinky curly, but what he had on his face was amazing. He sported huge bushy eyebrows and a large handlebar moustache. To tourists who visited the place, Phil appeared to be a carnival clown, but to the locals he was just one of the guys.

Phil knew Sam well. He knew what he wanted and just how he would order. He pointed at Sam, lifting his thick dark eyebrows upward. This movement translated to '*Hey Sam, how you doin'? You want the usual or you wanna discuss a new order?*' Sam returned a thumbs up to Phil, meaning, '*I'm fine Phil, just the usual please.*' Neither man cared for small talk.

There was some activity at the laundromat on the opposite corner, but Sam paid no attention. He turned to his newspaper, the *Times Picayune*, delving into the news of the day.

A police car with sirens blaring screeched its tires and stopped at the curb. This got Sam's attention. He peered through the haze of residual cooking fat that coated the market window and noticed two cops jump from the patrol car and run quickly into the laundromat. Sam was not interested in police activities and returned to his paper.

Phil came to Sam's table, setting a large heavy white mug down, followed by another heavy-duty dish holding three beignets, oppressively covered with powdered sugar. As he served Sam, Phil's attention was distracted. He saw through the dirty window that there was some police action across the street.

"Hey, what's going on over there?" Phil asked.

Sam ignored the question, took a sip of the coffee and a bite of his beignet. For those not in the know, a beignet is the French version of an American donut, but never the twain shall meet. Phil moved closer to the window and pulled a counter towel from his belt. He wiped a clean spot through the grease to gain a better look.

Phil was getting excited. "Now they got two more cars! What the hell is it?" Sam took a slow breath as he looked out of the window. Just then a carriage, drawn by a mule, stopped outside blocking his view. Eduardo, the driver of the carriage had two tourists in the back, and he was evidently explaining how the NOPD did their job.

Eduardo was one of the best-dressed carriage drivers in the Quarter. He was immaculate in his black frock coat with formal pleated tails that hung almost down to his ankles. All of this was capped off with a marvelous top hat, reminiscent of one worn by Abraham Lincoln; not as high as Lincoln's, but just high enough.

The carriage was also a thing of beauty. Two seats faced each other, with space for three on each seat. There were four garish vases at each corner of the carriage and each day Eduardo would fill them with colorful bouquets of fresh flowers. Finally there was the mule, Piccolo. His ears were stuck through a large straw hat, which had a beading of furry balls surrounding the brim. This took care of the flies that occasionally came to bother Piccolo.

Sam decided to leave the market. Phil and four other customers who were inside followed him. Everyone wanted to see what was happening. The narrow street allowed parking only on the right side, but a single line of cars could drive down the one-way street. If the cops had a problem here, traffic would be totally blocked in a matter of moments. Sam motioned for Phil to hold up at the front door of the market and he would check it out. As he started to cross the street, Sam paused in front of the mule, Piccolo, and offered half of his beignet in his open palm. The animal quickly lapped up the food. Eduardo laughed as he acknowledged Sam. He leaned forward and tossed his head in the direction of the laundromat. "Hey mon, what's shaking in there?"

A husband and wife, both tourists, leaned out on one side of the carriage, spotting Sam. He casually patted the mule on the cheek, in an effort to clean the dry powdered sugar from his palm, which sent up a small puff of white powder. Seeing this, the female tourist reacted.

"What was that?" she yelled out. "I saw that! What was that? Did you see that Larry?" she said to her husband.

Eduardo did his best to ignore the conversation from behind him.

"Did you see what that man gave to the horse?" The woman again asked her husband.

Eduardo turned to the couple. "What you sayin', lady?"

The woman was becoming frantic. She was sure she had seen a dope transaction and wanted real some action, right now. "The horse, the horse, that man gave something to your horse!"

Eduardo looked around for a horse and spotted Sam moving off to the laundromat. "Lady, this thing here is no horse, it's a mule." He gave a clicking sound with his mouth, snapped the reins, and the carriage moved on down Bourbon Street.

In only a few minutes a small crowd had gathered in front of the laundromat. There were now five police cars present. Traffic had quickly developed into an aggravating problem, with a single line of traffic stopped. A gridlock of great proportions was created. One officer was left outside, busily tying down the traditional yellow crime scene tape to divert all civilians from the area. When Sam reached the yellow tape the policeman looked up and recognizing him, quickly raised the tape, allowing Sam to slip under and move ahead.

Inside the laundry, three more cops were moving around the room. The place was small, only ten washers stacked against the north wall and ten dryers against the south wall. Sam's eyes quickly darted around, counting the living. There was only one civilian there, perhaps she was the owner, Sam thought. She was a black woman, heavy-set, middle-aged, wearing a white house dress. Her head was covered with a sheer off white cap, showing the back of her hair in curlers. He ignored her for the moment, and moved toward the cop located at the rear.

Officer Jim Fisher noticed Sam first. "Hey Sam, this you're case?" Jim was a fine cop, thirty-two years old, with a good attitude.

Sam smiled at Jim and flippantly said, "I just came in to get my socks. What do you boys have here?"

Jim smiled at Sam, catching his cynicism. He motioned to the last dryer, in the row of dryers at the back of the building. "She's right over there, in the dryer."

Sam's eyes squinted at the dryer, a large unit with a clear glass front window mounted at eye level. He moved closer to the unit and from the darkened corner of the room he could make out the body of a woman. As he drew closer, he saw she was younger rather than older, yet it was difficult to tell since she had been badly beaten about the head. Her face was pressed against the glass door, her mouth stretched open in a grotesque fashion.

"You guys keep everything clean?" Sam asked.

Jim moved in close to Sam. "I told them not to touch a thing."

"That's right, that's right," Sam replied, showing a feeling of sincerity. He then moved to the woman he thought might own the place, took his wallet from his coat breast pocket and flipped it open, displaying his badge number 218, along with his ID. "I'm Detective Pennington," he stated. "New Orleans police department."

"Oh God, they told me you'd be comin' to take control of this thing. I'm glad you here."

"Thank you, ma'am. And you are?"

"I'm Lila Washington. Do you have any idea what a dead body in my clothes dryer can create? Nobody in miles will want to use my dryers again. Any idea what that will do to my business? Huh? Do you?"

Sam opted to ignore her questions. "Did you see who did it?"

"No! Absolutely not! What kind a place do you think this is, anyway? I was next door for only a half hour. I got back here an' the place was empty. Then, after I was cleaning up and I found it. I was shocked to hell, I'll tell you that."

Just then Sam noticed a black car pull up onto Bourbon. Detective William Joseph Mays got out of the car followed by his deputy carrying an ID case. They headed toward the laundry. Sam's eyes focused on Mays. He was fifty-two years old, about five feet ten inches tall and thirty pounds overweight, with a small bald spot developing in the center of his head. Sam stood six feet tall and could easily see that bald spot.

Mays always wore a light gray suit with a white shirt, which was too tight for his fat neck. As though that wasn't enough, there was that usual yellow and blue tie. When he buttoned his jacket, it pulled tight around his enlarged belly, which pleated the coat at his middle. Today, his coat was open and what a break that was for everyone.

Mays worked out of Division 2 which was on the fringe of the Quarter, just on the other side of Rampart Street. Sam was assigned to Division 8, located on Royal Street in the heart of the Vieux Carre, the French Quarter.

Sam watched Mays as he neared the entrance to the laundry, then his eyes flicked back to Lila Washington. "I'll tell you what, ma'am," he said with great authority. "They have sent you a specialist in laundry murders. He's on his way in here right now. You answer his questions and he'll solve the crime." Sam headed for the door. Mays arrived as Sam left.

"Hello Sam," said Mays suspiciously. "You on this case?"

"Nah, just slumming." As Sam moved off, he glanced back over his shoulder. Mays stood there for a moment, looking after him.

Sam walked on, passing Phil still standing in front of the market.

"What is it, Sam?" Phil shouted. "What's going on?"

Sam gave Phil the OK sign and whispered in his ear. "They found a dead woman in a dryer. Last one at the rear. Avoid using that one and you'll be fine."

The Orleans Parish Police Headquarters was located on Royal Street, four blocks from Canal Street. Sam approached the building and quickly walked through the front door. It was a busy morning, lots of incoming arrests and outgoing releases. The cops basically dealt with the scum of the earth. Sam waved a hello to those cops who noticed him and moved into a small room at the back of the building. The sign on the door read 'Burglary & Homicide Division.'

The room was modest in size, with four desks for four detectives. The first two were empty. They were for Detectives Carey and Kennedy who were on assignment in Baton Rouge. In the back of the room, near the Mr. Coffee machine, his new trainee assistant, Wally White, was on the phone. Wally was a young man, with a white father and a black mother, not unusual in this city. He had been on the force for seven years and after prodding Sam to get him in the detective unit, Wally passed the detective test and now he was a trainee. Sam liked Wally a lot.

Wally hung up the phone and looked at Sam. "I was checking on the whistle," Wally said. "They can't hear a thing."

Sam walked over to Mr. Coffee and grabbed two cups. He looked at Wally with eyebrows raised, in silent question.

"No, thank you, I've had enough," Wally said. "Well, maybe a half a cup."

Sam poured two full cups as Wally ran through the messages. Then he looked at his watch. "You gotta be in court at ten o'clock. The assistant DA called. I was about to page you when you walked in."

Sam's body sagged for a moment, then he firmed himself up and set the two cups on Wally's desk. "By the way, I have no idea what you were talking about." Sam asked. "What whistle?"

"Oh yeah," Wally said. "The guy at the garage put your car up on the rack and ran it. Says he can't hear a thing. I told him we ran it above thirty-five and it drove us crazy and he said…"

Sam interrupted. "You take care of it." Sam headed for the court.

The Superior Courtroom was not nearly ready to start the day's calendar. A sign on the outside door read "Judge Marshall Williams" and below that was the case to be heard, "City of New Orleans vs. Joshua Skannes, Jr." When Sam entered the courtroom it was all but empty. Sam surmised that Jerry Weinstein and Judge Williams were probably in chambers. He didn't see any defense attorneys either, but there was a Court Clerk, a lovely black woman in her mid-thirties, sitting behind her desk. Sam walked up to the railing that divided the witnesses and the general public. He leaned over the railing, smiling warmly and caught her attention. She wore a plastic name tag, pinned to the lapel of her smart navy blue suit which read "Ms. Clara Williams."

"Excuse me, my name is Sam Pennington. Are you related to the judge?"

Giving him a questioning look, she replied, "No, why do you ask?"

Judge Williams was a new judge, recently appointed and not one whom Sam had not encountered before.

"Well, I noticed that this was Judge Williams' court and from your name tag that your name is Williams, so I was wondering if the judge had a pretty daughter." It was a phony line and Sam knew it, he just thought it might break some ice.

Ms. Williams provided a demur smile and tittered lightly. She spoke crystal clear English, unusual for an African American in the South. "No, actually Williams is a common name. How may I help you?"

Sam reached for his badge. "I'm a police officer, Sam Pennington, witness for the prosecution. Would you advise Jerry Weinstein that I am here?" Ms. Williams smiled at Sam, picked up the phone and dialed a number.

Sam withdrew to the back of the courtroom and took a seat. He opened the briefcase that Wally had prepared for him and started to formulate his folders of information for the trial. When he looked up, he saw Jerry Weinstein walking toward him.

Jerry was a fidgety man in his late thirties. Sam had a good word to say about every person he had ever met, with the exception of Jerry Weinstein. Jerry had a need to use blue language. He felt its use would cause him to sound more important, manlier. It only succeeded in making him sound crass and boorish.

Jerry was constantly worried about what others thought about him rather than what he provided to the situation. He was a lousy lawyer and, when challenged by the opposition, he often sought help from others. Jerry slid in the seat beside Sam.

"Good morning Sam, glad you made it."

Sam knew this was going to be a long day. "Hello Jerry, what's holding us up? As if I didn't know?"

Jerry hesitated, then looking Sam right in the eyes he said, "They want to plea bargain this one down to Manslaughter Two! That puts him in for ten years and he'll be out in four."

Sam's head fell to his chest. "And that's for killing a cop?"

Jerry put his hand on Sam's shoulder. "That's right! I said no fucking way!"

Sam had been in court with Jerry on at least a dozen occasions. On each of these situations, Jerry would always have Sam standing by, just in case he needed some quick behind-the-scenes reasoning, a backroom meeting in chambers, or at the very least, advise how they should approach a specific challenge the defense wanted to propose.

"Who's representing him?" Sam asked.

"Who do you think?" Jerry stated. "It's The Kingfish, Donald Mosely. That prick is making sounds like he intends to challenge every single bit of evidence we have. He's all smoke and mirrors. This is a simple little case, but these guys are going to drag it out like it was the most important front-page issue since the assassination of JFK! I'll tell you what Sam, you better be ready, and because I think they are going to keep you on the stand for at least two days. The whole shooting took only three and a half seconds. Bang and then two quick, bang bangs!"

"Take it easy Jerry, I'll be ready."

Jerry was getting frantic. "They have an expert to deal with the bullets in the body and the shells left in the gun. Your testimony has the first shot fired at you. It missed you and hit your car. Made a hole right through the driver's door. You never found the slug, right?"

Sam shook his head, no.

"Mosley will challenge that! Then they got an expert to challenge the cops on how they handled the collection of the evidence. Finally, they'll hit you guys for being racists!" Jerry looked steadily at Sam. "Have you seen Skannes Jr.'s rap sheet?"

Sam shook his head. "No."

"From age thirteen to seventeen he has been arrested and charged with fourteen felonies. How about that?"

Sam had a slight smile on his face. "But don't forget, he's got a rich daddy," Sam said. "It's the Big Easy."

Jerry was serious, no room for smiles and Big Easy jokes. "His rich daddy threw him out of the house two years ago," Jerry opined. "He's a bad-ass kid." Jerry took a glance at the door to the judge's chamber. "We took a five minute piss break, it's about over," Jerry stated. "You be here when I need you. You be ready when I need you." He leaned down to Sam's ear, talking very softly. "Listen to me carefully. The judge will not allow Junior's record to be admitted. He was just seventeen, a minor, and a child. A thieving little bastard who would have killed you in a heartbeat. Instead he got your partner. Hell, I've been fighting this case for six months. What Mosley plans to do is charge the cops with messing up the investigation. He's out to challenge you, my boy."

Jerry wasn't just venting his feelings, he was afraid. He started to walk away and stopped turning back to Sam. "I'll tell you something else. If you don't make a mistake, they will twist it around to make you look as bad as possible. If you do make a mistake, Mosley will hang your ass. That's what he does and on top of that, the judge is with him."

The door to the judge's chambers opened wide, revealing a dapper man in his early forties. It was Donald Mosley, the attorney for the defense. He was an impeccably dressed black man, wearing a navy blue Armani suit, with a matching blue French-cuffed shirt. His cuff links were brushed gold and silver and his tie was cream colored with a smattering of gold and silver dots. His haircut was fashionable and blow dried to finish.   Mosley's eyes quickly darted around the room. Upon seeing Jerry and Sam, he merely looked at the Rolex watch on his wrist, then back up at Jerry. He held both hands apart as though asking a question.

Jerry acknowledged Mosely. Under his breath he uttered through his teeth, "Okay you bastard, let's get it on."

As Jerry walked back across the courtroom, Sam ran his fingers through his hair. *I think I need a haircut.* Sam had a further thought about Jerry. He was a man who allowed himself to be bullied by a guy in an Italian suit. Sam decided right then and there he would work hard on this case. He'd prove the cops did the right thing and furthermore he'd prove that Skannes, Jr. murdered his partner in cold blood, by blasting his chest and stomach to pieces, with hollow point 'dum-dum' bullets. If Sam had anything to say about it, Jr. would be in Angola Prison for the rest of his life. That's what happens to bad-assed kids! He went back to his paperwork and thought about his partner, a lovely guy named Jack Arnold.

Jack Arnold was a good cop, tall with a rather pointed but handsome face. He was a 'no fooling around' type of guy. 'Just the facts, ma'am.' Jack was married to a pretty girl named Billie. If the truth were known, she was not thrilled with Jack being a cop. That was one of the reasons Sam didn't care for Billie, she wasn't standing squarely behind her man. Then all hell broke loose.

Six Months Earlier

Sam and Jack had spent the day in Baton Rouge, an hour's drive north from New Orleans. They had an exhausting time preparing for the Senate investigations concerning some illegal operations in the city.

They arrived back in New Orleans around six-thirty that evening. Jack was driving the black Pontiac four door Pacifica, Sam's newly assigned cop vehicle. It was Sam's pride and joy. It even had fake llama carpeting placed on the floorboards. Sam loved to take his shoes off and curl his toes through the fake thick fur.

As they swept over the high-rise bridge that carried you into the city, the Super Dome came into view. Sam always thought it was the most beautiful view one could possibly experience. The Super Dome was a magnificent domed stadium, home to the New Orleans Saints pro football team. Directly behind the dome was the rest of the city, its tall beautiful office and hotel buildings on the right and on the left, the lights of the French Quarter, the Vieux Carre. He could see the Hibernia Bank building, with its tower brightly lit to welcome visitors.

Jack pulled off the I-10 interstate at Canal Street and headed down toward the Mississippi River. He decided to take a left turn and head into the quarter onto Bourbon Street, just to look around before checking in for the night.

As usual, traffic on Bourbon was heavy stop and go. A late-running garbage truck was slugging its way up the street just ahead of them. There was trash pick up every night in the quarter, but usually they were finished by this time. Checking out Bourbon Street was a bad idea on a night like this, so instead Jack decided to follow the truck to the next right turn street and make it over to Royal and the parking garage.

Due to the trash truck, Jack was forced to stop in front of the Dixieland Bar. He rolled his window down so he could hear the music. Sam sat up also, looking through Jack's window. He looked past the open French doors of the Dixieland to get a better view of the band.

An African American boy was moving quickly through the club, heading toward the side doors leading onto St. Joseph Street. He carried a brown bag in his left hand and a revolver in his right. The boy carried the gun low down, beside his right leg. He had the look of a practiced thief. His hair was braided in dreadlocks that hung down to his shoulders and his clothing was a stained tee shirt and trousers baggy enough to hide guns, ammunition and enough dope to start a third world war.

The band continued to play. Many of the customers did not even notice what had taken place. Leonard the bartender stood motionless, breathing heavily. He had just faced a guy with a gun in his face.

Sam and Jack moved into the attack mode, each anticipating what the other was doing. Jack flipped on the running lights and Sam started dialing his cell phone. The boy left the club onto St Joseph Street. Just then the garbage truck moved forward, allowing Jack to pop into drive gear.

The car jumped forward and turned left into St. Joseph Street. Sam made his cell phone connection. "This is Detective Sam Pennington badge 218. Chasing armed robbery suspect."

Jack pulled the car even beside the running boy and screamed from his open window, "Stop, police! Stop, police!" The boy looked to his left and spotted a house with an open alleyway. It was two feet wide with space for one person. He forced the gate open and darted down the alley and into the darkness.

Jack pulled to the right curb, hit his brakes and brought the car to a screeching halt, threw the gear into park and jumped from the car to give pursuit.

Sam ran out of the passenger side and around the front of the car, cell phone in hand, screaming at high level. "Officers in pursuit on foot at the 1700 block of St Joseph Street! Need assistance!"

The house was a double shotgun, at 1720 and 1722 St. Joseph. The place was dark, it appeared no one was home. There was a wrought iron gate at each end of the house, with two alleys leading to the back. Jack reached the narrow alleyway at the left first, and peered into the darkness.

"Don't go in there, Jack!" Sam screamed. "Lay back." Jack concealed himself at the side of the house, while Sam sought cover behind the iron gate. "We're backlit from the streetlights," Sam whispered. "Hold fast, I got help coming."

Jack took a few quick peeks into the small alley while Sam backed off, looking around the perimeter of the area. Sam looked back down the alley to talk to Jack, when a shot rang out!

The flash of the gun indicated the shooter was standing on something high, since the muzzle flash came ten feet above them. Sam heard the bullet as it whipped past his head. Sam was only inches away from having his brains blown out. The sound of the shot echoed into a deep dull thud.

Sam followed the sound and saw his car, which was in direct line to where the shot was fired, from the dark alley. Sam used his phone again to coordinate with the police. "We need a chopper with a light," Sam screamed into his mouthpiece. "And an ambulance may be necessary. People can die out here! Let's go, let's go!"

Out of the corner of his eye Sam saw something moving down toward the second gate to his left. Jack saw it too. It was a shadow or something. They both raised their weapons and took aim. Jack was on the sidewalk first. The boy could be heard moving near the second gate. Jack ran down to the gate exit, took careful aim and screamed as loud as possible, "Stop, police!"

Two shots rang out into the night and Jack took both of them into his body. As his form collapsed on the sidewalk, the boy appeared at the gate opening and looked toward Sam. Sam dove behind some trash cans on the sidewalk and spotted a patrol car on Bourbon, getting ready to make the same left turn, that he and Jack had made minutes earlier. The wheels of the cop car quickly screeched off Bourbon and raced up St Joseph.

Hiding from view, Sam stole a look and again saw the boy. He was running back toward Bourbon Street, but when he saw the patrol car coming toward him, he turned and ran back up St. Joseph, toward Sam.

It would have been so easy for Sam to lean out and take a shot at the boy. In one instant he could have ended this fiasco, but he didn't. In a nanosecond, Sam recalled his police training.

Before you shoot you must call out a warning. Then if possible you must fire a warning shot. By the time Sam did all of that, the guy would have fired his remaining three rounds of ammo at him.

Sam gave further thought to his situation, and came up with a plan. *As he runs by me, I stick out my leg and trip him,* Sam said to himself.

At that moment the boy's foot landed on the sidewalk about an inch from Sam's face. Sam's right leg was prepared to move. Then he whipped his right leg forward and it crashed into the boy's shinbone. The instant the connection was made the boy smashed headlong into the pavement like a melon, breaking his nose and ripping the flesh from his forehead.

Sam was on him instantly, grabbing his arms and pinning them behind him and handcuffing him in one fluid motion. The back-up cops were there and quickly took control of the boy.

"Ambulance! Officer down!" Sam screamed into his radio, as he ran to Jack. He could see that it was bad and he ripped Jack's shirt open, revealing his wounds. One bullet had hit him in the upper chest and the second in the lower portion of his stomach. Two small holes and very little blood, but as Sam looked at Jack's face, more blood had filled his mouth as he gasped for air.

Jack was fighting for some clean, fresh New Orleans French Quarter air and was just drawing stale blood into his lungs. He pulled Jack's body over onto its side and the blood from his mouth ran out onto the sidewalk. Sam could hear him gasp for air, and as he did, there was a gurgling sound. Some air was getting to his lungs. It was the best Sam could do for now.

There were sounds of the ambulance arriving and that of the chopper overhead. Occasionally the light from the chopper would spill down onto them and then again there was semi darkness. When the paramedics took charge of Jack, Sam stood and found his own body shaking. He looked down at his clothing and saw he was covered with blood.

Sam saw two cops picking up the boy from the sidewalk, the kid struggled for a moment, and then decided to accept arrest. They moved off toward a squad car. Sam also saw the gun. He moved in, reached out and carefully grasped the weapon, a .38 Smith and Wesson Police Special.

The chopper was making noise, people were running all over the place and cops were calling out orders that Sam couldn't hear. He was the man in control of the situation and he had to sit down and take a breath.

There was a stoop at the front of the house. It was painted French Quarter green and had three steps leading down from the house to the street level. Sam sat on the stoop and took several deep breaths. He tried clear his mind – he had to think clearly. He saw the paramedics working on Jack, trying to insert a tube down his throat. He looked up and saw the suspect being placed into a patrol car. He rose and crossed to the policeman. His badge read Sgt. William Miller, number 435, Division 8.

"Excuse me Sergeant." Sam displayed his badge.

"Yes sir. Are you okay?"

"Yeah, fine." Pointing at the boy cuffed in the patrol car. "Listen, this guy is my collar." Miller knew of Sam and he knew this was not a man to be toyed with. "You take this kid to Division 8, right over there on Royal Street," Sam added.

"Yes sir," replied Miller.

"Tell them to book him on Robbery and with the shooting of a police officer. Tell them I'll be there as soon as I can."

"Yes sir." Miller turned and took a large plastic evidence bag out of his car. "I can book that thing for you too. Is that the gun that did it?"

"Yeah." Sam dropped the gun into the bag. "Thanks."

Charlie Wong, the forensics man from Division 8, arrived twenty minutes later and Sam directed him to his parked car across the street. Charlie was thirty-six years old, of Chinese descent. He was five foot seven inches tall and weighed close to two hundred fifty pounds. He looked like a Buddha, with a round face and full black hair, and was often mistaken for a Chinese Communist. The boys at the station called him Chi Com behind his back. But Charlie was an American-born Southerner.

"Hey Sam, I got a call at dinner." Charlie said, with a southern drawl you could cut with a knife. "What happened heah? Who got shot?"

"My partner, Jack," Sam said.

"My God. Is he gonna be okay."

"Jack? Jack's tough. He'll be fine." Sam didn't believe for a moment that Jack would be fine. "Just find a bullet for me, Charlie. It's over here at my car."

"You got it," He answered.

Charlie crossed to the car and started to look for the bullet. It had cut cleanly through the front door. He would have to do some hunting inside to find the slug.

While the chopper was still present, Sam enlisted it to help search the rear of 1722. The chopper flooded the back area with light and the police were able to recover the bag of money that had been wedged between a large storage bin and the outer cinder block wall. Sam concluded that the thief was trying to make his escape and jumped onto the storage bin. When he moved to the back, he was thwarted by a high brick wall, covered at the top with broken glass that had been cemented in amidst decoratively pointed wrought iron. It was precisely put there to prevent burglars an easy entrance onto the property.

It became all too clear what had transpired here. The thief aborted his escape over the glass-covered wall, turned back to the street and spotted Sam, who was sticking his head around the corner. He took a shot at Sam but missed him and the bullet hit the door of Sam's car across the street. He next jumped from the landing and in doing so, dropped his bag of cash between the shed and the back of the wall. Unable to retrieve the bag, he made a run for it, through the opposite side entrance. There, Detective Jack Arnold confronted him.

Sam called his Chief, Carl Witherspoon and apprised his of the situation.

Carl would go to Charity Hospital while Sam went to Jack's house to notify and pick up Jack's wife Billie.

Charlie Wong approached and told Sam that he was unable to find the slug. He suggested they would have a full search done on the car tomorrow, in the daylight hours. Sam agreed.

When Sam and Jack's wife Billie arrived at the hospital they were met by Carl, who had orchestrated everything. Billie was immediately taken to Jack's room, leaving Carl and Sam to sit and wait.

"You want some coffee?" asked Carl. "I'm gonna get some coffee."

At first Sam didn't answer, he just stared at the floor. "Carl, I really appreciate your coming down here." Sam said. "You can go home now, if you'd rather."

"No, I couldn't sleep. Maybe you want to be alone." Sam looked up at Carl. "I just didn't want to impose on you."

Sam's voice cracked a little as he said the words. "I'd really rather you stayed."

Carl looked away, pretending to search for the coffee pot, and then he too looked down at the floor.

Two and a half hours later the doctors informed them of Jack's prognosis. In surgery they found massive damage done by the hollow point bullets. So extensive were the wounds, they returned Jack to his room with no hope for survival.

Sam walked into the room where Jack lay dying. Billie sat beside him, holding his hand and whispering encouraging words to him. This was the lady who hated cops, couldn't stand violence, but she was a policeman's wife. She got tight around the eyes when some bastard shot her husband, then she became a woman of strength and courage.

"Hi, you okay?" Sam asked.

Billie's eyes never left Jack. She was a rather pretty lady, the housewife type, never enjoyed police activities, nor the housewife Teas the other wives took pleasure in. "I'm okay, I'll be okay." As she held Jack's hand she began rubbing it, as though she might be able to help him through the voyage he was about to take.

"Excuse me, I need to use the men's room," Sam said. He walked into the bathroom and was finally alone. He turned the cold water on and started splashing his face. The water began to mix with his tears, his body convulsed as he struggled to hide his sobs. It was the manly thing to do.

Day 1, continued

It was close to noon when the door to the judge's chambers opened and Donald Mosely along with two of his aides left Judge Williams chambers. Mosely was smiling and beaming with pleasure. He had obviously won his battle. They walked right past Sam without even a glance in his direction. Mosley knew who Sam was and he knew disregarding Sam was definite insult. Without stating a thing, Mosley was saying, *I ignore you, and you belong to me!*

Jerry was next to leave the chamber. He too was smiling, a real happy camper. He now 'tap danced' his way across the room to where Sam was seated. "We got it," he said with enthusiasm. "Now we start getting the jury set up, after we have lunch."

Sam looked at Jerry and said wryly. "What's the charge, Jerry?"

"Manslaughter two! We've nailed the little prick!"

So much for killing a cop. Sam thought. What a shitty business he was in.

At eight o'clock Sam, left the station and headed for home via Bourbon Street. It had been an uneventful day, which he spent most of his time doing paperwork. Now he walked several blocks, heading north, and started to hear the sound of good Jazz playing in the distance. Sam thought it must be Red Moon and his group at the Dixieland Bar. He decided to take a look. Red sounded real good tonight, and it was worth a glance.

Sam finally reached the Dixieland and walked through the front door. It was just as he had seen the place last weekend and the weekend before and six months before when his partner Jack got killed. The entire area, including the bandstand was open to the public from the street. A series of French doors allowed pedestrian traffic to stop and visit a slice of New Orleans without going inside or buying a drink. It was the best advertisement on Bourbon and the club was always packed. And Red Moon was there.

Red was an African American in his mid sixties. They were booked to play eight hours a night, six nights a week. More often than not, they would play ten hours, just for the tips. They just loved Jazz.

Sam headed for a seat at the bar. Leonard, the bartender and owner, spotted him walking in. Leonard grabbed a bottle of Glenlivet twelve-year-old single malt Scotch whisky. Sam squeezed his way passed a fat lady who was dancing with herself to an up-tempo jazz tune and made it to the open seat. Leonard was already there, and had poured the drink. The bottle had Sam's name written on it, with a fine-line Sharpie marking pen.

About two months earlier, Sam had seen a lovely girl who had caught his attention. He asked Leonard who she was and he said, "Kelly." She was a waitress, looked about late twenty to early thirty. What Sam liked most about her was her sweet smile.

"How's it by you, Leonard?" Sam asked.

"Okay Sam, and you?" Leonard retorted.

Sam nodded and sipped his scotch. "Good scotch." Then he changed the subject. "That waitress, Kelly, she been around?"

Leonard threw a quick glance around the room. "She may be on a break or in the back. I'll check it out for you." A waitress stood in the service area waiting for orders to be filled. "I'll be back." Leonard took off.

Sam took another sip of his drink and studied the area. He searched one more time for Kelly. Sam was feeling a bit blue. He was looking for some conversation. He was thinking of, perhaps, a tete-a-tete with a lady. Then he thought to himself, *Perhaps I was a little early. Possibly this was her night off. Maybe she was married with five kids.*

Chapter 2

EIGHT MONTHS EARLIER

KELLEY LEE JONES was born in Miami, Florida. Her father ran out on her mother when Kelly was eighteen months old. Her life had been fraught with moving into fifteen various apartments, attending many different schools and finally working several part-time jobs, some of which do not even deserve description. Her best position was the one she currently held, that of a receptionist at a local beauty salon in downtown Southeast Miami.

She was a tall girl, about five feet ten inches, with blond hair. She had the high cheekbones and chiseled features of a movie actress. When she smiled, it turned her face into the picture of a star. Her body was nothing to be afraid of either. She was a well-proportioned female animal, prepared to do the right thing, should anything of interest come along. So why did someone not take her? Because she lived in downtown Southeast Miami! Little Havana, they called it. Too tall for most any man, too skinny, not a Catholic, and when she smiled there were too many teeth showing.

For Kelly to have a chance at success, she would have to change her location. She would have to dig her way out of the pain she had suffered for a lifetime. Kelly had a father that had deserted her and a mother who would rather screw a stranger, than to properly help her daughter get a head start.

Momma had a boyfriend that she would see two or three times a week, or whenever else he might need servicing. She would check his dip stick, and if needed, fill his crankcase. Now at thirty-three, Kelly decided it was time to start thinking of the right thing to do. Getting out of Southeast Miami was definitely the right thing to do.

She kept the appointment book for the *Skin Deep Beauty Salon* and lent an appearance of business decorum to the establishment. At closing time, after putting in a ten hour day, she would spend an hour, if not two, cleaning up the place. There were six chairs and five hair dryers in the salon. Every work area had combs and scissors to arrange and sterilize and hair from the floor to be swept up and bagged. There were magazines to be arranged in the waiting room and phone calls to the next day's customers to confirm their appointments. Finally she would lock the back door and drag at least two large plastic bags to the trash Dumpster. Never once did she have the opportunity to meet anyone special, or to know anyone of any importance.

Kelly still lived with her mother, who was seventeen when she brought Kelly into this world, without the benefit of having a father to help her grow up. In addition, her mother had developed a case of failing health. Doctors could not specifically tell Kelly what her mother actually had, but it was somehow related to "failing health." Kelly suspected it had something to do with a raging case of alcoholism.

Then one day, a young girl named Cheryl came into the salon. She didn't have an appointment, but needed some attention, *fast*. It seemed that her carry-on bag was stolen when the plane landed in Atlanta and it contained all of her hair equipment. Cheryl cried out in a voice loaded with passion, "God, you gotta help me, I'm dead if I'm late. We go on in three and a half hours!

Kelly glanced around the room. Five chairs were busy and one was open. That was Maria's chair. Maria was a Cuban lady and she was having lunch in the back.

"It'll cost more money," Kelly stated. "Can you handle that?"

Cheryl was elated. "I own the stinking band. Let's go do it!"

For an extra fifty, Kelly got Maria out of the back room. Maria started Cheryl on the Skin Deep Beauty Make-Over. One hour and fifteen minutes later she was sitting under the dryer. Now that the panic of the day was over, both Cheryl and Kelly started sizing each other up.

Kelly noticed that Cheryl had come in with extra cash in hand and owned a band that was currently employed. She was possibly a Latina, had a rather nice figure and was about Kelly's size. But she was older, most assuredly she was considerably older. Cheryl determined Kelly to be a knockout lady, about her size, had a rather pleasant figure and a very pretty face. Her smile was quite radiant. At one point the two stood watching each other. Kelly felt nervous by the stare and rather than shake it off, she moved over to Cheryl.

"I'm sure everything will be just fine," Kelly said. "I know Maria will do your hair just great."

"Let me ask you something," Cheryl asked. "What are you doing at eight o'clock tonight?"

"Why?" Kelly wanted to know.

"Well, I got another problem. We have a three night-gig at the Boogy Boo. You ever heard of that club?"

Kelly was becoming confused. She did not have a massive education. Moving from school to school made her spelling and arithmetic a bit cumbersome. Besides, what the hell was she talking about, the Boogy Boo and a three-night gig?

"Okay fine, so you don't get it." Cheryl stated. "Trust me on this one." Cheryl then started to list the company policy. "Okay, we start at nine o'clock and play till one. That's four hours. I got a dress for you; it's gold lamé. You'll look great in it."

"What do I have to do?" Kelly asked, slightly amazed.

"It's simple, we got one dance step for all the numbers. They all sound alike." Cheryl jumped from the dryer and stood in front of an imaginary microphone. "Okay it goes like this. We gotta do sixteen bars of music, you here on my left," Cheryl grabbed Kelly and placed her on her left, "And me here on the right."

Kelly was trying hard to understand, but it was all confusing. She assumed she would be singing in sixteen bars throughout the town.

"Now you wiggle your ass with the beat of the music," Cheryl said. "Count the beat in your head, four beats to the bar. Just keep smiling. Look at the audience and keep smiling." Cheryl started to dance, counting off the beats and swinging her backside to the imaginary rhythm. "One, two, three, four."

Kelly started the swinging action, following Cheryl's lead.

"Now we do the same thing again,." Cheryl said, counting. "One two three four. Then one, two, three, four. Now here's the dance step. You exaggerate the swing of your ass and step forward with two steps to the microphone. Take a mike in your right hand, lean into it and sing with me. Ooo Ahhh Ooo Ahhh. Then go back and do it all over again."

"What's the song?" Kelly asked.

"Who the fuck knows?" Cheryl shouted. "These bastards scream so loud, I can never hear the lyrics. Look, I need you for three nights and I'll pay you four hundred a night, for four one hour sets."

Kelly looked around the room and noticed that everyone had stopped working on hair and were watching them with a very strange look. But it didn't bother Kelly. It didn't take a rocket scientist to quickly figure she would make an easy twelve hundred bucks for the job!

"I'll do it," Kelly replied.

"Great," Cheryl responded, as she hopped back under the dryer.

Kelly walked over to the owner, a middle aged Spanish woman named Margarita. "I need to take a few days off, Margarita. I'll be back first thing on Monday."

"What the hell you talkin' about?" Margarita screamed. "Who gonna clean the place, an' get all dees phones message?"

"Well, you could handle the phone and perhaps each of the ladies could clean up their own area," Kelly stated. "Then it's a 'take a number' to decide who handles the trash."

"I don teenk so," Margarita replied. "Jou owes me to do jour jobs. Jou got one big obligation here."

Kelly thought for a moment. She made one hundred dollars a day for six days a week. She worked eleven, sometimes twelve hours a day, for a total weekly pay of six hundred bucks. Now in three days she could get on a stage for a total of twelve hours and net twelve hundred bucks!

"I don teenk so," Kelly said. "I'm going to party!"

What happened next was Kelly Lee Jones' fifteen minutes of fame! She was a woman with very little background, brought into a situation by a stranger. Kelly took the reins in her hands and slapped the mule on the back, which changed the rest of her life.

Kelly and Cheryl took a cab to the Gator Motel, which was only half a block up the street from the Boogy Boo Club. First they went to Cheryl's room. She opened her suitcase and pulled out an overly fancy gold lame dress, along with some fancy gold shoes, and a copy of Jacqueline Kennedy's pearl necklace. She informed Kelly that she could stay in the room next door, in a room she had reserved for another girl from New York who did not make the trip. Cheryl was responsible for Kelly's room and all meals, which was part of the deal.

They next left for the Club, which had once been a movie theater. You could still see the words STRAND THEATER painted on the side of the building, under several layers of painted overcoat. A medium crowd had gathered and it was growing by the minute.

Kelly felt like she was in a dream. She and Cheryl went into the theater and Kelly got her first look at a legitimate stage. It was amazing. *There must be over three thousand seats in here*, she thought to herself. Cheryl dragged her backstage and into a dressing room.

"We only got about an hour," Cheryl told her. "If we don't get a chance to rehearse our moves, don't sweat it. Just do what I do as soon as you can do it. If you miss a beat, or the entire fucking song, who gives a rat's ass. No one can hear anything anyway! All they want to see is a beautiful girl. Now go to the dressing room, right next to this one and get yourself ready. Do your make-up, look great and keep flashing the smile. You got great fucking teeth!

"Excuse me, Cheryl, but I don't have any make-up."

"Well, here you go my dear," Cheryl reacted. ""Do not stand on ceremony." Cheryl grabbed a shopping bag and emptied its contents onto a chair. She next moved to her dressing table and began to divide the goods. "Here's some pancake, rouge and eye stuff." Cheryl looked up at Kelly. "Do you need some color for your body?"

"No thank you," Kelly responded. "This will be just fine."

She took the make-up from Cheryl and started to leave, but paused at the door. "When do I meet the guys in the band?" Kelly asked.

"Oh you mean Snake? I'll tell him I hired you. He'll check on you soon. Don't panic."

"Is Snake his name?" Kelly asked.

"No, it's Willis. George Willis. But don't get hooked up on that. He's a singer, he's a screamer, and he's got a guitar that he knows how to play. And he's a 'Snake!' Don't worry, I'll tell him about you."

Armed with her shoes and make-up, Kelly moved into the hallway. Three boys were moving cases of what looked like musical instruments toward the stage area. She was walking against the grain, trying to get to her dressing room.

"Excuse me. I'm sorry," she said as she bumped into more baggage. She found her room, opened the door and entered. This was it! Her first dressing room! Her own private dressing room! There was only a chair and a make-up table in the room, but by God, they were hers. She placed her make-up onto the table and examined the stuff, when there was a knock at the door.

She turned and opened the door. Standing there, without a doubt, was the strangest person she had ever encountered in her life. He stood five feet seven inches tall. Kelly was five ten and she looked down on him as if he were a kid. She forced back a laugh when she saw his head covered in dreadlocks.

Kelly had seen dreadlocks before, either on homeless people or worn by million dollar football players. As she looked down she could not miss that he wore no shirt, a pair of baggy black pants, no shoes and had a tattoo of a giant snake. The tattoo started on his left arm, ran up the front side of his shoulder, wrapped around his neck, then back down his right shoulder, ending up with the head of the snake, with its mouth open and fangs displayed, on the center of his chest.

"Hello Snake," Kelly said.

Snake did not answer. He was looking her over as quizzically, as she had done to him. She waited for him to finish his looking. "My name is Kelly," she said. "I'm part of your band. Cheryl hired me. I'll really try to do a good job. Good luck to you and the boys tonight." She smiled brightly. Snake continued looking her up and down and then nodded in the affirmative.

Now it was '*show time.*' The band consisted of four men, the keyboard man, drums, one second guitar and Snake, who was the lead guitar. Of course there were the two girls. The auditorium was almost packed. The kid audience paid twenty five bucks downstairs and fifteen in the balcony, for one hour of music. Then they would empty the room and do it again, three more times, throughout the evening. Out of all this, Kelly would make four hundred a night.

Kelly stood on the stage, frozen with fear. She had done her make-up as well as possible, had the dress and shoes on, but worried about everything else. She had no pantyhose and wondered if her legs looked all right. Tomorrow she would buy some pantyhose. Just then a roar erupted and Snake appeared on stage and the crowd cheered. This little man was a major hero with these fans.

He pranced out to center stage, like the cock of the walk and started playing and screaming his latest hit song. Kelly was unable to hear who announced the song, or what song it was and she was unable to hear the one, two, three, four of the bars of the music. Kelly tried to follow Cheryl by wiggling her ass. When it came time to do the Ooos and Ahhs, there was no microphone available for her. She just went ahead and Ooo'd and Ahh'd, then stepped back to wiggle her ass. That's how it went for the entire night.

In addition, there was a problem in shifting the audience. Someone who did the job of management did not figure how long it would take to change from one audience to another. The group had four sets to do in five hours. The crowd outside grew larger, while the crowd inside wanted to see more. Snake and his boys continued to play on and on and on. And the girls continued to do the Ooo's and Ahh's. They did their best, could not even remember how many sets they had done, and by the end of the night, they were all ready to collapse.

As they shifted the audience for the final set, a young boy who had been eyeing Kelly approached with his program. He was tall and skinny, with a face covered with adolescent acne. He drew closer to Kelly and she began looking for someone to give her aid, but she stood alone. Her mind raced. If he were to kidnap her, he would take her to a dark road on the outskirts of town and rape her unmercifully. Then he would throw her in a ditch where she would die in immense pain. He handed her his program and asked. "Would you please sign this for me?" His eyes looked down as he asked. He was ashamed to ask for an autograph from someone who was that beautiful.

Kelly took it and looked at it. It pictured the band. Snake with three other boys and two girls, one of whom, she was not. But the young man did not care. Kelly was something special to him. He had watched her for an hour, as she sang and danced and now he was close enough to touch her. He was thrilled. Kelly felt his thrill also. She looked for a pen and hollered over the noise of the departing crowd. "I'm sorry, I don't have a pen."

The boy was all but panicked! He quickly searched through his pockets, finally coming up with a nub of a pencil. "Here," he said. "Will this do?"

"Yes," she answered. "This will do just fine." She signed her name, Kelly Lee, avoiding the Jones part. She had a notion this would be a better stage name. Kelly asked the young man his name.

"Jimmy," he said.

"Okay, I'll put, 'To Jimmy with love.' Is that okay?"

Jimmy nodded, while his breathing started to grow stronger, heavier. After she had finished she returned the program. When Jimmy took it, he finally looked up at her, showing a big smile of braces on his upper and lower teeth. His breathing was now heavy. Standing before a star, he could not conceal his excitement and neither could Kelly.

The next two nights were basically the same. Cheryl finally paid her off, adding three hundred more, to make her three-day stint a cool fifteen hundred dollars.

"I wish we could have done more," Cheryl said. "You were great to be with but this was Snake's last gig. He's decided to something more classical."

"What's he going to do with that snake tattoo all over his body?" Kelly asked.

"I believe in his next gig, he plans to wear a long black frock coat with a white church collar. He'll call himself 'The Father.'"

When she got home, Kelly found her mother fornicating with a new stranger. She could hear them humping and pumping in the back bedroom. The sound disgusted her. She wanted to leave Florida more than anything in the world. It was a place of depression, a town of loneliness and despair. She remembered the one time as a child of ten when they got out of Florida.

Her mother had a new boyfriend, John, who loved to gamble. He called them from New Orleans, Louisiana. John had hit something called a Quinella where, before the first race, you bet on a horse in each following race to win. John won, big time. As a result of his good fortune, he sent two first-class plane tickets for Kelly and her mom to join him there.

When they arrived, Kelly saw the most beautiful city ever. She was surrounded with people full of love and happiness. The town was a continuous party and the food was delectable. When they went to the fairgrounds, she saw her mother's lover lose four thousand dollars on the first five races. It wasn't all that simple.

John had won eighteen thousand on the Quinella, but as it came out, he had an investor in the deal. So John only had half of the money for his share. John and Kelly's mother had a lengthy argument. He started out with nine grand and paid the airline one grand for two round trip tickets. He had just lost four thousand, and with his current expenses, had a net bankroll of two thousand dollars and change.

Being a lucky fellow, he parlayed that money into a sure thing. The final horse he bet on, ran twelfth in a twelve horse race. When the deal was concluded, her mother cashed in their return plane tickets, gave the excess money to John, and she and Kelly returned to Florida on an overnight bus. But New Orleans would always remain a distant goal for her.

Now, at age thirty-three, Kelly no longer had anything to hold her. Not her mother, not that house, not her job, not the State. She pulled one piece of luggage from her closet and threw some clothes inside. When it was filled, she was packing nothing more in it. She headed for the front door and called back over her shoulder, "Ma, I'm leaving."

"Alright dear, take care," her mother responded.

In an almost inaudible voice Kelly said, "I'll write when I get work."

Kelly walked twenty-four blocks to the bus station at East and Fillmore Street and bought a one way ticket to New Orleans. The bus left five hours later. Kelly used that time to think her thoughts. She had a chance to be something special. She had that moment when she was selected by Cheryl to work with her in her band. The opportunity arose where she would be one of the stars of the show, have her own dressing room and she was paid fifteen hundred dollars. She met a tall boy who admired her talent and asked for her autograph. However, none of this met with her final fifteen minutes of fame.

On her way to New Orleans, the bus stopped in Biloxi, Mississippi, for a one hour lunch stop. Kelly made her way across the street to the Grand Casino, a gambling barge that floated in the Gulf of Mexico. She had decided to gamble with twenty-five dollars. Kelly walked up to the first slot machine in sight and ran five one dollar bills into the machine, pulled the handle and won thirty-two thousand dollars. That was Kelly Lee Jones' fifteen minutes of fame.

Day 1, continued.

At the Dixieland Bar and Grill, Red and his band started up a fresh set of great music. Sam leaned onto the back of the padded barstool and glanced around the room. The single malt scotch had caused him to be even more amorous than before. He was now a man with a mission, a predator, on the hunt if you wish. He needed to get laid and there was no doubt about that. He needed a *tete-a-tete* with a pretty lady, one who showed deep interest in him.

Sam was a bit shy. He would never start a conversation with a woman, but rather allowed her the first opening. She would have to show him that she was interested in an alliance with him. Then, only then, if he were also interested, would he take charge of the situation. Sam spotted Kelly moving around at the front tables taking orders. She was a lovely looking lady.

The band had kicked into high gear. Red was pushing it up a notch.

Kelly moved past the patrons, always smiling, but never looking in Sam's direction. Eye contact for Sam was important. When you were on the hunt, it was eye contact that made the most meaningful signal of all. The first rule of the game was never being caught looking at the other person. If she was looking at you, you must never let on that you are, or were ever looking directly at her. But if you can catch her looking at you, then you have established definite interest.

When Sam first turned to scan the area, his eyes did not stop on any one person. It was as though he were looking for someone else, or scanning the bandstand. What it was actually about, was searching an area for a great piece of ass. If the situation did not present itself on this evening, Sam would have to resort to returning to his apartment and threading up an old porno on his VCR. But that was not the case here.

There was a stand at the bar where waitresses would place their orders, located halfway down the bar from Sam. Cleverly, Sam's eyes never focused directly on Kelly. Instead he would look at the back wall, leading or following her movement. Then he would concentrate on his peripheral vision to see if she might ever look his way. If her gaze stayed with him for at least two seconds, he would cause his gaze to drift away from her. Sam was being coy.

Kelly first got a glimpse of Sam when he entered the bar on the first day she worked at the Dixieland. He was a good-looking guy with a mysterious air, wearing dark clothes and a dark tie. She liked what she saw and asked Leonard who he was. Leonard told her his name and that he was a detective with the NOPD. Leonard added that he came in about every Friday night and stayed for a few hours, listening to music.

Over the next two months she became fixated with Sam. When he arrived, her attitude would change. She was not serving tourists at the tables, she was showing off for Sam, using that sweet little smile that she had learned from Cheryl and that little ass wiggle as she turned and headed for the bar. When she turned to look back, she scanned the area where he sat, but she never caught him looking directly at her. His eyes were always focused on something else. Sam was still being coy. But that was when Kelly first worked at the Dixieland. That was then and this was now.

Leonard placed a second double Glenlivet single malt in front of Sam. He looked back up searching for Kelly. Then it happened! After two months, she finally slipped, she made an error! She turned her head and looked directly at him. He was not watching her, but rather looking past her. He could see her looking directly at him from the corner of his eye. He wanted to move his gaze on toward the bandstand, but quickly decided not to do that. Instead, he shifted his eyes toward her and they locked. It was only for two seconds, but they locked! She was interested!

Kelly struggled her way to the bar. The place was getting crowded now, people standing two deep near the serving area. She had wanted to move to Sam and introduce herself, but that was impossible. She was now caught openly staring at him and he at her. The music was loud and everyone was talking. If they leaned in across the bar, they could get glimpses of one another.

"Hello," Kelly shouted over the din.

"Hi. Name's Sam Pennington." His voice shouted back.

"Kelly Lee, dancer, singer, now between jobs, currently waitressing at the Dixieland Bar and Grill." She offered him her biggest, warmest and most friendly smile to date. It was the kind of smile that just about melted Sam's socks off. She knew it, too.

"I know this is going to sound phony, but when do you get off?" Sam asked.

Kelly looked at her watch. "One more hour, then I get a free drink on Leonard. Care to join me?" Sam smiled and gave her thumbs up. No need to shout any more, it was a done deal.

The patio was in back of the club. It was mainly used for the workers and the boys in the band, for access to the two restrooms. A few palm trees had been planted which had failed to grow over four feet. Sam and Kelly sat at a table and a slow blues number could be heard in the distance. Leonard had prepared Kelly a Grasshopper, a drink of crème de menthe and cream. Since she had a friend, he made a pitcher which was now three quarters empty. Grasshoppers made Kelly talkative; she was in the process of telling Sam about her entire life, right up to running into Cheryl and meeting Snake.

Sam was feeling mellow, but in no way drunk. While she told of her magical life, he concentrated on her lovely face and radiant smile and weighing his possibilities.

Nice story. Cute kid. Getting late, Sam said to himself. *I'll find a spot when she breaks, tell her it's late and excuse myself. If she wants to come home with me, I'll take her. Wouldn't mind a little sex. Then I'll call a cab and send her home. God, will this stupid story never end!*

"Well, enough about me," she stated, her voice sounding a little tipsy.

"Leonard tells me you're with the cops?"

"Leonard told you huh? Yeah, I catch bad people," he said.

Kelly looked at him for a very long moment and touched his hand with hers. "Tell you what, Sam. I'm getting real tired. Why don't we go to my place, have a nightcap and snuggle. That okay with you?"

At that moment, Sam could feel a twinge at the head of his penis. It wasn't all that special, just a signal from his body telling him everything was ready to go forward and accept the challenge.

Sam stood up. "I can see myself doing that," Sam said with a wry smile.

They went three blocks South on Bourbon and headed over to Toulouse Street. As they walked, Kelly made note of the beautiful building in the far distance, located across Canal, a few blocks up into the city. The building itself was about twelve stories high with a tower at the top, which was brightly lit with white lights.

Kelly grabbed Sam by the hand and walked him across Bourbon to a small art gallery. There in the window was a picture painted by an unknown local artist of the exact place where they stood now. It was priced at $350.00 and was a rather exciting replica of the people strolling in the Quarter, the Tower of the Hibernia Bank building, with its shining white lights in the background.

"That is my bank," she said. "Do you know Bourbon is the only street in the Quarter where you can see that building?"

"No, I didn't know that."

"Well, that's true. You take a ride on one of the carriages and the only place you will see it is right here on Bourbon Street."

"Well, there you go," Sam said.

They moved on up to Toulouse Street and turned into a small courtyard that had originally been slave quarters. A cool night air covered the Quarter and fog had started to roll in.

"Fog's coming in," Kelly announced. "You may have to spend the night."

The interior of her apartment was decorated in a warm and pleasant fashion. To Sam that meant someone actually cared about the place. It was a studio apartment and off to the left was a small kitchen. Behind the kitchen was a door to a rather large bathroom with tub and shower. Kelly watched Sam as he entered the apartment and looked around.

"What do you think?" Kelly asked.

"I like it, it's very nice," Sam said.

Kelly moved into the kitchen and took a half bottle of Apple Brandy from the fridge and two glasses. "I gotta tell you, Sam, this isn't my way. I normally don't bring men home and I don't want you to get the wrong idea. Leonard said you were kinda special. So I took another look and I must admit I liked what I saw. I've never even kissed you and now I'm thinking about cuddling." She flashed a marvelous smile and said, "I think we should get a little acquainted. Tell me about what kind of a cop you are?"

Sam took her by the hands and gently pulled her to him and lightly kissed her on the mouth.

"I catch bad people," he said.

"Leonard confirmed that."

They kissed again. This time it was a dual, deep tongue extravaganza. After a few moments of heavy breathing and unrequited passion, Kelly pulled away. "I'm going to go freshen up," Kelly said, still gasping for air. "Won't you make yourself comfortable?" She turned and went into the bathroom.

Sam was beside himself. His penis was at half-staff and he cleverly concealed that with his coat. He kept his body turned slightly away from her as she left the room. He would have to talk it down to normal before she returned.

Sam opened the Apple Brandy and poured one glass, taking a sip for taste. Sam recalled a time when he was a kid in Atlantic City and some neighbors took he and his pal to the local circus. There they purchased two candied apples. His friend loved it and finished it in no time. Sam didn't like it because it was too sweet. However, being such a sweet and loving child, Sam went ahead and ate half of it. What followed was the most embarrassing time of his young life.

First he threw up! Not just once but many, many times. He became so sick that they had to go home early. That night he had stomach aches and the following two days he had the runs. From that day forth he had not eaten candy or apples again.

So Sam took a sip of the apple brandy and shuddered and his penis immediately went soft.

Kelly came back into the room, walked over to him and gave him a peck on the cheek. "I'll open the bed, it'll be more comfortable." Sam excused himself and went to the bathroom.

There he removed his shirt and looked at himself in the mirror. *Okay, we're both tired, we'll just make this a quickie and head back home.*

When Sam returned Kelly had already pulled the bed open and was lying on her stomach in the center of the bed, with her face in the pillow. It was a large bed, but Kelly had sprawled out in the middle of it, leaving no room for Sam to join her. Sam hung off the bed, trying to get some place to nestle his face in the crook of her neck, just below her left ear.

"Hey baby," he whispered in a soft voice. "This is Sam, one of the good guys. I'm gonna get you." He nibbled at her neck, kissing it tenderly. Kelly moaned, lifted her head from the pillow and said, "Hi Sam." Then she fell back onto the pillow.

The question was whether she was awake or not. Sam was perplexed. She wanted him and she invited him to cuddle and offered him a drink of Apple Brandy. How could a judge find him guilty of rape at a time like this?

Sam slowly arose and sat on the bed. He looked at Kelly and smiled, picked up his drink and made a toast. "I hope this was as good for you as it was for me." He swallowed the drink in one swig.

Sam quickly dressed and headed for the front door. He heard her stir and looked back over his shoulder. Slowly Sam returned to the bed and lay down beside her. As he did so, Kelly moved further to her right giving him even more room on the bed.

He slowly slipped in beside her and placed an arm around her waist, which caused her to turn toward him. Her eyes fluttered open and she saw him.

"Hi Sam, I guess I got a little drunk."

Sam smiled and kissed her lightly on the cheek.

"Thank you for that." Kelly whispered. "I'm so sorry, Sam. It was too many Grasshoppers. I never drink that much. Hope you'll give me a rain check?"

"You're fine and I'm fine and I have an early call tomorrow." Sam said. "Go to sleep baby."

Kelly leaned in and gave Sam a sweet kiss on the lips. "I'll see you out."

She hopped up from the bed grabbing a robe and moved quickly to the door and opened it up. A surge of dense fog rushed into the room. She looked at him and shrugged her shoulders. "Maybe I should have asked for a fog check?"

Sam laughed and took her into his arms and kissed her. There was a need in both of them and soon it would be fulfilled. He turned, looked back at Kelly who was standing in the doorway. She was beautiful, the porch light causing a halo of brilliance around her hair. She blew him a kiss, which he caught and blew back to her. Sam walked down the stairs and disappeared into the fog.

It was easy walking through the Quarter in a dense fog. All you needed to do was call off the name of the streets you crossed, without seeing a single sign and then turn onto the street you wanted. As he walked, he thought of Kelly. *She was just a nice kid. She talked too much, silly stuff. I don't think I'm interested in a major relationship with her. I don't have time for this. It's got to be the most stupid thing I did in my life. I'll have her over to my place, show her how I live. I'll cook her a good dinner. That ought to take care of it.* As he walked on he thought more about Kelly.

Chapter 3

Day 2

IT WAS THURSDAY, March 2nd. At six a.m., Sam decided to 'take a jog'. He was dressed in a tired old sweat suit and a vintage pair of tennis shoes, with a hole in the top of the left toe. He ran from east to west and then reversed directions to north and south. He was running through the Quarter, seeking a landmark. Kelly was right. The only place you could see the Hibernia bank building from the Quarter was on Bourbon Street. Finally satisfied with his experiment, he returned home to change his clothes for work.

Sam picked up a *Times Picayune* newspaper from the front of the St. Ann Street Market and walked inside. As he moved to his stool, next to the window, his eye caught Phil's and they exchanged sign signals for the order of the day. When he sat down, the headlines caught his attention. There was a picture of Lila Washington, the lady Sam had met at the Laundromat yesterday. The headline read, "Dead Body Found in French Quarter Laundry Dryer."

Sam looked out of the window where Phil had cleaned a clear spot. The laundry front door had a sign on it that read, "Closed For Vacation." Sam read on in the article and found it to basically be old news and turned to the continuation on page four.

There, he found a photo of Detective William Joseph Mays being interviewed by several reporters. Billy Joe Mays, a.k.a. William Joseph Mays, was being asked about his knowledge of the identification of the victim.

"'How did you identify the victim as Beth Hayden from Blanco, Texas?' A reporter questioned.

'We found her driver's license taped to her backside,' Billy Joe responded. Sam read further. The reporter's questions were fired out in machine gun fashion.

"'Can you give us her address?' 'Who do you suppose taped her license to her backside?' 'Was that the person who killed her?' 'Do you know if the murderer was a man or a woman?'"

Billy Joe quickly concluded the press interview. He had found out that his assistant, Sgt. Ron Farley, had divulged classified information regarding the case and shot his mouth off when he shouldn't have.

Sam reached the station and walked through the lobby toward his office. He stopped at the service desk to get his evening messages. The first was from Carl Witherspoon, who wanted to see him when he got in.

Captain Carl Witherspoon was a fifty-two-year-old white man, whom Sam had known for ten years. He had strong features and a warm smile. He also possessed a wry sense of humor that Sam appreciated. Nothing ever bothered Carl; he took things as they were presented to him. Sam entered Carl's office without knocking and moved directly to a small alcove, holding a coffee pot. He pointed to Carl and then to the coffee. Carl shook his head 'no' and waited patiently. Sam poured himself a cup and sat in front of Carl's desk. Carl leaned forward with a stern look on his face.

"I need help," Carl said. "I got a problem that needs your kind of help."

Sam took a sip of his coffee and looked up. "Give me the name and address and I'll go kill the bastard."

Carl sighed. He needed to get Sam in an aggressive mood, not one of jocularity. "I really need your help. Come on, let's go downstairs." Carl rose and moved to the door.

Sam dropped his head. He knew what those words meant. "Why don't you just tell me, Carl? I don't need to see it." Carl paused at the door and turned back to Sam. "I want you to see it. I want it to make an impression."

They walked down the stairs to a basement hallway. As they walked, Sam asked, "We goin' to see Weird Arnie?"

Carl glanced back at Sam. "We're going to meet with Arnold. We don't need anymore problems here. Only you, Arnold, and I are going to know about this, got it?" Half way down the hall was a heavy set of double wooden doors. On it was the shield of Louisiana and below was the name, 'Dr. Arnold Feenie, Coroner." Carl tried to open the door, it was locked.

"Let's go down to the morgue," Carl said. They walked down anther fifty feet and arrived at a plain door with a single sign which simply read, "MORGUE."

Carl opened the door and walked inside, followed by Sam. It was the main storage area of the morgue. There were twenty-four bays on each side, all ready to handle the 'city's' dead bodies. Sitting at the desk, at the rear of the room, was Arnold Feenie, a timid man of fifty-two, who spoke in a very controlled manner, as if he had rehearsed every line he uttered.

"Good morning gentlemen," Arnold said. "Nice to see you again." Sam tried to be enthusiastic.

"Hi Arnold."

Carl wanted to get it over with. "Let's do it!"

Arnold led the way to the right of the room and stopped at a box of latex gloves that was attached to the wall. He put on his gloves before pulling open drawer, "Q14." The "Q" indicated the Quarter, the vicinity where the victim was found.

As the drawer came to an open rest, Arnold pulled the sheet from the body. It revealed the same girl Sam had seen yesterday. The right side of her head had been savagely beaten with a round solid blunt object.

"Do we have any I. D.?" Sam inquired.

Carl pulled a small packet from his jacket pocket. Her driver's license had been covered with a piece of clear tape, about an inch and a half wide. It was the same type of tape used to seal a box for shipping.

"This is what was taped to her back," Carl stated. "It's a Texas driver's license."

"Can they lift a print from the tape?" Sam asked Carl.

"The tape itself is clean," Carl answered. "But they may be able to get a print off of the license. I've ordered a chopper to take this to Baton Rouge. The lab guys up there will use a chemical to slowly pull the tape free and check the face of the license for prints. It's a long shot, but we'll try."

Sam took the license and studied it. Her name was Beth Hayden and the address was 2340 Auburn St., Blanco, Texas. "Has her family been notified?"

"They'll be in town tomorrow to make a positive I.D.," Carl responded. Sam looked at the girl's picture with interest. She didn't look even remotely like the body lying in front of him. The date on her license placed her age as twenty-three, but she had been beaten so savagely, she could have been a hundred.

Arnold spoke quietly, not wanting anyone out of this secret circle to hear his words. "This body was found at a laundromat on St. Ann Street yesterday, at 8:45 am. She was found nude, inside a clothes dryer. The time of death was between nine and eleven o'clock the night before."

Sam listened and smiled slightly. This secret information had already been printed in the Times. Arnie was now running behind the times.

"The autopsy I performed indicated that she had been beaten to death with a medium round object, such as a pipe. I removed her scalp to chart the blows. Let me show you." Arnold placed his gloved hand at the top of the scalp, intending to display his handiwork.

"No, I don't think that's necessary," Carl said.

Arnold felt a moment of disappointment, then with a quick and a somewhat sardonic move of his hand, he flipped the rest of the sheet from her body. He showed that Beth Hayden had been mutilated. A feeling of nausea overwhelmed Sam. He feigned a slight yawn and sucked some fresh air into his lungs, but his eyes could not move away from the havoc the autopsy had wreaked on her body. Beth's entire body cavity had been laid open for the world to see. Sam quickly gasped two more sucks of air, but now the atmosphere didn't seem all that refreshing.

"I next proceeded to check the rest of the body," Arnold continued. "When I first inspected the vagina, my finger came in contact with an object about the size of a cigarette."

Carl took over from there. He withdrew a piece of paper from his jacket, now enclosed in a clear plastic envelope. "This is what Arnold found."

Sam took the article from Carl and studied it. It was written in red ink and read:

Do not go here. She's mine.

3

It was the number three written at the bottom that interested Sam the most. "Any prints here?" Sam asked.

"Nothing," Carl said, shaking his head with resignation.

"What protected the ink?" Sam asked.

Arnold stepped up and looked at the note. "It was wrapped in a condom," he said.

Sam did not like the situation. "Let's get this straight. We have a crazy person who murders a young girl and then tapes her driver's license to her body, showing her name and address. He next placed a note in a condom inside of her body so we can find it? Is that what we got?" Both Carl and Arnold remained silent. Sam took another look at the note. "Okay. Did she have any sex?"

"There were no traces of sperm in the body and none on the condom." Arnold said. "I don't believe this had anything to do with sex."

Carl was searching for an answer. "So what about the note?"

Sam thought for a moment. "We have a very sick person on our hands and there is a good possibility that this girl is the third person in a chain of serial killings."

"Right," Carl said. "Or the three may be his IQ level." Sam started to laugh, then, thought better of it, as another wave of nausea came over him. Carl continued.

"We ran a check on her. We arrested her twice before. She was a known prostitute."

"Okay, keep that quiet," Sam suggested. "We should find out how many hookers have been killed in the last year."

Upon hearing that, Arnold perked up. "I've got another girl right over here. She's a Jane Doe, been here for a little over two months. We hold all the Does for three months, then the city takes them and buries them in Potters Field. Actually, she has three more days before we turn her over."

"What makes you say she was a hooker?" Sam asked.

"I don't know," Arnold said. "Nobody asked about her, nobody knew her. If she walks like a duck and quacks like a duck, she's a duck."

Sam shook his head in amazement. Arnold's mentality never ceased to amaze him.

"Arnold, did you cut on her?" Carl asked. Arnold seemed surprised at the question. As the Coroner, he was ordered to perform any process he deemed necessary. This was a Jane Doe. So who cares about a Jane Doe anyway?

"No sir," Arnold answered. "She's right over there, if you want to take a look."

Carl's body stiffened. He knew how Sam hated this stuff, and now even he too was starting to feel queasy. "I don't think that will be necessary."

"What was the cause of death?" Sam asked.

"I don't recall," Arnold said as he moved to another cabinet and pulled the drawer out to full length. The body was also covered with a sheet. He removed the medical report that was placed bedside the body, and silently read through the report. Sam and Carl became more interested.

Arnold looked up and said, "Body was found in the trunk of a car in New Orleans, on Airline Drive. It's a used car lot. Death by blunt force to the head."

"Any idea what the weapon may have been?" asked Sam. "Might it have been something like a pipe?"

Arnold immediately got the drift of Sam's question. He had two women murdered, both stored in his morgue, both having been beaten to death with a blunt instrument. Arnold was the best the City had to offer. He was underpaid and overworked. If he put in for overtime, he was lucky to collect. He had reached a station in life where he belonged. A man who was over his head, making bottom money, working his ass off and
getting little respect from those at the top. Arnold thought he was being challenged, but then, he should have made a mental note regarding the use of a blunt instrument.

"I didn't associate the two murders," Arnold stated. "I never thought about that. You guys aren't suggesting that I…"

"Relax, Arnold," Sam said. "We are all on he same team." Sam glanced at Carl who looked away. There was no need to chew on Arnold. Just take it easy and make it work.

"Here's how we do it, Arnie," Sam said. "Do the autopsy and let us know what you find."

"What am I supposed to find?" Arnold responded.

"See if you can find another note," Sam said.

Arnold immediately jumped into action, reaching for a fresh pair of gloves. "I'll get started right now!"

"We're outta here," said Carl. Both Carl and Sam walked quickly to the door.

The two men moved into Carl's office and closed the door behind them. Sam pulled down the shade, sealing off the view from anyone walking by. Carl slid into his chair and Sam headed for Mr. Coffee. "Okay, Sam, let's talk hypothetical."

Sam filled his cup and moved to a chair in front of the desk. "Good idea Carl, let's let it all hang out."

Carl put his feet up and leaned backing his chair. "Let's assume that Arnie finds another note in Jane Doe. What then?"

"Then I want to see Ms. Washington."

Carl looked at Sam and asked, "Who's that?"

"The woman who runs the Laundromat."

"Where do you know her from?"

"I was there. I walked inside and saw the dead girl in the dryer."

"The Mays case?"

"I was having breakfast across the street when I saw the cops arrive. Went over to check it out. Mays arrived a few minutes later and I turned it over to him. That was it."

"So, you got there first."

"A few minutes, yes."

"So you are the detective on this case?"

Sam thought about this for a moment. "Carl, are you planning to withhold evidence from Detective Mays regarding this case?"

"Absolutely not," said Carl, sounding a bit indignant. "I was just asking you for some help here."

"Then you plan to turn over that message you found stuffed up this little girl, what's her name, Beth?"

"Hayden," Carl said.

"Beth Hayden. Is that what you're planning to do?" Sam asked.

Carl had not completely thought out the situation. He looked down at his desk, then up again at Sam.

"Okay, here's what we do," Carl said. "First of all we confirm that this is a serial. We wait for Arnie's...Arnold's report. Then we talk again. If it's a serial, I know you should handle it. That's it." The fact of the matter was they had to deal with police politics. It was a constant issue for Carl, from one division to another, to say nothing of Parish to Parish.

"This Beth Hayden girl is Mays' case," Sam said. "The potential serial murderer is my case. I don't want Rampart Division dealing with a serial murderer. You can't turn over our file concerning the note found in the girl's body, because that relates to a serial and the serial belongs to us. Aside from the fact that Mays is about to be retiring in a few weeks from now, I don't want anyone asking him to stay on to finish up on our serial case. It's that easy."

"Okay," said Carl. "I'll buy that for the moment. Sounds good to me."

Sam walked back to his office. Wally was busily organizing the files. When Wally was first brought into the office, after Sam's partner Jack was killed, Carl told Sam of a cop named Wally White, who had a photographic memory. Sam was intrigued by that and thought he would be a great guy to have around, if only for note taking.

"Okay Wally, listen up," Sam said. Wally grabbed a pencil and a yellow legal pad and began taking notes. "Everything I say is top secret. Nothing goes out without my direction." Sam stopped for emphasis, looking Wally in the eyes, and said, "You don't know anything, you got that?" Without waiting for a reply, Sam continued. "Where's the address of Ms. Washington, the woman who…"

"Right here." Wally handed Sam a folder which contained the information he sought. "That's the woman who runs the laundromat," Wally added.

"Good, that's good. Where did you get this file?" Sam glanced quickly through the file. "Is Ms. Washington in this file?"

"Yes sir. I read about her in the newspaper this morning, so I entered her name on the computer. I put the reference in different files. All the files are cross referenced, with other parishes and divisions. In a police file, I found out that a Laila Washington was arrested five years ago, doing a naked lady dance at a Veterans of Foreign Wars affair in Metairie."

"Oh my God." Sam sighed.

"To each his own. So that's where I got her address."

Sam started studying the file. There were three pages from the investigating officer, Detective William Joseph Mays. The rest of the pages in the file held all information concerning the murder, including the address of Lila Washington. Paper clipped to the back of the folder was the newspaper article of the story, given to the press by Detective Mays.

Sam gave some deep thought. Wally had been with him for six months and had never failed him. He was bright and attentive and had never missed an opportunity to allow his photographic memory to show Sam that he was the right man for the job.

"Tell you what," Sam said. "I'll never question you again as to how and where you gathered information. I will just assume you know what the hell you are talking about."

What followed was a hard working day. Arnold sliced and diced Jane Doe and Carl was in his office at the computer. He had begun to isolate and date all prostitution activities. Wally was busily setting up a suspect book, while Sam took a walk to Bourbon Street to see if he could make contact with Lila Washington.

Sam knocked on the door of her small apartment, which was located one block from the laundromat. Lila opened the door and as soon as she recognized Sam, she slammed the door shut.

"That's it!" she shouted. "I had enougha your type. Y'all can go pig-sticking for all I care."

"Ms. Washington, I have an idea how to save your business." Sam stood at the door for a long moment and then the door opened, until the safety chain caught. Only her left eye could be seen peering out.

"So, what you got?"

"All I want is some information and I promise to give you an idea that I almost guarantee will work."

She unchained the door and let him it. Sam walked in and stood in the middle of the room looking around. Not only did Lila run the laundry, she did some sewing. There was a sewing machine against the wall and clothing of various descriptions hung all around the room. Lila was looking at Sam and she rolled her eyes and said: "What you want to know?"

"There's one thing I wondered about," Sam said.

"An what is that?"

Sam started pacing around the room. "I know you weren't there when somebody put the body in the dryer."

"Honey, you can say that again."

"Now, think about the day before, even two or three days before. Did any guy come in the laundry that acted a bit unusual? Someone you didn't know? A new person that made you sorta suspicious? Anybody like that?"

"Nooo, I don't think so."

Sam stopped his pacing and focused on Lila. "Maybe late at night. Maybe last night, when it was slow. Late last night?"

Lila thought a moment regarding the question. No one had ever taken this approach with her before. She had only been asked what she had seen at the moment, but never once did they speculate on anyone that was there before the incident.

"There was a man there, about one fifteen in the morning. Nice guy, tall with a round face. He made me laugh."

Sam drew closer. "He was a funny guy?"

"Kinda funny, yeah. He had on a sweatshirt, with the sleeves cut off at the top. He made some jokes. I'd never seen him before."

"What kind of jokes?"

"I don't remember them, I don't know. Just funny guy stuff."

"So what was he there for? Did he use a washer?"

"All he had was a dress shirt, white dress shirt with some wine stains on the sleeve. I used some of my grape stain remover and it came out fine. Then he put it back in a plastic bag, paid me for the cleanin', and left."

"And that was it?"

"That was it, 'cept he never put his shirt in the dryer."

Sam had something. As meaningless as it was, it was something. "If I get an artist over here, do you think you might help him make a sketch of this guy?"

"Yeah, I can do that. Now what are you gonna do for me?"

It was Sam's turn to tell of his idea to save the laundromat. He really didn't have an idea, just some notions, but he decided to think it out as he talked.

"Okay, here goes. We live in a city that makes its living off of tourists. We don't make that much money cleaning their clothes. So if we change our thought into exciting the tourists, instead of cleaning their clothes, you may make more money."

Lila stared him down.

Sam continued. "The guys drive carriages full of tourists all over town. They show them Lafitte's Blacksmith Shop, the place where Marie Laveau the Voodoo queen lived, cemeteries and every ghost story they can think of and people love it."

"Okay, okay I know that. I live here remember? What's with my problem?"

Sam's idea started to formulate. He was becoming inspired. "Here's what's with you." He withdrew the front page of the *Times Picayune* newspaper from his jacket pocket and opened it in front of Lila. "There you go. You are the star of the show."

Lila looked at the paper, the one printed this morning, with her picture on the front page. She pointed to a large stack of papers piled in the corner. "I already got me four dozen of them things right over there."

Sam was ecstatic. "Well there you go! That's it. You got it! The headline says it all. 'Dead Body Found in French Quarter Laundry.' You have it all, you are the star."

"You crazy?" shouted Lila. She turned around and headed for the door.

"No, listen. You put a sign up that reads, 'Dead Body Found Here.' Then you tape a bunch of these newspapers on the front window. After that you make a shrine back by the actual dryer where the girl died, like the Catholics do."

"I'm a Catholic," Lila volunteered.

"Well there you go again! Then you get a mannequin and put it in the cloths dryer, like that Tussaud's House of Wax, and people will be able to see where the body was found. You could charge admission and sign autographs. I'll get my friend Eduardo to bring his carriage by. Hell, Eduardo was there the day they found the girl. He'll conduct a tour!"

"I ain't got no money for no sign," Lila said.

"Fine, when my guy gets here to draw the sketch, I'll convince him to do the laundromat sign, free of charge. Your customers will come back, they'll be doing their laundry in a National Shrine!"

Lila continued staring at Sam with a deadpan face. She thought it over, studied his intentions, analyzed his motivations, and then she smiled. Sam knew he had her hooked.

"Ms. Washington, I'd appreciate it if…"

"Call me Lila," She interrupted. "You got a good brain on you, boy. We gonna go far."

"Yes ma'am…Lila."

"How would you like some coffee? An' I got some cake in the fridge."

Sam smiled. He would love some coffee and cake. Anything for a picture of the suspected murderer.

Sam walked on down Bourbon and stopped at the gallery where Kelly showed him the painting the night before. The painting she liked was still there. Sam knew the Quarter well. This was a place for tourists, and as such, Sam understood that the price tag seldom fit the goods. He noticed the signed name on the front of the painting to be none other than Jerome Whitaker, who just happened to be a man he had arrested for check fraud three months ago. Jerome was still serving time in Angola prison.

Just to the upper left was another painting by Francis De La Hoya. It was much larger, a scenic painting of a beer garden someplace in Europe. What caught his attention was the care the artist paid to the people. They were having a feast of wild boar, drinking beer and wine and having one hell of a great time. Sam had noticed this painting the night before. It was priced at $1,675 and Sam knew exactly where this painting would hang in his apartment.

Sam also knew the artist, whose real name was Frank Hogan. Frank would happily paint him the same scene for $450. As a matter of fact, Frank Hogan was the very artist he would soon meet at Pirate's Alley to convince him to do the sketch for Lila Washington.

New Orleans is a party town, not unlike many others in the U.S. When you come to a party town, you are prepared to spend money and therefore be taken advantage of by those of a somewhat unscrupulous nature. Sam was not of that mind set. He desired fairness. He wished to obtain proper value for goods sold. Realizing that those involved in this establishment might have previously been absorbed in nefarious activities, he still wished for all to make a profit for their work. However, in no way should one son of a bitch ever try to take him for a sucker!

Seymour Lott looked up from his desk located in the back corner of the room. He was a small, gentle man with large glasses that seemed to frame his entire face. Sam recognized him and realized he had stepped into a gold mine. New Orleans had just become an even smaller town than before. Mr. Lott had been arrested some years ago for involving himself in selling pornography to a juvenile. Lott served eighteen months for his indiscretion and was now out on parole.

"Yes, may I help you?" said Lott, with a half smile.

"Right. I'm interested in the La Hoya painting, in the window. It's marked at $1,675."

"Ah yes, the De La Hoya, you have good taste, sir."

"Look, I don't want to play any games here, okay?"

Seymour was heading for the front window as Sam spoke. He paused and slowly turned around. "What games do we play?" Seymour asked.

"I'll make it easy. I'm about to go meet Frank Hogan. He's got a spot down on Pirate's Alley. I can get him to make one of those up for say, five hundred bucks, then I bring it here and get you to frame it for another hundred. But rather than go through all of that, let's say I give you six-fifty and call it even?"

Seymour quickly became concerned. He well knew that Frank Hogan was Francis De La Hoya, but he didn't recall exactly what he had paid Frank for the painting. "I'll have to check my book." Seymour headed back to his desk, as Sam stopped him with another proposition.

"I'll tell you what, I'll make it even easier. How about seven hundred and you throw in that painting in the window of Bourbon Street with the Hibernia Bank Building in the background. A Jerome Whitaker, isn't it?"

Seymour was once again taken aback. "I beg your pardon?"

"Jerome Whitaker. Isn't he still doing time in Angola on a bad check rap?"

Seymour's body stiffened, his breathing became more agitated. Sam crossed to him and put his hand on his shoulder. It was a friendly placed hand, a hand that said, *You do me a favor and I'll do you* a favor *right back.*

"I tell you what, pal, this is my final offer. I've got only seven hundred bucks for the two paintings. If you paid more than that and can't make a profit, then I'll just walk out and forget it. I'm gonna see Frank in about ten minutes and if he tells me different, I may just come back and talk to you about it."

Seymour stiffened once more. Then Sam delivered the coup de grace.

"Look I'm a detective, I work out of the office on Royal at..." Sam snapped his fingers trying to recall the address.

Seymour interrupted. "It's 348."

"That's it, 348." Sam smiled, looking him in the eye.

"Listen if I had known you were a cop, I'd have..."

"Don't worry about it," Sam interrupted. "I just want you to make enough..."

"No problem," Seymour re-interrupted. "I've got enough. Let me get these ready to go."

As Seymour raced to the window to collect the paintings, Sam moved to a small desk containing gift cards.

"I want one delivered to an address on Toulouse Street and the second one to my office. My name is Sam Pennington. My assistant is Wally, leave it with him."

Sam pulled two cards from the many that were placed on the desktop. They were both a picture of a baby seal playing in a snow bank. It made no sense to Sam what so ever. Why a baby seal in a snow bank in New Orleans? First he wrote the address and phone number of Laila Washington on one and slipped it into his pocket. On the second he made an executive decision which might have some meaning for Kelly. Below the other photo of the playing seal was an open area for Sam to express his thoughts. He pondered for a moment and then wrote:

Dear Kelly,

You were delightful last night. This morning I decided to jog through the Quarter. I kept looking, but only when I crossed Bourbon Street did I see it. You were right, it can only be seen from Bourbon. Your bank! Now I've seen the light.

P.S. How do you like the baby seal playing in the snow?"

With love, Sam

Sam walked over to Royal Street and on down to Pirate's Alley, which bordered the Cathedral on the south wall. There he found Frank Hogan, an artist of fine quality if you could catch him before three o'clock in the afternoon. Like Sam, Frank was a man of few words. He tied a red bandana over his head and wore a large straw hat over that. He also had a ponytail which hung down in the back, just below his shoulders. His look was one of raw character. A scraggily face with tanned skin, covered with a pattern of age wrinkles and scars that seemed to date back to the dark ages. His manner always disguised his true feelings. No matter what he said, when he said it, how he acted, or if he meant it, Frank was always the sweetest and truest friend in the world.

After a moment of brief discussion, Frank agreed to do the job. It wasn't his art or the money; it had to do with Frank's willingness to stay on the right side of the law. They were surrounded by artists, some good, some not so good, others possessing great promise. Frank had the ability to do quality portraits. Sam handed him fifty bucks and also passed him the card, with a baby seal playing in a snow bank, with Lila Washington's address on it.

Frank was doing a pastel of a young girl which was in the final stages of completion. She was a beautiful dark haired child of about ten and her parents looked on as he continued adding various shadings that were needed. As he placed two white dots in the eyes, they seemed to come alive. The entire drawing came alive. It was this quality that made Frank special. The parents were ecstatic and left with the special painting of their special girl.

Frank sat back in his chair and looked at the card Sam handed him. "What the hell is this stupid thing with a seal in a snow bank?" Frank asked.

"Oh it's just something I picked up to write on."

"That's the dumbest thing I ever saw, a seal in a snow bank, in New Orleans."

"Forget the seal," Sam said impatiently. "Forget the snow bank."

"How the hell can I forget it, you handed it to me."

"What the hell does it matter anyway? What's important is the name and address I have written on the card."

Frank took a pair of glasses from his pouch that hung from the back of his chair and put them on.

Sam decided to change the subject. "I just bought a painting by Francis De La Hoya. I got it from a guy named Seymour Lott over at the gallery on Bourbon." Frank just ignored what he heard. He now studied the photo of the seal in a snow bank. "Actually, it's not bad. I like the way the sun reflects across his body. I may wanna paint this someday."

Sam dropped his head to his chest. Frank was in a strange mood. "Frank, I need you to get over to Laila Washington as soon as possible," Sam said. "Get the drawing done by three o'clock. Is that okay with you?"

Frank changed pace again. "How much did you pay for the painting?"

"Seven hundred," Sam replied.

"You must be doing pretty good."

"I'm alright."

"That the one with the people having a party and getting drunk in a German beer garden?"

"Yep."

"Hold on to that one. A de La Hoya is gonna be worth big bucks, after the bastard dies."

"Can you get this done by three o'clock? I really need it."

"Okay."

"You got to stay with her and make her confirm it. She sees the drawing and confirms that is the guy, right?"

"You bet. I'll deliver it to the station."

"There you go. One other thing, I need a hand-lettered sign for the laundry on Bourbon Street. Shouldn't be a big deal. Like the one you did on the Acme over on Bienville."

"Okay," Frank answered.

"Don't make it special, just readable, okay?"

"You got it, Sam. Want me to paint your house for you too?"

Sam smiled at that one. He knew he was taking advantage of a fine artist. "I'll pay you extra for the sign when you're done."

Sam arrived back at the precinct at eleven forty-two, just as his beeper went off. He pulled the unit from his belt and checked the message. It read 911 and followed with his office number. The 911 signaled an emergency. Sam walked the ten more steps to his office door and went inside. There he found Wally, Carl Witherspoon and Arnold Feenie, standing in surprise at his quick response.

"You rang?" Sam asked.

Wally had just hung up the phone and was anxious to speak. "You gotta go back to court. They just got a jury and they'll start the procedures at twelve thirty."

"Okay," Sam stated.

Wally picked up Sam's briefcase, as if to move him quickly from the room. Wally checked his watch. "Court starts in forty-five minutes."

"Hold on," Carl interrupted. "We got time here. We have a major problem." Carl held a plastic envelope over his head. Sam slowly moved in and took it. Through the plastic he could easily read a note, written in the same handwriting as before.

Do not go here. She is mine.

At the bottom of the note, a number:

1

Sam studied the note. "Okay this is it. We have a serial."

Carl moved to the center of the room. "Everybody just sit down and relax. I've got a meeting with the Mayor and the Chief of Police in about an hour. Here's what I will do, and what I want everyone else to do."

They all took seats: Wally behind his desk, Arnold at a chair by the window. As Sam sat on the edge of his desk, he noticed a gift basket of cheese and crackers, along with a fifth of Glenlivet Single Malt Scotch, placed on the other edge.

"What's this?" Sam asked Wally.

Wally looked up. In the midst of all these emergencies, he had to pay attention to the important things in life.

"That came from a guy named Kelly, delivered by someone from the Dixieland Bar on Bourbon. There's a note in the basket."

Sam picked up the note. It was another card like the one he gave to Frank Hogan, with a baby seal playing in a snow bank.

Carl became agitated. "Can we get back to our problem here?"

"Sure thing," Sam answered, but he continued to read the note.

"I got a meeting with the Mayor and the Chief of Police at one o'clock,"

Carl said. "Can you people help me out on this one?"

"I got to leave for a court date at twelve-thirty," Sam answered. "Hang tough a minute."

At the bottom of the card the note said, *"See reverse."* Sam flipped the card over and read the note.

Dear Sam,

I hope last night wasn't a failure for you. I promise to never drink any more Grasshoppers or serve any more Apple Brandy. Furthermore, there will always be a bottle of Glenlivet for you to relax with.

Love Kelly

Sam put the card into his side pocket and slipped into the chair behind his desk. He quickly cleared the old paperwork from his workspace, including the basket from 'Mr. Kelly,' which he pushed under the desk, with his right foot.

"Okay, Carl, go," Sam announced.

Carl started pacing. "I'll meet with the Mayor and the Chief, fill them in with the details as we know them, but I have no idea what the hell these people will want to do until then."

"Most important is getting the hookers to understand the problem," Sam said. "We have to let them know that their lives may be in danger. Wally, let's advise all mobile units within twenty-five miles of this area, that we are looking for a suspect who has potentially murdered two, and possibly three women."

"You got it," Wally responded.

"May I next suggest that we do not tell the media about a serial killer," Sam said. "Carl, tell the Mayor, tell the Chief, but tell them to keep it quiet."

"I don't think I can tell them 'dick squat,'" Carl replied.

"Okay, fine," Sam said. "Then you offer that we're searching for a suspect. We need time to find him. Is that okay?"

Carl took a deep breath. "Oh God, here we go with the bullshit."

"You got a list of the hookers?"

Carl pulled a batch of papers from his jacket pocket. "My computer tells me that we got five prostitutes listed as missing and that's all. Now I have here a list of all the working prostitutes in the New Orleans area, and that list will choke a fucking horse."

"Okay," Sam added. "Wally, go for it. Prepare a list. Get ready to rock and roll. The instant Carl is out of his meeting, we go to press. And we need more help here. Carl?"

Carl realized this thing could get out of control. "I'll take it up with the Chief."

"The Chief is a good man, but he doesn't know what we know," Sam said. "There may be another woman murdered in the next twelve hours. There's a freako out there. A pussy-stuffing, sick son of a bitch, bastard freako out there! At seven o'clock tonight there will be a roll call in every division in this city. I want them to be given notification about this sick person. I want them to warn the hookers. May we at least give the hookers of our city a chance to breathe one more day?"

Carl looked harshly at Sam and Sam sternly looked back. Sam was speaking of police work and Carl had to speak about Social Sciences.

"So let's get Frick and Frack back in here," Sam said.

"Excuse me," Arnold spoke as he stood up. "I really should go back to my office. You guys can handle this." He turned to leave.

Sam stopped him. "Oh no you don't. Carl said you, me and him were the only three people to know that this was a serial. I'm the one who added Wally to the list. So you stay put here, Arnie. You stay."

Arnold stepped back to the filing cabinet, placed his arm onto the top, relaxing into his favorite position.

"You gotta be firm here, Carl," Sam said. "You the man! You call Frick and Frack and tell 'em they got to get back to work here by nine o'clock tomorrow morning. Tell them you will empty their desks and filing cabinets and they can pick up their shit at the front desk."

"And who do you replace them with?" Carl asked. "I don't know if I can do that. There are unions here, you know? I don't know if I can just fire two cops like that."

"Just fire them, Carl. By nine o'clock tomorrow morning. If push comes to shove, we'll draw two cops off the street. We need help here."

Carl glanced over at Arnold, who still leaned against the filing cabinet. Arnold would add nothing to this.

Sam slowly looked around the room. Of the three people he was speaking to, only one had a total concept of what was happening. He directed his next focus to him.

"Wally, at about three o'clock I have an artist coming in. His name is Frank Hogan, an older guy with a ponytail. He'll bring in a drawing of a suspect I got from Lila Washington."

"Who's that?" Carl asked.

"I told you earlier today," Sam said. "She's the lady who runs the laundromat where Beth Hayden was found dead in a dryer. Wally, I also want you to take Frank Hogan down to the morgue. Get him to do a drawing of Jane Doe. Do not pay him anything. Tell him I'll take care of it."

"You got it," Wally responded.

Sam left the room, saying, "Okay people, there you go."

Sam walked out of the precinct, carrying the briefcase that Wally had dutifully prepared for him. He walked quickly while estimating his time to go to his car, drive to the courthouse, park his car, walk to court and get into his seat. All of this in opposition to jogging directly to the courthouse.

After his jog he reached the courthouse with seven minutes to spare. He hit the men's room on the second floor for his first afternoon whiz. He freshened up with two paper towels and placed his black tie on his black shirt. Sam stood at the mirrored wall and took a final look at his image.

"Okay kid, let's go get 'em."

He left the men's room and went half way down the marbled hallway to Judge Marshall Williams' courtroom. On entering the room he found the entire chamber empty, except for a Deputy Sheriff who was eating a sandwich at the clerk's desk. The Deputy told Sam they had called lunch about fifteen minutes ago and they would be back at one-thirty.

It didn't bother Sam. People much bigger than this had crapped on him and he still survived. So he walked to a seat in the back and waited for justice to commence. He was actually thankful for the time he would have alone. He thought about Kelly and that sweet basket of stuff she had purchased for him. She was a great kid, but only that, just a kid. He then thought about Atlantic City, when he was a kid, and his time with his mother and father. And he thought about Vince.

Chapter 4

FLASHBACK:
FORTY-TWO YEARS EARLIER.

SAM PENNINGTON WAS born in Atlantic City, New Jersey. He grew up in an apartment located above the Pennington Hardware store which was owned by his parents, Roy and Martha. In his first sixteen years he saw the town start to fade. Atlantic City was reaching toward the poverty level, which would make it one of the most desperate of East Coast cities. Even the famous boardwalk on the Atlantic Ocean was starting to crumble.

The Boardwalk was a long structure of wooden 'herringbone' shaped wooden walkways, constructed on the beachfront. It was about fifty feet wide and ran about a mile, bordering the beach establishments with the Atlantic Ocean. It was built in the late 1800s and all through the 1940s and '50s, thousands of people would come on a sunny weekend to enjoy the atmosphere. It was here you could rent the world famous rolling chair. A guy could seat his date in the chair and push the cart over the rippling hardwood flooring and he could be a hero to the damsel who rode in style.

When Sam was sixteen, he was already well versed in the hardware business. But there was a new problem on the immediate horizon. Usually there would be an average of fourteen shoppers flowing through the store, but now Sam could only count seven or less and his father, Roy, was forced to release one of the three salesmen. Sam pitched in and helped at every opportunity.

Roy had started life as a carpenter and taught Sam all the magic of woodwork. Sam learned how to handle every electric tool in the store. On the weekends, Sam would set up a small shop in the side parking area and would teach people how to use the tools. He was a success, and one weekend Sam sold four worm gear 16-inch radial saws.

In February of that year his mother became desperately ill. The following August she died. Sam was devastated by his loss and his father thought his life had ended. They buried Martha Pennington at the Seaside Memorial Park Cemetery, and twelve of their friends came to show their respect. There would have been more, but many people had left the city seeking a better life elsewhere. There was a promise of legalized gambling, but that had not happened yet.

Soon Sam would reach his eighteenth birthday and he would be considered an adult. He still had one more year of high school to attend. Sam started his final summer vacation and he decided he would get a job. He would simply avoid entering his last year of high school, since there was no time for that now. With the economy sinking so fast in Jersey, who would spend the time looking for one truant high school senior? He read the want ads and applied to the Boardwalk Bar and Grill, a rather famous restaurant with the reputation for fine dining. He chose the Boardwalk because it was the only job in the want ads that required no experience. There were also no ads for trained carpenters. They proudly advertised the restaurant as "The finest dining on the Atlantic Coast."

The place wasn't really on the boardwalk, but about twelve blocks south of where the real boardwalk ended, located on a high knoll, overlooking the Atlantic. Sam took a bus to get there and then had to walk twelve blocks to the location. He had lived in Atlantic City all his life and had never seen the ocean.

The Boardwalk Bar and Grill stood alone, built out onto a flat piece of land that was as close as possible to the ocean without actually being in it. It was a one-story building, not all that fancy, painted white with blue trim. It was the small things that made it special. There was the black and gold awning that ran from the entrance to the parking lot, to keep people dry in bad weather. There were five golf carts with the same black and gold awning material that were parked at the side. The parking attendants would pick up customers who needed a ride and deliver them to the fancy wood carved front door.

Sam was dressed as well as he could be, but in this environment he felt like a hayseed. His black windbreaker jacket was his only special wearing apparel, which he zipped half way up and smoothed it straight. Under that he wore a white shirt with no tie, a pair of black Levis and white sneakers.

He did the best he could with what he had and moved on. The sign read SERVICE ENTER THROUGH THE REAR and Sam complied. When he walked to the back of the restaurant, he found himself in a rather beautiful seaside garden area. A three-foot brick wall had been built along the side of the cliff, overlooking the ocean. The wall was built to prevent the customers from walking too close to danger. There was also several large gas heaters positioned high above the table area, to provide heat for the cold night air. There were twenty tables located in the area, which was covered with the same black and gold canvas material. To the left were French doors which were left open, so that service people could easily move about and prepare for the luncheon crowd. Through the windows, he could see the main dining room with another thirty tables. The windows were covered with a dark gray film, protecting customers from the direct sunlight.

Five people were working, busily preparing for an eleven o'clock lunch hour. Each table was perfectly set, with decorated china plates, crystal and silverware. The final touch was a small nosegay of fresh flowers on each table. It was then that Sam noticed a lovely young girl about his age, with strawberry blonde hair. Sam was of an age, when beautiful young girls easily caught his attention.

She was dressed like everyone else, black shoes, black slacks, a white man's shirt and a black bow tie. Her hair was pulled back with a pink ribbon. That pink ribbon, holding her lovely strawberry blond hair, made her the most beautiful creature he had ever seen. He quickly looked away back toward the ocean, then he would glance at her from the corner of his eye, but she didn't notice Sam. If he got the job, if he ever got the guts, someday he might say "hello." Then he smelled something. He tasted the scent of it all. The freshly cut flowers, joined with the smell of the sea. Then there was the aroma coming from the kitchen. It was eggs, and bacon and many other things. Sam realized he was hungry.

He moved across the walkway to the kitchen. The kitchen was rather small. Too tiny for a place with this size operation he thought. He would soon learn that the size was just right. A large kitchen makes for wasted steps. Compact was efficient when it came to a volume operation. There were five people in the kitchen. The chef, Pierre La Forge, was a large man weighing about 270 pounds. He wore the standard master chef's outfit: black and white checked trousers, a white jacket with an extra large white table napkin tied in front of his neck and a large high hat, or *toque*, perched casually on his head. He also carried a cane with carved silver molding on the sides and a large silver handle. When he spoke he punctuated his instructions by pointing the walking stick, making sure nothing was mistaken.

One person, a lady, took care of the salads and bread. The rest of the staff were all men. One of them worked on the appetizers, while a *sous-chef* and his assistant took care of the entrees. It seemed impossible for five people to work in such a small space, but they seemed to walk through the kitchen, anticipating each and every one's move. There was never a mistake. It was a symphony and Sam watched in awe.

"You the kid with the appointment?" a voice said.

Sam looked up quickly. "Yes sir."

Chef Pierre crossed to him, hobbling on his walking stick. Sam held out his hand to the chef. "Nice to meet you, Chef." Chef La Forge took his hand and they shook. "Yes sir, I'm Sam Pennington. Nice to meet you, sir."

"What have you been doing before this?"

"Working for my dad. He owns Pennington Hardware."

"Yes, I know that place. Want some breakfast?"

"No thank you sir, I'm…"

Pierre interrupted. "Charlie, make the kid some eggs." Charlie grabbed a frying pan from a large rack about the counter and started with Sam's breakfast.

"You been here before?" Pierre asked.

"No sir, first time."

"Okay, let me show you how it works."

As he spoke, Sam had the notion that the chef was not French. From his accent he sounded Brooklyn-born. Pierre moved into the main dining room and Sam followed without question.

"We run one of the best places on the East Coast." Pierre paused in the hallway leading from the front door. Dressing the wall was displayed many photographs and awards given to the restaurant and of Pierre himself, showing the more than twenty years he had been there. He was pictured with celebrities, the Mayor of New York, councilmen and Senators.

"Here's how we do it. We cater to the best of the best, serve them lunch and dinner, six days a week. We are closed on Mondays." Pierre pointed to one of the pictures. "That's me with Mayor Lindsay in '69."

As Pierre spoke, Sam again noticed the girl with the strawberry blonde hair. She came in from the patio and glanced over in his direction. He thought he may have seen a smile directed at him, but that was just a guess, then she simply moved on about her work. If there was a God, Sam thought, *please give me the strength to say hello.* Pierre continued to ramble.

"We get our beef flown in from Kansas City, corn-fed, the best you can buy. Lobsters from Maine, best you can buy. All the rest from the docks right here, best you can buy. People who work here are the best you can buy. You want to be one of them?" As Sam drew his breath to answer a "yes sir," Pierre headed back to the kitchen. Sam followed.

They walked into the kitchen and there was a table which was now completely set, just as though it were in the main dining room. Everything was placed perfectly. With his walking stick, Pierre pointed to the chair. Sam slowly sat at the table while the waitress served a small breakfast bread, covered with a napkin. Pierre moved to the stove area, checking on his two large Barons of beef roasting there. He spooned more *au jus* over the baking meat. Then Charlie served Sam his breakfast, a medium breakfast steak, Kansas corn fed, the best you can buy, with three eggs over easy and a side of cottage-fried potatoes. Dressing the plate were three asparagus, placed in a decorative fashion.

How good can this get? Sam thought. It got better. When he tasted his steak it was from heaven. It was tender and juicy. Sam decided then and there that he wanted to become a world-class chef.

"You want some sauce for the steak or eggs?" Pierre asked, holding a pot in his hand. It was béarnaise but Sam did not recognize it.

"No sir, thank you, I'm fine."

"Here, try it on the asparagus." He spooned two dollops of the sauce on the vegetable. "Okay, just holler if you want more."

Sam ate like a king. It was the finest breakfast he had ever had. He tried a breakfast roll from the covered basket but it was too hot to the touch. There was a small bowl with what looked like white butter and after the bread cooled a bit, he spread the stuff on the roll. It was a delicious soft cheese. Everything was delicious. At the end of the meal Sam was served a small salad with a sweet and sour dressing. It was a delicious finish to a fine meal. The salad at the end of the meal was Pierre's signature dish. He liked it that way.

Pierre once again basted his roast. He then sat down at the opposite end of the table. "Okay kid, here's how it goes. I pay you ten dollars an hour and that's top dollar."

Ten bucks an hour! Sam thought. *Ten bucks an hour would buy this guy a trained uniformed driver.* Sam's heart was palpitating.

Pierre continued. "Everyone here works for ten hours. You will be part time so that's five hours a day, okay?"

"Yes sir, that's fine." Sam would be assigned the use of the company van, a twelve-year-old Dodge panel truck with the name of the restaurant painted on the outside. Pierre gave him the address of Vince Lockwood, whom he would drive to the market.

The next day he started at four o'clock in the morning. Sam dressed quickly and took the van to the restaurant to pick up the chef's shopping list, which was stapled to the rear kitchen door. Next, he went to the home of Vince Lockwood. He and Vince drove to the docks to the wholesale river market. Vince was past seventy years old and had a severe arthritic condition, particularly in his hands and knees. As Vince rubbed his knurled hands together, Sam asked if he took something for the pain.

"Aspirin," Vince said. "Aspirin does me just fine."

"My dad has a touch of arthritis too. He has a cream to rub into his hands. Says it does the trick."

"Not me, waste of time and money, aspirin does the trick."

The aspirin didn't do the trick. Out of the corner of Sam's eye, he could see Vince grimace as he continued to massage his hands.

Later, when Sam got some money together, he bought Vince some of his father's arthritis cream. Vince slipped the tube into his pocket without saying a word of thanks. It was four weeks later that Vince would ask Sam if he might get him another tube of that stuff. Vince ponied up a ten dollar bill, which Sam took. Sam told Vince that he would get a receipt and the change tomorrow, and they both dropped the subject. However, they both knew the real truth. Vince's joints had greatly improved.

They arrived at the Market Service Central, around five o'clock in the morning. This was a market that only dealt with those in the restaurant business. It was here, at Vince's direction, where Sam learned about the complications of running a first class restaurant. They moved through the place, choosing the best food available. Vince chose a melon and would say loudly, "Sam, this is too green," or "not ripe enough," "This is too soft, it's past its prime." Once he studied an ear of corn and stated, "This is shit. We'll have to go with white shoe-peg corn. Sam, go get me two of those big boys of white corn." Vince held his hands about fourteen inches apart, showing Sam the size of the can.

Sam wandered around, looking for vegetables in a fourteen inch can and he wondered, what the hell was shoe-peg corn? So it went until they finished that part of the market. It was now time to move into the seafood section.

They picked up the Maine lobsters which were shipped to the Boardwalk that morning. Vince picked out any other fish that was on his list. He also asked what the fresh catch of the day was. It was here that Vince displayed his true art: that of checking the fish and bartering the price.

"Hey, you bastards!" Vince said. "You got to help me out here. I'm on a budget. If you can't help me out here, just give me ten pounds of bait. We'll feed them that. An' we'll advertise where we got it!"

After much haggling they finally knocked a nickel off the price per pound and Vince acted as if he had been stabbed in the chest. As the fishmonger packed the fish in boxes of ice, Vince and Sam sat down for coffee. Sam noticed that Vince was in bad condition. He was having trouble holding his cup. He used both hands to get the cup to his lips. After taking a few sips to clear some room at the top, he reached into his pocket and came up with a small crinkled brown bag. It contained a half pint of some golden colored liquid, which he poured into his cup.

"So how long you been doing this?" Sam asked.

Vince looked up and smiled. "All my fucking life." Vince poured again from the brown bag into his coffee. By now the brew was growing stronger.

"What's that, brandy?" Sam asked.

"This is from my doctor, Dr. James Beam. When bone meets bone, it hurts like a son of a bitch and this elixir from Dr. James, oils the tortured joints and makes them easier to move. I'd offer you some but you're still on duty and I'm now off for the rest of the day."

"How old are you, Vince?"

Vince looked steadily at Sam, and then with a far-off gaze, he said, "I guess it's how you look at it. If I were dressed properly, with a clean shave and in a dark alley, I could pass for sixty-five." He looked at Sam with an impish smile. "But today with circumstances as they are, I'd have to say seventy-five."

Vince took another sip of his "coffee." "Let's make that seventy-nine and be done with it. He finished his coffee and placed the cup on the table. "I'm eighty-three and that's my final answer."

It took until nine-fifteen for Sam and the market boys to pack the van. Sam was worried about not being back by nine o'clock, as Pierre had told him, but Vince insisted that ten o'clock would be just fine. As the last load of lobsters were packed on board, Vince walked next door to the local market and when Sam arrived with the van, Vince came out with a fresh bag of Dr. James' elixir and hopped into the van. By now he had mellowed out from the hard-ass he was to a rather nice person, one full of information. Sam was ready with the questions.

"So what's this all about? I got the job and it's a great place, but I don't know anything. Why me?"

"That's easy. I'll bet you got the whole show, right?"

Sam didn't know what he meant.

Vince continued. "They set a full table and made you a fine meal. You gotta know the restaurant business. Look at it this way, we sell food, but the food is only half the battle. Sure, it's great stuff, but if you put the same meal on as a buffet, or smorgasbord, I guarantee you there would be very few people who would like that presentation. And for sure, not at those prices."

Vince was getting into it and he continue. "That buffet shit is served just a little better than that miserable fucking fast food hamburger crap. At the Boardwalk we do the presentation, that special moment. The atmosphere and the chef is what really sells the show." Vince looked Sam straight in the eye. "Got it?"

"No," Sam answered, a bit confused.

"Okay, a steak dinner costs George about five bucks."

"Who's George?" Sam interrupted.

"George is Pierre. I'll tell you about that later, too much now for your little pea brain to absorb. Let's get back to the show. So George spends five bucks on the meal. This could be the same as your mom cooks at home. You got music playing while you eat at home?"

"No, usually the TV is on."

"No TV at the restaurant, it's a special place. You and your lady are going out! You aren't going to watch any fucking TV game show. You arrive at the restaurant and they pick you up from your car and take you right to the big carved front door. You wait, just enough time for you to take in the pictures of Pierre with the Mayor and other celebrities. Makes you feel like you are on the inside too. Then the Maitre'd comes over and welcomes you to the restaurant and directs you to your table. You are seated in a beautiful setting, with lights dimmed and music playing softly. No fucking game shows on TV! Got it so far?"

"Yes sir, I think I get the picture."

"While you are waiting for dinner, you enjoy delicious hot French bread, with a fancy cheese spread on it. You and your girlfriend are drinking Mai Tais that you ordered from the cocktail waitress. Your girlfriend didn't notice the lady who served the drink, but you remember. You know, the one with the long hair and tight pants that were stuck half way up the crack of her ass? The thought of missing the game show in your mother's kitchen no longer bothers you. You are in a world of delight. Just like the Mayor and those other celebrities you saw pictured on the wall. When that steak comes to your table, sizzling, you are involved in a show. It becomes a special night, of total attention and entertainment."

Suddenly Vince grabbed his chest, a startled look on his face. He gasped for air and quickly searched his pockets.

"What is it, Vince? What's the matter?"

Vince finally found a small bottle of pills, opened the cap, poured out a nitro glycerin tablet, and popped it under his tongue. Sam pulled the truck over to the side of the road. Vince was breathing heavily, gasping for air and holding his hand over his chest. In a moment it subsided. "Boy, that feels better. I'm fine. I'm alright."

They both sat silent for a time, then Sam said. "Was that a heart attack?"

"Oh yeah, happens all the time."

"Oh boy! I'm wringing wet. You scared me, Vince."

"Sorry about that. A little over a month ago I had the really big one. Wound up in the South Bay Hospital. They kept me there for two weeks and two weeks home to recoup. So George comes over and he is hysterical. Not because I had a heart attack, no way. He's upset because he will be buying the morning supplies while I recuperate. For the next two weeks he has to rise at four-thirty in the morning. Now instead of putting in a twelve hour day, he's putting in sixteen. If you think I had a bad attack, you should have seen George by the end of the last week."

Sam finally figured it out. "Now I got it! He brought me in and cooked me breakfast and went through all of that, so he could spend four more hours in the sack."

Vince started laughing, and then coughing and laughing and then just coughing. Sam pulled over to the side of the road again, this time he simply slapped Vince on the back. Finally Vince gained control.

"Oh yeah, he got you alright. Did he show you the picture of him and Mayor Lindsey?"

"Oh yeah," Sam said. Vince started laughing again. "Then they sat me down in the kitchen and everybody started serving me this beautiful meal on the best dishes in the house." Vince started all over again laughing and coughing with Sam slapping him on the back.

"So what about Pierre?" Sam asked. "How did that come about?"

"His name is George Forge. We both worked at this small place in New York. It was back in the late fifties. George got this offer to go across the river to the Boardwalk so he became Pierre La Forge. He thought it looked better on the menu."

Vince rambled on for the ten minutes it took Sam to drive him to his apartment. After dropping Vince off and seeing that he was all right, Sam made it to the restaurant shortly past ten.

Pierre was out of the back door quickly and two bus boys followed him to unload the van.

"Everything go alright?" Pierre asked.

"Yes sir, fine."

"Come on inside and have some breakfast."

The meal was as magnificent as yesterday's. This time it was eggs Benedict served on the beautiful china with hot rolls and cream cheese. Sam realized he had not been set up yesterday. It was just how Pierre treated everyone. When he finished his meal, Pierre handed him fifty dollars for the day's work and went back to basting his new roast. Sam decided right then to do a great job for George "Pierre La" Forge.

DAY 2, CONTINUED

It was now twelve-thirty and the courtroom was rapidly filling up. The prosecution team was present: Jerry Weinstein and his associate, Frank D'Jorno. After a moment, Donald Mosely moved into the room. Mosely was wearing a beautifully cut, light blue serge suit with matching shirt and tie. Sam couldn't see his feet and wondered if his shoes and socks might also be a matching blue. As Mosely crossed to the jury box, Sam stood up to get a better view. There it was! Light blue suede shoes with matching socks. He was in fact the perfect Blue Boy. Sam wondered, *Could that be...might that be...a fresh haircut?*

Sam sat back down. A small audience gathered around him, mostly African American people, wanting to see justice done. Sam had been racing through this trial for two days now, and all he wanted to say to everyone was:

'*I saw this guy do it. He killed my partner. Now let's hang his ass and get on with our lives.*'

The bailiff announced the judge's arrival and all stood up. Judge Marshall Williams was a distinguished white man in his mid-fifties. Sam took a quick look at the Clerk, Ms. Williams. He found her eyes staring directly at him, with a knowing smile on her face. He had asked her if the judge had a pretty daughter. Now Sam smiled and dropped his head. The gavel came down and the jury was brought in. The opening arguments commenced. Next was Mosley's turn.

Sam had been involved in over one hundred trials. He received critiques from many lawyers. He was trained by specialists in the art of testimony and was considered one of the best NOPD had. Now he watched Mosely perform. He was no doubt what many called the best in the business. Forget the Blue Boy outfit. That didn't mean much. What really counted was what he had to say and how he said it. It didn't matter what Mosely thought and it didn't make a hill of beans what Sam thought. For that matter, even the judge did not count. It was all on the jury. Make them like you and believe in you and you are a winner. If push came to shove, make just one of them believe and trust in you. That is what Mosely set out to accomplish.

His voice was deep and warm. He had a casual approach to everything. Mosley could have started by saying, "Ladies and Gentlemen of the jury…" But that would have been too cold. Official yes, but frozen with the lack of emotion. Instead, Mosely opened with a warm smile and a soft statement: "Hello." Then he paused and looked at each and every one of the nine men and three women on the jury, making solid eye contact with each of them. "My name is Donald Mosely and I represent a young boy named Joshua Skanes, Jr.."

His speech was perfect. Every syllable well pronounced, every diphthong properly distinguished. It was the perfect All American speech – the King's English, if you will. Those on the jury had to be impressed. When he spoke of Joshua Skanes Jr., he always referred to him as 'this young boy,' or 'a child, not yet an adult.'

Sam looked over to his left and saw Junior Skanes, sitting at the defense table. He thought back to when he first interviewed Skanes at the station, early in the morning after the killing. There he was, sitting at the station, in handcuffs, with his sneering expression. There was the arrogance that he had shown that night, as he raised the gun in his hand and pulled the trigger…twice. Sam could hear the nastiness of his words and the foul-mouthed attitude that he spewed forth for all to hear.

Sam did not quickly recognize this. Six months earlier, his hair had been in dread locks. Now it was styled as if he were Joe College. He wore a white shirt, open at the collar, with a light gray V-neck sweater. Sam thought he looked like one of the Menendez brothers. They wore pullovers also, to look more youthful and innocent. However, the only sad thought was that the Menendez brothers were finally found guilty of brutally murdering their parents.

Now here it was again. Mosely had this sick murderer whom he now portrayed as someone he was not. He even had him wear glasses, to provide a more studious appearance. Sam was hard put to listen to the rest of Mosley's opening arguments. He described Junior as a desperate child who was petrified of the police. Those cops had so brutally attacked many of his friends, he feared for his life.

'*Bullshit,*' Sam uttered under his breath. Then Sam was on the stand. He was sworn in and now it was his lawyer's turn. But Jerry never left his chair. He simply sat there referring to his notes and asked questions with no emotion. Sam responded truthfully and honestly. That was it! It was over! More than ever, Sam knew what a sacrificial lamb felt like.

Next it was Mosley's turn. He stepped forward and looked directly at Sam, a soft smile crossed his face. "Good afternoon, Detective Pennington." His silky voice smoothly slid its way through the chamber.

"Good afternoon, Mr. Mosley," Sam responded.

"What I wish to do is start at the beginning." Mosley stated. "On the date in question, you arrived in the French Quarter at what time?"

"As I recall, it was around six-thirty p.m."

"Was it your usual job to drive around the Quarter at this hour?"

Sam thought a moment about the question. *Just tell the truth,* he said to himself. *Don't get fancy.* "We had to get to the garage in the Quarter. So, if we wanted to park the car, we'd have to go into the Quarter." Sam looked over at the jury. He studied them for a moment. Mosely continued to smile.

"But you decided to go up Bourbon Street. You had a long day in Baton Rouge and then the long drive back. Why up Bourbon Street?"

"I love the music, I love the people, and I love Bourbon Street."

"Isn't it possible that one of you said, 'let's see if we can find some trouble on Bourbon Street?'"

Sam got the drift of where this was going. "We were both off the clock. Other than hearing some music on the way to the garage, we wanted to park the car and go home. Royal is where the garage is. Royal is one way, heading south. The only way we can get there is to pick another street that heads north. We chose Bourbon. We intended to drive up Bourbon, find a street that went one way to the east, then turn right on Royal, and head south to our garage. The Quarter can be a little confusing."

"Alright, Detective Pennington, let's assume that is what happened."

Sam usually loved it when someone called him Detective. It was said with respect to his position, like being referred to as *Judge* or *Sheriff*, someone in authority. The way Mosely said *Detective Pennington*, it sounded dirty. Mosely said it nicely. He didn't seethe or snarl showing his teeth, as he spat out the name, but his intention was clearly meant to cause the jury to dislike him and his testimony.

Mosely took a position closer to the witness stand. "Let us start from the moment you first saw this young boy inside the Dixieland Bar. You had testified in your deposition that your partner had stopped the car. Then you stated, and I quote: 'A black boy was running through the club heading for the French doors, leading out to St. Louis Street. The band had continued to play, many customers did not even notice what had taken place. Over at the bar, Leonard, the bartender stood motionless.' Was that your testimony, Detective Pennington?"

"Yes it was."

"And when you first saw the defendant, he was moving away from the bar. Is that correct?"

"Yes."

"How bright were the lights on Bourbon Street at this point in time?"

"It's well lit. You can clearly see everything that happens."

"And the club, the Dixieland, what is the brightest spot that one could see?"

"That would be the bandstand."

"And how bright were the lights at the bar?"

"It's dimmer at the bar. But we saw Mr. Skanes running from the bar, past the bandstand and out of the door. He had a paper bag in his left hand and a gun in his right."

Mosely looked up at the Judge, who was paying little attention to all of this and asked a question. "Your honor, if I may? I suggest in the spirit of conducting an expedient trial, that the witness should be advised to answer all defense questions as simply as possible. His answer was, 'It's dimmer at the bar.' And now I must object to all that was said after that."

The judge looked over at Jerry Weinstein, who did not react.

"Objection sustained," The judge stated. "Please confine your answers to a brief *yes* or *no* whenever possible. Do not elaborate. I instruct the jury to disregard everything of the witness' testimony after 'It's dimmer at the bar.'"

"Thank you, Your Honor." Mosely turned back to Sam. "When did you have your last physical?"

"About eleven months ago."

"And you had your eyes checked then?"

"Yes, they were. Yes."

Mosely walked back to the defense table, one of his soldiers held out two pieces of paper. Mosely took only the top sheet and stood with his back to Sam, reviewing it. The assistant was a new guy whom Sam had not seen before when he saw Mosely and his staff leave the courtroom yesterday. He was an African American male, wearing a gray suit that seemed too large for his body. As Sam studied him longer it was obvious that the man, in an effort to feel like a bigger person, had indulged in the art of weightlifting. Now his small body had grown much larger in its girth, but his head remained the same size. As a result, he looked like a pinhead in a large gray suit.

Mosely turned and moved a few steps toward Sam. "I read in your ophthalmologist's report that you had a left eye problem, which might cause you to need corrective lenses for your vision. Is that correct?"

Sam opened his ledger containing all items prepared by Wally. He well knew there was no mention of this report in the ledger. He also knew that Mosely had the report. Now it was out in the open anyway, and Sam decided to play the game. He continued to sift his way through the large file. Finally, Mosely became impatient.

"Is that correct, Detective?"

"I can't seem to find that letter you are reading from in my file. If I may have a moment longer." Sam continued his search.

"If I may approach the witness, your Honor?" Mosely asked.

"Yes you may," the judge responded.

Mosely moved to Sam and handed him page one, of his doctor's review.

Sam took it and studied it. Then he looked up at Mosely. "Where did this come from?" Sam asked.

"That is not the question, Detective," Mosely said. "The question was, is that correct? Did you in fact, have a potential left eye problem that could cause you to use corrective lenses for your vision?"

Sam looked over at Jerry, who was going through his notes, attempting to arrange future stupid questions. The fact was, Sam needed to take a leak. He had been in that courtroom since one thirty, and he would do nothing to hold up the trial. He crossed his legs and tried to relax his bladder.

"Does my lawyer have a copy of this?" Sam asked.

Suddenly, Mosley's face became frozen. He quickly turned and moved back to his table, leaning in and asked a question of pinhead.

Sam had decided this was the time for him to assert his persona into the case. He well knew that his report was to be placed in his police file as a general record of his health. Sam wanted to stir up trouble, just to get Mosely to back off. By bringing up Sam's eye condition, Mosely was attempting to cause a false question in the minds of the jurors. If only one juror had eventually voted that there was a conceivable problem with the prosecution in the charging of this case, the entire trial could be thrown out, or it could even become a 'hung jury.' Sam did not want that to happen. He would now spend every opportunity to cause Mosely more pain than gain. Just as Mosely had now challenged his eye exam, Sam would now challenge the privacy act!

"Isn't this against the privacy act?" Sam asked.

Mosley quickly jumped in. "Your Honor, this paper just came to my attention last night. I have a copy of it for the prosecution."

"But this is my medical report," Sam said with alarm. "This is only for me and my doctor and my chief. How can you, how can anybody, how is possible for anyone to see this? This is private. This is against the Privacy Act! In Congress!"

The judge banged his gavel down. "Side bar!" he shouted. Mosely moved quickly to the judge while Jerry stood up, clueless as to what had just happened. He fumbled his way out from behind his table and grabbed a yellow legal pad so he could take notes. Sam could see that Mosely was making apologies, while Jerry was condemning every action he could think of.

Sam looked over at the jury. They were twelve loving and kind New Orleanians, including one woman about the age of sixty. She wore a pair of thick glasses that looked like the bottom of two shot glasses and seemed to be staring at him. Sam gave her a subtle smile and she quickly turned and looked away. Sam knew then that this could be his enemy.

His eyes gazed across the room to Joshua Skanes, Jr. who sat quietly with a passive expression. He was actually a rather handsome young man, with his proper haircut and the dread locks gone. What was about this boy that made him so wrong, that made him so evil? Then his eyes refocused on the people sitting behind him.

It was Mr. and Mrs. Joshua Skanes. Mrs. Skanes was in her mid-fifties. Her hair was covered with a brightly colored bandana, tied at the side, which then flowed down over her left shoulder. Her dress and jacket were a light brown with gloves that matched. Her jewelry placed her in a position of wealth. A large gold chain hung around her neck, which flowed into three tiers. As best that Sam could see, she wore three rings, one of them a diamond to die for.

She sat frozen with the lessons of a lifetime. Her mouth ran down on each side and her steely brown eyes peered out into the courtroom, as though she saw nothing but bad people, doing nothing but bad things to her child. She had raised her boy well, causing him to be the person she had created.

Then he looked over at Mr. Skanes, Sr.. It was like day and night. He was in his late fifties, but looked more like sixty-five, a large man with handsome features. He wore a dark shirt with a light gray windbreaker. Sam noticed his hands. They were wrapped around each of his arms. They were the hands of a laborer. They were strong hands, hands that had dug in dirt and cement all of his life. His face was passive.

His countenance suggested that he had the done best he could in life and now he was now sitting in, suffering the slings and arrows of outrageous fortune. In short, his kid should pay for the crime he committed.

The side bar concluded, with Jerry seeming angry and Donald Mosely wearing a smirk on his face. The judge made an announcement. "This file is permissible under the court's authority to accept it. The defense had a legal right to obtain this report."

The judge also challenged Defense Attorney Mosley for not instantly handing this report to the Prosecution Attorney Jerry Weinstein. The deal was done. Mosely returned to his spot at the witness table and requested the clerk to read the last question that was asked.

The court reporter, a white female of modest secretarial abilities, quickly ran through her paper file located at the back of her machine. Sam noticed that she also wore glasses.

"I can't seem to find that in my file," She stated. "If I can have a moment longer."

Mosely was becoming more impatient. He wanted to provide the jury with a nice neat package and now it was becoming unraveled.

"What was the witness answer to my question?" Mosely asked. "Please go back and find the original question I asked."

The reporter searched on through her paperwork and finally found the question. "Yes, here it is. 'I read in your ophthalmology report, dated January 22, 1999, that you had a left eye problem that could cause you to use corrective lenses for your vision. Is that correct?"

Sam continued looking at the first page of the letter.

"Will you answer the question, Detective Pennington?" Mosely asked.

Sam looked up and asked, "Well yes, if I had the rest of the letter."

Mosely quickly moved back to Pinhead, grabbed the second sheet and started to move back to Sam. Then he caught himself and froze for a moment.

"May I approach the witness, your honor?"

The judge stated, "Yes you may."

Mosely moved in and handed Sam the second sheet of paper and then stepped back a few feet. Sam read it and stated, "Okay, I've read it."

"And what is your answer?" Moseley asked.

"Well, the second page reads and I'll quote, 'This situation is not now thoroughly evident but, should be considered for future evaluation."

"Since you had this report made in January of 1999 and this shooting took place on the following July, is it not possible that you had failing eye problems at that time?" Mosley asked.

"Not really. The eye problem in my left eye was regarding my reading ability. I may need reading glasses in a few years, or maybe never. That's what I was told anyway, but as I sit here, I can still read just fine."

Sam was confident that they had just spent over twenty minutes of valuable court time on this issue and that Sam had won the battle. He had seen everything that happened at the crime scene. His eyes were fine. His doctor's report had said that. But then Mosely smiled broadly and turned to the jury. He softly clapped his hands together as if to say, *I have you and I have won the battle.*

What the hell was he doing with the handclap and the big blue boy smile? Sam wondered to himself. *Does this guy think the jury wasn't listening to my testimony? Does he think everybody in this room is STUPID?'* Sam looked over at the jury and caught the eye of the lady with the shot glass glasses. She was looking at him and smiling. Sam smiled back. He had just made a friend.

Sam had tagged Mosely out at first base, but with a smile and a handclap he rounded first base and headed for second. The only umpire on the field was the judge, who simply sat behind the bench thinking about his next golf game.

It was all a joke. Sam knew it, Mosely knew it, even the judge knew it and Jerry didn't have a clue. But there might be one member of the jury who possibly didn't know it. That would be the one person who might cause a hung jury. *God, but this is a lousy business!* Sam thought. *I really need to take a leak.*

Mosely and his boys moved two easels out and then displayed a massive board, four feet high by eight feet long. It was the perfect drawing of the scene of the crime, showing the area of Bourbon Street, the Dixieland Bar and Grill, along with St. Louis Street. The diagram also included the front and rear measurements of the house located on St. Louis St., every measurement assessing one inch equal to one foot.

There were four vehicles, three white cars and one large cement mixer truck. The first white car was marked DETECTIVE, the remaining white cars were labeled POLICE and the cement truck was labeled TRASH. Evidently the toy store where they bought these vehicles did not have a trash truck. It was like sticking notes on your refrigerator. Sam surmised that there was a magnet on the bottom of each vehicle, and a backing on the board that contained a metal sheet of some kind, allowing the cars and truck to hold to the surface. The vehicles were also marked in the index, at a ratio of one inch equals one foot.

Mosely then asked the judge to allow the exhibit to be placed as Exhibit A and next asked the judge to accept his following items as Exhibit 1, which listed it as the emergency phone call from the witness, Detective Sam Pennington. The judge agreed and Mosely set about his next confrontation.

Sam now sat through the most painful series of questions he could be asked. Blue Boy had created some confusion, purposefully designed to baffle and puzzle the jurors. Even Sam started to sweat. The jurors were trying to keep up with the questions and answers, a few of them keeping notes on a pad of paper.

Mosely asked, "What time was it when you first called the emergency police number?"

Sam knew the answer to that. It was in his phone record. The time of that call appeared on the print out. It was public knowledge. It was even published in the *Times Picayune* newspaper. All of these questions were asked and answered during the deposition a month ago and again today with his answers to Jerry, the City Attorney.

Sam re-opened his book to the proper page, making sure the jury saw his action and read the telephone report. "The phone company report states that my original call was made at six-ten plus twelve and one-tenth seconds."

"And that call was made as your partner turned onto St Louis Street?"

"Yes it was."

"But there was a pause between the time when the defendant moved from the Dixieland Bar and when your car actually turned onto St Louis Street?"

"I'm not sure what you mean?"

"Well, isn't it true that the trash truck had not yet cleared the area in front of you, Detective Pennington?"

"That is true," Sam said. "I actually made contact with emergency as we turned onto St Louis Street. While we were still parked on Bourbon and the boy ran out of the side door. The trash truck was just starting to move ahead. Jack, my partner, had to wait a brief second before the trash truck left him room for us to move through onto St Louis."

"A brief second?"

"Yes. I would say it was three seconds and then we turned onto St. Louis."

"Might it have been four?"

"It was an instant. I would say three seconds."

"Alright, we have changed it from a brief second to three seconds. That would be a thousand one, a thousand two, a thousand three. That isn't a lot of time for a heavy truck to move ahead and out of your way, is it?"

"The truck started to move earlier. We turned onto the street in three seconds."

Mosely moved to the display. He placed the car marked DETECTIVE and the TRASH TRUCK onto the diagram. "Is this where these two vehicles were on the night in question, Detective?"

Sam studied the layout. It was exactly as Sam had remembered both of them being situated. "Yes. That's about where they were."

Mosely removed a piece of white tape covering a series of black arrows, showing where Skanes, Jr. ran from the club. The black arrows showed the boy had started at the bar, moved through the club and then made a left turn onto St. Louis. But Mosely tore the tape off before the arrows got to the house on St. Joseph. "Is this the movement that you saw the defendant make, Detective Pennington?"

"Yes, that's about it."

Mosely moved the truck forward and then moved the detective car turning it on to St. Louis. "Then your car turned on to St Louis? And you made an emergency call on your cell phone. At the same time you looked up and saw the defendant moving quickly forward. But you had lost sight of him for three seconds. Thousand one, thousand two, thousand three. Is that correct?"

"Yes."

"And when you next saw the accused, as he ran up St. Louis Street, how far had he gone?"

"He had gone about five feet."

"Five feet in three seconds?"

Once again Sam's bladder was crying for some relief. He shifted in his seat to the other side and re-crossed his legs. In doing so, he felt he might have given the wrong signal to the jurors, a signal that might cause them to be unsure of his testimony.

"All of this happened very quickly," Sam said calmly. "If you wish, I could use my phone record, which has the exact timing of every word I said. They even report what they heard my partner was saying. They can hear the gunshots. I mean, this guy could have moved five feet or ten feet, three seconds or five seconds."

"And until you turned onto St. Louis and made that first emergency call, you can't be certain of the exact timing."

"I am generally accurate in my timing."

"And when your car moved onto St Louis, you and your partner were concentrating on the accused?"

"Yes."

"You made a cell call."

"Yes."

"Stating, 'This is Detective Sam Pennington badge 218. Chasing armed robbery suspect.' Is that so?"

"Yes."

"And your partner screaming, 'Stop, police, stop police.' Is that right?"

"Yes."

"And your adrenalin was rushing?"

Suddenly Sam stopped. He held his breath. He had just stated four quick "yeses" in a row, and now he stopped and looked around. Mosely stood there and smiled inquisitively at him.

"I'm more than able to control my adrenalin."

"I'm sure you are," Mosely responded. "But are you able to tell how far a young black boy can run in three seconds?"

There was a light tittering from the crowd at that response. Mosely moved closer to the witness stand, carrying Sam's courtroom deposition. He read from the document. "On page one of your deposition, and I quote: 'This is Detective Pennington, badge 218. Chasing armed robbery suspect.' Is that correct?"

"Yes. I've so stated that."

"And where were you when you made that comment?"

"We were just making the turn onto St Louis."

"Are you aware that this young boy, accused of murder, is able to run over half a block in three seconds?" Mosely asked. A low chuckle erupted from the audience.

"No, I'm not aware of that."

"Well you should be. Because if you had been, he could easily have passed that house half way up on St. Louis Street. Three seconds." Mosley tapped. "One thousand one, one thousand two, one thousand three. I'll bet even you can run about that far in three seconds."

A third chuckle came from the audience. They were enjoying this. A few even clapped their hands.

Finally Jerry stood up and made a comment. "I object your honor. Council is badgering the witness. It's not a matter of who can run the fastest, but rather what actually happened. I recommend…"

"Sustained," The judge announced. "I'll ask the question. After the trash truck cleared your vision and you made the left turn onto St Joseph Street, what was your view of the defendant?"

"At that point he was walking. Slowly walking. It was a though he didn't want to draw any attention to himself."

It was late in the day and the judge was getting tired. Having saved ten minutes of meaningless testimony from Detective Pennington, he relaxed back onto his deep-seated leather chair and temporally closed his eyes. "Continue, Mr. Mosely, the Court awaits your next line of questioning."

"Yes your honor, the real question here is what or who did the Detective actually see? So I ask you, Detective Pennington, who did you actually see?"

"I saw the boy moving up the street."

"And who else did you see?"

"I'm not sure I understand the question?"

"Weren't there people standing on St Louis Street, watching through the open French doors of the Dixieland Bar?"

"Yes there was, a handful, about five."

"About five. Might that be five or six?"

"Five or possibly six at the most. The defendant ducked under a rope that keeps people out of the club. He went under the rope and headed up on St. Louis toward Rampart."

"And is it not possible that one of those six people could have been an accomplice, Detective Pennington?"

"An accomplice? No, I don't think so. No definitely not. There was no accomplice."

"No one who could pass a gun to him as he ran out from under the rope?"

"No. No one."

Now Mosely took a stern position, crossing his arms and leaning back slightly. He lowered his head and stared at Sam from just under his eyelids. It was a look that Mr. James gave him back in high school. That look of: "Are you telling me the truth, or what?" *Where in the hell did Mosely learn that look?* Sam asked of himself.

"Well we'll just table that for the moment," Mosely said.

From that point on the situation played out exactly as Sam said it happened. The chasing of Skanes, Jr., running up to the hones on St. Louis Street, then Sam and his partner Jack leaving their leaving the car, and crossing the street to the house. Sam with his phone still open, telling his partner: "Don't go there Jack! Lay back! We're backlit from the street lights. I've got help coming!"

Then Mosely dealt with the street lights. How bright were the street lights, where were they positioned, what could you actually see? Once again he challenged Sam's eyesight. Sam felt as though he might need a white cane and a Seeing Eye Dog just to get back to his office.

"Now I wish to concentrate on an issue of great importance, that being of the first shot that was fired," Mosley stated. "I now address the following statement you have made concerning your previous deposition, which I now offer to the court as our next EXHIBIT."

"So received," Judge Williams confirmed.

"You have a copy of your deposition?" Mosely asked Sam

"Yes I do."

"You've testified a gun was fired at the back of the lot on St Louis Street and the bullet hit your car which was parked across the street. Furthermore, you testified that neither yourself or the criminalist, nor any of you assistant staff members, were able to locate the slug that struck your car. Is that correct, Detective?"

"Yes. But I did not..."

"That yes was sufficient, Detective. Your Honor, I now wish to offer the gun as Exhibit B and photographs of the detective's car as Exhibits C through G."

The judge made notes on a pad of paper. "So ordered."

Sam had walked into the courtroom at twelve-thirty. It was now four-thirty. That was about four hours since his last pit stop. Then God made a statement! A force from above made it clear that Sam was to be placed in a position of miraculous Grace. As Mosely turned around to face the witness stand, he bumped his arm onto the large display situated on the easel. His motion knocked the display down, causing the left edge to crash onto the floor. The four by eight foot sketch of the crime scene was split in two and the four vehicles became un-mounted and they also crashed to the floor.

Judge Williams, upon seeing this take place, banged his gavel down. "This court must provide a sentence for an existing trial in the morning. Court is adjoined for this matter until one o'clock tomorrow afternoon." He then banged his gavel down.

Sam left the witness stand and headed for the washroom in the outer hallway. He left Blue Boy and Pinhead to pick up the pieces. Sam needed nothing more than a refreshing pee and a cold Scotch.

Chapter 5

DAY 2, CONTINUED.

WALLY WAS AT a standstill. It was now three o'clock and Sam was still on the witness stand. Earlier, he heard Carl Witherspoon call the Baton Rouge police department and talk to Frick of Frick and Frack. Frick would be George Carey and Frack, his partner, was David Kennedy. These were the missing detectives on leave to the Baton Rouge Bureau.

Carl gave George Sam's line: they must be back in New Orleans by nine tomorrow morning or they would be replaced. George then said something and Carl answered, "I don't give a rat's ass what you have to do up there! Get back here by nine o'clock tomorrow morning. Do not call me back, just show up, or I'll pack up your shit and leave it in the lobby!" Carl then hung up the phone and left the office.

It was a side of Carl that Wally had never seen before. It was then that Wally started to realize that Sam and Carl had both decided they would do whatever was necessary to make the job work. But Wally knew that Sam believed in Frick and Frack. Wally wondered where those names came from. Sam told him he would tell him later. That was Sam's way of telling him to forget about it. There was a knock at the door and it opened, revealing Frank Hogan.

"Yes sir, may I help you?" Wally asked.

"I'm looking for Detective Sam Pennington." Then Wally spotted the ponytail.

"You Mr. Hogan?"

"Right."

Hogan carried all of his stuff. He always carried all of his stuff, some of which he towed behind him on a 'carry-on' baggage handler.

"I got a drawing for him," Frank said. Wally held out his hand and Frank gave him the drawing. "I don't suppose you'd have anything to drink around here?" Frank asked.

Ignoring Frank's question, Wally glanced at the picture. He noted it was a charcoal drawing of a middle-aged man in his late thirties to early forties, a bit overweight with a round chunky face. His hair was cut short and appeared to be black and kinky. Black kinky hair. Frank Hogan had drawn a picture of a black man. In addition, Mr. Hogan supplied a further description in the margin of the artwork. 'Wanted for questioning. Six feet, two inches tall, weighing about 200 pounds. No name.'

"Hey, this is pretty good," Wally stated. "But Sam told me it was a white guy with the same description."

Frank moved quickly to Wally and grabbed the picture from his hands. "Don't tell me that!" Frank said with some alarm.

Wally gathered his notepad and thumbed through the pages until he found the proper description.
"Here it is. White male around thirty-five years of age, six feet two inches tall, weight about 200 pounds."

"Don't tell me that!"

"If you want, we can call Ms. Washington and confirm the description."

"No. Don't do that! I never asked her if he was black or white! I just assumed that anybody that would do a thing like that would be a black man! She was black! Black people always talk about other black people! She never said anything about white people! I'll do it again right now!"

Frank was in a vocal pitch of a high leveled yelling fit. As he screamed, he un-strapped his easel and drawing paper, along with a bag of charcoal.

"This is the guy as she described him! I even did a quick sketch of his face! She agreed to it! She liked it!"

"Did she check out this final version?" Wally asked.

Frank looked at Wally with a belabored expression on his face. It was as though he were saying, *help me out with this problem, kid, and I'll provide you with free family portraits for life.*

"Didn't Sam ask you to have her check this out?" Wally added.

"She had to leave her apartment. I sat there alone and did the drawing. She went to her laundromat to move some furniture around. Said she had to get the place ready for a memorial service or something. She had to get some candles from the church. She was really excited. When I finished, I came over here. Jesus, why me? I'm an artist, for Chrissake."

"Okay, you draw another one. How long will it take?"

"About forty-five minutes," Frank said.

"That's fine. I'll call Ms. Washington and make arrangements to pick her up and have her here in an hour. Okay?"

Frank was sweating. He made some preliminary swipes with his charcoal. "You won't tell Sam about this, will you?"

"Sam will not know about this. This about you and me and Ms Washington."

Frank smiled, wiped the sweat from his face with his cleaning towel and went to work.

Sam walked into the courtroom men's room and headed directly for the urinal. The place was totally empty. By the time he made five steps into the area, he had unzipped his fly and had the lizard in hand. When he reached the porcelain urinal, he arched his back and let the stream begin. It was a thing of true magic. It was as though he had stretched his being into a moment of bliss. As it continued to flow, he thought of only the good things in life, like mom and apple pie. Then after about thirty seconds of easing pleasure, it started to cease. Sam zipped up quickly and washed his hands. He went for a paper towel but the dispenser was empty. He realized this was still the Big Easy. Wondering what the hell Mosely was trying to do, he crossed to an empty toilet, entered the enclosure, locking the door behind him.

He was alone in a toilet, a place to think things out. If it were to be known, it was one of Sam's favorite places of solace. The seat of the toilet was open with no cover, just the seat itself. Sam lifted his coat and sat down on the open seat. Leaning back, he pondered his situation.

There was nothing that Mosely had asked that was not open knowledge. It was how he asked his questions that made Sam look foolish. When they broke, Mosely was about to ask about the first shot fired, the slug that hit the car which neither Sam nor his people could find. It didn't cause any problem for Sam's department, but Sam was sure Mosely would turn this into a big deal.

The hole in the side of Sam's car was a clean, neat penetration. They figured it had to be a metal jacket bullet. When Sam checked the gun at the scene of the crime, he noted that three shots had been fired, and three were left in the gun. Left were two metal jacket bullets and one dum dum. Dum dums were hollow point lead slugs. These slugs were designed to be aimed at an animal. When the slug struck the animal, it would mushroom on impact, causing massive damage to the body. The metal jacket slug would also tear through the body, but would often find its way through the soft tissue and come out on the other side.

There were three rounds of dum dums and three rounds of metal jackets that had been loaded on this night. The first metal jacket entered Sam's car, the next two being dum dums that struck Jack. This meant the bullets Skannes, Jr. had loaded into the gun were miscellaneously distributed.

Normally, one would load a gun from a single box of shells. In this case, Skannes, Jr. may have taken them from a bowl, or a drawer, or wherever he stored his miscellaneous ammunition. It didn't matter to him whether they were dum dums or armor piercing, as long as when he shot they would stop the person from trying to stop him from doing his evil business of the night. At least this would be conclusive proof that this gun was fired at Sam and then struck his car! Where did that slug go? Then as he thought longer, it finally came to him.

It was eight months earlier that the department purchased ten new police vehicles. One of them was Sam's. He drove it from the dealership in Kenner, located out near the airport. He had driven the car for almost two months before the fatal shooting. Not on a single occasion could he recall hearing that high pitched whistle emanating from somewhere inside that car. Three days after his partner's death, he was driving through Metairie and there was that whistle. He didn't think much about it at first. It was just an annoying little thing. The hole where the bullet went through the car had already been repaired. But there was still that car whistle!

The door to the men's room opened and someone moved to the urinals. Sam arose from the throne and flushed the empty toilet with his foot. He wouldn't want anyone to think he had left an un-flushed toilet.

As he left his stall, he saw it was Pinhead who was just zipping up. Pinhead crossed to the basin area and started to wash his hands.

"Hey there, how you doin'?" Sam asked.

Pinhead just looked at him, not responding.

Sam added, "Great day to be alive." He then checked himself out in the mirror and noticed that Pinhead was full of soap lather, washing his hands.

Pinhead glanced at Sam's hands and then up to Sam's face. Sam caught the look. He glanced down at Pinhead's hands, which were frothy with soap, while Sam's hands seemed unwashed and dry.

"No thanks," Sam quipped. "I don't wash." As he left the toilet he shouted back. "See you guys tomorrow, bye now."

When Frank was about finished with his revised drawing, Lila Washington entered the office. She was a thing of beauty. Her wig was basically auburn, with golden tips sprayed at the ends. It was quite large. It looked like much too much hair or her head. She wore a Hawaiian mumu, like a tent if you will, which totally draped her body so as to completely hide what was hidden beneath. However, it was also covered with extremely loud colors. The tent hid the body while the colors amplified it. Go figure. Her mumu was covered with large yellow and red hibiscus flowers!

For her finish, she wore a myriad of colored beads. Most likely they had been gleaned from the many throws during the Mardi Gras parades she had attended. Smaller ones hung around her wrists and larger ones around her neck. The 'Big Daddies' were tied around her waist. Wally introduced himself and then reintroduced Frank.

"I met him over an hour ago," she said, regarding Frank. Then she directed herself to Wally. "I got business to take care of. I got a show to do." Frank was making his final touch ups on his drawing. "And you was supposed to make me a banner," she said to Frank, "When was that supposed to start?"

"I'll do it tomorrow morning." Frank tore the paper from his drawing pad and handed it to her. "There you are. This do it for you?"

"That's him! That's the man that killed that little girl! May God have mercy on that little girl."

Wally thanked Lila for dropping by and things got quiet as soon as she left.

"Nice job," Wally said to Frank. "Thank you."

"Thanks. Got anything to drink?"

"Sure thing. Got some coffee, some Coke and Sprite."

"That's great. I'm talking about a drink."

"Oh yeah. Let me check Sam's desk." He spotted the basket on the floor that Mr. Kelly had sent to Sam. With his right foot he casually slid the basket deep under the desk, in an effort to conceal its belongings. He searched through the drawers, finally coming up with a few drinks left, of Johnny Walker Black Label. The label itself was old, dried and half cracked off. "This might do it." Wally said with some pride.

Frank took the bottle from Wally and studied it suspiciously. "Looks like it came from a museum."

"Yeah, well..."

Frank poured two fingers into a coffee cup and took a good swig. Then he looked up at Wally and started to sputter. "I think it's gone sour."

"Look, let's go across the street to the market and get some new stuff."

"It's okay, I'm getting used to this." Frank poured the balance of the Scotch into his cup and took another long drink.

"The thing is," Wally added, "Sam's got another emergency drawing for you to do. He needs it right away."

"Who's the subject?"

"We've got a dead girl downstairs, another prostitute."

Frank swallowed, and then gasped for air. "You mean, downstairs in the morgue?"

"Yes." Wally answered.

"Oh my God!"

"Is that a problem?"

"Oh my God."

"Look, if that's a problem, I can try to get someone else to take care of it."

Frank quickly gulped down the last of his drink and placed the cup back onto the coffee rack. He quickly stood up. "Okay, let's go do it."

Arnold was seated behind a desk in the back of the main Coroner's room when Wally and Frank entered. Frank's eyes were somewhat shocked at the florescent lights and the look of the room. It was cold and ugly. The large storage drawers on either side of the walls held hidden death.

"Arnold, this is Frank Hogan," Wally announced. "We're here to do a drawing of Jane Doe."

Arnold moved from his desk. "Alright, she's over here." He went to a row of drawers on the left side and slid out one the one containing Jane. Frank and Wally moved in beside Arnold looking down at the girl. Frank was pale.

"Oh my God!" Frank uttered, sucking in his breath.

Arnold glanced at Wally. He wasn't sure what he should do. Wally wasn't sure either.

"Oh my God!" Frank said again.

"Listen, I can really get someone else to do this," Wally said with great concern.

Frank quickly dropped to his knees. "Let us pray."

Both Arnold and Wally were Catholic from the get-go. If anybody said "pray," they were on their knees in a Cajun second. However, Wally considered himself a thinking Christian. Very slowly, Wally started to sink down on one knee.

"Dear God please help this hooker," Frank lamented, following with an "A...men"

As Wally's knee hit the floor it was over and Frank and Arnold jumped back up. They both knew that when the Amen was said, you jump quickly off of those sore knees.

"Alright, let's go to work," Frank commanded. "Arnold, you got a comb or a brush?"

"Yeah, I got a comb." Arnold pulled his comb from his back pocket and Frank grabbed it. Wally pulled himself to a standing position.

"Wally, get that goose neck lamp off of Arnold's desk," Frank commanded. "We'll light the subject with that."

Wally moved to get the lamp while Frank opened his case of art supplies. He had really gotten into the project and now started directing the set. He spoke with authority. "Arnold, pick the lady up and hold her in your arms."

Arnold did not move. He would kneel and pray at a moment's notice, but holding a three month old corpse in his arms was out of the question. Frank looked back at Arnold.

"What the hell do you want me to do?" Frank screamed. "I can't make a picture of her lying down!"

Arnold glared at Frank with contempt. *Who the hell does this guy think he is?* Then he realized this was Sam's gig. He decided to do it for Sam. He moved to the body and placed his arms under her armpits, dragging her up into a sitting position. Her head hung down to her chest.

Frank was setting up his easel and Wally was looking for an electrical outlet to plug the gooseneck lamp into. Frank looked up at Arnold.

"Can you please help me out with this one?" Frank asked Arnold with passion. "I want to do a good job here, for Sam."

"What do you want me to do?" Arnold asked

"Could you grab the back of her hair and make her head look straight?"

Arnold looked closely at the back of her head. It had happened in the right rear quarter portion of her skull, that section running from just behind the right ear and up past the back of the head. This was where the victim died. Someone had savagely beaten her head with a blunt instrument. This area of her hair was matted with dried blood. Arnold grabbed a clean hunk of her hair on the opposite side, and pulled her head into an upright position.

"Well Arnold, that looks a hell of a lot better," Frank said.

Wally finally located an outlet and plugged in the lamp.

"That's good Wally," Frank said. "Now hold the light higher and phase it a little more to the right."

Wally did as he was told and Arnold was holding her head straight. "This is going to be a long night," Arnold muttered to himself.

Frank moved toward Jane's face and said, "Now let's see what color her eyes are." With his two hands, he placed an index finger and thumb over and under each eye and pried the lids open. "Oh my God, they're blue. I love a blue-eyed babe."

Frank moved to Arnold's desk and looked around. He finally found a large paperclip, and returned to Jane. He opened her left eye and delicately placed the paperclip under her upper and lower lid. The eye now remained open in a rather grotesque fashion, with the dead eye itself looking out through a paperclip triangle.

Frank stood back looking at his handiwork. "Now her hair." He took Arnold's comb and carefully combed her hair and after a few minutes in had it in a peek-a-boo style. He stepped back to review his subject.

As Frank crossed to the door, he asked, "Now how do I get these stinking fluorescents off? These fuckers will cause you to go blind. They flicker all the time."

"Over there at the right of my desk, on the wall," Arnold said.

Frank walked to the switch, turned it off, and the room fell in semi-darkness. When he turned back into the room he could see the tableau he had directed. Arnold held Jane in a perfect position and Wally held the light at just the right angle.

"Fantastic!" he shouted, and moved back in, placing himself behind the easel. "Now we do it, now we make it happen. It'll take about forty-five minutes to finish. Don't anybody move." He started to draw with his pastel chalk. Nobody moved.

It was nearly five o'clock when Sam walked from the court. He pulled his cell phone from his coat pocket with one hand and took his tie off with the other, slipping the tie into his coat pocket. He next pressed the fast dial on the cell phone. It was his private number at Division HQ. No answer after five rings. Wally must have left, he thought. He then punched another programmed number, this time it was Charlie Wong.

"Hello theah, this is Charlie," his cheery Southern voice said.

"Charlie, this is Sam. I need you to do a big favor for me."

"Hey Sam, what's goin' on?"

"Listen, I'll make this short. Six months ago in a shoot out my partner died and a bullet hit my car. I pulled you in but you couldn't find the slug. Do you recall that?"

"Where you at, Bubba?"

"I just left the courtroom. There is a problem with that slug that hit my car. I didn't look any further for it. When I drove the car I started to hear a whistle when I would hit about thirty miles an hour."

"You still on that case?" Charlie interrupted.

Sam was now walking across Canal Street, jaywalkin' his way to the median. He had to duck his way around a parked red streetcar taking on passengers.

"My car is on the second floor of the police garage on Royal, dark blue Pontiac. Keys are on the top of the passenger side, on the front tire. Call Jimmy at the motor pool. He leaves at five. Tell him you're coming down and he must prepare to stay late. He may need help, you stay with him. Show him where the bullet entered the car. Show him where you think it went out. Tell him I'm an asshole for not following up on the bullet. Just do what you can. I need that slug."

"You got it, Sam," Charlie said. "Bye."

Traffic on Canal was getting thick. Sam finally skirted his way around several cars and moved up toward Bourbon Street and the Quarter.

A few blocks later, he turned right on Toulouse Street and walked a half block down to Kelly's apartment. When he bought the painting for her, she was out purchasing his gift, and she did not see it until later that day. So her thoughts were purely for him. Unselfish thoughts, with total care for his happiness.

Sam took his phone in hand and dialed her number. There was a phone in her bathroom and he had noted her number listed there. It rang four times with no answer and he was about to hang up when he heard her voice.

"Hi, Kelly here."

"Hello there."

"Oh Sam, is that you?"

On this day, Sam had even gotten shit from Carl. He had gotten more of the same from everyone else he had met. He still had friends, people who liked him and wanted to work with him, but nobody but Kelly would say, 'Oh Sam, is that you?' with that warm, friendly, loving voice.

"Listen, I still got work to do. Come out on the porch. I want to look at you again."

There was some hustle going on inside, as though she was trying to hide something. Then the door opened and she came out, a hand towel wrapped around her hair and a larger towel wrapped around her body. She was barefoot, still holding the phone to her ear.

"Hi Sam. I was taking a shower."

"You look fine." His voice was soft, speaking into the telephone. Even though they could publicly be seen, their conversation was private.

"I try hard." She smiled and twisted from side to side, her bare feet squeaking on the wet wood floor "Would you like to come in? I'll show you a painting a friend just bought me."

"Can't, got work to do. I got a nice basket from a friend of mine also."

"Oh, who could that be?"

Sam just smiled back at her. He had been through a grilling with Mosely and didn't want to talk too much. "What's your deal with the Dixieland? What time do you get off?"

"Well," she said in a cutesy pie manner, "I sort of get it my way. That is, I can work whenever I want, and get off whenever I want. The only problem is, when I don't work, Leonard's wife covers my station and she hates the music."

"I was thinking of having you over for dinner at my place."

"That would be nice. I could do that."

"Leonard's wife gonna cover your station?"

"You got that one right."

Sam smiled. "This is Thursday, how about Saturday? I'll have you picked up around seven-thirty. My place, about quarter to eight. That work for you?"

"What do I wear?"

"Whatever you like. This is a dinner for just you. See you then."

Kelly watched him as he walked over toward Royal Street. She truly liked Sam, even though she had been involved with him in a disastrous, almost one-night-stand. She didn't know much else about the guy, but you could bet she was going to find out more on Saturday.

Sam walked quickly into his office and found it empty. He grabbed the phone and called the operator.

"This is Pennington. Looking for Witherspoon or Detective White."

"Captain Witherspoon got here just ten minutes ago and I directed him down to the morgue. I have nothing on Detective White."

When Sam entered the morgue he saw a strange configuration of four men working their brains out to accomplish the job of one. His loyal assistant Wally was seated on a chair near the table rubbing his shoulder. He was trying to get the blood to flow again after holding a light in an awkward position over forty-five minutes.

Carl had taken over the lighting job, directing the light at the subject. Arnold was not faring well either. The corpse had slid down to a much lower position and Arnold was desperately fighting fatigue. Sam flipped on the fluorescent lights and the room immediately shifted in mood.

Frank screamed in disgust. "My God, that is horrible!"

Sam moved across the room. "It's okay, Frank. Just pretend you're out in the sunlight.

As Sam arrived at the corpse, he also got a good look at the drawing. Frank had accomplished this one in color.

"Looks good, very good," Sam said.

The drawing was beautiful. Her face and eyes seemed alive. It was as though Frank had created a positive photograph of this person that one could actually touch and feel. Her skin was radiant and her blue eyes jumped out from the page.

"You take care of that sign at the Laundromat?" Sam asked.

"I told the lady I'd have it done tomorrow morning," Frank said.

Sam looked over at Carl. "So what happened with the Mayor and the Chief?"

"I waited and we talked. They thought and we talked. They met and we talked. Then they decided I should do whatever I wanted."

"That was it?"

"That was it."

Sam turned to Wally. "Wally, you got the letter done?"

Wally reached for his legal sized clipboard, which he always carried with him. "Yes sir, right here."

He handed Sam the first draft of the fax intended for the Orleans Parish Police Divisions, concerning their wanting to question the man Lila Washington met on the night of the murder.

Sam took the page and glanced through the copy. He then handed the copy to Carl. "This is very good," Sam said.

Frank finally looked at the drawing and announced, "I'm done."

Arnold released his hold on Jane's hair and her head dropped to the table with a thud, the paperclip dropped from her eye and landed on the floor.

"I'm going home now," Arnold said. He was exhausted. Pulling off his white jacket, he walked to the door. "Good night." He tossed his jacket on the chair by the door and left the room.

Carl finished perusing the letter and handed it back to Wally. "Nice. Good job, Wally. You don't say anything about murders, serial or anything. It's good."

"Make sure it's not to be posted," Sam added. "Just hand them out. They'll get around."

Carl looked at his watch. "Wally, let's go to my office. I'll get the girls to help send this shit out."

As they were leaving Wally added, "I need about ten minutes on my computer to put the letterhead on and room for you to sign."

Sam sat in silence looking at the corpse. She had been lying here in this cooled-down room for almost three months. She had a family, friends, people who loved her. Now she was deserted. If for no other reason than that, Sam wanted her to have an identity. He flipped the sheet over the body and shoved the drawer closed. He headed for the door, turned off the lights, set the lock and left the room.

Once in the hallway he scanned his reserved numbers on the phone and finally found the one for Jimmy at the motor pool. The speed dial wasn't set so he started to dial. Then he thought of something and stopped, looked back down the hall to the door of the Morgue. He moved back to the door and placed his ear against the glass panel. All was quiet inside so he tapped gently on the window.

"Frank, this is Sam." He waited a few seconds and then tapped again. From inside, Sam could hear a faint disturbed voice.

"I'm trying not to trip over anything," Frank said from within. "I can't get out of here. It's dark in here."

"Take it easy. Just follow the light to this door," Sam said calmly so as not alarm Frank more than he already was. "You'll be fine."

After a moment, Frank's head appeared in silhouette at the etched glass door. He put both of his hands on the glass. "Oh thank God! I've made it!"

Sam said, "Alright, open the door."

Frank's right hand grabbed the doorknob and twisted but the door didn't open. The knob just wiggled in the locked position. "It's locked! Oh my God it's locked!"

"Listen to me, Frank..."

"I'm locked in the fucking morgue!"

"Frank, listen to me. This is very easy. Take a look at the lock."

"I can't see the fucking lock! What do I look at if I can't see the fucking lock?!"

"Okay, calm down Frank, I'm right here. You can turn on the light."

"Where's the fucking light switch? This is horrible! I'm locked in the fucking morgue with no light!"

"Okay, Frank, do whatever you want. If you want out, I'll tell you how to open the door. If not, I'm leaving. See ya later."

Frank's voice quickly changed from panic to whimper. "Sam, please don't leave me here."

"Okay Frank, put your hand on the knob. Do you have it?"

"Yes."

"Now feel around to the center of the knob. You feel a little button there?"

"Yes."

"Now catch the little button between you thumb and forefinger. You got that?"

"Yes."

"Push the button in and twist it to the right. Got that?"

"Yes."

"Now open the door."

A moment later, the door opened and Frank appeared. His eyes squinted with the light from the hallway windows. He wheeled his baggage into the hallway and headed for the stairs.

Sam reached in, reset the lock and closed the door. He caught up with Frank on the fourth step. "Sorry about that, Frank, I just got some stuff on my mind. You should have called for me to wait a minute."

"I've never been locked in with dead people before and with the lights out! That can really scare the piss out of you. I was kneeling down behind my easel breaking it down to put it away when all of a sudden, it got dark and I literally froze. As I looked up I saw the door close and all I could see was the window on the doorway across the room. I fiddled with my stuff in the dark and finally got it together. Then I stood up and decided to move toward the light at the door. I couldn't see the floor so I slid my foot along in front of me trying not to trip over anything. As I moved on to the door, my heart started pounding and my breath became heavier. I swear to God, I thought I would die."

"Well, I really do apologize for that."

"It's okay."

"Listen, do you want a drink?"

"You mean that Scotch stuff in your office?"

"Yeah."

"Wally gave me some earlier. I think I'll pass."

Sam thanked Frank for a good job and offered to have a car take him home but Frank declined. Sam knew Frank was a fine artist. He didn't know much of anything else about him, not where he lived or if he lived with someone. Sam did know that he had made improper use of his talents. At the very least he caused him to paint a sign at the laundry on Bourbon, and Frank was most certainly not a sign painter.

Sam reached into his back pocket and pulled out his wallet. He quickly withdrew four C notes. They were four 'used' one hundred dollar bills.

"Take this." Sam said. "That's a total of four hundred, over what we agreed to."

Frank took the money. The last time someone gave him four hundred dollars was when the sky fell in. He studied the bills for a moment. "I'm not supposed to make this kinda money until after I'm dead."

Sam walked down the hallway, glancing into Carl's office. Wally had already accomplished his detail on the computer and was now working with Carl and his staff of ladies, to fax out the material to the outlying parishes. Sam moved on down the hall to his office.

The room was becoming dim. He crossed to the window and looked out. A bright flash of light lit up the background as though it was high noon, then it instantly grew darker. There was a beat of only three seconds when a crash of violent thunder hit, causing Sam to jump back from the window. This was New Orleans weather, the type of stuff you only get in the South. Particularly in New Orleans. Living in a sub-tropical zone made life interesting. It would be here one second and gone the next minute. But he never got used to it. Sam decided he wanted a drink.

He opened his lower desk draw and searched for the old bottle of Johnny Walker Red. Not seeing it there, he glanced around, looking for the basket from Kelly. It was not to be found either. Sam started to have suspicions of

Wally.

Giving up, he sat at his desk and called the motor pool. The voice that answered the phone belonged to Charlie Wong. "Hello theah. This is Wong speaking."

"Charlie, this is Sam. What's goin' on?"

"We found the travel of the bullet. It put a hole through that thick rug of yours and went unnoticed. Then it drove into the spot between the door and the floor. We removed the door and now they're about to cut out a hunk at the bottom panel, so's we can get our mitts on the grits. Where you?"

"I'm in my office. I'm on my way."

When Sam arrived at the second floor garage on Royal Street, there were two men who had just about finished removing the bottom section of the door jamb. Nick, nicknamed 'Nick the Knife,' was busily forcing the saw downward in order to finish the cut.

Charlie saw Sam first and waved. Sam crossed over and watched Nick the Knife as he continued his vicious attack on his car. Nick was the type of man that would do anything to make a buck. If he and Jimmy had been doctors performing a hemorrhoidectomy, they would have already removed the entire asshole from the body.

The right hand front passenger door had been removed and was leaning against a brick wall. Sam could only imagine the scrapes and scratches the door had suffered. On further inspection, he noted that they had trouble removing one of the main bolts that held the door to the frame. The head of the screw had been stripped and Jimmy had pried it from the opening, using something like a crowbar. His actions had in fact remove the screw and then the door. In accomplishing this feat, Jimmy managed to bend the door out away from the frame of the car, and the frame of the car in and away from the door. At about fifty miles per hour, this would cause something like a jet stream of air blowing into the car, hitting directly on the passenger side. But that didn't bother Sam as much as what had happened to the carpet.

The city assigned him this car eight months ago. It was a Pontiac and there was nothing really special about it, except for the carpeting. The car was navy blue and the seats were dressed out in dark brown leather. It was really vinyl, but it gave the impression that it was leather. The dark brown against the navy blue gave it a rich look, one that was most appealing to Sam. Then there was the carpet.

It was also dark brown and had the feel that someone had skinned a llama just to add to the luxury. When they would go somewhere, Sam would get Wally to drive. Then he would slide into the passenger seat, slip off his boots and feel the luxury of man-made llama beneath his feet. He would power his seat back and with his toes gripping at the soft carpet, would easily drift off into never-never land. But now that was the end of that!

When they tried to pull the carpet up, they found that it was glued to the hard metal flooring. As they continued pulling it back, the carpet separated from its foundation, leaving patches of the finished material like small furry animals fighting to stay alive. Finally, to remove the bottom of the rug, they had to use a hammer and chisel to scrape it from the metal floor. It did not come up easily. As they pounded, scraped, and pulled, they finally found the thirty-two-caliber hole in the right side of the car, just below the lower doorframe.

With the door removed, Nick the Knife was in position to make his cut. Finally, his reciprocal saw went through. A foot length of the car's lateral foundation fell from its base structure. Charlie was kneeling in position, holding a piece of toweling to catch it. Like gold diggers hoping for a strike, they went to the worktable. Using screw drivers and a pair of vice grips, they opened a slot at the top of the one foot piece of the frame. It fell free! The bullet that had haunted Sam for six months had finally shown itself. Jimmy assured Sam that his car would be ready to travel by ten o'clock tomorrow morning. Naturally, Sam believed him.

Sam and Charlie walked back to the office. If they could make a match of the bullet to the gun, Charlie would prepare a full forensic report. If there were no connection with the bullet and the gun, Charlie would simply forget that they had even tried.

"I'll wait in my office for the results," Sam said. "I really wanna know what you got."

Charlie smiled. "You got it, Bubba."

When Sam arrived at his office, Wally was packing up to leave. He looked up and smiled as Sam entered the office. "Hey, how's it going, Sam?"

Sam ignored his question. "How'd you guys do on the mailing?"

"Got it all out, no problem. How'd it go with the car?"

"All solved."

"Great." Wally put his hands in his trouser pockets and sat on the edge of his desk. "I had some problems with Frank the painter. He got a little freaky."

"How's that?"

"I don't think he wanted to go down there, to do the painting in the morgue."

"So?"

"So he wanted a drink." Wally volunteered. "So I remembered that you kept a bottle in your drawer. I noticed he was looking around for something so I pushed the basket you got from that Kelly guy under your desk so Frank wouldn't see it. Then I took the Johnny Walker from your drawer and poured him a drink."

"So?"

"Well, so, I figured that's what you'd do under the circumstances."

Sam took a look under his desk and spotted the basket. He gave Wally a strong thumbs up. "Nicely done, I couldn't have done it better myself."

Wally gathered his things and headed for the door. "I'll be here by nine tomorrow to see if Frick and Frack get in."

"That'll be fine. By the way," Wally turned back to look at Sam. "I just want you to know, I think you're doing a great job."

"Thanks Sam, I appreciate that. Good night." Wally left the room.

Sam promised himself that he would never again challenge Wally's integrity. He reached under his desk and pulled out the basket from Kelly. He decided it was time for him to have a party. After ripping the cellophane from around the basket, he withdrew his favorite Glenlivet. He found a small box of crackers from Spain and a jar of Russian caviar. After all was spread out and ready to eat, the phone rang. It was Charlie.

"I got it!" Charlie proclaimed. "I took two shots of the gun that you confiscated and compared them to the one shot at your car and bingo! same markings, same bullet."

"That's just great! Can you make up a file on this and get it to the court in the morning?"

"You got it, Sam."

Charlie hung up the phone and Sam got back to his party. For a while, life was great. He ate his caviar and drank his Scotch. Sam knew he had just spent over a thousand dollars of police money for work on his car to quell all additional questions regarding a spent bullet. He knew this had nothing to do with the case. He knew that Mosely knew that too. But Mosely would spend every bit of time and money the police might have available in order to get his client free of all charges.

So be it. Sam closed the jar of caviar and wrapped the crackers along with everything else in sight and placed all in the rear of his upright filing cabinet. After tossing the paper-made basket in the trash, he was left with only the Glenlivet. He poured another drink, when another heavy lightning strike flashed through the room. He started counting, *one, two, three,* then the sound of earthshaking thunder hit. He gulped the whisky as thunder crashed and he realized he had lived another moment in eternity.

Chapter 6

DAY 3

IT WAS FRIDAY, MARCH 3rd, and Sam needed a few days off. His period of service with the department provided him with a long overdue free weekend. The first thought he had to take care of was this day's business. He left his apartment at eight-fifteen a.m., walked left on Barracks St. and turned right down Royal St.. There would be no time to play games with Phil at the St. Ann Market on Bourbon.

When he got to his office, it was close to eight-thirty. Wally was there, on the phone, checking out the faxes from the precincts of the surrounding Parish Offices of the night before. He was already meeting with difficulties. Wally kept talking while silently acknowledging Sam as he came into the room.

Sam went to the old Mr. Coffee machine, purchased years ago as a result of TV ads created by "Jolting Joe" DiMaggio. He found no coffee waiting for him. Wally always had the coffee made by the time Sam arrived. This morning, there was nothing. However, Sam had never arrived a half hour early, either. While Wally continued to talk to Division 14, Sam was looking for a coffee filter. He searched the cabinet below and found none. Wally waved at Sam and mouthed, *'I'll do it as soon as I get off this call.'*

Finally, Wally hung up the phone and took another that had been on hold. It was Division 19, with yet another problem. Wally rolled his eyes. Sam started to look in various drawers in the cabinet and finally found a stack of filters. He placed one in the coffee holder and looked at Wally with the silent question of, *How much coffee do I put in?*

Sam had never made any coffee. He could cook, he could handle the bad guys, but he had never made coffee. When he was home, his coffee came from jar of instant. He held the coffee can up high with one hand and the coffee measure in the other, hoping to get Wally's attention. But Wally was concentrating on his call and waved Sam off. Sam started filling the filter with enough coffee to do the trick. Once in place, he poured water into the unit and pushed the 'brew' button. As Wally continued his conversation the other phone rang. Sam answered, and the voice asked for Detective Wally White. Sam put the call on hold and looked at Wally.

"That'll be fine," Wally said. "Thanks a lot." He hung up the phone and turned to Sam.

"This is for you," said Sam, "I got the coffee solved. Anything I can do to help?"

Wally just looked at Sam, saying nothing. He picked up the phone. "Hello, this is Detective White. How can I help you?" Then it all started again. Another precinct with yet another problem. Then Mr. Coffee started to drip.

Sam hit the third open line and dialed Bob Riazzi of the Crystal Market on Decatur St.. Bob would always attend the Thursday night poker game at Sam's place. But Sam also had those special 'Private parties,' ones that required extraordinary attention. The deal was, if Sam placed an order twenty-four hours before the special event, Bob would personally see that it was properly covered by showtime.

"Whatcha got going, Sam?" Bob asked. "I got some great catfish."

"Forget your catfish, this dinner is for two. Tomorrow night we have shrimp, barbeque shrimp, big ones. That's for an opener. Then a nice salad, like the one I make for the game. For the big deal I figure a good steak, with a lobster tail and a rice pilaf. A simple dinner with a statement. You writing this down?"

"What's after tomorrow night?"

"That's it."

"That's it? What about for breakfast?"

"Well, that's a possibility. I'll make my crabmeat and eggs benedict," Sam said. "Gimme the white lump crab meat and some truffles."

"Okay Sam, you got it. You need some help with this thing?"

"Call me at ten o'clock Sunday morning. If I'm alone, come on over and have some breakfast." Sam hung up the phone and looked over at the coffee.

The pot had just about filled itself by Mr. Coffee, which had a way of dripping long after it had completed its major brewing task. There was a dark brown stained paper towel that Wally used to collect this residual effect. Sam quickly exchanged the pot with the towel and poured himself his first cup. At that, moment Frick and Frack entered the room. Sam was pleased to see them. "Well look at that, my favorite detectives."

These guys were the perfect policemen. George Carey was "Frick" and David Kennedy was "Frack." They had both been in this department for nine years. Sam coined the "Frick and Frack" name because they were such a matched pair.

George was a good looking guy with prematurely gray hair. A well-dressed man about thirty-five years old, he stood about six feet one. David was smaller, maybe five ten. His dress was more casual. They never stood or sat together. One of them always positioned himself far away from his partner, just to protect the other's back.

George Carey moved in to shake Sam's hand and David held back by the door, looking around the room. They were in a detective's office, in the police station, a place of safety. They each had a desk located in the room, but they both had habits they had developed over the many years in the business.

After shaking Sam's hand, George turned and moved to the door. David crossed to Sam's desk and offered his hand. They were like a square dance, *Ladies in the middle and Men turn around*. Hence, Frick and Frack.

"You guys look beat," Sam said.

It was George who did the talking. David was more of a floater. They were both unmarried, George lived in the Quarter, about three blocks from Sam's place, and David had an apartment in Metairie. As a result of this, rumors had developed over the years as to whether or not Frick and Frack were gay. George once had a conversation with Sam. "I'll never marry," George said, "because I won't allow any woman to get into the jeopardy of being involved with a cop."

"We worked through the night," George said. "No big deal. Left Baton Rouge at seven this morning, had a good breakfast on the road and here we are."

George took a chair at Sam's desk while David countered at the door. Sam picked up the pot of coffee. "How's about a pick-up?"

"Yeah, great," George said and then looked back at David.

"I could use some," David responded. Without thinking, he moved from his assigned position and walked to Sam's desk. Sam poured two extra cups.

He recalled exactly how Frick and Frack liked their coffee. They were one hundred percent American. None of that French shit. No *café au lait*, full of milk and sugar. Just a good hot black cup of American. Sam picked up his cup and toasted the two men. "Glad to have you boys back." They acknowledged Sam and all took their first swigs.

Sam was careful with his coffee. As he drew the cup to his lips, he slightly blew over the cup to temper the extra hot liquid. He drew some of the brew into his mouth. It was then that the smell of the concoction, combined with his taste buds, told him this was a bad idea. It was the odor that attacked his senses first. It smelled something like hot skunk oil, combined with an after taste of boiled-down cow urine. For a second Sam held the liquid in his mouth, looking around for a place to spit. Thinking better of it, he decided to take the best of all options and quickly swallowed the foul mixture.

The pungency of the liquid quickly reached his eyes and they started to tear. As the drink moved over his lips they started to swell. As it flowed down his esophagus, he felt a burning that resembled a glass of cheap tequila in a dirty cantina.

Sam looked up at George and David. George was steadying himself, holding onto the back of a chair. David had a different reaction. He looked up and said, "Boy, this really does it for me." He took another big swig. "Gimme another cup of this and I'll never sleep again."

When Wally got off the phone, they all sat down and went over the program. They advised George and David of the facts of the case. Sam carefully avoided any mention of a serial killer. They established three dead hookers, but only two had been found. Their main job was to patrol Bourbon Street and locate anyone who might know Jane Doe, the first hooker found. They should also locate whomever might be about to identify the drawing of the male person Lila Washington had described.

By ten a.m., the boys were filled in with all the details. Sam suggested they both go home and get some rest before starting out on the street. George agreed, but David was ready to rock and roll. It must have been the coffee. As they left the room, they were arguing about how to work the case. Sam left Wally with his fax problems and walked to Carl's office.

He could see through the half open blinds the mom and dad of the third murdered girl, Beth Hayden. Detective William Joseph Mays was there, performing his task as the Big Kahuna of the case. Sam classified the parents as "looking old." They were both skinny, a bit under-nourished. She wore a housedress that she had obviously made herself. And she was crying, drying her eyes from a box of tissues Carl had offered. Her father was chain smoking a pack of non-filter Camels. He wore old western boots, worn Levis, and a faded blue shirt that hadn't seen an iron since the day it was purchased. His cap was a green John Deere, stained with the sweat of plowing thousands of acres of Blanco, Texas red clay.

They were good, church-going people. *What could they have done wrong with Beth?* Sam thought. *She had to have been a poor girl from Texas, living no doubt in a trailer park. Got some money together and came to New Orleans. Got into dope. Found a pimp, then got murdered.*

Sam waved his arms in the air, getting Carl's attention. Carl spotted Sam. Sam motioned, *Do you want me to come in there?* Carl crossed to the door and opened it.

"You want something?" Carl asked, speaking quietly under his breath.

"I wanted to know if you needed me for anything."

"You bet. You wanna take these two downstairs and get them to identify their dead daughter?"

Sam gave Carl a long silent stare. "I think that would be a good job for Detective Mays," Sam answered.

Carl looked back into the room at Mays. "Thank you for that suggestion. You have made my fucking day." Carl closed the door and returned to his desk.

Sam walked out onto Royal Street. He wanted some good coffee. There was a place a block down toward Canal that served a magnificent large cup of café au lait. As he walked, he thought of his early life in Atlantic City. He compared his life then to what he had just seen with Beth Hayden's parents. He remembered what it was like to be dirt poor. He thought of his son. He wondered what was he doing, and did his boy ever think of him, or even know of him? That subject would deeply bother Sam for the rest of his life.

Flashback:
Twenty-three years earlier.

Sam was seventeen and thought of only the moment. He didn't have a clue as to what he would do with the rest of his life. Vince once told him about the finest place in the entire world that he had seen. A town in the

South, where men were men and women were women and never the twain would meet. That town was New Orleans, Louisiana.

Vince had been a worker on a Christina Line Cruise, a boat that sailed from New Orleans to the Bahamas. He worked as an assistant chef, but his duties belabored the title. An assistant chef simply meant: clean up the kitchen. That was mop, polish and clean it up. Vince did his job well.

The ship arrived back in New Orleans at dusk, and the crew was given a twenty-four hour leave. That night, Vince and his friends made it to the French Quarter. His buddies were all Lithuanians, hot-blooded men, looking for action. Their pockets were stuffed with their pay. The usual tourists met with the boat tourists and they had what Vince remembered as the most beautiful time of his life.

It all started on Bourbon with the music and the booze. They drifted down to La Louisanne, a famous five star restaurant, where the food blew Vince away. They strolled to Decatur Street and as they walked, Vince noticed that there were more than eight restaurants per block, and each of them was excellent. "If you ever want to go someplace in the food business, you'd best head for New Orleans," Vince said.

They next made it down to Tujaques. This restaurant had been there since the late eighteen hundreds. They ordered more drinks and each had a large bowl of gumbo. The gumbo was fantastic, but that wasn't what started the fight. Something else had happened with his shipmates. Remember, those were Lithuanians.

"Anyway, a fight broke out and I tried to stop it," Vince said. "There was some great Dixieland music being played across the street, so I tried to get them to listen to some music, which I hoped would cheer up the bastards. And for good measure, I also threatened to throw them all in the river."

As it turned out, Vince was somehow knocked unconscious, and left in a doorway to heal himself. So much for Lithuanians. He was arrested early, at around two the following morning, and charged with sleeping in a public place. Once in jail, sleeping was difficult for Vince. Drunken/screaming prisoners kept him up the rest of the night.

The following day, his boat left without him. It was at this point in time that things started to change for Vince. He noted that the people of New Orleans were nicer, more human. He found that whenever you needed something, there was always someone to help you out. He walked down Toulouse Street, heading for the river and passed a one-story apartment with a sign that read 'Single Furnished Room Available.' He knocked at the unit next door and a man answered with a happy "Hi theah."

With only twelve dollars left of his paycheck, he paid the first and last with a check on his New York bank. There was not enough money in the bank, but if he got lucky he would fix that. Vince moved in.

It was a single room with a small cooking area on one side and a bathroom that had a basin, toilet and open shower. When the shower was turned on, water covered the entire floor which ran out into the living room. In order to solve that problem, Vince avoided taking a shower. He went to bed that night and watched TV on a twelve inch black and white set.

He awoke the next morning with a rumble and a shake. It felt as if it were a minor earthquake happening. He quickly stumbled from his bed and ran for the front door. When he opened the door, Vince got a true look at the French Quarter in all of its glory. There were three steps leading from the street to his room. As he looked out, he stood four feet above street level. Toulouse was a one-way, small residential street that led to the river. Directly in front of him, there was a sixteen-wheel New Orleans tour bus and Vince stared directly into the eyes of forty-two tourists. There was no more than ten feet of separation between Vince and the passengers. It was the heavy bus that caused the rumble that awoke Vince from his sleep. He saw a young boy held in the arms of his mother. He waved at the kid and the kid waved back at Vince. His mother, on the other hand, saw this with disgust. When Vince closed the door and stepped back into his room, he realized he had been standing in the street wearing only his Jockey shorts.

That day Vince walked around the city and tried to find work. After walking to thirty places, he found a joint on Bourbon Street – a coffee shop – and they hired him to come in and aid the breakfast staff. That meant mop, polish and clean it up. He stayed in the city for eight months, was promoted to the position of flapjack cooker, until he got a call from George Forge. It was an old friendship that took precedence over the love of a city, and Vince headed back to New York.

Sam continued to work with Vince, and then Vince had another mild heart attack. He arrived at Vince's apartment early one morning and found him sitting in his chair.

"Listen kid, I can't make this run," Vince said. "I got a big hurt going on here." He was pointing at his chest.

"I'll call the doctor!" Sam said.

"It's okay, don't bother and don't tell George about this. You know what a pussy he is. You go on and make the buy. You got the list?" Vince asked.

"Yeah, I got it," Sam said.

"Okay, I'll sit right hear and heal." Vince rested his head on the back of the chair and closed his eyes.

Sam started to leave, then paused at the door. "How will I know you're okay?"

Vince reflected for a moment and said. "Well if when you get back I'm still sitting here and I'm breathing, then you know I'm okay. If not, call George and tell him he's a pussy."

Vince was an amazingly and resilient person. He actually started a mild jogging routine. Every other day Sam would go shopping and Vince would speedily walk around the market parking lot. Neither of them ever told George about Vince's attack. They agreed to keep it their little secret. Then, of course, there was the girl with the strawberry blonde hair.

Her name was Shelly, Shelly Roberts. She was nothing but a party girl and if you ever met a boy who needed a party, you could just take a close look at young Sam. On the fifth day of his job, Sam accidentally ran into her. She was sitting on the patio taking a break when Sam came out to remove the last of the day's purchases from the truck. He noticed that she was looking at him. Perhaps a smile crossed her face. He quickly looked away and moved into the back of the vehicle. Once inside he would occasionally jump up and peer at her out of the window. On his last jump up and peer routine, he caught her looking again.

This was a positive sign for Sam. He left the truck and moved across the patio toward her, carrying a bag of supplies. She was sipping a Coke, her lovely legs 'parked' on a side chair. Without a doubt, this was the most beautiful girl Sam had ever seen. Her face was chiseled in alabaster. She was like a Queen of Beauty. Her body flowed like an angel, drifting from her head to her heels. Her breasts, her thighs, her whatever, gave him the most excited feeling he had ever felt in his entire life.

He paused for a moment, desperately trying to conceal his heavy breathing. Then he spoke. "You want some chips to go with that Coke?" Sam stood holding a twenty-five pound bag of Tortilla chips. She smiled at him and said, "Sure."

Sam quickly tried to tear open the bag but the plastic wrap was not giving. He fought with it for a moment and said that he'd get a knife.

"That's okay," she said, "don't bother. When I first saw you I just wanted to get to know you better."

Sam was about to involve himself in the most dangerous venture of his young life. This woman, who had a face of chiseled alabaster, a Queen of Beauty, who flowed like an angel, was in fact a lying slut. But it took Sam a little over nine months to figure that out.

To be fair, some of what she told him was true. Her father was a control freak and her mother a wimp who would not lift a finger to help her. That was true. They lived in the posh beach area of New York known as The Hamptons in a big gated house, that also was true. When her dad wanted her to go to college she had to be home by ten o'clock, no dates on school nights, never drink alcohol and pass every class with no less that a B grade. All true, true, and true.

But now we come to the flip side. In desperation, resulting from her father's ridiculous requirements, she finally ran from the house with a boyfriend named Josh Honeycutt. He was a musician who needed someone to aid him in backing his band. A lie. Josh Honeycutt was really Leroy Harvey, a dope dealer. Shelly really knew that. They moved into an apartment on East Oriental St. in New Jersey, where Josh/Leroy continued with his clandestine dope trade.

So why would a rich girl like Shelly want to hang out with a scurvy devil like Josh/Leroy? Because Josh/Leroy was also into some very kinky sex stuff.

Other than being a slut, you might also call Shelly a nymphomaniac. Blow in her ear and she's follow you anywhere. On many occasions Josh/Leroy would bring home strangers, men or women or any sexual combination that might strike his fancy. His goal would be to arrive home before the party, get Shell all hot to trot, slip some booze into her body and get her to smoke a little dope. When the people arrived, things would start to really groove.

Shelly loved sex. The high point of every night was for Josh/Leroy to watch her having sex with two strange men at once. The girl with the beauty of a Goddess, and the purity of a nun was, unbeknownst to Sam, nothing more than a white trash whore.

She and Sam had their first sexual adventure in the van while parked out in back of the Boardwalk Café. It was beautiful, even memorable, considered by Sam to be a holy experience. The reason this happened, the reason Shelly gave Sam her 'come-hither' look was that Josh/Leroy had finally left her and joined a real band. He was the harmonica player.

So that she might have another stud to service her needs, Shelly took Sam under her wing, stuffed him in between her legs and allowed fornication to happen at every opportunity. A few months prior to this, Sam had developed a small case of acne, a condition that was prevalent to most youths of his age, from twelve to eighteen. Now after a month and a half in the sack with Shelly, his face cleared up brighter than a baby's ass. Then he got the news.

"I'm pregnant," she said.

"What? What happened? How'd that happen? What are you telling me? My God, pregnant?"

She ignored his stupid questions. They had had intercourse over fifty times. Who cared what happened? She was pregnant! Now came the big discussion.

"What do we do about this?" she asked.

Sam, in his own magical way, a person who had matured beyond his age, declared: "I think we should get married and have the baby."

Of course, Sam did not know of Josh/Leroy, or those people Shelly had involved herself with in those clandestine sexual activities. She was now pregnant and Sam had done it. Was it possible that pregnancy could alter a woman's feelings about life? If a woman who had hundreds of men suddenly became so taken with the experience of getting knocked up, she would actually choose motherhood over sex orgies? Well, that's what happened.

She turned her life around on a dime and became as pure as the driven snow. Shelly read every book she could find on pregnancy. There was no smoking or drinking as she had a living person growing inside of her body and would now provide it a chance to be a complete and healthy human being.

A Justice of the Peace married Sam and Shelly at the local courthouse. At the time, he had to be twenty-one to be married without parental consent. He was only eighteen and so he lied about his age. Shelly told Sam that she was nineteen, but she was actually twenty-one. They both lied.

The next four and a half months were beautiful. Sam moved into her apartment. She continued to work at the Boardwalk. He still made the early morning trip with Vince and got a second job with Pierre, playing the water boy at night. This job entailed taking dirty dishes from the table, hauling them back to the kitchen, and making sure every table was provided with fresh water.

When Shelly began to show, Sam convinced Pierre to let him take over her job. He developed the habit of sleeping in two shifts. Sam bought an air mattress which he placed in the van. After his duties with Vince were over, he would get into the van around ten o'clock in the morning and sleep for three or four hours. He was back in the restaurant at two o'clock in the afternoon and worked until midnight. He would finish off by doing the final load of dishes. After that he would go home, sleep until it was time to pick up Vince and the day would start all over again.

During the eighth month of pregnancy, Shelly became a bit more agitated. That was the nature of a pregnancy. Women become more charged with childbearing than what their husbands were doing to keep the ship afloat. When he arrived home after midnight, he would find the apartment a mess and no food for him. Shelly would be sound asleep after a hard day of watching TV and eating. After ten hours of hustling food, it was now necessary to go home and clean up the kitchen. Sam was young and tough, he could handle it. To add to this problem, Sam had to deal with his father and Pennington's Hardware.

Sam had made a study of the hardware business. He found that there was a mall being built North of town, which included a 'Classic Home Hardware Company.' This organization would become a household name in a few years, having over a thousand stores from Maine to California. Their buying power alone would cause Pennington's to crumble in the dust. Sam decided it was time for his dad to get out of the business.

Roy Pennington had already tried to sell his store but no one was interested. Their current inventory showed Roy had two hundred eighty six thousand dollars left in the store, give or take. He further surmised, after paying all debts, back bank payments, money to the venders, payment to the newspaper for advertising, and a final salary for all the employees for the sale itself, Roy might clear one hundred grand after the sale.

It was the first week in June. They met at Roy's place at the kitchen table early one morning, when his dad was totally sober, and Sam made his proposal.

"We go for the Fourth of July weekend," Sam suggested. "The fourth falls on a Sunday. That way we get three days for the sale. Everybody gets Monday off for the Fourth of July. We take a full page ad on the first Saturday and Sunday and we make it a full 'ONE HALF OFF,' on everything. We sell like crazy.

"I'll put one exit at the front door and a person at every register we own. I'll buy us a security guard at the door. Nobody walks out without a sales receipt. On Sunday we advertise the final sale day as Monday July fifth. FINAL SALE. EVERYTHING MUST GO. 75% OFF."

His father looked at Sam. He was a smart kid and he knew what he wanted. "Okay, that's fine. You make it work and get me at least a hundred grand."

"The deal is, I make one third," Sam said. "That's the deal. When it's over we just walk away. That one third pays for my kid's education. You owe me that."

"No," Roy said. "Make that twenty percent. Twenty thousand sounds good to me. I wish I'da had twenty thousand in my kick when I was a kid. That's it, twenty thousand."

"No!" Sam said. "I get one-third of what we net. That's the deal." Sam held his hand out and his father took it. The deal was done.

Sam advised Pierre that he needed the Fourth of July weekend off. He needed to sell the hardware store. Pierre bitched and moaned and finally gave in. On the evening of June 25th, Sam got an emergency call at the Boardwalk. While serving a large tureen of bouillabaisse, Pierre stepped up behind him, which was unusual. Pierre never came into the dining area, unless there was a well-known politician and a camera available.

"Your wife went to the hospital. You have a baby boy. Go to her, I'll serve the soup," Pierre said.

Women do crazy things when they are pregnant, but until a man can see his child, only then it can happen for him. Sam had a son, a baby boy and Sam was a father. At his age, eighteen, he was a daddy. And the world was right! They named the boy Roy, after Sam's dad.

Then it was Saturday the 3rd of July. Sam had moved back into the family house for the three day sale. He prepared for another young girl, Rosie, to stay with Shelly and help with the new baby. Rosie was a part-timer at the Boardwalk. Not too bright, but Sam felt that she could do the job.

Sam had planned everything perfectly. He and two assistants, started the day at five in the morning. They had to totally rearrange the store by five a.m.. All the old merchandise was brought up from the basement and four cash registers were placed at the end of the sales line. The lines were created with yellow plastic tape, wrapped around orange road safety cones.

The signs that Sam spent hours to prepare were stationed throughout the store, advertising the 50% off price tag. The day was a major success. Sam walked up to his dad's apartment, and brought Roy three shopping bags full of cash. He first counted out everything they owed: the payment to the bank, and the total bill for their inventory and the money for the working staff. At the end of it all, there was forty-eight thousand dollars left! They had managed to make a profit of forty-eight thousand dollars in one day! It was better than Sam had expected.

Sam couldn't sleep well that night. He arose at four thirty the next morning, went down to the store and started again. There were gallons of paint that did not move quickly enough, so Sam pulled them from the back area and placed them in large stacks near the front door, with a new sign that read, 'DESIGNER PAINT-ORIGINALLY $9.95 – NOW ONLY $5.00 EACH.' This was a big hit. Eighty percent of the paint sold, along with most of the big stuff such as radial and chain saws. It all amounted to another thirty-six thousand, and there was a final day left!

Sam called Shelly around ten o'clock. She sounded groggy. He told her of his excitement. She seemed pleased but very passive. It was late, Sam thought, she had obviously been asleep. He would reach her during the day tomorrow and surely get a better response.

On Monday, July 5th, all hell broke loose. It was a madhouse! It was the time when the scavengers arrived, those who would steal, rob and hold hostage. Sam made a deal with a man who wanted to purchase all of the remaining steel and wood shelving. Sam knew that his dad had spent a total of fifteen thousand dollars for those units. Even though some of them were broken, most still had value. He offered a close out of seven thousand dollars and the guy accepted!

The man had come with three helpers and two trucks. They moved in and started pulling the shelves apart, like rats searching for food. By six o'clock that evening they had managed to dump all the small stuff, nails, screws and whatever, onto the floor, packed their trucks and left. It wasn't until much later that night that Sam realized he hadn't collected the money.

Sam was young, things were moving fast, the security guard was on a break and they just drove off with the goods. Sam could have called 911 and filed a police report on the incident. He had a description of the men but no license numbers on the truck. Sam decided to move on. Seven thousand dollars of old shelving, so what the hell.

By six o'clock, they had made what Sam calculated: about one hundred thirty-eight thousand dollars over the three day weekend. His advertisement stated that they would be open until ten o'clock that evening, and this was a good time to call home and tell Shelly his good news.

He had tried to reach her earlier, but there was no answer. This was the fourth time and still no answer. Worried, he found Rosie's phone number that he had tucked into his wallet and dialed it, hoping to find someone home. It rang a few times and Rosie answered.

"Hey Rosie, what's going on?" Sam asked. "Where's my wife. How come you aren't with her?"

"Hi Sam, how you doin'?"

"I'm fine. What's going on?"

"I'm doin' fine."

"Rosie, what I'm asking you is, where's my wife and why aren't you with her?"

"Oh well, I think her father came to get her."

Sam stood silent. He was waiting for additional information from Rosie but nothing was coming. He prodded her further. "What makes you think her father got her?"

"Well she called him earlier today around one o'clock and she said she was tired of her situation and she wanted him to pick her up cause she wanted to go home and that was it. I thought you knew all about it."

"What made you think I knew about all of that?"

"Well, I just thought so."

"Thank you, Rosie. I appreciate your help."

"That's okay."

Sam hung up the phone. Her final statement, 'That's okay,' proved to Sam she had the mentality of a five year old.

Sam drove under the Hudson River to New York. He made it down to the Hamptons. It was a classy residential area, full of wealth and opulence. Each home he saw was more beautiful than the last. He and Shelly had driven down here once, just around the time they were married. She wanted to show Sam where she had grown up. They never attempted to see anyone, that was it for her. Now Sam was back and ready for war.

The house was at the end of a cul-de-sac. He pulled the van up to the closed front gate. Just to the left was a panel containing a small light and a button to press to gain attention from someone inside the house. He gave the button a long push and waited.

He felt good about this wait. It gave him a moment to gather himself. He opened his mouth wide and sucked in some of that beautiful sea air which constantly permeated the area. Sam was starting to relax. He would be calm. He would talk to her father or her mother and he would make sense with them. These were not unreasonable people.

No one responded and Sam started breathing heavily again. He rang the bell twice more and honked the horn of the van, then another long ring on the buzzer. Still nobody came. He opened the door of the van and stood up, peering into the darkened yard.

The two story house was painted white. It was situated about five hundred feet from the gate. There were only a few lights controlling the area. Sam left the motor running, with his headlights on. He jumped to the ground and moved directly to the gate. 'Maybe they're not home,' he thought.

Then he heard the sound of an electric motor and he could see a white golf cart pulling forward from the back of the house. It turned onto the driveway headed toward him. A large man wearing black trousers and a black sport shirt drove it. It stopped by the front door of the house. After a moment a light switch was thrown from the inside, which turned on lights that covered the front door area along with at least thirty Malibu-style driveway lights. Finally the front door opened.

The man who came out must have been Mr. Roberts. Shelly had told Sam that he was in his mid-forties, but this guy looked closer to sixty. He had the body of a person who had survived a major car crash or a massive birth defect. He used two aluminum canes, one in each hand. They had extensions that clamped onto his upper arms. He wore a white sweatshirt which concealed his body, but by his movements it was obvious that he endured great pain to move.

As he walked he placed one cane forward, clicking on the cement, and then the other cane, clicking behind. It was *click, shuffle,* then *click, shuffle.* He finally made it to the steps and then five steps down to the cart. Sam made a move back from the gate. *How the hell long will it take for this guy to get down here?* Sam said to himself. *I could have easily driven my van up to the door and met him on the porch. All I want is to see my wife and son. I just want to find out why she left. What's going on? This is pathetic. This guy has all the money in the world but he can't buy a life.*

By now Roberts had seated himself in the cart. His twisted legs hung out on the side and his left arm grabbed an overhand pipe, used to steady him. His cane hung down from the clip on his left arm, rattled and banged against the side of the cart, as the guy in black drove on down the driveway. The big guy in black stopped just before the gate, turned the key off and got out of the cart. He moved to his right where a panel was located. Simultaneously, Roberts got out of the cart on his left side and with great difficulty made his way to the gate opening. The big guy pushed the open button on the panel but held it only long enough for one person to pass through. The gate held in its partially opened position.

Sam got a close look at the man his daughter accused of being a control freak. He had steel gray hair and wasn't five feet eight, due to his physical condition. His back was twisted and frozen, causing him to bend his head upward at an awkward angle in an effort to look up at people. He held his mouth slightly open with his lips spread wide and his teeth showing. It wasn't a smile, rather an effort to breathe easier. He sometimes saw this expression on Vince, when he sucked for air while suffering one of those heart attacks.

"Mr. Roberts?" Sam asked.

"You must be Sammy?" His voice sounded mean, full of double bad hate.

"Yes sir, my name is Sam. I just wanted to talk to my wife and see my boy. I just want to find out what happened. When I talked to her yesterday she said…"

Roberts interrupted. "I don't need to hear any of that! Listen, I'm going to do you a big favor, kid. I'll give you twenty-four hours to walk away from this whole mess you created."

"What mess? What did I create?" Sam asked.

"Either that or I'll create more misery for you than your little life has ever seen."

"What are you talking about?"

As Roberts continued to speak he started to move closer and closer to Sam. *Click shuffle, click, shuffle.*

"My lawyers are now preparing a case against you that includes at least thirty charges of rape and holding my daughter prisoner!"

"What are you talking about, we're married. I've got a certificate!"

"When I get done with you boy, you'll be spending thirty years in a fucking jail. I will annul your stupid certificate and your life will be over!"

The big guy in black moved through the gate and passed an envelope to Roberts.

"Now here's my big favor to you. There's five thousand dollars in this envelope. You take it and get out of this town, permanently. If that word is too complicated for you, it means for good. Don't call, don't fax, and don't ever show your face around here again. I give you twenty-four hours and if you're still here, my attorneys will serve you with our action. Police will be with them, at the Boardwalk Bar and Grill, to take you into custody. He handed Sam the envelope, turned and shuffled away.

Sam stood motionless, looking at the man who was about to start a war and finish it, if that was the case. Roberts was back into the cart and the big guy jumped in behind the wheel. Sam crossed to the gate, wading up the envelope into a tight ball.

"Shelly, Shelly!" he screamed. "You got it, baby! You got it your way!" He pitched the wadded money through the bars of the gate, landing on the front seat between Roberts and his goon. They paid no attention to that. They had a problem and they took care of business.

As the cart backed up the driveway, Sam saw the front door to the house open. It was Shelly. She had heard him scream and looked out to see what was happening. She stood there like the goddess he had always known. She wore a light blue robe over her white nightgown, with the wind blowing gently through her hair.

Sam was desperate. He made a final plea for her help. "It's me, baby. Come on, let's go home."

She stood at the open door with a frozen face. Suddenly, the situation he could never dream of happening had become a horrible reality. The golf cart stopped at the landing and her father got off. He shuffled and clinked his way up the stairs. *She heard me*, Sam said to himself. *I know she heard me.*

Her father reached the top step and, moving past Shelly, he looked back at Sam.

"Twenty-four hours, kid, that's it!" he screamed, as loud as his miserable body would allow. "If you're still here we'll make your life a living hell." He walked past Shelly and worked his way into the house.

For the first time this day, Sam was alone with his wife. The bozo with the golf cart had already backed it up the hill and now disappeared around the corner of the house. Sam grabbed the bars of the gate, holding on.

"Listen honey, I just made over twenty thousand dollars. We got something to start with now. We can do anything we want, you, the baby, and me. Come on, honey, let's go. Go get dressed and get our son and let's get out of here!"

Shelly looked at him as if he were the most pathetic creature she had ever seen. She kissed her hand and waived the kiss to him. Then she smiled, raising her head high, and moved into the house closing the door behind her. After a moment, the outside Malibu lights were turned off and Sam was left standing alone in the headlights of the van.

"Is that all there is?" Sam said aloud, with a degree of sarcasm. Suddenly the smell of the fresh night sea air presented itself with the odor of dead fish.

Sam pulled back into the parking lot at Pennington's Hardware at nine-forty-five. He walked inside and saw total destruction. Phil, the security guard, sat on a chair at the front door, finishing a beer.

"Hey Sam, how's it go?"

"Looks like we did it." Sam responded.

Phil quickly swallowed the last of his beer, wadded the aluminum can into a tight ball and pitched it onto the floor. "You got that right. It was a hell of a sale. At the last minute, I got a guy come in and buy every one of them cash registers. Nobody was here, so I said gemmy five hundred bucks and you got 'um. So he gave me five hundred bucks. So a little later, when I saw your dad, I gave him the five hundred. He said thanks, paid us all off in cash and he just took off. Nice guy, your dad."

"My father left?"

"Oh yeah? We helped him down with a bunch of bags, loaded up his station wagon and he took off into the night."

Sam went to his apartment, hoping to find his father there, but not expecting a miracle.

"Roy, you son of a bitch!" Sam said out loud. "I'm paying you off with one hundred eleven thousand dollars and fucking good riddance!"

As he looked about the place he noted the total destruction the two women left. Food on the floor, the couch and side chair stained with wine and broken glass. They had removed all of Shelly's clothing and other stuff, leaving him with nothing but the barest of necessities. Sam didn't have time to clean the place. He had a bus to catch.

Sam threw his things into a single bag and said to himself, *Thank God they had the heart to leave a bag for me.*

He drove to the Boardwalk Café, which was normally dark on Monday, but a special party was just concluding. Pierre sat alone in the kitchen finishing a bottle of Piper Heidseck. Sam sat on the other side of the table and tried to explain.

"The thing is my life has fallen to pieces. I gotta get outta here quick! My wife is gone, she's got my kid. My dad is gone, he took all the money. I feel like I'm on a squirrel hunt and I'm the squirrel."

Being the good man as Pierre was, he leaned forward and offered Sam a drink. "Here you go, kid. Things are never as bad as you think."

"Well, I tell you what. Any worse and I'll be in jail. What I need is for you to loan me five hundred bucks. As soon as I get work, I'll mail it back to you. Promise."

"Wait a minute. You string me out with these sob stories so I can lend you money?"

Sam reached in his pocket and withdrew the keys to the van. "I'm totally broke, George, dead broke. My dad took it all. I'm leaving town tonight and I need the money. Please give me the money. I'll pay it back."

"Who told you my name was George?"

"The same guy who told me to tell you that you were nothing but a fucking pussy!" Sam jumped up, grabbed his bag and headed for the door. Pierre was right behind. He was fuming. "No you don't. It was Vince, wasn't it? That bastard is always talking about me behind my back!"

"In ten months you taught me a lot," Sam said. "Even showed me how to cook, and I'll never forget that. Thanks a lot." Sam left Pierre standing in the kitchen and headed for the highway.

Sam walked about a half a mile. He figured another mile and he'd be out of town. There he could hitch a ride south, or west, it didn't matter. One way or the other, he'd make it to New Orleans. He knew he had only twelve bucks in his pocket and he had to smile at the five thousand he threw back at Mr. Roberts. From behind he heard a horn honk. He turned and saw it was the Boardwalk van driven by Larry, the kid who did the late night wash the dish routine.

"Hey Sam," he shouted. "Hop in." Sam jumped into the shotgun seat and Larry pulled off down the highway. "Pierre said I was to take you to the Greyhound," Larry said. "That's where you want to go?"

"No, but you can drive me to the freeway. I'm hitching to New Orleans."

Larry handed him an envelope. "Pierre said this was for you."

Sam took the envelope and looked inside. It contained a thousand dollars in twenties. Sam closed the envelope and looked outside. "Yeah, Greyhound will be fine." Sam didn't want Larry to see the moisture in his eyes.

Sam arrived in New Orleans at noon on the third day of his travel. He found a room on Toulouse Street with three steps up to the front door, located just off the street. It was a single room with a small cooking area on one side, a bathroom that provided a toilet, washbasin and an open shower. It was exactly as Vince had described to him.

Sam took the room and proved he was smarter than Vince. He placed a towel on the floor between the bath and the bedroom. Then he forced the door closed over the towel. Sam then figured, if you took a quick shower, turning the water on and off just to cover the rinse cycle, the bedroom would stay dry.

He moved through the Quarter, looking for work in a restaurant and found nothing available. Every place had its own chef and each chef had his own staff. A newcomer didn't have much chance in this town. He finally got a job serving coffee and beignets at the Café du Monde. The money he made there barely paid for his meager existence.

Then one day at Armstrong Park, listening to a Dixieland band playing their brains out, he saw a billboard in the distance. It was an advertisement for the New Orleans Police department. Good Salary – Good Benefits.

Sam went to Division Eight on Royal St. and signed up. But he would have to show them his high school diploma! After checking the yellow pages, he took a streetcar to Tulane College and enrolled in a high school correspondence class. It took six months to pass and Sam did it in spades, graduating with As in every subject. He next passed the test needed to join the academy training. He was sworn in as one of New Orleans' finest.

After receiving his third NOPD paycheck, he made a doctor's appointment and had a vasectomy. That would be the last time he would be in the position to contribute to a child who didn't have a father.

Chapter 7

DAY 3, CONTINUED.

BEFORE SAM WENT to the courthouse, he stopped off at the garage on Royal St. to look at his cop car. It was amazingly 'finished.' He first checked the right front passenger door; the fit was magnificent. He opened and closed the door several times and it snapped shut like Tupperware.

He had already glanced at the new carpet. Actually, it was no longer a carpet but more of a 'standard commercial rug'. They had removed the llama from the back section as well, and now the new goods were small loops of blue and gray shiny fiber.

Originally, this car was an accident, state of the art, the *avant garde* of automobile manufacturing. Somehow, someway, they managed to make an average everyday roadrunner look like something very special. On occasion when parked on the street, he would return to his car and find a guy standing there looking into the interior. When he would open the door, the man would come around to his side and ask what kind of car it was.

It was really the color that did it. The navy blue paint job against the chocolate brown leather seats and the dark brown llama carpet made it look special. Now, it was just another cop car. No one would notice and no one would care. He was given something special, and now he was reduced to cleaning the bathroom toilets.

Sam climbed inside and felt the rug with his feet. It was as though he put them directly on the metal floor. He next put his key into the lock and tried the windows. First, the driver's side window, down and up. Then the passenger side down and almost up. Then down again and almost up. The window stuck about an inch and a half from the top.

"I'll drive," Sam said softly to himself. "I'll have Wally ride shotgun."

Sam walked into the courtroom at exactly one o'clock. Judge Marshall Williams was just climbing the steps to the bench. Everyone was present and in their proper places. As the judge sat down, he noticed Sam crossing down the aisle and gave Sam a smile and a nod. Sam smiled also.

Nice of you to be on time, Your Honor, Sam said to himself. *Let's get it on.* As he crossed to the prosecution table and sat down, he noticed Charlie Wong was seated just behind him. Charlie gave him a thumbs up and Sam acknowledged it with another nod.

Then Sam was back on the stand and Donald Mosely approached. Today, he wore a beautiful moss green suit with a pale green shirt and the same moss green color tie, and of course, moss green suede shoes. Sam's thoughts ranged from the sublime to the ridiculous. *I wonder if he has the shoes made first, and then matches them to the suit, or if he makes the suit first and then has the shoes made*, Sam thought. *I'll bet you he gets a swatch of the suit cloth and takes that to his shoemaker.*

"Good morning, Detective Pennington," Mosely said, interrupting Sam's thoughts.

"Good morning, Attorney Mosely."

Mosely quickly decided to avoid using the title *Detective*. He also decided to avoid discussion of the bullet that hit Sam's car. He had already seen the report from Charlie Wong, so that would be a wash. Mosley decided to cut to the chase.

"I now wish to move to the conclusion of your testimony in this matter," Mosely stated.

The instant Charlie Wong heard those words, he leapt from his chair and headed for the exit. Sam saw him go.

Thanks Charlie, Sam said to himself. *Thanks for helping me spend taxpayer's money to find the bullet. Thanks for proving it was meaningless. And thanks for aiding the garage boys in screwing up my car.*

Mosely was now in his stalking mode. "I will to start with the testimony delivered by you in this courtroom yesterday. The same testimony was delivered by you to a Grand Jury six months ago."

Sam casually opened his book and pulled out his testimony. "I have to refresh my memory," Sam said, reading from the page. He took a moment to glace over his statement. "Ready when you are, sir."

Mosely smiled. "I didn't ask you to refer to your testimony, but I thank you for helping me out." There was a small chuckle from the audience. Sam noted that a few of the jurors smiled and turned to one another.

"On both occasions, the first day of your deposition to the Grand Jury, and then again yesterday in this court while being examined by Mr. Weinstein, you have stated as follows: 'The boy could only be heard moving near the gate.' How did you know that it was the boy's movement? And by the boy I indicate the defendant Joshua Skanes, Jr.."

"It happened very quickly. I heard two quick shots, my partner fell and then he appeared. He, being Joshua Skanes, Jr.. It all happened in a split second."

"Let us please go back to where you heard the movement behind the gate."

"Yes sir," Sam knew that Mosely was just getting started.

"How did you know it was this boy, or only this boy, who stood behind the gate?"

By now Mosely had moved back to his diagramed show card display that fell to the floor the previous night. He pointed to the house on St. Joseph Street, showing where Jack was and where Sam was. Then he pointed to the spot where Sam had said Skanes, Jr. was, just before the shooting. But now there was a piece of tape there, and instead of the name Skanes, there was a question mark.

"And this is where you assumed the defendant was coming from. Is that correct?"

"No sir. That is were I knew the defendant was coming from."

"You couldn't see who was there, could you?"

"I saw who it was the instant he moved out. A split second. That was it."

"Mr. Pennington – may I call you Mr. Pennington?"

"Yes you may."

"Mr. Pennington, I will later attempt to find out what a split second is, as compared to three seconds. For now, I want to find out what was in your mind just before the moment you heard the two gunshots that killed your partner. Can we handle that?"

"Yes."

"At the moment you heard someone moving behind the gate how did you know who this person was?"

Sam looked at Mosely for a moment. "We saw no evidence of anyone else behind the house. Only the defendant ran from behind the house. After we apprehended him, we went back and checked the back of the house. No one could have gotten in or gotten out. Nobody. There were glass bottles buried in the cement, in a ten foot wall at the back of the house, over behind a trash bin. That was where he was when he fired at me." Sam was rambling. He caught himself.

"So after you apprehended the defendant, you went to the back of the house and checked it out?"

"Yes."

"What were you looking for?"

"We were confirming that no one else was behind the house."

"But you just stated that you saw no one else behind the house, that only the defendant ran behind the house. Why would you need to confirm that?"

They hadn't even gotten to the point where Jack had taken two slugs into his body. Mosely had managed to make a big case out of slight bit of movement, by a person behind the gate.

"There is always doubt when a detective hasn't already seen the area," Sam said. "Someone else may be present. It was after our inspection that a definite conclusion was made. That no one else was present."

"Now we've come full circle, Detective – ah, Mr. Pennington. So I ask you once again, before the shots were fired, how did you know it was Mister Skanes, Jr. behind the gate?"

Sam just stared at Mosely. Basically, they were both on the same page. Mosely had nothing to win other than his client's life. Sam had everything to lose, the pride of his department and retribution for Jack.

"With bullets flying and people dying, who can tell in an instant exactly what's going on?" Sam said. "It's not a matter of a split second, or one thousand one, one thousand two, one thousand three. It's a matter of what you are trained for, it's a matter of right and wrong!"

Then it was the prosecution attorney, Jerry Weinstein, who finally jumped up into action. "Objection, Your Honor. Mr. Mosely is intimidating the witness. We've heard all this before, what's the point?"

"Sustained." The judge slammed the gavel down. "Sidebar," he demanded.

As the lawyers moved to the sidebar, Sam took a glass of water from his tabletop and had a long drink. He studied the room looking for Jack's wife, Billie. He had talked to her on the phone several days before but she had not been present, either yesterday or today.

Mosely was tenacious. After the sidebar was over, he managed to totally ignore what Sam had just testified to and went through, what a split second was and how that may relate to what three seconds were. Next he went into the lighting on the street, how bright and how dark the areas were. He went further into the possibility that there was another man, an associate of the defendant, who was there from the start, and who was the first to move behind the house on St. Louis. This was the man, Mosely suggested, who actually killed Sam's partner.

Much to his benefit, Jerry kept objecting. Everything that Mosely set out to uncover was nothing more than stupid excuses, and anyone with half a brain could see through it. There was absolutely nothing more that Mosely could manufacture that might alter Sam's testimony. As Sam continued to tell the who, what, when, where and why of it all, he would make a point of always talking directly to the jury. He would study their faces and try to think what they were thinking. The only thought that would come to his mind that there was someone among them stupid enough to believe any angle Mosely proposed. When that happened, it would be a hung jury!

Donald Mosely concluded his cross-examination of Sam at ten minutes after five in the evening. It took Jerry Weinstein a half hour to rehabilitate Sam's testimony. Sam was dismissed and court was adjourned for the weekend.

Win, lose or draw, Sam had done the best he could for his dead partner. If he failed, if Joshua Skanes, Jr. was found innocent or if it became a hung jury, it didn't bother Sam. He would just hide in the trees and wait for Joshua Jr. to make one more mistake.

Sam walked into the men's bathroom and crossed into his favorite stall. He took a quick leak, flushed the toilet lowered the seat and sat down. Sam was exhausted. After two days of bullshit examination from Mosley, he had about decided to take the rest of the day off. Then his cell phone rang.

"Hello."

"Sam. This is Carl Witherspoon."

"Hello Carl."

"Where are you? You sound like you're in an echo chamber."

Sam answered dryly. "I'm in an echo chamber."

"Okay, that's fine. Listen, we got a quick answer from Baton Rouge. It's about the dead girl's driver's license."

"What do you have?"

"They lifted the tape cover on the license and found no fingerprints. But they found something else. They found a smudge of makeup, not what the girl wore. She wore pancake. This makeup was an oil-base. Actors call it grease paint."

"Grease paint?"

"Yeah, grease paint. This guy could be an actor, or a wanna-be. So he changes the way he looks. How about that?"

"Okay. So he puts on a fake mustache, or a beard, or a wig. Like a chameleon."

"Yeah, something like that."

"Thanks Carl, I appreciate that."

As Sam walked back to the Quarter, he called Wally. He told him that he was now officially off for two days, and asked Wally not to bother him unless it was either major loneliness or a desperate emergency. "And you can forget about loneliness," Sam, added.

"How's the car?" Wally asked

"Fantastic. A thing of beauty. You might stop by and take a look on your way home,"

"Yeah, I'll do that. Okay Sam, have a nice weekend."

"I got one more thing for you to do."

"Shoot."

"I want you to take that drawing of our suspect and make a bunch of copies. Then I want you, or somebody, to make changes in each of them. Give one a mustache, another with a mustache and a beard and another with a dark curly wig. I want all our cops to know, this guy can change his look."

"You got it, Sam."

The sun was just setting on Bourbon Street and things were kicking into first gear. A tall, heavy-set man wearing a dark blue suit with a white dress shirt moved through the small gathering crowd. He was 43 years old, with curly dark brown hair and wore glasses. He, like everyone else, was looking for entertainment.

As he walked down Bourbon, the man paused in front of the Cabaret Bar located near, Toulouse Street. He tried to gain a peek into the bar. He was approached by a hawker, who would try to draw customers inside.

"Hey buddy," the hawker said, "we got the best time of the evening going on right now. It's *double cocktail time,* even as we speak. You wanna see a great show? We got it all. Step right over here and take a look."

The man smiled. He knew exactly how the ruse was played. He had already moved his wallet from his rear pocket, and placed it in his front jacket pocket. His mamma didn't raise any idiots. He walked toward the door, just as Sam moved to pass him in the opposite direction.

"How ya doin'?" Sam said to the stranger.

The man looked at Sam directly in the eye, from a distance of five feet. "Fine," he said. They both walked on.

Two blocks later, Sam stood across the street from the Dixieland. Four bands had been playing all day long, and now Red and his boys were setting up. Sam couldn't see Kelly, but Leonard was behind the bar preparing to rock and roll. Sam thought he would stop in to hear a good jazz set and have a drink. Then Sam thought of something else and quickly made his way back to the Cabaret Bar.

When he arrived at the Cabaret, the hawker moved on Sam like fresh meat. As he drew breath to speak, Sam flipped him his badge.

"You had a big fat tall man out here?" Sam asked. "You let him inside?"

"I don't know."

"He was a big heavy-set guy. Had thick dark curly hair. Wore some glasses. You sure you don't remember him?"

"Oh, yeah. I remember him."

What's your name?"

"Jerry."

"He still in there?"

"Yes sir, I think so."

"You think so?" Sam initiated a quick dial number on his cell phone.

"Yes sir, he's still in there."

George Carey answered the private number. "George Carey here."

"George, this is Sam."

"Yeah, Sam."

"I'm a block and a half away from you. You know the Cabaret Bar?"

"Sure do."

"Get here as quick as you can." Sam disconnected the call. He then moved just outside the door and looked through the parted curtains. It was very dark inside, even including the stage area, which was lit by two three hundred watt mushroom bulbs. Your eyes would have to adjust just to see the girl on the stage.

"How many people you got in there?"

"Twenty-six."

"How do you know it's twenty-six?"

"I get paid by what I bring in."

"An' how do you keep them in there?"

"I tell 'em the good stuff starts after dark."

"An after dark, what do you tell 'em?"

"I tell 'em another lie."

"You're a real scumbag, Jerry, you know that?"

Jerry was speechless. He had never been spoken to like that by a policeman. Sam spoke again. "I said, you are a real scumbag, you know that?"

"Yes sir, I know that."

A few minutes later George Carey and David Kennedy arrived in the front of the club, driving a police car. They left the car, leaving their running lights blinking. Sam met them on the sidewalk.

"Whatcha got here?" George asked.

"I saw a guy. He's the right size, the right facial shape. I figured we'd check him out."

"Okay, let's go do it," George answered.

David quickly moved to the curtain and took a peek inside.

"I don't want to make a big deal out if this," Sam said. He turned to Jerry. "Here's what you do. Once we go in stay in the back with us. Get on a table or a chair. See if you can spot him, okay?"

"Yeah, sure."

George moved in. "You tell us where he's sitting." They were playing Jerry like a banjo.

"You bet," Jerry answered.

"Alright, let's go!" Sam said.

When they got inside the music was deafening. The place smelled like the bottom of a bat cave during a humid summer day. Added to that, you had to deal with the stench of cigarette smoke along with the aroma of stale beer and foul wine. A female dancer was onstage, wearing a two-piece bikini swim suit, covered with a baby doll nightie. She was flipping the hem up and down, so as not to show too much flesh. A waitress walked around the tables, offering the use of a flashlight for a buck. The waitress was doing a successful business.

When the dancer saw who had the flashlight, she would move to the front edge of the stage, directly in front of the customer. The guy would turn on the light and direct the beam between her legs as she danced around, pulling the hem of her nightie, from hither to thither to yon. The customer would lean in, and was now able to get a direct look at the golden view of her crotch.

This was not great. Her crotch was always covered with that bikini and there were shouts from rowdies, screaming at the back of the room to get naked. She then peeled off the baby doll and gave the crowd a good look at what a fat little girl wearing a two-piece bathing suit looked like. The guys in the room applauded, hoping and believing they would see much more. They even threw money on the stage, which she happily picked up and stuffed in her bra, always leaving the ends of the bills sticking out to inspire others to join in on this sexual depravity.

As the horrendously loud music continued, George and Jerry were standing at the rear of the club. George had placed Jerry onto a chair, so he could have view of the entire audience. Jerry peered over the crowd, and spotted the 'mark' sitting at a small table in the center of the second row. Sam was standing fifteen feet away, watching as Jerry bent down to George and screamed something over the music. George looked over at Sam and held up two fingers. Sam looked down the second row and spotted where fat boy was seated. Sam looked across the room and saw David, and he held up two fingers. David acknowledged the message.

Then the music stopped and the silence was deafening. The girl strolled off the stage and a voice from over the speakers crashed and reverberated across the room.

"Alright ladies and gentlemen, you wanna to see more?" They roared and cheered. The voice spoke again. "We're going to give the little lady a few minutes to cool down. Then when we start again, she'll be ready to show you what she's really got!"

It was now time to hustle drinks. It was also time for George Carey to make a move on fat boy. Sam moved himself closer to the center of the stage. David held his position, and George moved in quietly sitting down at Fat Boy's table. As he moved in, George took a quick glance at the suspect. He seemed a likeable fellow, with both hands on the top of the table. He withdrew his badge and placed it in front of the man.

"I'm Detective Carey, New Orleans Police. I need to ask you a few questions."

Fat Boy looked quickly at George. "What's the problem?"

"Just relax and stay calm," George said. "I need you to keep your hands in front of you. Do you understand?"

"Yes."

"What's your name?"

"Alex Kroman. Here, I have my..." Kroman reached for his inside front right pocket, but George quickly interrupted, reached out and grabbed his arm. "Hands on the table," George firmly commanded.

"My God, what's happening here?"

"Here's the deal. You know who I am but I don't know you. I don't want to make a scene here. You lock your hands together chest high. Then get up and head for the front door. Walk slowly, with no false moves. You'll be met at the left and right by two more detectives and we all walk outside. Got it?"

Kroman started to hyperventilate. "Yes, I got it."

"Hands clasped."

Kroman clasped his hands. "I got it."

"Chest high."

Kroman raised his hands. "Chest high, I got it."

"Now, let's move out."

The two men rose and headed for the front door. Both David and Sam met them at the half-way mark and they all walked outside.

The instant the four men cleared the door opening and found their way onto Bourbon Street, George spun Kroman around facing the wall and held him there while David quickly searched his entire person for weapons.

"He's clean," David stated. George released his hold.

Alex Kroman had been through a short, quick visit to hell. He slowly turned around and leaned his back against the wall, breathing heavily. He was sweating profusely and his skin had turned sallow. Sam stood a few feet back, allowing George to make an arrest if necessary.

"I'll need to see your ID," George said.

"Yeah sure, I got one right here."

Alex reached into his back pocket, then realized he had moved his wallet to the front. He withdrew a Louisiana driver's license and handed it to George. George glanced at it then handed it to David, who walked over to the cop car and got on the radio. Sam moved in closer to Alex.

"What's your name?" Sam asked.

"Alex Kroman. I'm a professor at Loyola University."

Sam studied his face for a moment. "You wearing a hair piece?"

"Yes sir, I am. I'm losing my real hair."

I'll make it easy on you," Sam said. "We have a witness that says you were in a laundromat on this street three nights ago. Were you there three nights ago?"

"Yes I was. It's about for maybe five blocks up the street there. I stopped in to get my shirt cleaned."

"What time were you there?"

"I don't recall. It was early morning, after one, maybe one-thirty."

"Did you see anyone else there?"

"There was a lady there. I think she was the owner. She helped me out. We cleaned the shirt."

"Anybody else?'

"Not really. Some people walking on the street."

"That was all?"

"I didn't see anyone else come into the laundry. I was in and out in fifteen minutes. I didn't even dry my shirt."

George crossed in and tapped on Sam's shoulder. Sam turned and George led him back to the car.

"This guy's clean," George said. "His license is good as gold. He's a professor at Loyola University. Been teaching classes on English History for seventeen years. Never even had a ticket. Never been busted. A pillar of the community."

"So why's he hanging around down here?"

"So he's a 'closet' dirty old man. Who cares?" George offered. "Hell, I got problems too."

"Yeah, right," Sam said.

"I'm gonna cut him loose," George said. "We got no reason to hold him."

Sam walked back down Bourbon, stopping across from the Dixieland. Red was into a hot number and Leonard was mixing drinks as usual. Then, near the bandstand, he saw Kelly and he smiled. He hadn't felt a smile on his face like that all day long. The mere sight of her cheered him up. He wanted to hear the sound of her voice, feel the touch of her hand. The fact that she talked too much was still a bother, but he'd work on that.

He wanted to go in for a drink, catch a set, flirt with her, but he decided against it. He was truly exhausted, not physically, but mentally. Instead he walked up Bourbon, four and a half more blocks and noticed a small commotion going on at the corner across the street from the St. Ann market.

The artist, Frank Hogan, had painted a beautiful sign, which hung at the top of the laundry. It read 'French Quarter MURDER,' on the first line, and then on the second line, 'It happened HERE!'

Next, were massive enlarged portions of the newspaper, showing the headline, 'DEAD BODY FOUND IN FRENCH QUARTER LAUNDRY DRYER', along with a large photo of Lila being interviewed by the cops.

I didn't give Frank any money for those enlarged photos, Sam said to himself. *Lila must have gotten some new investors for this.* In addition, someone had run a string of Christmas tree lights above Frank's sign, to light the front of the building and make sure all pertinent information was legible.

There were three people standing in a short line outside, waiting to get to a washer, which were all being used. Lila was there, dolled up like a woman in deep sorrow. She wore a large black caftan with a string of pearls. Her hair was now long, black and flowing, obviously a wig. She sat at the door signing autographs. Who knows why she was asked to sign, or what she signed them on, but sign she did. Behind her, in the far back corner of the laundromat, was a small table full of glowing candles. Another small pinpoint of light was placed just above the dryer where Beth Hayden was found. Sam could not tell if someone had placed a mannequin there. Perhaps that would have been too much!

It had created a bit of a traffic jam also. As cars moved up Bourbon Street, they would pause to see what was going on. Several carriages were there too, with their drivers explaining to their customers just how dangerous the Quarter could be.

Sam crossed St Ann Street and entered the market. Sally, an older woman who took the evening shift, greeted him. He asked where Phil was and she called to the back of the room. As Sam slid onto a barstool, Phil arrived.

"You see this shit that's going on out there?" Phil said in an outrage. "Are you believing this shit? What asshole gave that woman an idea like this anyway?"

Sam peered out through the window and nodded his head in agreement. Phil took out a fresh towel from his belt and started wiping the front window. "What the hell does she think this place is, fucking Disneyland? Look at the traffic, for crying out loud." He turned back to Sam and smiled. "What you want Bubba, coffee or a drink?"

"A drink would be great."

While Phil went back for the booze, Sam glanced back across the street. It was about forty feet from where he sat to where Lila presided, over her shrine. She spotted Sam, and was standing there waving at him with a large warm smile on her face. He had been the man who had designed this tribute. Sam looked around and saw that Phil was out of sight. He smiled back and waved at Lila.

A few miles south was the warehouse district of New Orleans. It was in this area that Eddie Marsh had his apartment. Upstairs, on the third floor, was where he prepared for his clandestine activities. One of the upper rooms was in pitch darkness. Eddie's heavy footsteps could be heard approaching the room. The door opened quickly and banged against the wall and the lights turned on.

Eddie stood at the open door, seething with anger. He crashed his way through the messy room and sat down in a chair facing a large makeup table, which was surrounded by ten lit 75-watt light bulbs. Eddie glared at his face in the mirror. The impossible thing had just happened. The police had made contact with him. He had no idea how or why they made contact with him. He could not now figure what information they had in their file to seek him out. But it happened.

He took large metal bowl from below his desk and poured some wood alcohol in it. Then, ripping the dark brown kinky wig from his head, he placed it in the bowl and forced it under the liquid. He then ignited the wig with a lighter, and it burst into a ball of flames. As it died down slightly, he reached into his left hip pocket and withdrew his wallet, taking out his driver's license, which he also tossed onto the fire.

Eddie added some more liquid to the keep the flames alive. Plastic and hair started to burn and shrink in size. "That does it for you, Mr. Kroman. I'll never be stopped again." Then Eddie took some cold cream from a jar and spread it on his face, and started removing the makeup with some Kleenex tissues. "And I will kill the bastard who tries."

Sam and Phil had finished their drinks. They bade each other good night and Sam walked to his apartment. He felt it might be wise to be honest with himself. Over the past three days, Kelly's face and name had cropped up in his mind many times. The fact was, she really didn't talk too much. The fact was he enjoyed hearing her voice and sharing her stories. In reality, he thoroughly looked forward to her company.

Chapter 8

Day 4

SATURDAY, MARCH 4TH. Kelly had worked a hard, long shift, starting at five Friday evening and ending at six the following morning. Leonard's wife was supposed to spell her, but on this occasion his wife was feeling a little fragile. Kelly worked through with a big smile and that fantastic attitude, and she managed to carry it off.

Kelly was tired and her feet hurt. She had already been shopping the day before to find a dress to suit the upcoming occasion with Sam. Kelly found a black cocktail dress, the mini hemline emphasized her lovely long legs.

She got home from work at six-thirty Saturday morning, removed her clothes and fell back onto the bed. She decided she would sleep until three and then get ready for the big evening. But sleep did not come easily. At nine she got up and decided to clean the house. She got out the vacuum cleaner, turned on the dishwasher, sat down with a coke and fell asleep on the chaise-lounge. At six she awoke and realized there was only one and a half hours left to prepare. That is when the preparations for magic came desperately into play. She quickly aborted the cleaning process, returned the vacuum to the closet and emptied the dishwasher. Now it was time to do her make-up and hair.

By six-thirty only the hair had not been done. She styled it at least four different ways, and decided it was either much too much or not enough. She started to get nervous because she had sprayed her hair with so much lacquer that it started to look like a wig.

She dampened a towel and tried to wipe the glue from the roots, and then blow it dry. It finished into a fluffy mass of golden curls. When she looked at herself in the mirror, she liked what she saw, sort of a cross between an Afghan hound and a shaggy Poodle. Then she dressed. At seven twenty-five, she opened her front door and sat on the couch to wait for her ride to Sam. At exactly seven thirty, Eduardo arrived.

"Hello, I'm Eduardo. J'ou Miss Kelly?"

"J'es I am."

"I here to deliver you a welcome to my mule, Piccolo, and my carriage named French Quarter tours. My mule and me are here to deliver jou presence to Mr. Sam Pennington. Jou ready to go?"

Eduardo had just made Kelly's day. She would now get a carriage ride, her first ever, and Sam had selected Eduardo. He was perfect, broken English and all. She stood, gathered her black and gold shawl and said, "Ready when jou are, sir."

Eduardo helped her into the open carriage. She was glad she had brought a shawl. A slight breeze was blowing. They drove down Toulouse Street to the river and turned left on Charters Street. You couldn't live in New Orleans without seeing a mule-driven carriage, but riding in one was an experience. Kelly felt like a queen, sitting back on the soft leather seats, enjoying the fresh air and feeling about as special as special could be. As they trotted up Charters, she knew people were looking at her, wondering who she was, wishing they were her. They passed the tall golden statue of Joan of Arc, riding her beautiful steed into battle. It was a magnificent sculpture and Kelly felt equal to Joan's challenge.

Finally they turned left onto Barracks Street, passing the Flea Market and the old mint which was now a museum housing Mardi Gras paraphernalia. Then they moved on into the lower residential area of the Quarter. As they completed the turn, Kelly caught sight of Sam standing in the far distance. He stood on the top balcony of a three story apartment building, and was looking in her direction. He was dressed all in white. A white pullover sweater, white cotton slacks and white tennis shoes. He looked like her white knight.

Eduardo pulled Piccolo over near Sam's front door. He hopped off and helped Kelly down from the carriage. From street level she could still look up and see Sam. This was a Sam she had never seen before, and her heart skipped a beat. She heard soft music playing from Sam's apartment: possibly a trio of guitars, perhaps it was gypsy music, but something that caused her to think of embarking on a great adventure.

Eduardo had returned to his carriage and took the reins in hand. He shouted up to Sam, "I got my phone on, boss." He held the phone up in the air. "Jou just call me when jou ready and I'll take the lady home." Clicking his reins, Eduardo guided Piccolo up Barracks Street.

"I'll buzz you in!" Sam said to Kelly. "Take the stairs up two flights; I'm right at the top." Sam moved inside and she heard a buzzer ring.

She pushed the gate open and walked inside, finding herself in a courtyard. It was decorated with lighting that came from the upper balconies, which created a mood effect in the area below. The centerpiece was a fish pond, with statues of three nymphs splashing their feet in the water, appearing to play with the beautiful specialty fish that were swimming lazily around. The rest of the courtyard was covered with flowers and various plants and a few large banana trees. Scattered around were benches and chairs wherever needed, but the lighting was what pulled it all together into the most romantic of places.

Just to the right was a long staircase leading to the second floor and beyond a smaller winding staircase to the top floor. As Kelly made her way up to the second floor, she noticed that some of the people were at home. She could see them through their shuttered doors and she glimpsed at them and the well-decorated apartments within. The place reeked of Old New Orleans. Finally she was on the smaller winding staircase. When she reached the top, there was a sign taped to the open door reading, "Welcome, Kelly. *Mi casa es su casa*."

She entered a small but exquisitely decorated foyer, with a marble floor and an antique crystal chandelier. The ceiling was higher than normal, as was the case with many older homes in the city. As she moved through the foyer she passed a half open door on her left. She pushed the door slightly and peered inside. It was a small but beautifully decorated bathroom. The lighting was dim but enough to show what the room possessed. The floors were marble here too, but not the same marble as the foyer.

The basin and surrounding areas were pink marble and the floor Carrera white marble. The tub was an antique, with large golden feet reaching out to the floor. It was the fixtures that really sold the place. The tub was plumbed from the outside and done with all brass fittings. The shower held a large, one foot wide circular shower unit made of brass and a face of polished golden bronze. The basin fixtures were two brass dolphins that stood at least a foot high with the water coming out of their mouths.

Kelly walked out of the bathroom and into the living area. Expecting a small area, what she was greeted with was a massive great room and kitchen. She was stunned! Kelly saw Sam still standing on the balcony, leaning back against the railing. He smiled and looked as if he had just stepped out of the cover of a movie magazine. Tanned and handsome, he raised his hands to Kelly, and opened his arms in welcome to her.

Kelly gave him a wry look, followed by a more wry smile. She thought to herself while smiling, *If he wants to play position games with me, I'll give him something he'll never forget.*

Slowly, she walked into the center of the room. Sam didn't move. He watched her as she took in the beauty of his work. The big room had fifteen foot high ceilings and there were three pair of French doors leading out to the balcony. When left open, they provided an excellent additional dining area. Sam had placed a table for two just outside on the balcony.

Kelly's attention was drawn to the kitchen which was built into one side of the living room. It was complete with a wet bar that was on the front side of the kitchen area, and the actual kitchen was behind. The kitchen was equipped with a large double sink. The refrigerator and range were in stainless steel of professional quality. Even the dishwasher was different, with none of the amenities one would find in a regular kitchen. There was no mistake made here, this was a pro's kitchen.

Once again she noticed the lighting. It was all built into the ceiling and streamed down onto the direct area that it needed to augment. There were small pin lights that fell only on the bar and not on the people at the bar, and larger lights that fell onto the range at the back, and also the refrigerator.

Kelly looked back at the table Sam had prepared. There, a single amber light flooded over the table top, but only over the table top, and each picture on the wall was lit with the same feeling of care and romance. Kelly turned to her right and saw a back hallway. She walked to it, ignoring Sam. She knew he wanted her to do this, and do it she would.

She lost sight of him as she moved into the hall. To her left was a closed door. She opened it and looked inside. It was his office, a cop's office. There was an old desk, along with shelves which held hundreds of books. Pictures and papers were pinned to awkward places all over the room. There was a fax machine and copier and an answering machine. This was a working guy's office, not a place for 'Missy' to play around with. She closed the door and moved on.

She next walked into his bedroom. It was a man's bedroom, stylishly decorated with custom furniture, all in supremely good taste. Yet there were touches a woman would enjoy. She noted the king-sized bed with an oversized headboard, a place to rest and to play. His massive closets were covered with antique shutters. And the television set, the biggest she had ever seen, was on a riser, providing anyone in bed with a fantastic view. Finally she moved on to Sam's bathroom.

This was the *piece de resistance!* If there were ever a place in this apartment that was designed to please a woman, this would be the spot. It was especially large and grand. All the paintings were original oils. Painted on a base of off-white, they were covered with many bouquets of flowers. The artist sealed his work with a gold glaze, which gave them an old world look. They were signed, "De LaHoya."

Everything was modern, the basin and fixtures were modern, the shower was modern, and the toilet and bidet were modern and the tub! The tub was a thing of beauty. It was also the biggest Jacuzzi she had ever seen.

She had been in a spa tub once before, when she was in Las Vegas with her mother. She remembered sitting there playing with her rubber duck that swam in and out of the bubbles, but she expected no rubber duckies here. This tub could accommodate at least five people, with water jets and pin point jets coming out from every spot imaginable. This would be a mega blast from heaven!

Sam stood out on the balcony, waiting for her return. When he saw her coming, he braced himself against the railing. He wanted to know what her reaction was. When she came back into the room, she noticed another De LaHoya painting, of Germans having a party at a beer garden. She recognized it as the one she saw the other night on Bourbon Street. Kelly smiled and walked over to Sam and without saying a word, wrapped his arms around her. He well knew that he had gotten to her, and he hadn't even fed her yet.

Kelly sat on the balcony in a stuffed chair. The music changed into a smooth string group playing a version of show tunes from the sixties. Sam moved to the kitchen and did his thing, gathering food items and placing them so as to excite the digestive juices. His first course was magnificent: two very tasty crab cakes. The second was a small bowl of his special gumbo. Kelly could have eaten more but more was not offered. She'd learn why a little later. Next Sam served the barbecue shrimp, a special and secret recipe he got from Vince. The gumbo was Pierre's. It was amazing how marvelously two New York chefs could master such delicious Southern dishes. Sam overdid the shrimp a bit, serving an extra helping, but he couldn't stop himself. Sam liked shrimp.

The entrée was next, lobster and steak with rice pilaf. Kelly managed a whole lobster and half the steak and no pilaf. Sam had a salad prepared for the finish. His cane vinegar dressing was special, and Kelly loved it. It was unusual to serve a salad at the end of the meal, but Sam told Kelly that he had learned the practice in a small town in the backwoods of New Jersey, where a chef he knew always served his salad last. "That's because he liked it that way," Sam said.

Kelly took a sip of wine while Sam changed the music to old tunes from the Big Bands of the forties, and they danced to "Moonlight Serenade" by Glenn Miller and his Orchestra. As they danced to the seventh tune the phone rang.

"That must be Eduardo," Sam said.

Kelly sat down on a bar stool in the kitchen as Sam answered the phone. She listened to Sam.

"Hello. This is Sam. Hey there, Eduardo. Well, I'll ask." Sam took the phone from his ear and covered the mouthpiece. "He wants to know if you're ready to go home."

By this time, Kelly had only done half of what she had planned. "Please tell Eduardo, I don't teenk so. Tell him I saw dees whole lot of apartment. Tell him I saw the big bedroom. Tell him I been fed real good and now I look for one big thrill in the big spa. Tell him hasta luego, Señor."

Sam returned the phone to his ear. "Thanks Ed," Sam said. "I'll catch you in a few days." Sam hung up the receiver. They got buck naked and jumped into the spa.

Her body was even more gorgeous than he had remembered, causing him to shake a bit in anticipation. He pushed several buttons that caused a massive display of bubbling excitement starting from the sides of the tub, squirting out and hitting the body in ways to cause one to anticipate the next. From the bottom, a massive amount of small bubbles erupted, and a relaxing flow of hot water drifted over their bodies. Then there was the final button.

"Okay, here we go," he said as he opened her legs slightly and pulled her down over one of the remaining silent spouts. "Now just take it easy, this one can cause nirvana." He pushed the final button and five of the remaining spouts came alive. Water shot up from the bottom of the tub, erupting in a rush of soothing water which flooded the top of the spa. Sam had pulled her body down placing her bottom right over one of the spouts. She felt like it was an intruder into her privacy. Her eyes grew wide, she grabbed for the side of the tub. She looked at Sam, who gave her a dispassionate look. He was, after all, just following the directions from the manufacturers of the tub.

It was impossible to see down through the water with all of the foam and bubbles, but they both knew exactly what was happening. Kelly released her stranglehold on the side of the tub and relaxed her body slightly, as the water continued to punch upward. Kelly felt it striking the tip of her love bud. She sat there for a long moment, wondering what would happen next. And happen it did. She reached an orgasm!

It wasn't a great orgasm, just a preliminary one. One of those orgasms that said, *here I am, I can do this, what's next?* What was next was another, and then another and then she was wasted in an orgasmic pool of complete ecstasy.

Sam shut the spa down. "You okay? Sam asked.

"I'm fine, just fine. I'll be fine in a minute. I'm just going to relax a minute. But I'll be fine, just fine, in a minute."

He dried her lovely body off with a fluffy white towel. As he wiped the beads of water from her flesh, she was once again invigorated. Her breathing became heavy once more. Quickly, they moved to the bedroom. Sam flipped the covers back onto the floor. She was dry but Sam was still wet. He ran his hands over her body and picked her up, lying her down in the middle of the bed on soft sheets. Then, like a smooth and gentle tiger, he began to devour her entire body.

She was sexed in more ways than she had ever read about. The tub orgasms were only a faint memory, a hint of better things to come. This was the real thing, and when he penetrated her, it was a though she had lost control of her very being. She had given it up to the manipulations of a gentler and stronger force. Kelly was in a dream world, experiencing pleasures she had never been told about. She finally understood why her mother liked the guy she was with. Then, it was close to over.

He took her face in his hands and gave her a deep kiss. It was the kind of kiss that said, *I love you baby*. With one final thrust, his body exploded into her, and it was totally over. He rolled over onto his back while Kelly lay there, catching her breath. It would never be better than that.

Day 5

At six o'clock, Sunday March 5th, Sam moved into the living room and cleaned up. It didn't matter when he fell asleep, his mental alarm clock always rang at six o'clock. By eight the place was as neat as a pin. He sat on the balcony reading the paper. After a quick scan, he put it aside; nothing interesting there. Sam removed his shirt and got some morning sun and at nine, the phone rang. It was Bob Riazzi of the Central Market on Decatur.

"Hi Bubba, how'd it go?"

"Hello Robert, I got everything connected," Sam said.

"I guess you don't need any help with the dishes."

"Thanks for calling, but no thanks," Sam heard bare feet slapping against the wood floor. Kelly was heading to the bathroom, followed by a voice. "If that call is for me, tell 'um I'm not here." The bathroom door slammed shut.

"I just got the word. She's not here."

"Love your style, Sam," Bob replied. "See you later."

They had a champagne breakfast that went really well. She helped, he cooked. The eggs Benedict with oysters and truffles were a designer meal that Sam had created. Actually, there was a restaurant down on Decatur Street that used his recipe and named it for him. As they sat on the balcony enjoying the morning sun, Sam offered a suggestion. "How'd you like to take a drive with me and see my boat?"

"You have a boat?"

"Sure, doesn't everybody?" Sam replied with a smile.

Not only did Sam have a boat, he also had a car. It was parked on Barracks Street in one of four small garages which fronted the apartment. It was an Italian sports roadster, a vintage Alfa Romero Spyder circa 1979. It had a removable hard top for when he wanted the wind to blow through his hair.

Sam opened the garage door and there was the car. Kelly's little squeal told Sam that she liked it. It was a cute little thing. It was red, an oxidized red that needed some polish or a new paint job. Sam said he would work on that soon, but for now, "It runs like a top." After he helped her into the car,

Sam jumped behind the wheel and prepared to start the motor.

"I haven't had this baby out for over a month. Hope the battery's okay."

He put the key in the ignition and turned it on. The car gave a wheezing try and went dead. Sam quickly turned the key off.

"Okay Baby, let's go," he said to the car. "Let's just get it together and move out onto the road."

Sam tried the key again. There was a slow grinding of the fly wheel and it managed to pick up speed and then caught! As the engine grabbed on and held, a massive plume of smoke filled the garage. Kelly started to cough. Sam raced the engine. He put Baby into reverse and started to back out onto Barracks Street.

"Boy, I love the smell of carbon monoxide in the morning."

For the months Kelly had lived in New Orleans, she had only been associated with the French Quarter. She would leave her apartment on Toulouse Street and walk to work at the Dixieland on Bourbon. She would go to the river, the mighty Mississippi, and shop for stuff and things. She would look at the twin Crescent Connection bridges that crossed to the Westside. Without a car it was difficult to get around, but now things had changed.

Sam entered the I-10 and kept left to the West bank, leading across the muddy Mississippi. This was another of Kelly's biggest thrills of the century. Last night her ride with Piccolo, and now she was in an Italian sports car driving over the Mississippi river. As they reached the river Kelly pushed up in her seat, glancing around, seeing the wonders of one of the finest scenes in the country and looking back behind her at the city skyline. There were the high beautiful buildings, with the huge Superdome in the background. As they continued on she saw the river. It was majestic! When she looked straight up, she saw the top of the bridge itself. It was marvelous.

They drove to the town of Lafitte, about twenty miles south of New Orleans. This was not a town as you might know it, more of a place. Located on Bayou Perot, Lafitte was an area of fun and happiness. There was a market on one corner and nothing but houses built for another quarter mile, then a church and more houses, then a spot with growing weeds and a small restaurant and bar.

They drove to the Town Market, Museum and Picnic Grounds. Sam introduced Kelly to George Wheeler, the old fellow who owned the store. George and his wife Mabel were sitting on two rockers in front of their place.

Sam purchased a museum ticket for a quarter and while Sam went to the market to buy some food, Kelly strolled the aisles of the museum, searching for...whatever. There was an old stove, an old clothes dryer, stacks of old dishes, a stuffed deer head and a display showing the death of John F. Kennedy in Dallas, Texas. The display contained three items: a Dallas newspaper showing the President's death, a snapshot taken of Kennedy and his wife Jacqueline moving in a distance through a crowd. There was also an envelope, hermetically sealed in plastic, autographed by JFK. George Wheeler stood at a safe distance, watching her with a delighted smile on his face.

With the shopping finished they moved another half mile south and wound up on the property of Judge Wilford Bean. It was an old rambling house on about four acres of land with a huge back yard that swept down to the bayou. Sam drove down the dirt road and headed directly for his boat. Kelly saw it parked in a dry dock, built from old timbers. It had been pulled into the dock by a very fat cable, attached to a winching machine. As they drew closer she caught the name of the boat on the bow...*Miss Lee*. She had used the name Lee also, because she thought it gave her some star value. *What a coincidence*, she thought.

The *Miss Lee* was an old shrimp trawler about seventy feet in length, but the boat had been transformed. A large cabin had been added to the center of the boat and the hull had been stripped of its paint. Actually, it looked as bad as a man with half a haircut. Sam told Kelly that all it needed was the final exterior paint. Work had been in progress on and off for years. Hard shrimping had caused sections of the boat to fail but now with some love, hard work and personal conviction, it had again become a seaworthy vessel.

As Sam parked near the boat, Kelly got a look at Judge Wilford Bean, standing on the poop deck. He was a man in his eighties and about six foot three, with steel gray hair. The judge was deeply tanned and walked with the vigor of a much younger man. They left the car and walked over to the boat. A temporary ramp had been built leading to the upper deck. Sam and Kelly climbed to the top and were greeted by Judge Bean.

"Permission to come aboard?" Sam said with a salute.

"Permission granted," the judge answered.

The judge had a smooth deep voice, well spoken and highly intelligent, Kelly immediately liked him and the way he smiled and looked at her. Kelly felt he liked her also.

"Kelly," Sam said. "this is retired Judge Wilford Bean, no connection to

Judge Roy Bean of Western fame." They shook hands and the judge took Kelly's hand and lingered just a bit before releasing it. Sam looked toward the rear of the boat where there was a young man working in the back section of the boat. Sam called out, "Pedro!" The boy looked up smiled and waved to Sam. "That guy over there is Pedro Sanchez, the head honcho of this organization. Isn't that right, Pedro?"

"You got that one right," Pedro answered.

Kelly noticed that Sam called Judge Bean "Judge," but she opted to call him by his Christian name, shortening it to "Wil." After the introductions she moved away and looked over the boat. "Hey Wil, this is quite a boat you boys have here."

With a big smile on his face, Wil answered. "Allow me to take you on a tour." Wil held out his arm and she took it and, offered him that famous smile she just recently developed.

"Thank you, kind sir." As they walked off, she turned to look back at Sam and she gave him a second smile as if to say, *Eat your heart out Bubba, I just made another friend.*

"Sam towed this garbage scow down hear about ten years ago." Will said, as they headed for the pilot house. "He told me he wanted to turn it into a high level luxury cruise vessel. I suggested we sink it and start from scratch, but he said, 'No way, I love this boat.' Well, I studied him long and hard and said okay, let's do it." Kelly laughed.

They walked into the pilot house. This was the operational part of the boat, the place where the sailors meet the sea. It was full of electrical equipment, radios, sonar, radar and an automatic pilot. There were also four television screens, monitoring every area of the boat, all with connecting cables running from one to another. They hung around like lights on a Christmas tree, in the process of being decorated for a big event.

Kelly stood at the wheel of the ship. She placed her hands on the spokes and screamed, "Steering aft you land lubbers, I'm coming through!"

Wil liked her sense of humor. He decided she would be a keeper. "So we pulled this puppy out of the water and placed it in my dry dock," Wil said. "Then Sam got a partner with some bucks in his pocket and we started to redo the engines. I got two of the biggest horsepower jobs that would fit in the engine room and two boys from the navy yard to hook them up. This boat will now haul...well, you know what I mean. Over here is a ladder leading up to the top. You can really get a beautiful view of the whole Gulf up here."

Next he took her into the main cabin. With the extension that had been built onto the deck, it became a huge area. Kelly started to see the possibilities. She noted the teak hardwood moldings that had been placed on the walls. The room had no furniture, but everything else was completed.

"Here you have the main living space, with the galley built right into it," Wil said. "Sam likes the galley and the living area together. Keeps people friendly."

Kelly quickly noted the similarities to his apartment on Barracks Street. The kitchen was completely finished with a refrigerator, dishwasher and an ice machine, all in place, and running. Wil took her by the hand. "Down here is the master bedroom."

They climbed down the ladder at the rear, to another large area. This one was also finished. The walls were varnished dark teak wood. There were custom-made reddish dark blinds over the three port holes on each side. A rich gray carpet was freshly laid and the bed was positioned in the back side of the room, complete with a massive head and foot board. A television at the other end of the room was placed with excellent "in bed" viewing. Truly a place to sleep and play!

Sam had taken the food from the car and was preparing dinner on the aft deck. The sun was just starting to set over Bayou Perot. They were all outside enjoying adult beverages and conversation. Kelly had met the rest of the team. There was the Judge's girlfriend, Norma Taylor, a lovely lady in her early seventies. And then there was Roberto Hernandez, a quiet man, in his late thirties to early forties. He was tall and skinny, and looked as though he had worked hard all of his life.

Sam, Pedro, and Roberto served the dinner. It was beautiful. The soft shelled crabs, corn on the cob and Sam's *etouffee*, a Cajun stew, that was made from an assortment of seafood and a large link of anduille sausage. He finished the meal with that now-famous salad which he had also served her last night.

"So what about you, Pedro? Where are you from?" Kelly asked

Pedro looked up at Kelly. "I'm from Honduras."

"He's Eduardo's son," Sam interjected. "Eduardo Sanchez. They guy who drove you over last night with the carriage ride."

Pedro excused himself. "Excuse me. I must get the wine." Pedro headed back to the galley.

Kelly looked questioningly at Sam. "So what's the story on his father?" she asked.

"Eduardo was a bank president in Honduras," Sam settled in to tell the story. "Banco Pacifica was one of the biggest banking chains in Honduras. Eduardo was the president of the bank in San Pedro Sula, a small city on the Caribbean Sea. That's just below the Gulf of Mexico. About ten years ago they were hit by a massive hurricane that nearly destroyed the entire country. It hit San Pedro Sula the worst. Its economy was wrecked. Eduardo's wife and daughter were killed in the storm. Eduardo and Pedro immigrated to the United States and they wound up in New Orleans."

Pedro came back from the galley with a new bottle of wine and three fresh glasses. He poured three glasses of the ruby liquid into the fresh goblets.

"I'm telling Kelly about your early life here," Sam said to Pedro. "Do you mind?"

"You can tell her anything you want. I like her. She's to be trusted."

Sam was in a mellow mood. He toasted Kelly and everyone else and sipped the wine. It was a vintage Syrah. "Good stuff, my boy, great choice."

Pedro smiled and gave a thumbs up. He then headed back to the galley. Sam picked up where he had left off.

"Eduardo got them a job on a tourist cruise liner. He worked in the galley, and he lied about Pedro's age and he wound up serving drinks in one of the ship's bars. Pedro was only sixteen at the time. So they wound up in New Orleans. I found them sleeping in a doorway over by the church. We became friends. I moved them into my place, it was an unfinished apartment then. Got Eduardo a job hustling tourists in a carriage."

"So what did Pedro learn in ten years?"

"Well, I taught him to be a pretty good chef. He learned how to steer a boat and he's now a licensed ship's navigator, with naval documents to prove it. And he's learned about construction, and wiring for television, and communication systems. I'm not sure how he learned the television stuff, but he got it from somebody."

Dinner was fantastic. Pedro came back and sat down beside Sam, joining the festivities.

"What's the schedule look like?" Sam asked.

"I think we can be in the water in a week," Pedro said. "We get the final load of furniture in tomorrow. Then Roberto and I will do the final two coats of paint on the outside skin. We let it dry for one day between each skin. We plan to move her out sometime next Saturday."

"I'll be here," Sam said.

Pedro gathered things from the table, and headed back to the galley and Roberto joined in. Sam stood also and said, "I'll give Pedro and Roberto a hand with the clean-up."

As Sam removed the last of the plates from the aft deck, Kelly also took a stretch and wound up strolling on the rear part of the deck.

Kelly watched the sun as it finally set over the horizon. She moved off looking for Wil, finding him leaning against the bulkhead of the starboard wall.

"Hey Wil, how're you doin'?"

She had caught Wil by surprise. He jumped rather quickly, hiding something in his hand.

"I'm fine. How 'bout you guys?"

"We're fine." Then she smelled the sweet aroma of marijuana.

"Sam's doing the dishes," she hastily added. "I'll go help him finish up." She quickly headed for the galley. It was an awkward situation and she didn't know what to do about it. She had just made a fool of herself by finding Wil at a time he didn't wish to be found. She entered the galley, finding Sam alone. Pedro and Roberto were on the deck, putting chairs and other stuff away.

"I've done a terrible thing," she said.

"What's that?" Sam asked.

Kelly looked at Sam for a long moment and said, "It's nothing. Forget about it."

Sam studied her face closely. "Okay," he said. "Where's the Judge?"

"He's out on the deck. I think he's smoking dope."

Sam quickly understood what happened. "Okay, so you caught him smoking dope."

"Yes, but I think something should be done or said."

Sam gave her a long look and a smile. He leaned in and kissed her on the cheek. "It's getting late. Let's just go home. I'll go talk to the Judge."

Sam left and Kelly started to gather their stuff together.

When Kelly came out of the galley, Sam and Wil were walking toward her. Both men were smiling as though nothing had happened.

"Well, goodnight ya'll," Wil said. "Hope you had a nice day."

"It was wonderful," Kelly said. "Thank you so much."

Sam and Kelly got into the car and he started the engine. She was in a state of confusion. Half way to the street Sam stopped the car and turned off the engine.

"'What we have here is a failure to communicate,'" Sam said. "Here's the deal. Judge Bean had been on the bench for twenty-six years. Then he developed an eye condition. They call it glaucoma. It wasn't caught early enough and he was advised he would go blind within a year. A doctor told him that marijuana would relieve the pressure on his eyes, to the point that blindness could be avoided. However, no one in this society would allow him to buy marijuana, nobody. So, the Judge found himself between a rock and a hard place.

"He got some dope, I don't know where, and he smoked it. He smoked six joints a day and his eyes got better. It relieved the pressure on his eyes. It was just that simple. No big deal."

Kelly looked at Sam dead straight in the eyes and said. "Okay then, it's no big deal. That's fine."

But it wasn't fine and Sam knew it. This could either be easy or a great big mess. Either way, he would give it his best shot. Once again, Sam gathered his strength. He spoke softly, so as not to cause any alarm. "The Judge retired at sixty-five and moved into this place with his wife. She died two years ago from cancer. Now he grows a patch of weed in his back yard, still smokes six, maybe seven smokes a day."

Kelly turned and looked out of the back of the car. The Judge was standing on the top deck. Norma stood beside him. He suddenly looked like a tired old soul. Sam caught the same view in his rear view mirror. She knew quite well Wil would never need a Seeing Eye dog or a white cane. She jumped from the car and trotted back to the boat. She arrived at the bottom of the temporary ramp and made a formal salute. "Permission to come aboard, sir?"

The Judge acknowledged her and when she came aboard Kelly crossed to him, providing him with a true feeling of regret. "I'm sorry for what I have created here tonight. I now understand everything. Please forgive me."

She placed her hands around his neck and gave him a big kiss on the cheek. The Judge responded with a hug and a 'smooch' of his own. Norma snorted a few times, but said nothing.

Sam remained silent as they drove back to the city. His mind was now on business. It had now been five days since Billy Joe Mays had picked up Beth Hayden in the clothes dryer on Bourbon Street. They had found one more, labeled Jane Doe, whom they believed was the victim of the same murderer. Now he hoped for some action. Kelly sat quietly also. Sam noticed this and he wanted to cheer her up. "Tell you what. I'm going to take us home another way."

It was nine o'clock when they lined up for the ferry in Algiers, a small city on the Mississippi, just across from New Orleans. They drove onto the ferry and parked near the bow. They both left the car and walked to the side to see the beautiful city with all of its lights. She had many firsts to remember from this weekend with Sam. Now this, her first ferry ride was also special.

As the boat turned its heading toward the city, the air kicked up and the wind blew against her face. "Who could have thought of taking a ferry boat to get home?" she asked.

Sam moved close to her and placed his arm around her shoulder. She turned and wrapped her arms around his waist. It was a cool night and the water was as smooth as silk. The boat glided its way to the Canal Street dock and Kelly noticed that Sam continued to be preoccupied. Perhaps he was thinking of tomorrow and what he wanted to accomplish. She hoped he was not dwelling on the situation she had created with the Judge.

Sam left the motor running and waked her to her door. He gave her a quick goodnight kiss. "I'll call you the first chance I get."

"Thanks Sam," she said. "Everything was absolutely perfect."

"Goodnight baby." He moved quickly to his car and drove off into the night.

Kelly felt the let-down the moment she entered her apartment. She sat on the couch and looked around her quiet small room. She thought about Sam and wondered if he would ever call her again. She was just a weekend fling, and now the weekend was over. *We seemed different on the way home,* she thought. Maybe she was borrowing trouble, so that when trouble came, it wouldn't hurt so much.

Chapter 9

Day 5, continued.

IT WAS JUST after ten o'clock when Sam walked into his apartment and went into his home office. There was a blinking light on the answer machine and Sam punched it into service. The voice he heard was Carl Witherspoon.

"Sam, this is Carl. Your boys think they've found a new hooker victim. Call me."

Sam picked up the phone and called the precinct.

When the receptionist answered, Sam asked for Carl but was switched to the morgue instead. George Carey answered.

"George, it's Sam. What's going on?"

"Hey Sam, we've been having a real good time around here."

"Can you fill me in quick?"

"Got a call on a dead body found stuffed in a frozen meat container. She's in the process of thawing out. Won't have any news for at least another hour or two."

"Okay, anything else?"

"Yep, we found out the name of Jane Doe. Penelope Andrews."

"Are you guys going to stay there?"

"Oh hell yes. We're waiting for the thaw to happen. See if we get another love note from Mr. Weird."

"I'll be there shortly." Sam hung up the phone. He went into the bedroom and took his detective clothes from the closet. When he removed the stuff from his old pockets, Sam noticed that his cell phone had a dead battery.

He quickly changed and headed for the station.

Sam had not given Kelly a moment's thought during this period of time. It was so typical of the male animal. His work became more interesting than his new girlfriend. Had he known, had he even suspected her deep sadness at that moment, he would have called her. Had he known about her feelings regarding dope and the Judge, he would have instantly dispelled them. But now, she was out of sight and out of mind. It is a terrible thing men do to women.

At ten forty-five Sam walked into the morgue and found all of his important people present. They were diligently waiting for the young lady to thaw. David Kennedy was sitting on a chair by the front door, while George Carey, Arnold Feeney and Carl were seated around Arnold's desk.

As Sam walked across the room he saw the body of the new girl on a gurney in the middle of the room. She lay there nude, totally uncovered. Sam studied her for a moment then looked over at George. "Okay George, let me have it again from the top," Sam said.

George stood up and took center stage. "Alright, here it is. We got fifty-five frozen food lockers gathered over at the Industrial Canal. These are basically meat lockers, rented to restaurants in town. They hold their meat until it's needed."

"So all of us here in this town are eating nothing but frozen meat?" Sam said, a bit alarmed.

"No. These are holding places for the meat that is shipped in already frozen. Like from Australia. Like a leg of lamb."

"Okay, go on."

"Now the meat in these lockers is checked every three months, four times a year. This morning a security guy finds a chain that has evidently been cut. It had to be opened with one of those big bolt cutters because it was a very heavy chain. When he opened the door of the locker, this body falls out on the ground."

"So, who got the body?" Sam asked.

George looked through his file. "Let's see. That would be William Joseph Mays of the Rampart Division."

"Here we go again," Sam said. "We couldn't have gotten there first?"

"I think it was a lady security guard, and she was a little shook. She called the number in her file and got Rampart. We heard the call go through, but by the time we got there, this guy Mays was already in charge."

"Okay, next," Sam stated.

"I've got her at one hundred twenty-eight pounds and five foot six in height." Arnold volunteered. "She's between seventeen to twenty-five years old, give or take."

Carl stood up to stretch. "Let me cut through some of this. This is another Jane Doe, but I understand George has a lead on the first one. Right, George?"

"That's right. Penelope Andrews." George said.

"Right," Carl said. "So the key to this thing that makes it all fit together is..."

Sam interrupted. "When did this hooker right here die?"

"Good question." Carl agreed. Everyone in the room focused on Arnold. Arnold looked around and noticed that everyone was staring directly at him. He stood up and crossed to the gurney. "Okay," he said. "Let's check her out." As he put on his rubber gloves, Wally entered the room.

"Hello everybody," Wally said. No one responded.

Arnold started poking at the body as though he was checking the cooked tenderness of a turkey. He probed at her stomach. With a rubber encased finger he raised her left arm up and pushed another finger at her arm pit. As he raised her arm, the body turned over slightly exposing the left side of her face. It looked a lot like meatloaf. She had been so badly battered that she was unrecognizable. Sam saw this and just stared at her face. Everyone knew they were dealing with a big time 'Monster of the Midway.'

Arnie took a scalpel in his hand and prepared to go to work.

"Okay," Arnold said. "I think I can start now."

"That's okay Arnie," Sam said. "We've got stuff to discuss. We'll wait in the hall."

Once in the hallway, they all gathered around in a bunch. Carl was the last out, closing the door behind him.

"Okay," said Sam. "One thing at a time. First, what's the deal with Jane Doe number one?"

George sifted through his notes, finally coming up with the information. "Here we are. We showed her picture to a young lady at the Galway Bar on Bienville. She identified her as Penelope Andrews. They had lived together for a month in September. Seems Andrews was looking for work and finally found a job dancing for private parties." George looked up from his notes. "I've got a major report in the works on this kid, waiting for the material to come in."

"What's the roommate's name?" Sam asked.

"Hironee Jessup. She's an African American hooker. She's not cooperative."

"Anything else?"

George scanned through his notes. "I asked her everything I could think of, but Miss Jessup didn't recall anything pertinent to this case. She didn't see a thing or know a thing…nothing."

"Let's bring her in," Sam said. "Arrest her for pandering. Keep her away from an attorney, if she has one. We sweat her for twelve hours, give her some sleep deprivation, and then we talk. There is no way two hookers can live together for a month and both don't know exactly what the other is doing."

David took out his cell phone and dialed, moving away from the group. He started an intimate conversation.

"Now about Detective Mays, is he a problem?" Sam asked.

"I've run into this guy numerous times and he's always one big hard ass," George said. "If he doesn't get his way, he's ready to chew you out, but this time he just signed the body over to us. Filled out the paper work and turned it over to me. So we got the body."

"That's great, George," Sam said. "Next, what's the number of this meat locker and when was it last opened for inspection?"

Again, George referred to his notes. Sam noticed that Wally was in the background, quietly taking down notes on his clipboard.

"The locker was 27F, and it was opened by the inspector on the eleventh of November," George said. "I don't know if anyone else entered the locker since then."

"Hold on!" screamed David. "I got it." He ended his cell phone call. "The restaurant came in on November fourth. That was their last entry. Next was the inspection report on the eleventh. That places the body there after the eleventh.

"Wally, make up a good calendar." Sam instructed.

"Already got one started." Wally proudly announced.

The door to the morgue opened and Arnold stepped into the hall. "Here it is." Arnold said. He held a plastic envelope high in the air. It contained the missing note, stuck inside of Jane Dow number two.

Sam took the envelope from Arnold and turned toward a hallway light. It was clearly the proper note. The instructions were legitimate. *"Don't go* here. She's mine. 2."

"Okay," Sam said looking intently at the group. "We now have a confirmed serial here. Let's go to my office and lay this whole thing out on paper."

Carl moved into the group. "I'd like to see a profiler on this case," Carl said. "I know an FBI guy I could bring in."

"Okay Carl," Sam said. "you do that right now. I want names, dates and usual suspects listed. Let's go."

When they hit the upper hallway, Carl moved into his office and Sam and his boys went to the left to Sam's. Once inside Sam's office they started to work on the wall of miscellaneous activities that had grown larger throughout the years. When he finished, Sam had a clear open space to stage his attack. At the same time, David was involved with another cell phone call.

"Okay, pictures right here," Sam said. "First victim Penelope Andrews, below that the name of Hironee Jessup." As Sam spoke, Wally placed the photo of Penelope, drawn by Frank Hogan, on the wall. Wally put a push pin through a piece of paper and made a hand note. *"Hironee Jessup. Hold 24 hours for questioning. No attorney."* He next placed a piece of white paper on the wall with the new name: Jane Doe. He reached for a photo of the last victim, Beth Hayden, number three. He placed it on the far right wall.

David ended his call and moved into the group. "That was dispatch. They just arrested Hironee Jessup on pandering."

"That was quick," Sam said.

The door opened and Carl came into the room. "Got hold of my FBI profiler," Carl announced to the group. "Name's Angelo Marino. He'll be here at eight o'clock tomorrow morning. Let's all be here and be ready."

Finally David Kennedy had had enough. He stood up and took center floor. "That's right, Mr. Marino will give us a wealth of information. First thing he'll do is advise us that the killer of these women is a loner, never been married, and comes from a broken home. He's had a bad childhood and most likely was sexually abused by his father. Sounds like one sick son of a bitch to me."

"Go on David, tell us more," Sam prodded.

"So, now he's looking for us to stop him. He leaves notes for us in the hope that we find him. The notes say, *'please stop me before I do it again.'*"

George headed for the coffee machine. "Suppose it's a black guy?"

George asked.

"Mr. Marino might agree with that," David added. "But Marino's file might show that black men are seldom involved in serial murders. This has got to be a guy willing to take the time to get to know a woman, gain her confidence. Then when he's finally alone with her, strips her naked and beats her to death with a club. Yep, one sick son of a bitch."

Carl shakes his head at the thought of such a man. "What makes him so angry with hookers?"

"Come on, we've heard all of this before," David said. "You got to go back to his childhood. We don't know why he does what he does. Maybe his mother was a prostitute, trying to keep their lives together. Or maybe she had an affair with another man. His father found out. Beat the crap outta her. Whatever happened, it left a bad mark on this child's evil little brain. The mark festered in his lonely life for thirty years, and it finally boiled over. The people who know him think he's a real nice guy."

"You believing all that?" George asked.

"Not for one second," David answered. "When push comes to shove, we see a guy that's motivated to be one real big sack of dung. What we've got here, is a jack-off who murders women on our streets. Our job is to catch him and stick him away in a deep dark place. Feed him nothing but bread and water for the first five years. After that we take away the bread."

"What do you think Carl?" Sam asked.

"You guys seem to have a handle on this. I'll call Marino tomorrow and cancel." Everyone in the room remained quiet. Sam moved to Mr. Coffee machine and poured a cup. "We'll need help," Sam added. "We'll need a cop or two in every spot in the city where hookers hang out. We need to find this guy in two weeks or we'll have to call in the big cop army and prepare for the worst."

Carl checked his wrist watch. "Well, it's just after twelve. I got to make a call from my office and then get some sleep." He looked at the group. "You guys make good sense. See you tomorrow." Carl left the room and a call came in on David's cellular.

"Hello," David said. "Yes, I got it." David signed off. He looked at Sam. "The boys are confirming that they arrested Jessup and will book her in fifteen minutes. Pandering's the charge and no one will be able to trace the booking number. She's asked for her lawyer. She gave the arresting officer his card. His name is Donald Mosely, of Mosely and Mosely."

Sam thought of Blue Boy. "Now that's really good news," Sam said. He swallowed the last of his coffee. It tasted like mud, but the burnt caffeine was his most pleasurable jolt of the evening. "I'll take Hironee," Sam offered. "What the hell kinda name is that?"

"She's an African American." George said. "It's spelled H-i-r-o-n-e-e."

"I know how to spell it. I just wanted to know if it meant something."

David Kennedy stepped up to the plate and took a swing at the answer with a chuckle. "I think it has to do with black women who are really pissed off with white guys."

"Okay fine," Sam said. "She's my type of gal. You guys go on home and get some sleep."

"Here." Wally said, laying down a stack of copies on Sam's desk. "These are the suspects that George and David came up with. I'll leave them here on your desk. I've also included ten more pictures of our bad boy with wigs and stuff." Wally said, as he started for the door. "See you guys later."

Sam picked up the stack of eleven copies of driver's licenses that Wally had prepared. Twelve, if you included the last one made of Alex Kroman.

"Where did you guys come up with this stuff?"

"We always make an enlarged copy of information on the suspects," David volunteered.

"Yeah, we got a copier installed in the trunk of our car," George said. "One of us talks to the dude while the other goes back and knocks out a copy of his license. A piece of cake."

David shrugged. "You never know how many suspects get released, only to find that they actually did the deed."

"A lot," George said. "You ever hear of Ted Bundy?"

Sam studied them for a moment, realizing why he felt Frick and Frack made one of the best teams in the bureau. "Okay, fine. Go on home, see you guys tomorrow."

"Goodnight Sam," George said as he and David left the room.

Sam moved in and pushed his foot around under the desk, searching for his stuff, his party basket from Kelly, but he couldn't feel anything. He moved from his chair and got on his knees, lowered his head to the carpet and made a good visual search. Nothing was there! He stood up and thought, *Somebody took my stuff. Maybe it was Wally.*

Sam turned around and looked at the filing cabinet in front of him. He opened the top drawer and found everything he was looking for. He poured some Glenlivet and reopened the caviar. Sam said to himself, as he sat at his desk with his feet up, *I'll never challenge Wally's integrity again.*

The phone rang. It was Melvin Teague, officer in charge of the nighttime lockup.

"May I speak to Detective White?" Melvin asked.

"You've got Detective Pennington. Let's get to the chase. You've just arrested a Hironee Jessup, and you're holding her incognito, is that correct?"

There was short pause, then the question from Teague, "What was that, incog...?

"Do you have Hironee Jessup up there?" Sam interrupted.

"Yeah, we got her. She's here with no information from nobody."

"That's fine. Put her in an interview room, I'll be there in a few minutes."

Sam scooped his finger in the can of caviar and threw down a wad of fish eggs followed by a slosh of scotch and was on his way to the jail.

Day 6

Monday morning, March 6

It was one o'clock when Sam walked up the stairs to the lock-up facility. This was a series of twelve cells with a capacity of four men in each. A series of "drunk tanks," if you will, for those tourists from Bourbon Street who made too much of a great evening.

Just beyond that was the women's jail, mostly reserved for prostitutes. Six cells for double occupancy. These cells were not for serious crimes. If you were guilty of murder you'd be delivered to a larger facility, Division 1 on Rampart Street.

Sam headed to the first of five small interview rooms. Sgt. Melvin Teague stood at the door to room one, holding a list of charges. Melvin was a big man, about six foot four. He was rather good looking and seemed slim and fit. Sam wanted to ask if he had played basketball, but the subject seemed out of place just now. Sam took the file.

"Thank you, Sergeant. I'll call if I need help." Sam entered the room. It was small. There was one table with a chair for the defendant and two on the opposite side for the detectives. The usual lamp hung from the ceiling, shining straight down, giving the place a *movie* look, from cop films of the past.

And then there was Hironee Jessup, a black woman, about twenty-five years old. She was tall, about five foot nine and rather pretty. She wore Levis with white pumps, no stockings, and a white high school sweatshirt. The school name had all but faded into oblivion. Her hair was neat and clean, an Afro with style and purpose.

"Hello," Sam said. "I'm Detective Pennington with the New Orleans Police."

"An' I'm Hironee Jessup, with one bad-ass attorney who wants me to call him right fucking now! You got dat?"

"Listen to me." Sam said calmly. "This has nothing to do with you. I'm not Vice, I'm with Homicide."

Suddenly Hironee's attitude changed, from deep anger to impossible rage. She banged her fists on the table top and screamed at the highest pitch of her voice.

"No you don't, you muther fucka! You white bastards wanna hang me with a murder? You better get one strong rope, cause my lawyer ain't gonna put up with this bullshit, no fuckin way! You got dat?"

The door to the room opened and Melvin and two other policemen jumped in and took charge. Hironee had just jumped across the table, grabbing Sam's shirt. Melvin and his pals quickly pulled her off of Sam and put her in cuffs. As they led her away, she screamed obscenities on down the hallway.

Sam sat quietly for a moment, trying to catch his breath, when Melvin returned to the open doorway. "You done with the lady?" he asked.

"Nope, just getting started. I'll be back in about an hour. I'll call first."

Sam returned to his office, finished the last of the caviar and opened a "soft" garlic cheese from France. He opened a box of gourmet crackers from Sweden which were covered with sesame seeds, and he munched away. There were other surprises left from the basket. He would try them all. It would be a long night.

After warning Melvin of his next arrival, Sam walked back up the steps to the second floor. It was one thirty in the morning. When he arrived at the interview room, Melvin stood at the door, with his pals seated on folding chairs at the side.

"I got her cuffed to the chair," Melvin said.

"You ever play any basketball?" Sam asked.

"No."

Sam gave that some thought. Evidently, every tall African American male did not play basketball.

"Thanks," Sam said, and entered the room.

Hironee would not say a word to Sam. She was at least quiet. He used his softest voice and expressed himself with his most polite attitude.

"This has nothing to do with you. I need to gather information about a girl who stayed with you. Her name was Penelope Andrews and she is dead. Her body is right here in this building, in the morgue. I need to know who she knew. I need to know who she saw or who was trying to get close to her. I truly believe you can help me to prevent another murder. Another prostitute on the street could become a victim and your information can help me stop this guy."

Hironee jumped into another fit of rage. Her right hand was cuffed to the table leg, but that left her room to swing at Sam with her left. Sam calmly leaned back on his chair causing her sweeping left hook to miss his face by inches.

"You accuse me of being a ho! I ain't no mutha-fuckin ho! I runs a hospitality business. I an honest citizen 'a this community, you cocksuckah!"

Melvin and the boys came into the room an dragged Hironee back to her cell.

In his office, Sam continued pawing through his basket stuff. It turned out to be quite an expensive present. There were levels of goodies there: more caviar, more cheese, a small can of pâté de foie gras. Sam opened the pâté and looked around for a knife. There was none to be found.

But a man alone, working in his office during the early morning hours, has discretion to do any task needed, in any manner he may deem fit, to perform. He grabbed the pate with his fingers, grasping it firmly and slowly pulled it from the can. In doing so, a few drops of fat dribbled onto the top of his desk. But that was okay. He was alone. No one was there to see his abominable table manners. The fat would be wiped up later with a 'Manpower' paper towel.

Then came the *piece de resistance*. Sam took a big bite of the hunk. Like a rat in heat, he took two more bites. It was beautiful. The very basic instincts of mankind, washed down with two sips of Glenlivet, one following the other, he managed to devour a gourmet meal.

It was now four-thirty in the morning and Sam headed back upstairs.

Melvin still waited. His two buddies sat on their chairs, eagerly hoping for this night to end. Sam moved in and motioned for Melvin to open the door.

Melvin was a showman. He opened the door and swept Sam in with the motion of his arm. Sam smiled. He crossed in and found Hironee sitting quietly there with her knees up holding her legs in her arms. It was as though her spirit had been broken. Was it that easy? Did she die on the vine? Or was it just one more pause before another major attack?

"Would you like something to eat or drink?" Sam asked.

"I wouldn't mind a Coke," she answered.

Sam jumped up and opened the door. Melvin was there. "We need a coupla Cokes."

Melvin started going through his pockets. He came up with some change, but not enough. "Hey, you guys wanna help out here?" he asked of the cops sitting in the hall.

His two pals started looking for change in their pockets. Sam found a quarter.

"Here I got fifty cents," said Hironee.

Melvin gathered the change and headed to the Coke machine. Sam stood at the open door, turning back to take another look at Hironee.

She was just about done. It was almost over. Finally, Melvin returned with the two Cokes and Sam moved in for the kill. He sat down at the table and opened Hironee's Coke. She took it in her hands and placed it to her lips. Tipping her head back, she poured the cold liquid deep into her throat. Ah, it felt good. She placed the cold, wet can on her forehead. The pressures of the night were relieved with one cold sensation of pleasure.

Sam took the point position. He looked her square in the face and offered the best situation he could come up with.

"Now, if you will just listen to me," Sam said holding eye contact. "This has nothing to do with you. You got that?"

Hironee sipped her Coke and set the can on the table. She was tired now. The hassle of the evening had started to take its toll. She felt a nervousness coming on. It was the bodily shakes of the first new day, when she had taken too many drugs the night before. Now she spoke softly, making each word crystal clear. "I'll say this one more time too. Real easy for you to understand. I don't give a rat's ass about that little white girl. I don't care about who she went with, what she did or how she did it. I don't give a fuck if she lives or if she dead. You got that? Now, if I don't get my phone call, you gonna be sucking swamp water, and you can kiss your fuckin policeman's badge goodbye."

Sam decided he had had enough of Hironee. He also knew that if she filed charges against him, he'd simply deny it.

"Cuff her," he said to Melvin. "Take her down the back service elevator and bring her to the morgue. Keep her quiet. Just you, bring her down. Nobody sees her. Got it?"

"Yeah," Melvin said. "You want my guys to come?"

"Just you Melvin," Sam said quietly. "Just you."

Melvin moved close to Sam and asked softly, "Hey, we doin' something illegal here?"

"Melvin, we are all doing something illegal here. That's what we do for a living."

Sam looked back at Hironee. "On second thought, better bring your two pals with you. If she gives you a fight, tie her up and carry her down."

The florescent lights were on inside the morgue. Sam pulled open the drawer holding the body of Penelope Andrews. She was completely covered with a sheet.

Melvin and his pals entered forcing Hironee ahead of them. Her hands were cuffed behind her back and her mouth was sealed shut with a wide strip of duct tape. Her nose was sucking for air. It was the only sound that could be heard in the room. The sound of a woman in panic.

"When we put her in the elevator she started to scream," Melvin explained. "We had to tape her mouth shut. That okay?"

"Sounds right to me," Sam said. "Over here boys, gonna give the little lady a first class exhibition."

They moved her a few feet from the slab, each of the boys holding her up by the armpits. Hironee was no longer in a fighting mood. The fight was gone and she was no longer in the mood to call her lawyer. Now, she figured she was about to die. Sam moved to within inches of Hironee's face.

"You got something you want to tell me?" Sam asked. As he spoke he ripped the tape from her face pulling those small hairs from her upper lip. She was shocked by the pain but she bit the bullet. She opened her mouth wide and sucked in the much needed air.

"What you got for me?" Sam repeated.

She started to gain control of herself, her breathing was coming easier. But she knew there was more to come.

Sam took the sheet in his hand and gave it a little flick, now showing only the top portion of her face.

"Wanna take a look? Wanna see what this little white girl looks like now? You know, the one you don't care whether she lives or dies?" Sam crossed to the other side of the slab. "Okay, nothing to say? No problem! Let me introduce you to Penelope Andrews."

Sam took the sheet in his right hand and whipped it over the body causing it to fall in a heap to the floor. Sam did not look down at Penelope, but directed his gaze at the four people standing before him. Sam was showing her the cadaver, and she anticipated what it would be like, but even in her wildest imagination, was she prepared for what she saw. It was a sight that she would carry with her for the rest of her life. She clenched her teeth and tightened her lips in an effort to avoid throwing up all over the sheet.

On seeing the nude dead body, Melvin took three quick steps back. His face showed deep concern. Sam glanced down at the body and saw what a good job Arnie had done. The first scalpel cut ran from just below her chest bone and opened her up like a gutted fish. It sliced her wide, down through her stomach and ended somewhere at the crotch. While the partying continued on Bourbon Street, this little girl lay on a slab with her guts and crotch exposed to the world, and somehow that didn't seem fair. Except for the fact that she was dead and that didn't seem fair either.

Sam looked up into the eyes of Hironee Jessup. The blood had drained from her face, making her look like she wore a thick layer of white powder makeup. And there were tears in her eyes. Her knees began to collapse and the boys on either side had to hold her up.

Sam looked back at the corpse. He had decided hours earlier that it would either be Hironee or him and he was winning.

"This mess down here…" Sam said, as he waved his arm over Penelope's exposed innards. "…our autopsy caused that."

With his right hand, Sam reached for the cadaver, and grabbed hold of the back of her hair. He pulled her body halfway up twisting her face to Hironee.

Hironee's face contorted. She uttered a sound of deep sadness, a moan if you will.

"But her murderer did this!" Sam said. Hironee dropped her head down. She was desperately trying to hold on but Sam was easing in for his final pitch.

"He beat in the back of her head with a club. See here, where her skull collapsed? See, right here. You can even get a look at her brain."

Sam was valiantly trying to control a gag. He slowly placed Penelope's head back onto the slab. He continued swallowing his spit in order to keep his stomach bile from erupting. The formaldehyde smell of a body that has been kept in the cold for over three months was nearly unbearable.

Melvin turned and headed for the door. He put his hands up on the wall to steady himself.

Sam crossed around to the front of the slab. He came as close to Hironee's face as possible. Her hands started to shake. This time she shook with emotion and horror at what she had seen.

"Tell me who did this!" Sam snarled. Then I'll send you home, right now, in a squad car. If not, your counselor, Donald 'Blue Boy' Mosely, won't even find your bones! You got that?"

Hironee stated to spill her own guts. "He was a tall man. Real big guy. Six two, maybe three. I only saw her about five times in the month we stay together. She told me about him, she kinda like him. He was gonna fix her up with something special. I only saw him once when he pick her up at my place. But I swear I didn't get a good look at his face."

What about his weight?"

"Two hundred eighty or ninety, I guess."

"And that's it?" Sam asked.

"Yeah, I swear to God, that's it."

"Was he a white guy?"

"Yeah he was white."

"And you never saw his face."

"No sir, never."

"What kind of car did he have?"

"It was white, no, kinda cream colored. And it had a silver thing on the front grill. It was a kinda bar that ran from the top left to the bottom of the other side. Like a slash thing, with a medal or something in the middle. I couldn't see what it say.

"A big car?"

"Yea. A four door, older type a car. An it had a big rust mark on the left front fender. Like it had been left out in the rain a long time."

Sam leaned back onto the gurney. He had gotten all he really wanted. Anything else would be lagniappe.

"Where did she work?"

"She work the streets. Did some strip dancing. I never seen the place. She move around a lot." Her tears started to flow again and the shaking got worse. Sam instantly understood what she was going through. If ever a person should give a break to a drug addict, now would be the time to do it.

"You want to go home or to the hospital?" Sam asked.

"Home. I wanna go home."

Sam walked over to Melvin, still hanging on the wall. "Okay Melvin, I'll sign the release. Drive her to her place. Make sure she gets inside."

"We never filled out an arrest order," Melvin said

"Very good, Melvin, I'm proud of you. You guys get going. If she starts to go into a seizure, change your course, and get her to Charity in a hurry. You got it?"

They all started to leave the morgue. Hironee paused at the door. "I'm sorry she dead," she said.

"Me too," Sam replied pensively.

Hironee burst into uncontrollable sobs, burying her head into Sam's shoulder and his new black shirt. They left the morgue, leaving Sam with the unceremonious job of putting the body away, along with the task of cleaning the mess from his shirt.

Sam walked into his office and poured a fresh Glenlivet. It was now just after five o'clock in the morning, Monday, March 6th. He had just a few hours left before a new day dawned. It was just starting to get light the streets were starting to get busy. He stretched out on the couch but sleep did not come. Just resting his frame had to be enough. Then he thought of Kelly.

In the short week he had known her, she had become the bright spot in his life. In the muck and mire he had to live through, she had provided him with the true link to happiness. He thought of her living in that small apartment on Toulouse Street. He thought, *Maybe I'll suggest she move in with me. Only temporarily of course, but she could use it as a weekend retreat.*

He remembered how much she enjoyed the evening she spent there. How she loved the spa. How much she enjoyed the big TV. *I'll give her a key.* Then as his body relaxed, he thought of Shandor and Svetlana.

Chapter 10

FLASHBACK, EIGHTEEN YEARS EARLIER.

SAM WAS A young police officer, having been involved on the job for two years. As a trainee, one with fewer than five years as a cop, he undertook additional off-duty jobs, one of which was aiding people moving in or out of the Quarter.

Having a policeman present when you made a move requiring a moving van or large truck, was a necessity. The Quarter streets were simply too narrow to allow traffic to pass while a moving van was parked there. Sam and other cops had to be hired by the mover, who would pay for an officer and police car to be parked across the nearest intersection, blocking any ongoing traffic. Civilian drivers were directed to go another way.

This was the fifth week of the New Orleans hurricane season, and an absolute hell was brewing some one hundred and twenty miles south of the city. The citizens of New Orleans were now being pelted by rain and deeply annoyed by twenty-five to forty-five mile an hour wind gusts.

Sam parked his patrol car across Royal Street, blocking all upriver traffic. As he sat in his car facing the river, he noticed a man moving three large 4 x 8 foot long sheets of dry wall from the flatbed of his truck, parked around the corner on Barracks Street.

He had seen this guy working there before, as long as at least a year earlier. He was working on a large three story apartment house, which was in a pretty bad condition. Once, while jogging past the building, Sam had noticed that the inside back staircase was totally unusable due to a massive attack of Formosan termites. He also had looked into a few of the units.

They looked more like hovels in a third world country. When he looked in the window of two apartments, he saw that the termites had had their way with the inside of them too. The little bastards had chewed their way through the floors, walls, and even the foundation was suspect.

The worker was about Sam's age, same height and weight. His hair was cut short and his face appeared to be Russian or Slavic. As the man picked up the parcel of 4 x 8 dry wall sections, the wind gusted. As he walked from his truck toward the apartment building, the wind blasted him and his goods, catching the sheet rock like a ship's sail, and blowing him back into the wall of the building. The wind picked up even more and pinned him against the wall.

Sam quickly jumped from the car and ran to give aid. When he got there the man was fighting to retain his balance, trying to gain control of his body.

"Hold on!" Sam screamed over the gale. "I'll give you a hand."

"It's okay!" The man screamed back. "I got it."

Sam stepped back. Suddenly the wind died down and the man was able to push the dry wall sheets from his body.

"Okay, I got it now," The man said.

He adjusted his hands on the heavy sheets and started to walk to the front door of the apartment. Just then an even stronger force of wind hit which almost picked him up into the air and blasted him back into the wall. The wind and plasterboard drove him back, causing him to crash back into the brick and stucco covered wall. Sam stood helpless as the sheet rock appeared to wrap his body in a blanket, split in the center and fall to the ground like a bag of dry cement.

The man started laughing wildly. "Boy, that's one big fucking wind!"

His laughter was contagious. Sam started smiling. "You want me to help you with the rest of this? Come on, let's get it inside before it rains."

"Okay. I got some twelve-foot-long sections at the bottom. Let's do it."

They both started moving dry wall into the patio, safe from the wind. At each run, Sam would glance at his patrol car and the moving van in front of the house on Royal Street. Everything was as it was before. Sam was convinced that he didn't really need to be there. When they finished off loading the supplies, the wind had stopped and the sun started to shine. So it was in the Big Easy.

The man's name was Shandor. They took a break from the job and sat in Sam's patrol car drinking Cokes from Shandor's cooler. Shandor loved to talk and told Sam of his life, his hopes and his loves. His current mama was

Svetlana, a Russian princess.

They had traveled to New Orleans to take charge of the apartment building Svetlana's father had purchased several decades earlier. Now it was to be Shandor's job to fix it up properly, and when it was finished, they would live in the apartment on the top floor of the building.

Then Shandor found out that Sevetlana was broke. To say the least, this was distressful to Shandor. He could not hire any help, so he did all the repairs himself. He worked odd jobs to make money to purchase the supplies he needed to put the apartment in shape.

"I got all the tools I need to do the job," Shandor said. "I been working on this for over two years now. The best I got to offer is that I uncover everything so I can see what's got to be fixed. What you think of that?" At which time he broke into hysterical laughter. It was infectious, you had to laugh with him.

They talked for a half hour, then Sam offered a suggestion. "I tell you what. I'm pretty handy with tools and stuff. I could start on one apartment, finish it up and move to the next. Whenever you sell one unit, you pay me for what I've done. How about twenty an hour?"

"I charge my fuckin woman fifteen!" This was followed by another peal of laughter.

"Okay, fifteen," Sam said.

"And you mean you gonna work for nothing, then I pay you when I get an apartment sold?"

"That's it. That's the deal."

"Okay, man. You got it." Shandor held out his hand and they shook on it. This was followed by another screaming fit of laughter from Shandor.

Over the next four and a half years, Sam and Shandor became close friends. There was no problem too big, no job too hard that could stand in the way of a good laugh from Shandor. Often, they would not work for a month at a time, while Shandor did odd jobs to earn money for supplies. After that they would both be back on the job, weekends and nights, continuing to put it together.

Shandor arrived with a truckload of 4x8 treated plywood that was finished on one side. Sam started on the floors of the bottom apartment. Shandor had the exterminators treat the apartment for Formosan termites when he started the job. Sam ripped up the thick "heart pine" wood that covered the floors. These beautiful floors dated back over a hundred years.

He was able to save almost a third of the wood from each of the five lower apartments. There were six apartments on the second floor and three larger units on the third, with Shandor and his lady's being the largest. Sam had planned to have enough original wood, to resurface the wood floor of Shandor's entire apartment.

After nine months, with both men doing part time work, they had totally completed five ground floor apartments and six second floor units. Not only did Sam finish the floors but he sanded, caulked and painted the apartments to perfection. Every electrical outlet was replaced.

"I got to take time off," Shandor announced. "Maybe six to ten months. I gotta save some money. Then I pay you and we go to the top and finish it off, okay?"

"Sounds good to me," Sam said. It really didn't sound good to Sam. He hadn't planned to take six to ten months off. He was geared to sleep eight hours a night and work seven days a week, eight hours as a cop and the rest in construction. Now with only police work to keep him busy, Sam felt like a ship without a rudder. He would jog by the apartment building about twice a month and sure enough nothing was happening. After nine months of inactivity and no call from Shandor, Sam decided to pay him a visit.

Shandor and Svetlana lived in a second story apartment on Royal Street, about three blocks from Barracks. Sam had been there half a dozen times and on each occasion he had only gotten glances of Svetlana. Shandor had called her the Prussian Princess, but Sam secretly accused her of being the Queen of Mean. Svetlana behaved like royalty. She never smiled and always kept herself at a distance. She invariably wore a flowered house dress but always looked stylish. Her hair was a long mane of reddish brown and what he could see of her body, under the copious flowered design, seemed quite lovely.

One day Sam called on Shandor, but he was in the shower. Svetlana was busying herself in the kitchen. She wasn't cooking, that was for sure, because she never cooked. Shandor was happy with a "Hambooga," as he called it; however she wanted to eat out at one of the many restaurants in the area.

Sam sat on an old wooden chair toward the front of the living room. As he looked around he saw nothing really nice. Everything was a step away from a thrift shop. There were at least twenty plants of various types and sizes. Some even had the name tags still on them. Svetlana must have had some green thumb. They were the only new things to be seen, because the entire apartment seemed to be full of second-hand things which suited the purpose, but never the taste.

Sam looked back at the kitchen. Svetlana was seated in the breakfast nook and was looking at Sam. It was not that cat and mouse look that he had gotten from women before. This was a look that he had never anticipated. This was a hard strong look, a look with meaning. She kept staring at him and he finally smiled at her, but there was no smile on Svetlana's face.

Shandor came down the hall wearing a pair of Jockey shorts, drying his back with a big towel sheet. "Hey Bubba, you ready to go back to work?" It had been less than a year since Sam had seen him, now suddenly Shandor was back on the job. "We go now and start the top floor." Shandor announced.

"Did you get money for the lower units?"

"No. No carpets now. First we do the top floor, then we carpet all at once. Let's go, Bubba."

All this ended with a manic string of laughter, as he moved back to the bedroom. Sam looked back at Svetlana. She was still staring at him. Her expression had softened slightly, mellowed just a bit. At first she had been challenging him, but now she was sizing him up.

Sam and Shandor worked on and off for eight more months. During that time they had repaired all of the outside stairs and banisters, railing and flooring. They had finished the two, side upper apartments and had finally begun on the master unit.

Over this time, Sam had noticed that Shandor had become a bit flighty. Normally he would buy two "hamboogas" and they would take their break and talk about sex and the world in general. Now Shandor had changed the pace of things. When they first arrived back at the apartment, he took Sam into the lower number one apartment. It was here that he had made his office. In the living room were two saw-horses, with the double strength of 4 x 8 pieces of plywood that served as his desk. The surface was covered with papers and tools. The floors that Sam had finished with 4 x 8 plywood were still okay, but now there was a refrigerator in the kitchen and a double bed in the bedroom.

Everything made sense except the double bed in the bedroom. Eating habits had changed too. Shandor now took delivery of lunch from a young woman who worked at the Mini Mart down on Decatur Street. She would ring the doorbell around one o'clock. Shandor would call out, "Lunch" and he'd scurry down to his office and disappear for at least an hour. When he returned, it was with a smile on his face and a hammer in his hand. Sam had seen the delivery girl on several occasions. She was a small, cute black girl, with a good body and a great smile. Shandor had once mentioned how fascinated he was with black women and now it seemed he had just proved his enthrallment.

While Sam worked in the big apartment, Shandor put on an entire new slate roof and he did it alone. They both painted the outside of the building. They used a new combination of colors and techniques and the place looked more appealing.

One day, Sam was in the master apartment, preparing to install forty-seven recessed lighting fixtures. This was a complicated job, dealing with hundreds of feet of various colored wires, to be run into the attic. All of this worked from dimmers located in rooms below. Sam had made a master chart of all the lights, where they would turn off and on, and which exact light would be used to accomplish which goal.

Shandor, on the other hand, could care less about this lighting job, but he gave way to what Svetlana wanted. To Shandor now, life was nothing more than hamboogas, black chicks and hard work. To Svetlana, it must have been a great lighting effect.

It was ten o'clock at night and Sam was climbing down the ladder from the attic onto the living room floor. He was pulling wires, installing light cans and strapping more wires into the wall boxes. It was definitely a two man job, but he had not seen Shandor in three days. He had assumed that Shandor had been finishing a job over on Decatur Street. Just then the bell rang. Sam crossed to the outside balcony and looked down, spotting Svetlana.

"Hello," Sam said.

Looking up at Sam, she said in a demanding voice, "Push da button and let me in."

She walked into the living room and paid no mind to anything that was going on. There were three work lights, for when he had to run electrical extension stingers, from the lower apartment. Svetlana stood and looked around.

"Dis place look like shit," she announced.

"It will look better when I'm finished."

"I going back to Russia tomorrow," she said. "My father is dying."

"I'm terribly sorry to hear that."

She looked at Sam for a long moment, with no emotion whatsoever. "Yeah, me too."

"Is there anything I can do to help?"

"No. You done enough."

"Where's Shandor?"

"He's a boom."

"You mean a bum?"

"Yeah, dat too. He one big piece of shit bastard. You know about his black girl?"

Sam shrugged his shoulders. She ignored the physical comment, opened her purse and withdrew a bunch of papers.

"I found dis in his drawer." She read from the paper. "I give him dis apartment for da work he has done, an' for which I pay him nothing. Is dat da deal?"

"Well, no. He was supposed to sell one unit and pay me off from what he got for it."

"What's da difference?" she asked. "Buy, sell, who cares? He owes you monies or you get apartment. Dat's da deal he make. Now I make a new deal." She was wearing a white long sleeved blouse and a dark long skirt, with a wide black belt. "You ever make love to a Russian woman?"

"No I don't think so."

The first thing she did was to remove the belt. "I want to have sex with you. I like your looks. You a nice boy."

She removed her blouse, revealing at the very least a D cup bra. The skirt followed, showing him what Russian women were made of. She stood before him in a thong panty, studying him with that "come-hither" look. She removed the bra and revealed the most magnificent breasts he had ever seen. Sam wondered what Shandor was doing right now with his black lady. What he was about to do with Svetlana, Sam knew he would be having much more fun.

She grabbed the nipples of each breast, with both hands, tweaking at them, causing them to become slightly enlarged.

"Okay baby," she said. "You ain't seen nuttin yet."

She dropped her panties and the young policeman, who had sworn to give all for God and country, was about to share his soul with fire and brimstone. He quickly removed his shirt, followed by his trousers, and his underwear, in one fell swoop. She looked down at his manhood, as it started pulsating and swelling. Slowly she stepped forward and took hold of his family jewels.

"Boy, you a lot bigger than that fucking Shandor."

"Boy, am I glad to hear that!"

Sam took her face in his hands and kissed her. His tongue moved deep into her open mouth, searching. Svetlana stepped tight to his body, placing her leg between his and began rubbing up and down. Her arms reached around his body and her nails bit into his back.

It was the mother of all orgies, a tribute to sex, a joy to behold, a night of total debauchery. They performed every known position written or dreamed of in the Kama Sutra. Svetlana was a tigress and Sam no longer thought of anything but the pleasure of now.

At two-thirty in the morning, Sam quickly dressed and ran down to the St. Ann Market and bought a loaf of hot French bread, a jar of peanut butter and a bottle of wine. When he got back he found Svetlana standing near a pile of rope she had found somewhere. She held her thick belt, which she lightly cracked over her hip.

"I tie you up first. Now we gonna get serious." The French bread got cold while Sam got hot. Sam learned more about sex in one night than he knew in all of his active years. Perhaps, if he knew then what he had just learned now, he would have saved his marriage. But that was history, and now he was making new history.

At six that morning Svetlana departed, leaving Sam with unbelievable memories and a legal document stating his ownership of apartment #301. He was a man of property, and what dreams he had for that property. He would turn it into a showplace.

Day 6 continued

It was Monday morning, March 6th. Sam awoke startled as he heard the door to his office open, and he saw Wally enter. He glanced at his watch. It was seven-thirty. Wally was surprised to see Sam.

"Hey there, you sleep here?" Wally asked.

"Yeah, must have dozed off, big time," Sam answered. "Make some coffee, will ya?" Sam slid his feet to the floor, stood and stretched.

"You got it boss. You feeling okay?"

Sam smiled. "Yeah, great."

Wally chuckled as he prepared the coffee. The door opened and George and David entered. They both looked rested, had a fresh shower and shave and appeared to be officers prepared to do their job.

"Good morning," George said with a big smile. "Everybody ready to give 'um hell?"

Wally was pouring water in Mr. Coffee and Sam was again stretching it out.

"Just fine, George," Sam said. "How's it with you, David?"

David said nothing and headed for the coffee. He enjoyed watching it drip. George crossed in close to Sam. "Hey Sam, you look like a tough night in a dog fight."

After a night like last night, and at this time of the morning, ignoring George was better than trying to come up with some verbal abuse of his own.

"What the hell did you spill on your shirt?" George added. "I got a guy that can clean that up for you and have it back here by noon."

Sam moved to the window and took some deep breaths. He did some more stretching and twisting exercises, determined not to let George get the best of him. But George was equally determined! He crossed and joined Sam at the window, looking out over the Mississippi. "Boy, do I love this city. It's great to be home." He looked over at Sam. "Whoa, hey there, you could use a shave." Wally and David are about to burst, trying not to laugh out loud.

Ignoring George, Sam turned and moved to the Mr. Coffee machine. Wally and David turned their backs away from Sam. George followed Sam to the coffee machine.

"I got a barber over on Rampart that'll give you a shave and a haircut for twelve bucks. That's a good deal. I can get you in right now if you want. We'll get your shirt done at the same time. I'll drive you over."

"No thanks, George," Sam said. "I'm in my bohemian mode. Thinking about growing a beard." Sam glanced at Mr. Coffee, it was just half full. "Okay, listen up everybody," Sam said. "Got some new information last night."

Wally picked up his writing tablet.

"I got information from the informant, Hironee Jessup. She said that Jane Doe, AKA Penelope Andrews, may have been murdered by a big white man. This white man was driving a three to five year old large white or off white vehicle with a large rust stain on the left front fender. She also provided a description of the front of the vehicle. It has a metal bar that runs from upper right to lower left and it covered the grill. In the middle was a medallion of some kind."

"Sounds like a Volvo to me," David offered.

"What did the guy look like?" George asked.

"What I've given you is all I got. Ask me no more questions. Wally, get on the horn and call traffic. I want them to look for an older model, cream-colored Volvo sedan, with a rust stain on the driver's side front fender."

"You go it."

"And add the driver may be armed and dangerous."

"Coffee's ready," David announced.

All in the room except for Sam grabbed a cup and headed for Mr. Coffee. Sam was now fully awake. He walked over to his desk and picked up the stack of twelve enlarged copies of driver's licenses that Wally had tossed there the night before. He also noted the stack of new retouched drawings Wally had supplied. "Here you go, George. Put a sign up on the wall that says, 'Suspects.' Pin these driver's licenses up also. Should a stranger walk in here, it will look like we're actually trying to catch this guy."

With coffee in hand, George moved in and took the file from Sam. David was tasting his brew, nose wrinkled. "This doesn't seem the same as yesterday. Who made this shit?"

"I made this shit," Wally announced. "You want the same shit? Here you go. Here's a jar of instant. Take two tablespoons'a this shit and dump it into your cup. Then you'll have the same shit as you drank yesterday!"

The office was getting a bit testy. David poured a small amount of instant coffee into his cup. George finished posting the driver's licenses on the wall. Wally was on the phone making a call to traffic. Sam casually walked to Mr. Coffee and poured himself his first cup. Everything became very quiet.

"Okay, that does it," George announced. He then walked over to his desk and sat down. He started going through his paperwork. Everything remained quiet.

Sam sat on a stool in the center of the room. He studied the file that George had pinned to the wall. Something was wrong, desperately wrong, with the driver's licenses. It was easy to see it now, when they were displayed together, but not so quickly seen, when they were observed individually.

There were eleven licenses, taken from the general population, and one taken from Alex Kroman, last night, but they were different. Sam stood up and crossed closer to the display wall. "Hey everybody, come over and look at this."

Everyone in the room closed in on the wall of pictures.

"What's wrong?" George asked.

"Well look at them," Sam stated. "We got eleven driver's licenses taken by the Department of Motor Vehicles, each one is the same. All are close-ups of each driver. Then we got one of Mr. Alex Kroman and his is different, a wider shot, different background. It's overall a darker picture. Can you not see that?"

George reached out and took the Kroman copy from the wall. "Look at that," George said. "His is different."

Wally reached into his pocket and pulled out his wallet. He quickly searched for his driver's license. "Here's mine," he said. "I had it taken in Laplace."

The three other men searched for theirs. They came up with David's from Metairie and Sam and George's from New Orleans. They all looked identical.

"Okay Wally, check with Loyola," Sam directed. "See if Kroman is there. If he is, get someone to bring down my car."

Wally was quickly on the phone.

"Want us to go?" George asked. "I'm the guy who screwed up the bust."

"Nobody screwed up the bust. We all go together, and nobody screwed up." Sam walked back to his desk, and took his first look at the new drawings Wally had prepared. Each of them was over drawings of the master created by Frank Hogan. The first had added a mustache, the second a beard. Then near the bottom of the stack, one was there with a kinky wig. It was amazing. The look of this picture had a close resemblance of the picture on the driver's license of Alex Kroman. "Look at this, boys."

George and David walked over and took the pictures from Sam.

Wally stood up from his desk. "Kroman's there. The car's on the way."

The morning "go to work" traffic was difficult. Sam drove while Wally rode shotgun. Wally was an unhappy camper. He loved to ride in this car. He enjoyed the dark brown plush fake llama carpet, and even more, he loved the tight fitting doors and windows provided by the manufacturer. He vowed to get a new carpet and the screaming window fixed as soon as they returned to the precinct. He was hiding his face from the wind blowing from the open window, shielding his face with his clip board.

They arrived at the LSU campus and parked in the secured area reserved for official vehicles. George and David arrived close behind, parking behind Sam. An old security guard was there to guide them into position. As they got out, they all huddled together.

Sam was looking around studying the lay of the land. The campus was quickly filling with students and Sam didn't want a problem to arise.

"Where's the classroom?" Sam asked Wally.

"It's that building, right over there, on the second floor, room 217."

They entered the building and climbed the stairs to the second floor, to room 217. Sam put his hands on the doorknob and looked back for George and David. They were walking behind him, about ten feet back, both with jackets open and guns easily accessible.

Sam twisted the knob and pushed the door open gently. It swung into an arch revealing the entire room. It was empty except for one man with his back to them. He was writing on the blackboard.

Sam moved quietly into the room. Wally followed and slid to his right, preparing to cover for Sam. They both slowly moved forward. George and David arrived and they moved into the room, taking back-up positions on either side of the door. No one drew a gun but all were prepared for the event.

Looking at him form the rear, this man was an exact duplicate of the person they had seen at the Cabaret Bar on Bourbon. He was six foot two and weighed at least two hundred thirty pounds, and had a full head of curly dark brown hair.

"Excuse me," Sam said. "I wonder if I might speak with you."

The man turned from the chalkboard and faced Sam. Sam immediately realized this was not the same Alex Kroman they had questioned at the strip club last Friday night.

"Yes? Yes? How may I help you?" Kroman answered. He looked around the room and on seeing four men who could easily be willing to "menace" him, he became agitated.

Sam asked, "Are you Professor Alex Kroman?"

"Well yes, yes. Yes I am. Yes indeed. I'm Alex Kroman. Yes."

"I'm Detective Sam Pennington, New Orleans Police department." Sam displayed his badge and ID card. He then raised his right arm and without looking back at his men, waived them off. The boys relaxed.

"Well yes. Yes. I'm Alex Kroman. Professor of English Literature, here at Loyola University of New Orleans."

Sam reached into his jacket pocket and removed the blow-up of Kroman's driver's license.

"May I see your driver's license?"

"Well yes. Yes you may." Kroman started fishing in his rear trouser pockets for his wallet, then moved to the front. There was no wallet there. "I don't have it. Where is my wallet?"

"Maybe it's in your jacket pocket." Sam offered.

Kroman went for the jacket pockets and finally came up with the wallet. "Ah here it is. I knew I had it." With a smile on his face he offered the wallet to Sam.

"Would you please remove the license from the wallet?"

"Yes. Yes, I can do that. Here it is right here." He handed it to Sam. "There you are, my license."

Sam took it and compared the license to the copy. Kroman leaned in to stare at the copy. "What is this?" Kroman shouted, pointing at the copy. "What is this? This isn't my picture. This is someone else's picture. Someone has put their picture over my picture."

Kroman looked up at Wally, George and David. He was asking for their approval. "Can you not see that this is not a picture of me?" Kroman asked. "I'm not the person in this picture. It's someone else. Can you not see that?"

Wally, George and David went down to the parking lot and waited for Sam. In the meantime, Sam and Professor Kroman had a cup of coffee in the faculty lounge. It was there that Sam got Kroman to calm down. He learned that a year ago he had somehow lost his wallet. He reported it to the local DMV and for a fee of five dollars it was replaced by mail.

So much for Professor Alex Kroman. But now they had what they believed to be a photograph of the actual serial killer. Sam would call Frank Hogan to paint a picture of how he really looked, without the fake hair.

Flashback

One year earlier.

It was during a Mardi Gras parade, when Eddie was walking up Canal Street. He was stalking a man who walked ten feet ahead of him. Eddie had stood for over an hour, watching this man eat dinner, peering at him through the window of the Oyster Bar on Bienville. At this moment in time, Eddie did not know his name, but he believed he himself could fit him to a tee.

He next saw him standing at the cash register paying his bill. He was tall, over six feet and weighed about two hundred pounds. He was older than Eddie, had a short beard, nicely trimmed around the neck area. His hair was shorter, a darker brown than Eddie's dishwater blonde, but Eddie could handle that.

Eddie continued following the man down Canal Street. The parade was wonderful the crowd was great. The floats were beautiful and the beads thrown from the floats to the crowds, rained down in gold silver and a myriad of colors to the waiting hands. There were shouts of those below: "Throw me something, Mister." But Eddie didn't care about this parade. He didn't even hear the music. And he hated the beads. If one landed on his shoulder, he brushed it off onto the street. He had only one thought on his mind.

After they crossed Canal Street at Bourbon, there was a slight break in the crowd. Eddie seized the opportunity and quickly moved forward. Now he was only five feet behind his target, then three and finally only one. There was no need to dally here. He would make his move fast and quick. Do it all in the same moment. Never give a sucker an even break. Do it now and with immediate action. Don't stop!

Eddie moved forward in lock step with the man. He bumped him hard on his right rear hip, the side he knew where the man had replaced his wallet after paying his bill at the Oyster Bar. Simultaneously, Eddie reached his hand in the man's right rear pocket and withdrew his wallet. The man was jostled off balance for a moment, then paused to look back.

"Excuse me, sir. I'm sorry," Eddie said. By that time, Eddie had slipped the wallet into his jacket pocket and had fallen back a few feet.

"That's okay. It's tough walking here," the man answered. This man was Alex Kroman. After changing direction, Eddie walked back down Canal to

Bourbon, turned right and then walked down Bourbon Street..

Eddie entered a small bar. It was crowded, wall to wall. He fought his way to the toilet and was met by a crowd of heavy duty urinaters. He headed for one of the three enclosed toilets, inching his way toward the toilet door. As soon as someone would leave, he'd take another step forward.

Finally he made his way into the stall, closed and latched the door and was alone. He sat down on the toilet and checked out the contents of the wallet. There was money there, but Eddie was not interested in that. What was the object of his direction was the man's driver's license, which he withdrew from a side storage area. It was the license of Alex Kroman. Other identification showed that he was a professor of English at Loyola University. He studied the license carefully. Kroman's beard was cut short, his hair had a curly look, everything was a medium brown.

I can handle that. I can look like this guy, he said to himself.

DAY 6 CONTINUED

Sam had everyone in the office working like beavers. Frank Hogan was there, manufacturing a drawing a charcoal version from the copy of the fake driver's license and no curly brown hair. George and David waited patiently for the finished drawing. They would then head back to the haunts on Bourbon Street, where the hookers could be found, showing them the updated picture of the suspect.. Wally was at his computer, completing his new top sheet to be faxed to all parishes. Sam sat in his chair with both feet up on his desk. He was exhausted, and glad his boys had a good night's sleep.

It was now late afternoon, March 6th, as Eddie waited patiently at the Café Du Monde coffee house, searching for the young waitress he had met earlier. Eddie was still doing his chameleon deal. He was dressed in a light brown suit and tie, and a pair of light green shaded sun glasses. His partially balding head was now out in the open. He did not wear a hairpiece, and with his general manipulations, appeared to be a much different person that he had been before.

She approached Eddie with a pot of hot fresh coffee. She was much younger than he, but that didn't bother her much. She was new in town and having a friend like Eddie, one who could only do good things for her, was a major plus. She was also a part-time hooker. Her name was Sally.

"Want me to freshen it up?" Sally asked.

"You can freshen me up anytime," he answered with a chuckle. He reached out and tried to tickle her on the side, but she playfully pushed him aside.

"Come on now, I don't want to burn you."

"You can burn me all day long. All night long too." He laughed, she giggled. "We still on for tonight?" Eddie asked.

"Yeah, I guess so," Sally responded. "I get off late, though. Ten o'clock."

"I'll pick you up right out front."

Chapter 11

FLASHBACK, THIRTY-FOUR YEARS EARLIER.

EDDIE MARSHALL WAS born in Leesville Mississippi, on August 14, 1960, the only child of Jeff and Irene Marshall. He arrived weighing nine pounds six ounces. Eddie was a big baby, but his father Jeff was also a large man who stood six foot two and fought to keep his weight down below two hundred. His mother Irene was a small woman, five foot two and weighed only one hundred twenty-five pounds. When they would enter a party, the comment was made: "Here comes Mutt and Jeff."

Shortly before Eddie was born, his mother had her final prenatal check-up. Due to the large size of the baby, and the fact that Irene would not dilate enough to have a natural delivery, this created a problem for Irene. When Eddie was born, she was advised not to have any more children for her own health. At eight months and one week into pregnancy, she would have to have a Caesarian Section, at which time the doctor tied her tubes. Irene would blame Eddie for these circumstances.

His father, Jeff Marshall had a good sense of humor. He had a joke to tell for every situation. Jeff had developed a mail-order catalogue of what looked like antiques, but Jeff called them semi-antiques, because they were ripped-off reproductions. He shipped the catalogues of furniture all over the southern area. One hundred fifty thousand catalogues every six months, with one of the most popular places for the sales being New Orleans, Louisiana. He would laugh all the way to the bank and say, "These people really love this shit!"

Jeff had a large factory on the east side of town, which employed around fifty people, working in a storage and shipping area that covered almost a half-acre. It was a profitable but tough business. If the manufactured product was poorly constructed, it arrived to the buyer in a broken or unacceptable condition. His returns on these items might well spell the end of the company and he had to watch out for that. This was the garbage furniture business of Mississippi. It worked well, as long as Jeff worked it.

The furniture was, in the main, manufactured in North Carolina. But some of it, the gold leaf stuff with the high lacquer finish, was built in Nuevo Laredo, Mexico. Twice a year his father would travel to the two manufacturing locations, to set designs needed to be created and constructed for the next season.

His mother, Irene, was very strict. Eddie always called his father dad. He called his mother "ma'am." There was a difference between the two. Dad was his father, while "Ma'am" was the person who established Eddie's rules of conduct. Irene was the town librarian, a person who fit everything into cubbyholes, and ran her family like she operated her library.

Their house was located in a middle class neighborhood of Leesville. It sat on an acre and a half of land. There was a large oak tree in the back yard where his dad built a tree house. The house was about twelve feet off the ground. In his early years Eddie would spend time there, getting away from his mother's constant haranguing. It was a place to be himself. There he gathered books and periodicals. It mattered not what he read, just that he was able to read without interruption.

When Eddie was just nine, after finishing his day's schooling, he would walk over to the library, only a block away. There, his mother would sit him down at a table to do his homework. She'd check it out and, if necessary, make him do it again. This may be the reason he never developed the sense of humor his father seemed to enjoy so much.

Eddie was more serious than silly. He would rather read a book than play with other children. He was not a joiner but rather a loner. His instincts were really quite good. He was always polite and always did as he was told. He tried very hard to anticipate his mother's orders.

His father loved sports, watched every game that was broadcast on television. Baseball was his favorite, and his team was the Atlanta Braves. When he returned from one of his trips to the Carolinas, he brought his son a starter kit to join the Little League team. He had purchased a Braves baseball cap, a fielder's glove and an aluminum Little League-sized baseball bat.

They would go out in the backyard every afternoon and practice the art of the game. His son was growing fast. He was, by now, almost as tall as his mother. His dad figured a boy of his size would most certainly become a major league star. But, that was not the case. The fact of the matter was Eddie had a problem with coordination. His years of sitting and reading books did not allow him to have the time to get the "hang" of catching the ball. His father would scream at him.

"Keep your eye on the ball!"

With bat in hand, while hitting "fungous" at him, Eddie would do his best to maneuver into the proper position to hit a long one. When the ball would zig, Eddie would always zag.

He never got it together. After losing two boxes of softballs, his father decided Eddie was a late bloomer. They would start again next year. But next year never came around.

After living some years in the house, his dad ordered some construction work. The one story home would have an addition, a second floor. In fact, it was to be a "camelback.' Jeff had the construction crew build a top level on the back of the house, adding a small staircase to get to it. As it turned out, his dad and ma'am would end up with a bedroom and bath on the second floor in the back of the house. The old master bedroom downstairs would be used as a home office for his father's company. Eddie's old downstairs bedroom would become part of the new enlarged kitchen. Eddie would be moved into the front of the house by the garage.

Eddie's new bedroom was much larger. When completed it had a massive closet, a queen-sized bed and an adjoining bathroom, which also contained the household washer and dryer. Eddie loved the construction and loved his room. If his parents were in bed at night in the upper back bedroom, he could play his music loud as it could go and they would never hear a thing. He would never have to go to that tree house again. Eddie finally had his privacy.

By the time he reached ten, Eddie was able to please his mother to perfection. Every school paper he wrote would receive an 'A.' His mind had developed into an almost photographic memory. He would rush to finish his school work, and then head for his reading. If he had to leave for school at seven in the morning, he would set his alarm for five. He could be up, showered, dressed, and make his bed. Then, he was ready to leave in forty-five minutes. He could relax and read his book. At about five minutes to seven, he was standing in the middle of his room, ready to go to school. He could hear his mother's footsteps heading down the stairs and walking down the hallway to his door.

"Eddie! You ready to go?" she would scream out.

"Yes, ma'am, I'm ready."

She would throw open the door and see him standing there and never acknowledge the fact that he was prepared and on time. "Alright then, your father is about to have breakfast."

"Yes, ma'am."

One day, while at the library, he came across the story of Billy the Kid. He found this in the non-fiction section. Prior to this, he was in the children's fiction section, which had grown stale for Eddie. He was rapidly growing and developing a style that would allow him to make history.

When he read the true life story of Billy the Kid, the entire story leaped from the pages and grabbed his imagination. He moved on through Jesse James, and Butch Cassidy and the Sundance Kid. Later he found Bonnie and Clyde, "Machine Gun" Kelly and "Pretty Boy" Floyd, to say nothing of two of his biggest heroes, Al Capone and John Dillinger. These people were all before Eddie's time, and he was searching for something or someone with whom he could identify.

At age twelve, his father told Eddie he would take him and his mother on a weekend trip to Nuevo Laredo, Mexico. His father had business to take care of with his Mexican associates. His dad told him about the bullfights in Mexico. Eddie had never learned anything about bullfighting. Living in Leesville, no one had ever spoken about a bullfight, and he had never seen anything on television about it.

"I'll take you to the bull ring on Sunday," his dad said. "It'll be one of the most exciting experiences of you life." Thinking back, Eddie remembered that he had seen a bullfight on the late night movies, with cowboys riding on the bulls' backs. But he never considered that to be the most exciting experience in his life.

"Sure dad, that would be fun," Eddie said. Jeff was pleased that Eddie would be looking forward to such an experience and he assured him, "It all has to do with the matador and how he kills the bull."

"Sounds good to me," Eddie said. He turned to his father and gave him a smile. When he got back to his room Eddie thought about what his dad had said. Somebody was going to kill a bull. A matador was going to do it, and his father was going to take him to see it. The more he thought about it, the more it became the thrill of his young lifetime!

The following day, after school, he went to the library. He had finished all of his homework in study hall and he made sure that he had dotted every 'I' and crossed every 'T.' When his mother looked it over, she nodded her approval. She moved away, leaving him completely at his disposal to the study of human knowledge.

Eddie had been rooting around in the card-ex files for three years now, always seeking more information, always searching for a new criminal personality to dream of, but today, he made a bee line to 'Bullfight.' After some mild searching, he found what he was looking for located under 'Mexico.' Eddie went to the section listed on the card file. It was at the rear of the building, just across from the bathroom. The rack listed simply 'Bullfight.' It was a good area to work in, because his mother would not quickly find him there.

The very first book he pulled from the shelf was a large black and white work from the author and photographer, Michael Kline. The date of the book was 1945. When Eddie opened it, there it revealed the magic of the great sport of bullfighting. As he thumbed through the book, he came across a picture of the greatest matador of all time, Manolette!

It was through Michael Kline's writing that he learned of the finesse of a real bullfight. There were magnificent pictures that amplified his words beneath them. The pages first explained the starting of the *coreda* or bullfight. Kline wrote, "This is not a sport nor is it a contest between man and bull. It all comes down to a simple truth. The bull will die. The manner in which he dies, depends on the excellence and finesse of the matador."

Eddie read on and learned that before the fight began, the participants, arrayed in costumes of varied colors and glistening hues, parade slowly and ceremoniously around the ring. A brass band played the music of the Creda, it's sound meant to excite the audience. At the head of the procession were three matadors, armed with a sword and wearing bright heavy *trajes de luces*, the suits of lights.

Next were the *Cuadriallas*, a six-man team that assisted the matador. There were also two men on horseback. Their horses were covered by heavy padding to keep the bull from gorging them, and they also wore blinders in order to keep the horse from jumping away from the attacking bull. These riders carried long poles with a short metal knife-like device, with which they stabbed the bull at the top of the neck. These were the *Picadores* and their job was to weaken the neck muscles of the bull, forcing him to lower his head, allowing the matador a clean kill!

Eddie heard footsteps coming down the hall. He grabbed his jacket, and covered the book. He met his mother as she opened door.

"Oh, excuse me. I was just leaving." Eddie said.

"Your father came home early," she stated. "Go home with your father. I'll be along in an hour."

"Yes, ma'am."

His father was quiet as he drove home. It had been a hard day for his dad, just one more problem with business. Thirty percent of the units the Mexicans had produced arrived broken. His people would have to unpack all items and spend precious time to repair each damaged unit.

"There goes the profit, here comes the loss," his father said. "Just one more thing to take up with the Mexicans."

His dad didn't like to fly so they drove early on a Wednesday morning, heading for Mexico. They took off with Eddie in the back seat of the Ford station wagon. Two hours into the drive, Eddie got his first glimpse of New Orleans. This was a place Eddie wanted to visit some day. As they swept down the I-10 freeway, his dad pointed out the Superdome and the twin bridges over the Mississippi. Eddie thought to himself, *This is definitely the place.*

It wasn't until around noon the second day, while Eddie was still in the back seat, he overheard a conversation between his dad and ma'am. They were nearing Laredo, Texas and were locked in a traffic jam. He had been asleep and they were talking in low tones. He awoke when the conversation raised a decibel, into a low level argument.

"Come on," his dad said to his mother. "I told the kid I'd take him to a bullfight. Mexico is a foreign country, for crying out loud! What the hell do we do in Mexico on a Sunday afternoon, go to a movie? We don't even speak Spanish."

"These people torture the bull and then they kill the bull." Irene said, glancing to the back seat to look at Eddie. He closed his eyes again, feigning sleep. Irene looked back at Jeff. "It's a disgusting thing to watch. Why would you want your son to watch that?"

"Look, Irene, you and I go to the race track. We bet on the ponies. A horse falls and breaks a leg. Doctors come out and check the horse. They decide to shoot it and they do it. Right there in front of God and country.

Then they haul the thing away to the glue factory. So what's the big difference here, what's the big deal?"

She glanced back at Eddie once again. He seemed to be sleeping soundly. Then she looked out of the window. "I just don't like the unnecessary killing of animals."

"When in Rome you do as the Romans do. Anyway, that's why they call them dumb animals." Jeff said.

They crossed the border at Laredo, Texas without incident, winding up in Nuevo Laredo, Mexico. They checked into the Prado, a rather fine place on the main Boulevard of Nuevo Laredo. Their room was on the fifth floor, and from their windows they could see the magnificent border city.

That night they went to dinner, heard a Mexican mariachi group dancing and singing and they ate Mexican food. Eddie didn't like the food, but being a dutiful, agreeable and cheerfully helpful young son, he pretended to love it all. He gleefully cleaned his plate right down to the last bean. However, what Eddie was actually looking forward to was, the bullfight!

The following day while his father went to do business with his Mexican partners, Eddie and his mother went shopping. This was the most painful experience he could imagine. It was absolute torture. She would move from store to store, looking and feeling every item she might be interested in. She would check the prices, feel the goods, decide to buy it, and later decide not to. It took two hours to move through the first store and then there was yet another one around the corner.

At one o'clock, it was time for lunch, and she ordered him the same food he had the night before, a taco, enchilada, beans, and rice. *This all tastes like it came from the same pot*, Eddie thought to himself.

At six that evening they all met at the hotel. Dad had a good meeting with the Mexicans, or so he said. They all agreed to create a better shipping method for the new items. His father had lost sixty-eight out of two hundred shipments. That was his profit. But all of that was swept under the rug. That night they did it all again. More dancing, singing and Mexican food. Eddie shoveled it into his mouth.

Eddie had the side bedroom, located as an auxiliary unit of the suite. It was designed as a single hotel room with a door that could be unlocked from the suite side, to accommodate an extra bedroom. To Eddie it was a hateful room. There was no TV, not that he wanted to watch anything. It was small, and the air conditioning didn't work properly. It was either too stuffy or too chilly.

Eddie climbed into bed that final night. As was with the night before, he did not remove his clothing. His parents never noticed he wore the same clothes from the day before. His mother was too busy shopping and feeling the goods, and his dad was too preoccupied with fixing his deal with the Mexicans, for either to notice Eddie.

As Eddie tried to sleep, he suffered from the hiss of the cooling/heating system. It would hiss and then get quiet. When it hissed he would flip the heavy blanket off and when it would be quiet he would flip it back on. He found no comfort in Mexico. It was only a matter of flipping and flopping. Eddie hopped his parents were having a better night than he was, in their palatial Royal suite.

Then it was Sunday, the day of the *Fiesta Brava*, "The Brave Festival," the *Creda de Toros*, "The Running of the Bulls." It was magic time for Eddie. He had read about it, dreamed of it, and now it was time to see it. He could see the ring from the back of the station wagon. It was a large grandstand, seating more than fifty thousand people. This was of course, from Eddie's point of view. It actually accommodated, in this small local town, a meager twenty thousand. But that was big enough for Eddie.

They parked the car and moved through the large courtyard into the area itself. It was beautiful and exciting. In the courtyard he saw a large poster of the favorite matador of the day, Manuel Ortega. Ortega was the new boy, the upcoming matador of Mexico. He demanded more money than any other matador on the ticket.

Eddie heard the music of a brass band and his blood started to boil. This was it! This is where it would happen! As they walked through the crowd he noticed that neither his mother nor his father paid much attention to him. Not that he cared, but he noticed it none the less. His ma'am was concerned with seeing a bull killed, as opposed to seeing a horse shot. His father was preoccupied with the deal he made the night before, hoping it would lead to more profit. Eddie just wanted to see something that was breathing, die.

As they entered the grandstand area, Eddie had to use the toilet. His parents walked him to the facility and waited outside for him.

It was a filthy spot of odor and scum, crowded with men lined up waiting to use the one urinal. The urinal was made of tin, welded together into one long trough, running from one end of the room to the other, about fifteen feet in length. Even at twelve years old, Eddie knew this was the best it was going to get. He took his penis out and started to pee. It felt good. Then as it ended, things started to smell worse. Someone was taking a horrendous bowl movement in one of the stalls. At that moment Eddie vowed he would never piss again in a Mexican public toilet.

He left, met up with his parents, and they moved toward their seats. His dad had purchased 'shady side seats' for them. The music changed into a high crescendo and then even more so, to a magical moment of driven passion. Just as they found their seats, with a grand view of the entire arena, the event began.

The parade was even more than Eddie had expected. All of the men who were involved in the bullfight, paraded across the bull ring. There were also the three matadors, one of which was Manuel Ortega. As they walked across the center of the ring, it was Ortega that stood out from the others. He was tall, at least six foot two. He carried himself proud, with eyes looking ahead, a stern face. Eddie had read that these men chose their three bulls, before the Correda started. There was no doubt, according to what Eddie had read, the three bulls Ortega had chosen would now be shaking in their boots. Eddie had now found a live, breathing hero.

Then when the parade ended, a bull entered the ring. There was a gasp from the audience as the bull snorted, pawed at the ground, displaying his fearlessness and his prowess.

The first matador was introduced over a loudspeaker. The announcer spoke in rapid Spanish, sounding like a screaming automobile auctioneer. Then Eddie heard the mention of a name, Carlos Rivera! Carlos, a young man barely twenty-one years old, entered the ring. As he walked into the center of the circled area, he accepted the mild applause of the audience. The public knew this was just a boy, a beginner. They all waited for Manuel Ortega.

When Eddie read the bullfighting books by Michael Kline, he never mentioned the condition of the bull. He never said the bull arrived in the arena in great shape, and went out like a sack of shit. Thinking back, Eddie realized he never mentioned the bull at all.

Now the Picadors were doing their job, shoving sharp lances into the bull's neck. It was all a matter of time and the bull was running short of time. Next came the Bandilleros, jabbing their colorful darts into the same neck area. The bull lowered his head even more. Finally the matador stepped up. It was time for the matador to have his turn with the bull.

The bull was breathing heavily, and stood in the ring in total confusion. The matador teased him with his cape, and made brave passes that avoided the bull's horns. The animal had been trained for this challenge, and the matador continued to show his bravery, and finesse with the cape. Then finally the matador wrapped the cape around his sword, as though to hide it from the bull. He did a few more passes with the cape and sword. He challenged the bull, and in a hypnotic state, the bull, worn out and bleeding, was in the right position for the kill.

The matador dedicated the bull to a lovely young woman, seated ring side with the dignitaries, saluting her with his hat. Eddie was beside himself with excitement. He was all eyes and as quiet as a mouse. The matador made a few more passes and raised his sword, and as the bull charged, the matador passed his body, over the horns and slammed the sword deeply into the bull's withers. The bull staggered momentarily, regained his balance then fell. The audience screamed and stomped their feet, yelling "*Olé! Olé!*" The matador was awarded an ear of the beast as a reward for his magnificent performance. Two ears and a tail would have been the highest award, but what the hell, he was just a kid. He presented the ear to his lady, and the crowd roared.

Eddie's mother stood and faced his father. "That's it. I've had enough. You want more of this, be my guest. I'm going home."

As the field crew, using two horses with a pull chain, drug the carcass of the bull out of the dirt field, his father, in an attempt to make his wife happy, began to move out. Eddie was in a state of euphoria.

His father yelled at Eddie, "Okay son, let's go."

Eddie looked around quickly. Hs father was leaving the stand. He spied his mother on the upper walkway, pushing past the vendors selling their tacos and beer.

His father yelled again, "Let's go Eddie. We've seen enough now."

Eddie stood up looking back at the arena. A new bull charged into the ring. It was massive. He was a huge bull, far bigger and stronger than the first one. *This is the bull that Ortega had selected*, Eddie thought.

He turned at looked back at his father. "Dad, he called out. "Dad, let me see one more fight!"

But his father was twelve rows up and half way to the exit. He either didn't hear him, or did not pay any attention.

"Dad, please! This is the big one! It's Ortega! Please Dad, please!"

His father kept walking his way forward. Eddie decided to try to catch him. He fought his way up the stairs. There was another deafening scream from the crowd as the announcer introduced Ortega.

This was to be one of the greatest bullfighters in the world, right here, today! The bull Ortega had chosen for his first fight was massive, with the power of a hundred men.

Out of the corner of his eye, Eddie saw Ortega enter the arena. Ortega was not concerned. He turned to face the bull that stood across the ring from him. He stood there, showing no fear in facing death. With his feet planted in the dirt, he faced the bull, as he charged with his first attempted onslaught.

Working his way through the mob of people, Eddie finally reached the tunnel and caught sight of his father, who had now reached his mother. She was upset and he was trying to comfort her. As they talked, Eddie looked back into the arena. There was a swell of *Olés* from the crowd and Eddie saw the finish of a beautiful pass that Ortega had performed. He turned and left the stadium.

Eddie was in a state of depression. He didn't care about his mother's angst over the death of the bull. He was there to see the fight, and he was missing the gallantry of Ortega. He would never forgive his mother for this.

As they walked toward the car, they were met by a hoard of venders, selling Mexican-made jewelry, pottery, crucifixes and colorful clothing which hung from a rack. There was a guy selling what looked like a small wooden miniature pig. He carried a three foot square table that he strapped around his neck. On the top of the table were around twenty of the pigs, made out of hazelnuts. Each nut had holes drilled in it for the four legs and in each leg was a match stick. The face of the pig was constructed with a large hole for the mouth which was plugged up with a piece of cork. Its eyes were painted on, and there were two pieces of wood, carved to resemble pig ears, and a tail. When put in place, they all somehow managed to wriggle around, as though there were a mechanical device inside the pig that made it all happen. Eddie's father was quickly attracted to this.

"How much?" Jeff asked.

"Five dollars," The vendor answered, with a toothless smile.

His dad handed the man five bucks and started to move his hand over the table to find the pig with the proper movement in the tail and ear area. It reminded Eddie of his mother, as she felt every item on their shopping tour yesterday. They were both on the same wave length.

When he found the right pig, his dad moved to the vendor and whispered something to him. The vendor chuckled and said something back to his dad. His father looked back at the pig he had just paid five bucks for, then back at he vendor. "Boy, you sure got me there." He smiled and moved his wife and son toward the car. He was happy with his purchase, and hoped Eddie would be satisfied too.

While on the road, his dad explained the secret of the inner workings of the pig. "They remove the cork from the mouth and put a live fly in the body," his dad explained. "The fly moves around for a day or so, causing the wriggle from the head and tail, then the fly dies. If you want that puppy to keep on wriggling, you better be ready to catch a fresh fly!" He laughed, very pleased with himself.

Irene was appalled. She gave Jeff a shocked and disgusted look. "I can't believe you'd buy that thing," she scolded. "That entire country is possessed with torture and death!"

"Come on, what are you talking about?" his father shouted. "My golly, you kill flies every day with bug spray!" Irene just looked out of the window.

They stopped at a motel in Orange, Texas and had a late dinner at the coffee shop, then turned in for the night. They all slept in one room, his parents in a double bed and Eddie in a roll-away. As they fell asleep, Eddie's thoughts were not of the bullfight, but more of immediate reflection of the future. He had checked his pig while in the car. The fly had already died. He pulled the cork from the mouth and shook the dead fly out onto his hand. His parents wanted to get home and get back to business as usual. Eddie wanted to get home and catch another fly.

They left Orange, Texas in the morning and arrived home just before midnight. It had been a hard drive, and his parents said a quick goodnight as they went up the back staircase to bed. For the first time in over a week, Eddie was alone.

He had now begun to stage his life for these moments. It was his time to read about his heroes, and to live his expectancy of a better time to come. Eddie did not realize this now, but he was in the process of becoming a full-fledged sociopath.

First he needed to rehearse the process with the pig. He pulled the cork from the pig's mouth and placed it on the sink. He would hold the pig in the palm of his left hand. Next he would grab an imaginary fly form the air, and place it into the mouth hole of the pig. Then, moving his left hand finger over to cover the mouth hole so the fly could not get out, he picked up the cork between the thumb and forefinger of his right hand, and quickly placed the cork back into the pig's mouth. It was an awkward process, but he worked it a dozen times or more, and finally it started to fall into place.

He went into the kitchen and took a clean jar from his mother's pantry, where she did her canning process. He put some sugar into the jar, keeping the lid at the ready for quick use. He placed a small amount of water into the jar, and shook it around, then went outside onto the porch, and waited.

At first it seemed that nothing was there, but after about fifteen minutes a fly flew by, then another and then another. They circled the jar. Finally one of them landed on the lip of the jar. Eddie stood still, with the lid at the ready. The eager fly sniffed around the top then decided to delve into the jar itself. His buddies were not that excited and remained flying around without attempting a landing. Eddie pounced on the jar, clamping it tightly closed.

He moved quickly into his room, concerned that the fly might die in the water. He stood at his bathroom sink, with the pig and cork nearby. Eddie carefully opened the cap and stuck his right hand into the jar as far as it would go. The mouth of the jar was too small and he couldn't get his hand in far enough to grab the floating fly. He tried tipping the jar forward, hoping to cause the fly to come closer to his hand but as he did so, the fly only floated away from his hand. Eddie became frustrated and he tried five times to catch the fly with the same results. He capped the jar and put it down on the counter.

Eddie stepped back and thought this entire matter over. Finally he came up with a solution. The fly was stuck in the water. By filling the jar with more water it would bring the fly up and he could grab it. It worked!

He held the fly by the wings but it was desperately trying to get away. He held him just tight enough to keep from killing it. With his left hand, he held the pig in place. He next moved the fly to the open mouth of the pig. It didn't fit! Try as he might, his thoughtful and well planned operation didn't work. It was a failure. He had caught a big fly, an adult fly. Eddie realized now that what came out of he pig last night was a small fly. He had failed! He had lost the war! If he had been a matador, he would have been laughed out of the arena!

Eddie studied his face in the mirror. He held the pig in his left hand and the fly in his right. He studied his plight, his frustration. The fly kept on buzzing, attempting to get free. He was stupid beyond belief. He was beyond control. He hated what he saw, the look on his face, the total stupidity of what he was trying to accomplish. And worse of all was the fly. One of his wings suddenly got free, and he now was about to tear his other wing off. Eddie opened his mouth wide, placed the fly in his mouth and quickly pulled his fingers out sealing his mouth shut. Eddie had the fly trapped in his mouth!

He first sealed his lips shut, at the same time he closed the passage to his throat. Then by opening a small air space at the back of his mouth, he was able to puff air into his mouth, causing his cheeks to blow out outward. Looking at himself in the mirror he almost laughed out loud. He looked like a blowfish with a fly in his mouth. It was really mind over matter.

He was breathing through his nose, waiting for the fly to make a move. The next step was for the fly. Eddie held his position looking in the mirror, with his cheeks bulging. His eyes were bugged out, and breathing through his nose became labored. But he held on, waiting for the fly to make his move. Then he felt it! He could even hear it! He couldn't tell where it was, but the fly sure as hell was flying around. Then he felt it! It was on the hard palate of his mouth. He could feel its feet sticking to the tissue of the bridge of his mouth. Then a buzzing sound as he landed at the back of his lips.

His lips were very sensitive and he could feel him moving around, looking for a way out. Saliva had started to slowly fill his mouth, and Eddie tried to relax. Then there was another quick buzz and the fly landed on the center of his tongue. He could feel it walking up his tongue toward the back of his mouth.

Eddie recalled a book he had read several years ago. It was a fiction story of a mother and her son who had eaten something that bothered him. Later that night he was suffering from stomach cramps. His mother took him into the bathroom and stuck a feather onto the back of his mouth, tickling the sensitive area of his tongue. As she did this and the feather went deeper and deeper, the boy started to gag. When this happened he started to feel a vomiting reaction. She leaned him over the toilet and he started heaving, but nothing came up. Then she stuck her finger down his throat as far as she could. In moments the boy was vomiting. He vomited up his last meal. Even though it was a terrible experience, he felt better when all was said and done.

Eddie fought the fly. It was persistent. Perhaps it was the fly's need to get out of his mouth that made it such a daunting challenge to Eddie. Then Eddie felt the gagging reaction. Three times in a row he gagged. Had this happened to a normal person, Eddie would have opened his mouth and blasted the fly into the sink. Eddie was not a normal person. He firmed up his mouth and cheeks, sealed his lips shut hard and closed his throat even tighter.

As the gagging continued, it was followed by the bile from his stomach. Burning, churning acid quickly made its way up his throat towards his mouth. Each time this happened, Eddie would swallow the bile back down waiting for another attack. He noted that the saliva in his mouth had stated to flow even faster. He tipped his head forward and saw in the mirror that his lips were covered with the liquid. The back of his tongue felt dry, but the saliva was about to get the fly.

This was the fly's moment of truth. Like the bull, it was the fly's time to die. Eddie looked into the mirror, saluted the President of the Correda, leaned his head back and swallowed deeply.

He opened his mouth wide sucking in much needed fresh air. But, it wasn't over yet, for Eddie could still feel the fly, stuck somewhere in his windpipe, just near his Adam's apple. He quickly swallowed again, but that didn't do it either, so he washed out the jar with the sugar water, filled it with tap water and drank it all down.

That was it. It was over. He had accomplished something he never thought he could do. He did it quickly, with no thoughts of failure or retreat. He had won the battle and he was the master of his soul. At least, that's what Eddie thought.

Eddie still isolated himself from most of the students, but he did manage to develop a small group of boys he shared information with. Eddie was shrewd. He stood on the side and listened. The others spoke but Eddie simply gathered information. Dean was the oldest, fourteen years old. He was the most seasoned and wisest of the group. Then there was Jimmy, thirteen, the clever one. If there was a sharp line to be heard, it came from Jimmy. Finally there was Larry a twelve year old with access to a collection of his father's dirty books. If it weren't for the books, Larry would never be in the group.

They stood out at the back of a baseball field. If anybody had a pack of smokes, here was the place to smoke them. Larry had last month's issue of a dirty magazine. When his father was finished, he would pitch the books in the trash, where Larry would quickly retrieve them.

"Take a look at this baby," Jerry said. "She's a real bitch." He opened the book to the centerfold and pulled it out. All the boys leaned in to take a look.

Dean made a remark. "Look at those tits, look at that pussy. Shit, I bet you guys don't have a clue what to do with that."

"What do you mean Dean?" Jerry said. "You know where to keep the shovel for the trouble?"

"You bet I do," Dean answered. "An' you know it too." He made a fist with his right hand and made a pumping action.

"Oh yeah, that," Jerry answered.

Finally Eddie spoke up. "What are you guys talking about?"

"You mean you never took your dick in hand and wanked on it?" Dean said with a big grin on his face. "You never drained the lizard, jacked off, you never masturbated?"

"Yeah, I done that," Eddie said. "I just didn't know what you guys were taking about." But Eddie had never done that. As he glanced at the picture of the centerfold girl he could feel his penis starting to swell.

"Okay, Jerry," Dean said. "Who gets the book first this time?"

"This one goes to Eddie," Jerry answered.

That afternoon, Eddie walked to the library. His mother had purchased him a new windbreaker jacket. He had outgrown the green one. This one was blue, and had large pockets on the side. There he would keep his stash of dirty books, along with stolen material from the library.

There was no homework for tomorrow as it was a national holiday. When he arrived at the library, his mother was busy doing an inventory. He moved to the back room where he had originally met Michael Kline and Manolete. He quickly walked into the toilet, locking the door behind him. His actions displayed a feverish intent.

His motivation was animal-like, a desire to cause an orgasm. Eddie dropped his pants and shorts and sat down on the toilet. He pulled the magazine from his pocket and set himself to the business at hand.

Eddie had never done this before. The boys had talked about it, they had acknowledged they had done it, had even described how it worked, but Eddie had never participated. Now it was about to happen.

With his penis in one hand and the magazine in the other, he started the action. It didn't take long. His mind was already filled with the potential excitement of the event. He looked at the girl with her legs spread open, at the same time creating a pumping hold on his penis. Within a minute he stated to feel his virgin sperm flowing up from his lower body. And then, Eddie got scared.

In a second he tossed the magazine to the floor and caught his penis in the other hand clamping it tight, causing the flow of sperm to end! And end it did!

Eddie was quickly out of the bathroom. He had hidden the magazine back in his blue jacket pocket. He needed something else to do, something to take his mind away from his current predicament. He walked over and started searching for more reading material, with no nude women.

It was then, while searching for a new and more modern thug to read about, he came across a book dealing with the life of Ralph Barkley. Unlike Billy the Kid, the name Ralph Barkley meant nothing to him. He saw the original cover on the inside of the front page. It read, "Ralph Barkley became one of the most horrendous mass murderers in the last century. From 1956 to 1963, he raped and killed over 18 young women. He now sits in a Florida prison awaiting his fate."

Eddie flipped to the front page and read, "Ralph Barkley was born on the 14th of August, 1935." That line caught his attention. He was born on the same day, August 14th 1960. What an amazing coincidence! He took the book back to his chair, and started to read. Of all the books he had read, this one hit closest to home.

Ralph Barkley was sentenced to die, but with no exact date. It was 1972 and Barley was going through yet another appeal process. How many women he killed would never be known, but they had concluded it was at least eighteen.

Eddie stuffed the book into the right pocket of his new blue jacket. The naked lady magazine was stuffed into the left. He hung around until five o'clock when his mother locked the library door.

On this night, Eddie's dad had a social job to take care of. He was honorary chairman of social events for the local Lions Club. They were meeting to see about setting up a 'Fair' fund raiser for the local children's hospital. His dad would be home late. Tonight it was just Eddie and ma'am.

Irene stopped at the market and bought stuff for dinner, Eddie helped carry the groceries. All the while he just wanted to get home, but there was a point in time when she was waiting in line for her number to be called. He noticed that she held number 23 and that number 7 had just been called.

There was a music section in the market. The kind of crap kids liked. As his mother waited for her number to be called, Eddie snuck off and purchased an album of a group called The Rage. He didn't care what it sounded like he just needed some new music.

He returned to the meat section and saw that number 18 was up next. He made up his mind right then and there, this time it would be different. When he got home he would go into the bathroom and this time he would go all the way.

They arrived at the house at around six-thirty. She told him dinner would be ready for eight.

"Yes ma'am, I'll be ready," Eddie said. He turned and headed for his bedroom and then directly to the bathroom.

There was no more fear in Eddie. This time he was going to do it. He removed his shoes and his trousers. Then he took his shorts off, opened the front of his shirt and sat down on the toilet seat.

He had an hour and a half before dinner, and he would make the most of it. He pulled the magazine from his jacket pocket and opened it at the first page. There was nothing there, just an ad for a sound system, but the anticipation of what was about to happen, had already caused his erection to materialize.

Then he got to the centerfold girl. There were more shots of her, even more provocative and raw than the first view of the centerfold he had seen. With penis in hand and his mind reeling, he easily reached a massive orgasm.

Sperm ejaculated over his bare legs, some of it landing on the floor. He was in a state of euphoria, breathing heavily, enjoying the moment. Then the door opened and his mother, carrying a basket of clothing to the laundry room, stepped inside. In his selfish goal for personal pleasure, Eddie had neglected to lock the bathroom door.

"What are you doing?" she screamed. "What has happened to you? My God, how dare you do a thing like this? How dare you abuse yourself like this?" She snatched the magazine away from Eddie and looked at the pictures. "Where did you get this magazine?"

Eddie struggled to cover himself. His mother was standing there shaking the magazine at him, furious at what he had become. "You like this book. Is that it? You enjoy seeing the foul pictures of women in this book! You are a disgusting human being! Shame on you, shame, shame. You are grounded.

You will be grounded for as long as I see fit!"

Still holding the magazine, she turned and headed for the door. Eddie stood from the toilet, pulling his shirt closed to conceal his nudity. There was nothing he could do or say. He could just stand there feeling like a fool. Then his mother paused and turned, looking back.

"I will have your father remove the doors from your room and the bathroom. You'll never be alone again. This is between you and me. Now clean yourself up. And while you're at it you can pray to God to forgive you for the unspeakable thing you've done here. Shame on you! Shame on you! For now, you leave both these doors open!"

She left and Eddie sat back down onto the toilet. He was still catching his breath. He started to formulate a decision. He decided he would murder his mother!

At eight o'clock his mother called him for dinner. It was a horrifying experience. His father was not there and they were alone. No music or TV was on. They sat quietly at the table and just ate, never looking or saying a word to each other.

When he returned to his room, Eddie was back to his plan for murder. A short time later, Eddie had to take a leak. He stepped over the clothes basket his mother had dropped when she had walked in on him and stood before the toilet.

He could hear his father entering the back garage door, walking down the hall past his bedroom. His dad saw Eddie through the open door of his bedroom, leading to the bathroom, as he was taking a pee.

"Eddie, what the heck are you doin'?" he said with a slight smile on his face. "You advertising?" He pushed the bedroom door closed and walked down the hallway.

Eddie lay down on his bed. He had pretty well figured out the rest of his life. Animals or human beings meant little or nothing to him. It was his pleasure, and fascination, that meant the world to him. He would hate to kill someone and get caught. That would result in his serving life in prison or death by execution. The death by execution thing was out of the question. He would just have to stay smarter than the rest. *Take your time and be right about the crime.* That was his new motto.

His mother's death would be his first major challenge. He had to find a way to do it, but make certain that being caught was never an option. He worked his way through numerous plans, all of which failed his review. The problem, he realized, was that his plans were too complicated. He must simplify.

It all boiled down to where he would do the job. He thought about out back, at the tree house. But neighbors might spot him, or see his mother there. They might call the cops. Then there were questions to answer and disposing of the body would be a pain in the ass. Other locations met with the same disapproval.

The best spot was in the house. It was perfect. He ran it through his mind again and again, fine tuning it, adjusting the when and how. He decided it would happen on a Saturday. This was the day his mother was home and his father worked at the office.

His father arrived home at about five-thirty. He would kill his mother at three-thirty. Then he would dispose of all the evidence have time to establish an alibi, and when his dad arrived they would both discover the body. It was perfect.

The following morning at breakfast, nothing was said about removing his bedroom or bathroom doors. Perhaps his mother had mentioned it and his dad said no. Perhaps she forgot about it but that was a no also. Perhaps she had a change of heart. It didn't matter, she would be dead soon.

On Wednesday the following week, he decided on the coming Saturday to be the date. He had made up a check list of thing to do. Just to make sure nothing was overlooked. The bottom of this list read, "Make sure to destroy this list."

He first located a periscope. His dad had bought it at a parade they had attended. As a young child he could sit on his father's shoulders and peer through the periscope, thereby seeing the parade from a distance, above the crowd. Eddie didn't particularly like the unit and had stored it in the back of his bedroom closet.

Thursday and Friday he would continue to gather stuff he had prepared on his list. He made up a small notebook of things to do to properly do the deed. Then on Saturday he spread everything out on his bed and went over the list once again. Everything was ready by two o'clock, an hour and a half before the murder was scheduled. He was filled with anticipation.

Eddie didn't want to move too quickly. Three-thirty was the time of her death. He had to make sure he followed his plan to the letter. He reviewed, for the last time, his 'things to do' list. Then finally it was time.

He stood in his room with his legs covered in the kitchen plastic wrap, from his feet to his knees. This was to keep his mother's blood from getting on his legs. Next he covered his upper body with an old rain coat. Nobody could possibly miss the coat. He hadn't worn it in over five years. On his head he wore a plastic shower cap, which he stole from his mother's bathroom, where she stored a box of them. He also found some plastic gloves that she had used to color her hair. One set would never be missed. He was now fully protected from the splatter of blood.

He moved to the door and opened it up. He placed the front of the periscope into the hallway and looked down into the kitchen. He peered through the scope searching for his mother, but he couldn't find her. It was now three thirty-five and he was becoming impatient. But impatience was Eddie's middle name, and he knew how to control it.

Finally his mother moved into view and stood by the sink. He could see the sink in full view, his mother standing with her back to him. It was Saturday, the day she made potatoes au gratin, one of his dad's favorites. She moved the sack of potatoes to the counter and started to peel them. It was time now, the time to do it to it!

Eddie stooped over and picked up his tool of choice, the aluminum little league baseball bat his father had bought him many years before. He moved quietly down the hallway, ready to do his evil deed. His mother was at the sink, still peeling potatoes. The radio was on, playing a station that advertised soft rock. Eddie moved into the kitchen behind her. The plastic he was wearing rustled, but the music from the radio muffled the sound.

He stood behind her with the bat raised high above his head. He waited for a period of time, wanting to seize the proper moment. Her head was not at the right angle. If he swung the bat now, it might catch the cabinet above her. He had to get her attention.

"Ma'am?" he said softly.

"Yes," she answered. She didn't raise her head up, just continued her work.

"Ma'am?" he said again.

"What is it?" she answered

"Mother?" he asked a third time.

"What is it!" she asked, a bit agitated. Then she turned to look at him.

At that moment he crashed his baseball bat onto the top of her head! Her body immediately collapsed, her feet splayed out and she crashed to the floor like a box of rocks. She sat there with her back against the lower cabinets, her head hanging down and her arms dangling at her sides.

Eddie took a step back. He waited for a moment to see what would happen. Nothing happened.

I wonder if she's dead, he asked himself. *How will I know that? How do I check her to see if she's dead? I've got to check her pulse. How do I do that? I should have known that!*

He stood up with bat in hand and made five more smashing blows to the back of her head. With each successive blow of the bat, her head bounced up and down like a rag doll. With each blow of the bat, there was no blood from the wound.

He kneeled down in front of her and looked up into her face. Her head hung down, with eyes open, staring ahead. Eddie confirmed she was definitely dead. He checked the time on the clock on the wall. It was now three-thirty nine. He had more than an hour and a half left to complete his duties. He was even ahead of schedule.

He went to the door of the kitchen and removed the plastic clothing from his body. He was delighted that he hadn't seen any blood. He wrapped the shower cap, leg covers and gloves up with the raincoat. Grabbing the bat in hand, he moved to his bedroom.

First he took his bat to the bathroom sink and washed it off, making sure no splats of blood were left there. He replaced it in the back of his closet with his other memories, his baseball cap and glove. He also returned his periscope to the side of his closet. No blood stains on that.

Next he placed a fresh pair of gloves on his hands, along with a black garbage bag and went back to the kitchen. Eddie had some apprehension as he approached the open kitchen door. He was looking for his mother to charge out like a wounded bull, but she was just sitting, in the same position as when he had left her. Now her head started bleeding. It started to run down the front of her house dress, causing a growing pool of blood to gather where she sat on the floor. *Make a note of that,* he said to himself. *Blood doesn't start quickly.*

He removed a small kitchen knife from his back pocket and proceeded to the front door. You could not see into the kitchen area from the front entrance of the house. He stepped outside and closed the screen door. Using the knife he cut two slashes in the screen. He next placed his gloved hand through the slash and opened the screen door. That being completed, he ran upstairs to the master suite.

Once there, he proceeded to destroy the place. First he got his mother's jewelry case. Most of it was just fake stuff, but some of it was actually diamonds. He threw the diamonds in the black trash bag and the fake jewelry onto the floor.

Next, he ripped the beds apart. In doing so, he revealed a .45 automatic handgun his dad had concealed between the mattresses. He tossed the .45 into the black bag.

He pulled clothes from the closets and prescription drugs from the medicine cabinet. By the time Eddie was finished, the room appeared as though a massive theft had taken place.

Then he was back to his bedroom, never once even taking a second glance at his mother. She was now history and Eddie was in the future. He tossed the plastic clothing from the murder, along with the items he had taken from the upper suite, into the black trash bag. Then he went to his check off list. He read it carefully. After confirming he had done it all, the check off list itself was the final item placed in the black bag.

Eddie waited until it got dark, about five-ten. The garage door opened and Eddie moved out to the trash. He was now pushing the envelope. His dad would be arriving in about twenty minutes and he didn't want to be out there when he got home.

He moved quickly to the front of the garage and pulled out one of the garbage cans to clear an area underneath. Eddie pulled a medium piece of driveway tile open, revealing a pre-dug hole in the earth that he had created. He dropped the black bag into the hole and walked back into the garage, returning with an old empty paint can, filled with dirt. This he dumped into the opening and the dirt completely filled the hole. Tamping the dirt down with his foot, Eddie placed the driveway tile back into place, positioning the garbage can back on top. He finally moved into the garage, closing the door behind him.

His bedroom door was now closed and finally Eddie sat down and listened to music. He turned on The Rage, the album he had recently purchased at the market. He kept it low for a moment, the sound emitting from his headset. He would adjust the level when necessary. Should anyone ever check out his volume level, they would have found that he could not have heard anything from the kitchen. It was a simple ruse. Always keep it simple.

At about five twenty-five Eddie heard his father's car enter the garage. His dad opened the back door and walked down the hallway past Eddie's closed bedroom door. Eddie had now turned the volume from The Rage up to a painfully high level. He now waited patiently. He laid back on his pillow, waiting for it all to fall into place but it took forever to hear his father's reaction.

What was he doing in there? Eddie thought. *How long is he going to take to find her?* Then he heard his father's voice.

"Eddie!" he screamed. "Eddie!" The door to his room opened quickly and his father took a step inside.

Eddie bolted upright, removing his headset. "Hi dad." He greeted his dad with a smile.

His dad was reeling with pain. He looked like a dead man walking. When Eddie saw him it was as though he had aged a lifetime in only a matter of moments.

"What's the matter?" Eddie asked with great concern.

"Nothing," he answered. "I want you to stay in here. I'll tell you about it later. You just stay in your room. Keep the door shut. I'll be back to get you. Stay here. You understand me?"

Eddie understood quite well. His father didn't want Eddie to see his mother lying dead in the kitchen. "Yes sir, I'll stay here if you want." Eddie appeared nervous and distraught, responding to his father's attitude. But he played the game, and remained in the bedroom. His father nodded and left the room, closing the door behind him.

The police arrived thirty minutes later. The coroner was there also. The cops interviewed Eddie, proving he had nothing to do with the crime. The following day the local newspaper, *The Leesville Independent* tabbed it, "Burglary Results in Murder." There was a photo of his mother, along with the usual description from the police. That was it. No one ever challenged Eddie with anything.

That night Eddie was filled with rampant adrenalin. He wanted to read the Ralph Barkley book, but his attention kept returning to the success of the perfect crime that he had committed. *It was a dirty job but someone had to do it*, he said to himself with a smile.

Chapter 12

Day 5, continued.

It was Sunday night, March 5th, just before 10 o'clock, when Kelly entered her apartment. Sam had just dropped her off at her door. It had been a beautiful day on the boat. She was in a state of euphoria, had been bedazzled by a magnificent weekend, and had decided Sam Pennington was a definite keeper.

She turned on a TV channel playing an old movie, stripped off her clothes and flopped into bed. After a few moments there was a station break, and a local commercial came on. It was an ad for the Crazy Cajun Car-man, located at 237 Canal Blvd.

Kelly grabbed her steno pad from the side table, and made notes on the page. Then the Crazy Cajun Car-man appeared on the screen. "Hi there, I'm Leroy Anderson, the Crazy Cajun Car-man, and I'm here to sell you a new or used car, at prices you will not believe."

Leroy was a young man, in his mid thirties. He wore Levis and a pair of cowboy boots, with a tight fitting white tee-shirt, with the "Crazy Cajun Car-man" printed on the front. The shirt was meant to display his well-conditioned body. Leroy obviously was a weightlifter.

As Leroy spoke, he walked down the aisle of cars, slapping the hood of each as he passed, quoting the outlandishly cheap price he would charge. "I got a 1995 Ford Taurus station wagon, Louisiana license number UlA 794. This car goes out clean, full power. If you can't find the power you want in a car, you are in the wrong place.

"We got air conditioning, intermittent wipers, power steering, driver airbag, cloth seats, deluxe wheel covers, rear defogger, tinted glass, luggage/roof rack, power mirrors, 4-wheel disk brakes, and recline lounge seats. In addition you can unlock this car with without a key, with hand control units or a numbered door lock, positioned on the driver's side.

"You are in this car and outta here for seven thousand, two hundred fifty-five dollars." Then he slapped his hand on the hood. "An' the Crazy Cajun guarantees this car will be here for you, with the Cajun Guarantee, of pure pleasure driving, at seven thousand two hundred fifty-five dollars." He slapped his hand on the hood once again and moved on.

Kelly wrote down as much information as she could handle, then finally turned off the TV and fell asleep.

FLASHBACK

It was six and one half months earlier when Kelly Lee Jones arrived in New Orleans. She had thirty thousand dollars in hand from winning one pull of a slot machine at a Mississippi gambling establishment. But this little lady had more than that piece of luck to deal with. She had much more to offer.

When she left the bus stop, she saw an ad on a wall at the bus station for the Hibernia Bank. *Looks good to me*, she thought. She took a cab to the bank, put the money in a checking/savings account, and moved into the French Quarter.

The cab driver recommended the Palace Inn on Burgundy Street. She rented a room which was fifty-three dollars a night. She would find a cheaper place tomorrow. Then she walked to Bourbon Street. She remembered this street well, from when she first saw it as a child.

It was early in the evening at the Dixieland Bar and Grill, and Red Moon and his boys were just setting up for the night's entertainment. She walked inside and sat down at the bar. Leonard, the bartender came over. "Yes ma'am, what can I get you?"

"I was looking for a job," she said. "I'm a pretty good waitress." Then she offered that great smile.

"Well, we don't need anybody right now."

The smile left her face. Then Leonard added, "If things get busy later on, maybe we could use some more help."

The smile returned. "Oh that would be great!"

She sat at the end of the bar, waiting for a call to action. She heard the music of Red Moon as he and his boys played the tunes America loved. She also had three glasses of water, even though Leonard also offered to buy her something to eat.

"No thank you, I'm just fine," she said. Then at the eleven o'clock hour, Kelly finally got her shot. Leonard came over to her, and made a quick deal. "I got one girl who didn't show up. There's some clean uniforms hanging in the back. Find one that fits. I'll try you out at her station."

Kelly wound up at the prime station, the one just to the left of the bandstand. She looked great in her waitress outfit. It was a black merry widow corset with red panties with black hose below.

Be it by instinct or something she had learned at the Boogy-Boo, by seven o'clock the following morning she had collected seventy-two dollars in tips, more than any other waitress in the place. It must have been that sweet smile and the shaking of her ass Cheryl had taught her that did the trick.

Leonard was amazed at how easily she had worked the room. She kept the people filled with drinks, made them laugh, and every one had a real good "Southern" time. Her personality was infectious, and Leonard could spot a good thing when he saw it.

He took some cash from the cash register and dealt out one hundred dollars. "Here ya go." He handed her the money. "That's what you get for one eight hour shift. If you wanna do it again, I'll put you on the payroll."

Including her tips, Kelly had just made one hundred seventy two dollars for an eight-hour gig. That was seventy-two dollars more a day than she made at the "Skin Deep Beauty Salon," working for at least for ten hours.

"Put me on the payroll. I'm ready to go."

Kelly went out to search for an apartment and found one on Toulouse St. It was $360.00 per month. She then checked out of the Palace Inn, moved into her one room shelter, and returned to work at the Dixieland at eleven p.m., starting her next shift.

At three o'clock that morning, Red Moon and his boys were taking a final break in the back patio when a group of six customers came into the club. They sat down in her section, just to the left of the bandstand. They had all driven in from Texas, and were out for a good time.

The leader of the party was an older man from "Big D." That's Dallas, for anyone who doesn't understand what "Big D" stands for. Kelly found out his name was Charlie. The room was only half full, and Charlie and his party were about to order drinks.

"My name is Kelly," she announced. "An' I'm here to deliver anything ya'll want. An' since ya'll's from Texas, I'll bet a dollar ya'll know exactly what you want."

Everybody ordered their usual pleasure, and then it came to good old Charlie. "I don't know," he said. "I gotta study that there menu."

Kelly reached into her apron pocket, pulled out a buck, and dropped it on the table. "There you go big fella, you win. While you study that menu, I'll get everyone else started."

As she started to leave, Charlie grabbed her arm.

"Hold on there. I read here you have Jack Daniels whisky. I'll have a double Jack, neat."

"That's a double Jack Daniels, no ice, no water." She left the table for the bar, and there were chuckles all around. Charlie studied the buck he had just won. He would now have to do her, big time. He would now have to "better" her, at least a thousand times that. Hell, his custom hand-made cowboy boots, the ones he now wore, the ones with the name "Texas" emblazoned on the sides and a big lone star in the front, the ones that were a duplicate of the boots worn by LBJ when he was President, the very boots that cost him more than a thousand bucks. And those were only one pair of twelve others, now resting in his closet at home.

As Kelly returned to the table with a tray full of drinks, Charlie reached into his deep pocket and pulled out a wad of cash that would choke a horse, if not a giraffe. He peeled off ten one hundred dollar bills and spread them out before him. Kelly placed the drinks on the table, winding up at Charlie. She also provided him with a glass of water.

"What's this for?" He asked.

"Well, I figured you might wanna brush you teeth after you swig down this class-act whisky."

The rest of Charlie's party laughed their faces off, slapping each other on the back.

"Well, I tell you what, little girl," Charlie said with a smug expression. "I'll bet you a thousand you can't get up there on that there stage and sing us a song."

Charlie held his hands out, displaying the money on the table. Kelly looked down at the cash. One thousand would do a world of good for her new apartment.

"Okay, you got a deal."

She turned and left the room for the back patio.

Red Moon was a man in his mid-sixties, or somewhere near his late nineties, nobody could tell for sure. In the late fifties and early sixties he had worked second horn with Al Hirt. Later he played first trumpet with Pete Fountain when Pete had his place on Bourbon. He finally made a deal at the Dixieland, and played there ever since. He was the consummate professional. No amateurs on his stage.

When she entered the patio, the boys were taking their final stretch. Kelly crossed to Red. "Red, I need a favor."

"Sure thing, honey. What's your name, anyway?"

"I'm Kelly Lee." She gave Red the million dollar smile and the ass wiggle. She glanced at his eyes as Red looked down at the wiggle. "I got a thousand dollars if I can sing a song on stage with you boys. What do you think?"

"I'm sorry, we can't do that, honey. Union don't let no amateurs try out here."

"I know all the words to 'Bill Bailey.' Here's what we do. You boys give me a four bar intro, with the full band. Then I sing the whole song through. Behind me, I need the piano and drums, with the clarinet filing in the holes. After that, you boys start again from the top, come in with the full band at full level, for the first sixteen bars. Then I'll join in for the last sixteen. You lay back a little when I start, and build with me till we close. Finally, give me a two bar reprieve, with a nice slow down for the big finish."

"Where did you learn to talk like that?" Red questioned.

"I used to work at the Boogy-Boo, in Miami Florida. I'm a professional. In addition, I'll split the thousand. That's five hundred for you and the boys."

A slight smile crossed Red's face. "So what's your key?"

Kelly was not sure of her key, so she sung the first four bars. "'Won't you come home, Bill Bailey, won't you come home.'"

"Yeah, we can play in that key."

The band came back into the room, and climbed up onto the stage. Red introduced "Miss Kelly Lee." They played a four bar intro while Kelly got onto the stage, and when she took the microphone in hand, the piano, drums, and clarinet took over, from the top, and Kelly sang.

She sang like a seasoned pro. Her voice was lilting but strong. It had authority. She even possessed a natural vocal wavering called a *vibrato*.

When she reached the end, the band started at the top, in full Dixieland swing.

Kelly took her sixteen bar rest, and looked about the room. She had been singing directly to the audience. They all sat looking at her. Even Leonard and the rest of the staff had stopped working, and were just watching her.

After the first sixteen bars and with the full band still playing, she started for the finish.

"'Remember that crazy evening, I threw you out, with nothing but a fine tooth comb. I know I'm to blame, it's a low down dirty shame. Bill Bailey, won't you please come home.'"

The song ended and there was a moment of silence, then all hell broke loose. There was applause from all, some were cheering, and a few screamed out, "More, more."

Kelly graciously acknowledged the crowd's appreciation, left the stage and moved to Charlie. She scooped up the thousand laying in front of him, walked to the "Tip Jar" that had been placed there by one of the boys, dropped five one hundred dollar bills inside, stuffed the remaining money into her bra. She then headed for the women's room, located on the back patio.

Red Moon moved from the stage and walked over to Leonard. He leaned in close, so no one else could hear.

"Listen," Red said. "You oughta make a deal with this girl. She's good. She's a pro. Sign her up for the band. She's special."

Once inside the women's room, Kelly was able to catch her breath. "I did it!" she said out loud to herself. "And I was good!" A few minutes later, she returned to her station. Leonard caught her eye, and she walked over to him.

"Hey there, you were good," Leonard said.

"Thank you."

"Listen, Red wants you to sing every night."

"Oh no," she said, playing a little timid. "I'm just a waitress. Then I'd need to join the union, and all that."

"How 'bout you just sing one song at the start of each set? Get the crowd warmed up?"

"No, I don't think so."

"Suppose I increase your pay to two hundred a day."

"That would be fine. Thank you."

Day 6

Kelly awoke at eight Monday morning, and instantly her thoughts and feelings were of Sam. She had only met him last Wednesday evening. In two more days they could have an anniversary of their first week together. But Sam was a special person, someone she could know and trust.

She thought she might call him, but remembered Sam telling her of his morning routine. Right now he would be walking down Bourbon Street and into the St. Ann Market, for some coffee and beignets.

She quickly showered, dressed and grabbing her check book and note pad from the side of the bed, she telephoned for a cab. The taxicab arrived on time and honked the horn. Kelly leaped inside and directed the driver to 237 Canal.

The Crazy Cajun Car-man, was a medium-sized lot which held about seventy-five cars. She took only three steps onto the property, when a guy bolted through the office door and approached her. He wore a Hawaiian shirt and a Polynesian straw hat. He was in his late 50's, tall, with a dark tan. The tan matched his hat and shirt.

"Hello there. May I be of help to you?"

"Yes, please. I want to see the Crazy Cajun."

"Well I'm the one. I own this lot. My name's Jimmy Stewart. I am the Crazy Cajun."

"Hello Jimmy. You're not the Crazy Cajun I saw on TV last night."

"No, we's all Cajun guys around here."

"Well, I's the person who wants to see the guy who talked on the TV last night."

Jimmy looked around the lot. "Excuse me a moment, let's see if I can find him somewhere." He turned and jogged back to the office.

Kelly glanced around the lot, her eye catching sight of a sky blue sports car, possibly a Hillman Minx, with a convertible top. It would fit the Quarter perfectly. Just small enough to crowd its way into a small parking space, and old enough not to be on a car thief's list.

Then Leroy Anderson appeared. Kelly was a bit surprised when she got her first real look at Leroy. He was the same cocky man she had seen the night before, wearing the same outfit, but he was only five feet seven inches tall. Kelly towered over him by three full inches. Kelly looked down at him as he walked up.

"How do ya do ma'am, good morning to ya."

"Good morning," she answered, glancing into her spiral note pad. "I was looking for the 1995 Ford Taurus you advertised last night at around ten thirty."

"Oh, I'm sorry dear, that one was sold last week."

"Well you were selling it at around ten o'clock last night."

Leroy started to smile. He was dealing with a lady who simply did not understand the television/car industry.

"The thing is, we make these commercials at the start of each week. We sell some of them. There's no way we can keep track of all of them, if you know what I mean. But if you want a car like that one, let's go check out the lot."

Kelly looked at him carefully. He was a used car salesman. She would play his game, and he would lose at hers. She knew, what with interest on her thirty thousand, salary and tips at the Dixieland, minus her food and decorating her apartment, she had a net spending account of seven thousand two hundred fifty five dollars. That left her thirty thousand nest egg untouched. "Okay then, let's check out the lot. And I want a car with your Cajun guarantee, for full pleasure driving."

"No ma'am, that was only a guarantee for the Ford Taurus. An that one's been sold. Some have the guarantee, and some don't."

"Okay, I can see that red car in the back corner of the lot. It's got a price tag of five thousand eight hundred dollars on the windshield, along with the guarantee."

By now three men had joined them, two more car salesmen and the mechanic wandered in from the back garage.

"Okay boys," Leroy shouted. "Lady wants to look at the red Pontiac. Let's dig it out."

It took time to dig through the back lot to just get to the red Pontiac, and when the four men finally arrived, it didn't start.

"Okay, we need a new battery here," Leroy commanded.

"Forget about that one," Kelly said. "How about the little blue sports car right next to it? It's got a price tag of five thousand two hundred fifty dollars. And it's got a Cajun Guarantee sticker on the windshield. How's it run?"

"Like a charm," Leroy stated.

"Motor okay?"

"Fine."

"Transmission, rear end?"

"Real fine."

"Everything else real fine?"

"Needs brakes," the mechanic stated.

Leroy quickly looked back at his employee. His face was hidden from Kelly and Leroy gave a look that said something like, *You speak again out of turn and you'll be back flipping burgers at McDonald's.*

The mechanic was a boy of around twenty-five. He was tall and skinny and weighed a mere one hundred and twenty pounds. His name was Rod, and he wore grease-saturated blue overalls and an old cowboy hat. Rod took a quick look over at Leroy, then back to Kelly. Rod was his own man.

"What's wrong with the brakes?" Kelly asked.

"Left front is worn down to the bottom. Makes a squeaky sound. Rest oughta be re-done too, so's as to balance 'um out."

"Then would you give it a Cajun Guarantee?" Kelly asked.

Leroy took a few steps toward Rod and Rod backed off a bit, then he stood his ground once again.

"It needs a minor tune-up to make it right." Rod announced. "New plugs an' points, new filters, and a change 'a good oil. Then it's a good little car."

"How long does it take?" She asked.

"Bout three hours. I'll toss in a new set 'a wiper blades too. Ought a have a new battery too; this one's about done with."

Kelly turned to the Leroy who was about to have a fit. He never liked people playing with his money.

"I'll be back in three hours," she said. "Have the papers ready. Five thousand two hundred fifty dollars, plus tax and license fee."

Leroy was already overcharging her one thousand for the car, so what the hell. Everybody did it. "Yes, that will be fine," Leroy answered.

"Anybody know where I can get a cell phone?" Kelly asked.

"We don't sell any 'a them," Leroy said.

Rod moved up to Kelly, he stopped a few feet away. It was as though he felt she was being used by the boys on their car lot. It was as if they all felt she was fair game. Rod was having none of that. "There's a place just up on Canal. Turn left an' go about half 'a block. It's called Phones R Us. Tell 'um Rod sent ya. They'll make ya a real good deal." It was obvious that Rod was infatuated with Kelly. He had never seen that sweet smile, never heard her sing a song, nor had he seen her wiggle her ass. It was just her presence that caused him to speak up.

When Kelly arrived back at the lot, the car was parked out front, and ready to go. Not only were all the mechanical things taken care of, such as brakes, engine filters, and wipers, she noted the car had also been washed and polished. In addition, there four brand new Dunlop tires, placed where the rubber meets the street. All of this was accomplished by Rod and his two assistants, and all in three hours.

She walked into the office and signed the papers. Rod was there, looking on. Kelly thanked Leroy for the good service, and left. Leroy was not a happy camper. His extra profit had greatly diminished, as a result of the words of Rod.

She got back to the car, and took the top down folding it back into its resting position behind the front seats. As she climbed in behind the wheel, Rod moved toward the car, carrying a gift for her.

"Scuse me, ma'am, I got a gift for ya."

"Oh, what's that?" Kelly said.

"They call this here a tonneau cover. Keeps the sun and dirt off a your seats when the top is down."

It was folded and wrapped in plastic. He pulled it open and attached it to the car, using the matching grommet points. When in place, it made the car into a sleek roadster.

"I want to thank you for all of your help," Kelly said. "You are definitely one of the good guys." Then she leaned in and, finding a clean spot between his left ear and chin with no dirt or grease, she gave him a soft kiss on the cheek. "I will be back for a check-up now and then. And my boyfriend has an Alpha. He needs attention too."

Kelly jumped into the car and started it up. It shot into life with its new battery. She put the gear into low, and took off, heading East onto Canal Street. Rod watched her go. It was his magical moment. He turned and headed for the garage. As he walked passed the main office, he saw Leroy standing out in front, glaring at him.

"Not a bad deal," Rod called out. "Least ya sold a car."

Kelly had decided to return to the happiness of yesterday. She wanted to do it all again. She wanted to show her new car to the Judge. She passed over the Mississippi River and headed for Lafitte. As she continued on she checked her fuel gage. The tank was full, thanks to Rod.

After stopping to ask a few directions, Kelly finally arrived at George Wheeler's Lafitte Market, Museum and Picnic Grounds. After having a chat with George, she purchased two twelve packs of Hebrew National hot dogs, four six packs of buns, an onion, and the usual variety of condiments. Then she gathered two plastic tubs of Cajun potato salad, and four cans of Hormel Chili and Beans. In her final pass through the market, she also picked up a jar of finely chopped peanuts.

Kelly turned right onto Judge Wil Bean's property, kept to the right of the dusty road, and headed directly to the boat. She was pleased with her car. It had driven well. With a new set of wipers what could possibly go wrong?

She parked near the boat, got out, and heard a whistle from up above. She looked up and saw Pedro there, looking down, waiving and smiling. She had made yet another friend. "Permission to come aboard?"

"Yes ma'am. Be my guest."

Pedro motioned for her to go around to the port side. When Kelly arrived there, she saw Wil Bean and Roberto were there, trying to understand why one entire gallon of paint had been quickly sprayed out in a glob about twelve by twelve inches square on the front of the boat. It had happened quickly and then ran down into a large white pool on the ground.

Roberto had been a professional painter, but one who was not used to using this new type of "Air Spray Unit." Wil had brought six rolls of paper towels from his house and they were both mopping paint from the front of the boat.

"Hey, I got an idea. Anybody for lunch?" Kelly asked.

Lunch was a major success. Pedro prepared the food, and the finely ground penuts on the top had made a world of difference. While the men ate their brains out, Kelly spent time reviewing the directions on the new paint rig. It had to do with the spray nozzle.

Kelley learned very early in life that men do not read directions. They prefer to feel themselves along, arriving at the proper conclusion. This was a paint rig that only sprayed the exact amount of paint on the directed surface, with no paint being wasted on outside air. There was no need to use any form of a protective mask on the face.

"Let me read this to you boys," Kelley offered. "After all interior units are in place, insert the master structure into the housing, forcing it to collapse the holding spring. With your thumb, twist the structure counter clockwise, allowing it to cam and seat itself firmly into the housing. This completes the arming of the spray head." Kelly looked up at the men. She held up the spray rig for all to see. "Did you do that?" she asked.

Armed with Kelly's suggestion, after reading the directions the spray system worked perfectly. Then two large furniture vans drove in with all the stuff they needed for the boat.

They ended their day at dusk, and all went to Wil's house for dinner. It was seven o'clock and chicken was on the barbie. They had corn and potatos and wine and good friendship and some grass for Wil.

At eight o'clock, Kelly bade them all goodnight. If they wanted her, she would be happy to return tomorrow. Wil came in from the outside porch, where he had been puffing away to keep his eyes healthy.

"Hey there," Wil stated. "No need for you to head back to the city tonight. It's getting cold outside. I got a back bedroom here for you to use."

Then Norma came over. "If you'd rather, you could go back to the boat and sleep in the big bedroom. Be good for you to check it out for Sam. He'd like that."

Kelly climbed up onto the upper deck. It was peaceful and quiet. She could hear the gentle water as it splashed against pilings leading to the landing. Kelly could have lived here forever. She made her way down to the master bedroom and turned on the lights. The lights in his room were all on dimmers. She moved around the room, turning lights on, up or down, in order to set a mood. It was a beautiful room. She knew Sam would love it.

It was Monday night, March 6th, when Sam arrived home shortly after ten o'clock. He was tired now, bone tired, stupid tired. He started seeing things out of the corner of his eye, would glance at them, and seeing nothing would look away. Sleep deprivation would do tricks like that. He had been up all last night with Hironee Jessup, and that had about 'done him in.'

After his morning session with Alex Kroman, Sam had tried to call Kelly, but there was no answer at her apartment. Apparently she had not set up her answer machine. While walking home, he stopped at the Dixieland, and talked to Leonard. After telling Sam that he looked like shit, Leonard told him Kelly had called during the day, and stated she needed a few days off for rest and recreation. So much for Kelly.

Sam removed his cowboy boots by one foot pushing on the rear of the other, then visa versa, and flopped down onto the bed. As he started to drift into sleep, he sat upright. He had forgotten to check his own answer machine.

As he moved down the hallway, he removed his coat and trousers, tossing them on a chair. He entered his office and crossed to the phone, hitting the play button. The first call was the voice of William Joseph Mays.

"This is Houston calling. We may have a problem. Give me a call."

The call was then disconnected and Sam hung up the phone. He stood for a moment, thinking about the situation. They had seldom used this as a need for communicating. They had talked about it, that someday it may happen, but over the last ten years, they had only had sporadic occasions to talk. Sam checked his watch. It was now ten eighteen.

He quickly dressed and left his building, walking up Barracks toward the river. At the corner of Barracks and Charters was a gay bar, an all-night place where people of the night hung out, paying due diligence to the true art of intoxication. Outside, in front of the place, there was an open pay phone. There was no booth, just a pay phone, located on a covered antique iron stand that was easily available for anyone to use.

Sam put a coin into the slot and dialed a number. He listened as the phone rang twice, then he hung up. Again he checked his watch. It was ten twenty-four.

He next went into the bar. It was about half full, with gay boys doing whatever gay boys do in a gay bar. Sam payed no attention to the customers. The bartender moved toward Sam.

He was an old queen, about sixty-plus, with bright blond streaks in his dark brown hair.

"Hi there. What you want, sweetheart?"

"Did you get the Glenlivet in?" Sam asked.

"Oh yes. You're the one. I remember you. It's been a long time. Yes, I have it." He turned and drew a fifth from the shelf and quickly returned to the bar.

"Double, neat," Sam said.

"You got it." The bartender poured the drink.

Sam hated bars. It didn't matter who was there, gay or straight, he just hated bars. He took a good swig from the scotch, and it felt great. Sam looked about the room. He was alone. The other boys in the room were all busy talking. They were the lonely people. Sam was a man with a mission. The phone outside on the street rang.

Sam moved out to the sidewalk and picked it up. He wanted to make sure it was Bill Mays on the other end of the line.

"Hello?" William Joseph said.

"Yeah, hello."

Sam looked around the area, seeing if anyone was standing near by to hear his super-private conversation. "You called me."

William Mays was sitting in a small bar, located across the river in Algiers. It was a few blocks from his house.

"How you doin' pal?" Mays asked.

"We gotta stop meeting like this," Sam answered.

"I'll make this short and quick. I was called into the Office of Internal Affairs earlier today. No problem, just the usual review of my status. The guy I met there was a junior, a cookie-cutter cop named Roger Gentry. He said, 'I understand you are retiring soon.' I said yes, so he pulled out my file and started going though the thing.

"We spent an hour going through my first twenty years with the department. He asked some questions and I gave some answers. So we move on. Then he asks what about this big drug bust, an' I said 'what about it do you want to know,' an' he said, 'what about your partner, Sam Pennington?' How the hell do you answer a question like that?"

"What did you say?"

"I said, 'Sam Pennington? What do you want to know about him?' And he pussyfoots around and says, 'let's table that for a moment,' and then he goes on. Do you know what these boys have been looking for, for ten fucking years?"

"No," Sam answered.

"Well I'll tell you what. They picked up fifty million dollars in the wholesale value of cocaine and heroin, and now the information they have shows that another fifty million dollars of this drug shit is still missing. You got that? Ten years ago, they figure they lost fifty million dollars of cocaine and heroin, now they want to question me about what the fuck happened. Did you get that?"

"Yeah, I got that. So how did it end?"

"I got done there at six o'clock. I hit the first pay phone I could find and called you. I go back tomorrow morning at eight. We go on for, I don't know, for how long."

"Have you ever talked to a guy named Lupson Deland?"

"The head guy? No. Never met him. I'm only good enough for the cookie-cutter guy."

"Okay, we just be patient and keep our eyes and ears open."

"I worry about you. I can handle me with no problem."

"Thanks for the information. You go out in what, around two weeks?"

"Sixteen days. I pick up my forty-year pin, turn in my gun and my badge, and then it's *hasta luego* for me. And my wife thinks we just sold our house."

"You sound good. Be patient and hold tight. I'll see you soon."

Four blocks away, near the river, Eddie Marshall had parked his car and stood outside of the vehicle, observing the front of the Café du Monde. He was dressed in a casual brown jacket with no wig or makeup. He appeared to be a Joe Average type of guy. He was waiting for Sally. It was now almost eleven, and she wasn't going to show. Eddie was upset.

He got into his car, the five-year-old white Volvo station wagon, the one with the rust stain on the front left fender, and drove past the restaurant. He drove slowly, peering inside, trying to spot Sally. Then he angrily accelerated the car, and moved on toward Barracks. He turned left, heading west.

Eddie passed Sam's apartment just as Sam was using his key to open the front gate. Sam could hear the car passing, but he didn't look back. Eddie saw a man opening the gate, but he wasn't concerned with him. There was only a ten foot distance between the two men as Eddie drove on to Dauphine Street and made a left, heading for Canal.

Sam walked back into his dark apartment. He went directly into his office and threw a switch, which activated or disconnected his telephone. All was now quiet, and he found some peace with the world. He started to leave the room, except he had not checked all of the phone messages of the day. He pushed the start button and heard the previous call from Mays. Then there were several miscellaneous messages, and finally one from Kelly.

"Hi Sam, this is Kelly. Well, I bought a car, and then I got a cell phone. My Cell phone number is 555-3126. I'm at this number whenever you're lonely or need anything. I'll call you at the office tomorrow. Love ya. Bye."

For now, Sam's life was complete. All of his business was done, and Kelly was somewhere where she could be reached. It was too late to call her now, tomorrow would be fine. He stripped off his clothes and fell into bed. Tomorrow would also be a good day to deal with the Bill Mays issue.

As he closed his eyes, he thought about the Skannes trial. Sam completed his testimony last Friday, and Mosley had more action to do today. He wanted to know how it was all going. He wanted to know when the jury would be sent away to mediate the outcome. He wanted to know what the verdict would be. Tomorrow he would ask Wally to check it all out.

Chapter 13

DAY 6, CONTINUED.

EDDIE DROVE HIS Volvo out of the quarter, crossing Canal and turning left on Poydras. Three minutes earlier he had passed Sam Pennington entering the gate of his apartment on Barracks St. They both did not notice one another. Eddie was upset with Sally. She had stood him up.

"Why did she do that?!" he screamed to himself out loud. "She knew she had a date with me! She fucking well knew it!"

Eddie was now on Poydras and pulled up to stop for a red light at St. Charles. He noticed another car that pulled up to his left. The driver, a man, was watching him curiously. Eddie stopped talking to himself, glared at the man for a second, and when the light turned green, pushed ahead for a block and turned right on Decatur.

He had already gotten too close to the cops. Perhaps it was best that Sally did not meet him on this night. It might be better for him to go into hiding for a while. He had already destroyed the Kroman driver's license, and had believed he was safe from any additional police interference. Eddies brain was now moving in waves of paranoia. As he drove, he thought of Ralph Buckley, the serial killer who wound up as Eddie's hero.

"What would Ralph have done in this situation?" Eddie thought. "I've played games with the cops and almost got caught. Now it's time to cool it. I shouldn't have gone to see Sally. No way. And I've been driving this car too long. Somebody may have already spotted it. The cops are out looking for me in this car!"

Eddie looked into his rear view mirror, trying to spot his hypothetical tail. He quickly drove around the block, pausing in an open parking area, and then around the block again. He found himself clear of any police interference.

He was now in the industrial section of the city, an area of some renewal development over the past years. He passed Emeril Lagasse's very popular restaurant on the corner, and moved on up to Tchoupitoulas Street. There in the middle of the block was a three story dilapidated structure, built in the late 1800s, that had been vacant for the past fifteen years. On the top floor, its final occupant had been a manufacturing factory for Mardi Gras T-Shirts, beads, and plastic cups, with the two lower floors constructing cheap, put-this-stuff-together-for-yourself furniture. When the furniture company went bust, the T shirts beads and cups went out also. Now the building belonged to Eddie.

FLASHBACK

Eddie had purchased the building five years earlier when he first arrived in New Orleans. He paid one million, two hundred thousand in cash, for the structure. It now looked no better or worse than the day he bought it. Eddie was not one to improve on anything.

He reached behind his sun visor, removed a garage door opener and pushed the button. A side single-car parking door opened into the night, and Eddie's car slipped inside. The door closed and he was once again safe from the nastiness of the outside community.

It was dark inside. Eddie left his car and slowly made his way to the private elevator at the right side of the building. The structure had large service elevators at the opposite side, but they no longer were in working condition. He entered the small passenger elevator and pushed the button to the top floor. He left the elevator on the third floor and walked into a dark room. The city lights streamed in from the street below. He threw the light switch on, revealing the entire room.

It was truly quite beautiful. After all, it was designed by a man who for ten years had managed his father's business. All four walls were painted red. There was an ornate, king-sized bed against the back wall. It was a handsome unit with gold trim, an antique four-poster, with style. It was finished off with a rose colored lacquer that was hand-buffed, just to give it that antique look. Just to the left of the bed area was an antique gold door which led to a posh, red-colored bathroom with gold fixtures on the sink, toilet and shower.

To the right of this area was the kitchen with all of the required accoutrements. The cabinets were installed by a professional. Eddie didn't want to try that one himself. They were also finished in red. The kitchen floor was also professionally covered in vinyl. It was also covered in the same shade of red.

The living room was located just before the elevator with a graceful selection of couches, tables and chairs, that would provide any home in the country a medal for good taste. All of those items had been manufactured in North Carolina, and the high lacquered gold finished items from Nuevo Laredo, Mexico.

Originally the ceiling was twenty-five feet high. Eddie did this one himself. It took him a month to finish the job. He bought three hundred twenty eight squares, of an antiqued tin stamped ceiling, displaying the design of the Olympic wreath in the center. They were beautiful. Painted in gold, with an antique lacquer finish, he hung them up on a grid he created out of wood strips. The strips were held secure by running wire from the tin squares to the original ceiling.

Then there was the final magic: well-chosen paintings and other artwork, along with green plants and bushes, well placed to give the room that perfect designer look. Even the floors were of hard pine, covered with Middle Eastern throw rugs.

This was the area where Eddie had committed his crimes. It was here that he murdered Penelope Andrews, and the second girl, named Carla Owens, who still remained in Division 8 of the New Orleans Police Department under the name of Jane Doe # 2. And finally, Beth Hayden was murdered here. It was also here that he had planned to murder Sally at a later date. At the time, he didn't even know her last name. But there were so may other women who had had been murdered by this insane man of misguided power.

Eddie walked into the kitchen, took a beer from the fridge and popped the cap. As he sipped the beer, he noted that he was standing before the red kitchen cabinets with the matching red linoleum flooring. The blood red color was not by design but rather due to necessity. When you beat many women to death with your aluminum Little League baseball bat, let their blood not show on the cabinets walls or floor.

Then Eddie walked to a hidden door at the right side of the room. One could not see the hinges or the seams of the door. He leaned on the wall and there was a clicking sound. When he released his pressure the door popped open. He threw a light switch on and entered into his actual living area. It was a huge room which ran the entire width and length of the building, excluding where he had built his fancy red apartment.

The entire area was lit by a string of florescent lights. The room was bright and you could see every detail of how this man had lived for the last five years. It was in direct contrast to the beautiful red room, the absolute garbage pail he was now standing in.

The Mardi Gras bead manufacturer went bankrupt some fifteen years ago. They sold all of their machinery that had any value and left what they couldn't dispose. As a result, the room was filled with a mess of unusable things, bags of beads, sewing machines that didn't work, bolts of cotton cloth used to make t-shirts, a photograph section with paint and printing devices used to print out messages and pictures on their t-shirts. Eddie had used this area and available equipment to manufacture his fake picture of Alex Kroman's driver's license.

In the nineteen hundreds, the owner had built two women's and men's bathrooms in the back corner near the steps that led up to the roof top. The bathrooms were filthy. They looked like a toilet in the back of a cheap car repair place, with sinks full of black grease that had been lodged there for over a century.

Eddie had replaced the commode in the men's room, along with the sink. That was five years before when he purchased the building. Since then, nothing had been cleaned.

There were clothing racks strewn all over the place. His socks and shorts and shirts were placed in old broken cardboard boxes. They sat on the floors in various locations thought the room.

Finally there was a facsimile of a kitchen. A large open sink built onto the wall, an old beat-up refrigerator, a wooden counter with open shelving above, and no stove or oven. He cooked on three hot plates. They were plugged into a series of extension cords that ran across the room from various master electrical plug in units. The place had the feeling of a Chinese fire drill, one that made a temporary connection but could result in a massive fire should something fail.

Then there was his makeup area, located in a deserted corner of the large room. It contained his grease paint, wigs, and all the other stuff actors wear. Beside the kitchen counter was his bed. It was large, a king sized unit, covered with a stack of single-sized grey colored bed blankets. No one could tell if or when this bed had ever been made. Eddie lived in this place like a hermit, a man who only had one goal in life: to murder the whores of New Orleans.

Day 6, continued

Eddie finally arrived in his apartment. It was now close to midnight. He walked through the majestic red room, and walked to a wall at the left side of the room, pushed at the wall, and an inside latch popped open. He then grabbed at a shelf and pulled a hidden door open.

He walked into a cavernous semi-dark area. He followed toward the direction of florescent lights, beaming from a room toward the end of the hallway. This room was Eddie's sleeping quarters. There was a large unmade king sized bed against the far wall. The place had the look of a semi-deserted room, where a homeless person had broken into and had lived in rubble free of charge for at least ten years.

Eddie was tired. He removed his shoes and clothing and flopped down onto the bed. He picked up a large electrical switch box. He pushed the number one switch to the on position, and his bedside light lit. He pushed the number two switch off, and the fluorescent ceiling lights went off. He stumbled into bed, and slept soundly for the next twelve hours.

Day 7

It was Tuesday, March 7th. Eddie went down to the ground floor where he had three cars parked. He concentrated his efforts on the white Volvo with the rust-stained left front fender. He carefully cut and pasted paper over every exposed chrome fitting and window glass area. This was the prep time, and it took almost three hours to do it right.

Then he hooked up his professional air pressure paint rig, the same type of rig that Kelly would be using to paint Sam's boat, and carefully sprayed a dark green paint to cover the white. It turned out beautifully, and Eddie stood tall.

Flashback

Eddie was twelve years old, and after his mother's death, life with his father was perfect. He was basically living alone with no interference from anyone. His dad hired a woman to clean the house and cook the meals. Her name was Miss Betty. She started at nine and left at five in the evening, leaving food for the evening dinner, in the warm up oven. Eddie ate his dinner, his father seldom did.

Eddie never said a word to Miss. Betty. As he best recalled, she had never even heard his voice. That's how Eddie liked things to work. If every one would simply leave him alone, to do as he wished, all around him would have a peaceful existence. Even he and his father had little to talk about.

After his mother's funeral, he noted his dad had become filled with such remorse over the loss of his wife that he started drinking heavily. His dad had always been into booze, but now it had developed into a bad habit, sleeping until one in the afternoon and arriving home after three in the morning.

And there was always the library. Eddie could now study every book in the place, with no remorse over who saw what, and who cared about what he was reading. Ralph Barkley, the man who had become a serial killer murdering eighteen young women, became a hero of Eddie's life. Barkley had been in jail for eight years, during which time his attorneys staged a massive amount of various plea bargains in an attempt for their client to avoid death in the electric chair. On July 14th, Ralph Barkley lost his final plea, and he was finally electrocuted on July 25th, 1975.

It was a bad day for Eddie. He would devote as much time as necessary to ensure the fact that he would never make the same mistakes Ralph had made. His mother was only a test case; well-done but not perfect.

When Eddie was sixteen he suspected his dad had a mistress, but even that didn't bother him. He checked into his high school and was given a paper for his father to sign. This was for him to acknowledge report cards, meetings with the teacher, or PTA gatherings. Eddie simply forged his father's signature and left him out of the loop. He knew that was the best thing to do.

At eighteen, he went to "Ole Miss" for two years of a liberal arts education and finally for two more years of Business Accounting. His father insisted on the accounting thing. It was really the only subject they had spoken about. When that was finished, his dad preferred he come to work at his factory. Eddie was depressed at the thought, but his father had paid all his bills with no question. When Eddie asked for a few hundred here, or a thousand there, it was always given. Now, he didn't have much choice in the matter. For the next ten years, he did his job at the mail order business. He worked in a small back office with three other people, figuring out what this small chair should cost, and how much that coffee table should sell for. In addition, Eddie, using what he learned at Ole Miss, was quickly able to figure what his father had made in this modest business. In fact, his dad was the king of catalogue sales in southeast America. He would ship his goods from Florida, all the way west to the Texas panhandle and from Louisiana, north to Kentucky. His dad knew the people, their likes and dislikes. Good and cheap, with a look of class.

His father had developed a small fortune. The house in which they lived was on a two acre parcel of land, with a value of some seventy thousand dollars. This was Mississippi property, a poor state. Most other states would value this land at 1.3 million, give or take. He also had investments and cash, which collectively came to 1.8 million.

Then there was the factory and all its holdings. With his finest pen in hand, Eddie calculated everything would sell for at least the total value of Jeff Marshall's life, around six million dollars. Eddie decided it might be time to kill his father.

But the thought of another family murder brought Eddie back into reality. His mind drifted through all of the various configurations of the crime scene he would create, but none of them worked out. They all had too many holes. The biggest one being: mom and dad murdered and their kid sitting in his room with a smile on his face.

His father died at the age of 58. He had consumed about a half gallon of booze a day for the past 10 years, since the day his wife was murdered by a burglar. His death was caused by liver problems, along with other complications, that Eddie did not wish to even remotely understand. He took his dad's passing with casual interest.

He cremated his father's body and took charge of the ashes, which he placed in a urn and left unceremoniously on the living room mantle for all to appreciate. Next, he swiftly closed out all of the family belongings.

The six million dollars for the business was finally sold to a man from Charleston, South Carolina, for a down payment of two million, with payoffs of five hundred thousand each year for the next four years.

But Eddie didn't care about the rest of the money. Forget about it. He had enough money to accomplish what he wanted to do. He could have sold the store for two million bucks and just forgotten the payment of the balance of another four million. He would never again even contact this person to collect his money! He sold the house to a guy from Mississippi, who wanted to move up in stature. Eddie gave him a good deal: five hundred thousand, as is!

Finally, he collected his dad's cash. His father was not in the stock market, just the cash market. He had around two hundred thousand stashed in his bedroom safe, another six hundred thousand divided in four banks, including one in Nuevo Laredo, Mexico, one in Jackson, Mississippi, and two more in Leesville. That left Eddie with three million, eight hundred thousand dollars.

But that also left Eddie with the taxes. He would have to pay inheritance tax: fifty percent of everything to the government. *Not so*, thought Eddie. He packed up his car with all of his personal belongings, including his favorate aluminum Little League baseball bat, and the $3,800,000 dollars he collected from his father. That was correct. Eddie had three million eight hundred thousand dollars in his car with him. He never intended to pay a single tax for anything. It all belonged to him.

He had covered his tracks well. Everything about Eddie was phony. He left an address and phone number to the man who bought his dad's business. He told him if there was ever a problem, he could call. He gave him a phony number. Eddie did not expect a call.

The guy owed Eddie another four million to be paid off in eight years. But for Eddie, to even be concerned with that money would mean the buyer would have to send him a check! Eddie didn't want the money, and he wanted no one to ever find him! He wanted to be left alone! Eddie wished to perform his sick style of life with no interference from anybody!

At six forty-five on Sunday morning, Eddie finished loading his final belongings into the Volvo. There was some space left for a few things on the top. So he opened the garage and took whatever tools his father had that could be of service to him. That included a standard shovel, a pick, an ax, and a large bolt cutter. This bolt cutter had the power to cut through a chain link fence. It wasn't that he felt he would ever need one of those, it just might have looked good displayed on his shelf, but he decided to bring it anyway.

He drove off in the morning fog, heading out of Leesville with no one in the world knowing where he was going. There was no track to his life, no person to find him late for an appointment, or too early for a meal. He rolled the window down and felt the fresh, cold air as it drifted through his vehicle. No one would ever again tell Eddie how to do anything.

Eddie was driving on the 59 highway, just south town, when he turned onto the I-10. A half hour later he was coming in to Slidell, Louisiana. He had already crossed the Pearl River and would soon be crossing a small, short portion of Lake Pontchartrain. Twenty minutes from that, he would be able to see New Orleans. But just as he was about to cross into the Big Easy, something to his right caught his eye.

Eddie noted there was a large green area, possibly swamp land, located near an off-ramp. How could he get there? And where the off ramp was located, was yet another question. But Eddie needed to check it out. He was looking for something special.

He managed to find a turn around, and then a second one, and found his way now heading back to New Orleans. He was in the right lane, driving under the speed limit at thirty-five. Then he saw the exit. It was hard to notice if you hadn't been there before.

Eddie took it off and moved slowly down the service road. It was now a quarter to eight and traffic was still quiet on this early Sunday morning. The freeway was just to his left. It was almost as though he was standing on the shoulder. Then on his right there was a six foot high chain link fence with an old gate, about fifty feet down the road.

He parked his car just before the gate, left his vehicle and looked around. There was something about this area that had a magical feeling. It was as though someone from up above said to Eddie, "This is the spot."

The gate had a padlock, securing an old rusted chain that was wrapped several times around the gate posts. Eddie walked back to his car, withdrew his dad's bolt cutter, proceeded to pop the gate lock and gain entrance to the field beyond. It was fate that made him bring the bolt cutter.

He crossed over a small hill, which led him down into a large meadow. As he walked, the sound of cars on the freeway all but disappeared. Just in front of him he could see Lake Pontchatrain. The lake was so big you could drive on a long bridge over the Causeway, and when in the center of the bridge, not see land from either side.

Eddie found himself in a strange place, a spot where he was the only person to be aware of a home to put to rest his children of the devil.

DAY 7, CONTINUED

It was Tuesday, March 7th. Sam awoke at six-thirty a.m. He felt amazingly refreshed. What he needed to do was go about business as usual. He took a quick shower and shave and arrived at his office by eight o'clock. Wally was already there, with coffee brewed and hot.

Sam sat at his desk and drew up a quick list of things that needed to be accomplished.

1. Take care of Kelly. Make sure she's okay. Give her a key
2. Check on the Skannes trial. Keep me advised.
3. How about my car?
4. Is everything now straight with our Serial Killer?
5. Take care of Mays and the Internal Affairs unit.
6. Make sure Eduardo is moving ahead. Advise he may quickly be starting the Police Benevolent Society of America.
7. Check on Hironee Jessup.

As Sam continued to write, Frick and Frack interrupted as they entered the room.

"What's with the serial?" Sam asked to anyone with an answer.

George stepped forward, pulling a pad from his jacket. "Got a list of volunteers from the office here, along with Rampart. Got fifteen good old boys to take turns on Bourbon Street. They sit in shifts in a bar for two hours, drink nothing but Cokes, an' watch the bimbos try to dance. The street is covered. When Fat Boy shows up, and he will, we nail him. David and I will be on constant vehicle patrol."

"Okay, that's good. Wally, I need you to stay in touch with the court, the Skannes trial."

"I'm on it," Wally answered. "Called the court yesterday. Right now the defense is starting with his witnesses. Take about two more days."

"That's good. Real good," Sam checked over his list. "I'll need my car. Some personal business."

"Ah, that's a problem," Wally turned from the Mr. Coffee machine. "I got the window fixed yesterday afternoon. But it's going to take till

Thursday for the carpet."

"What's the problem with the carpet?" George asked.

"It's not llama," Wally stated. "We finally tracked down some chocolate brown Llama from a dealer in Boise, Idaho. It'll be in late tomorrow, and the boys will lay it in." Wally looked over at Sam. "Sam, you can take my car if you like."

Sam ignored that comment and called Kelly's new cell phone. It rang four times and she answered.

"Hello, this is Kelly. How are you doing today?"

"Hey there."

"Sam, is that you?"

"One and the same."

"Oh Sam, it's nice to hear your voice."

"Where are you?"

"I'm at the boat. I came down yesterday to give the boys some lunch and spent the night. It's beautiful– the boat I mean. We painted the entire hull with a spray rig, all with a white base coat, and we're putting on the second coat now. Maybe Wednesday we can start the finish coat. An' Pedro's almost finished installing the cables for the TV system. It comes in crystal clear. Wait till you see it."

"I've got some stuff to take care of here today. Maybe I can get there tonight."

"How do you feel?" she asked.

"I feel great, and I love you and miss you."

Sam thought about her last statement. She was there for him, helping out as best she could. He never once accused her of talking too much. He now loved the sound of her voice, and the excitement she displayed in what she was doing.

"When are you coming back into town?" Sam asked.

"If I'm going to stay here for awhile, I need to get back to my apartment tonight and get some clothes. Do you think you could make it here?"

"I don't know for sure. Got a lot of stuff happening."

"Okay. Maybe we could meet at the Dixieland?"

"That's an idea. That would work out. What time do you plan to get there?"

"I didn't plan. I could call Leonard and tell him I could come in and do my song."

"What song?"

"'Bill Bailey.' I sing it at the start of every set. Five nights a week. I always wanted you to catch it but you were never there when I did it."

"What time would you start tonight?"

"First set is seven o'clock."

"Okay, I'll be there at seven."

"That would be great. I'll see you at seven."

"If I'm not there, I had a problem."

"What problem?"

"I'm a cop. Cops always have problems."

"Gotcha. I understand. When we next get in bed, I'll sit on your chest and sing the song then."

"That sounds like a good idea. I'll add it to my list of tricks."

Sam hung up the phone and next placed a call to Hironee Jessup, but there was no answer. He thought he might stop by and see her, check if she was alright.

Sam's next cell call was to Eduardo, who was parked in the service area in front of Jackson Square.

"Hello, Eduardo speaking."

"Eduardo, are you on Charters?"

Eduardo quickly recognized Sam's voice. "Hey there! Yes, I'm here. Waiting to go to work."

"I'll be walking up to you in about five minutes. When you see me, pull on down the street and pick me up."

As Sam left the office, he grabbed two Creamy Puff doughnuts from the coffee area and stuffed them into both of his two front coat pockets. He walked over to Charters Street and turned left, heading down to the Cathedral. He saw Eduardo in the distance and waved at him. Eduardo clicked the reins on Piccolo's back, the mule kicked into gear and started down Charters toward Sam.

The animal immediately recognized Sam and pulled over for a stop directly in front of him, nuzzling his mouth against the front of his crisp clean black shirt. Sam gave him a pop with his hand, right on the nose.

"It's not nice to be a nudge," Sam said. He reached his hand into his coat pocket and offered the mule a doughnut. But Piccolo was not one to be worried about a flick in the nose, and was more into a treat from the street offered by an old friend. Sam hopped into the carriage, sat riding backwards in the front seat, just behind Eduardo.

"My cleaning bill is getting out of hand," Sam said.

"Tell me about it."

When Eduardo spoke, his accent had diminished greatly. His English was all but perfect. He was indeed a man of letters.

"Go down about three blocks and turn right to Bourbon, go to a building about a block up I want you to see."

Sam had now gotten Eduardo's interest. "So what's happening? You have something happening?"

"I think we are about to move into stage two."

"That quick?"

"Yep."

Eduardo turned right on Bourbon and headed up about half way through the quarter. Then Sam directed him to "park" at the end of the block. There was a refurbished building on the corner which had once been a home, or and office, three stories high. It was painted soft yellow with dark green trim for the shutters and doors. A sign was hanging on the right front door: "Legal Office," and another sign of the left side advertising "For Rent."

Sam leaned in close to Eduardo. "I figure they have about eight rooms on each of the top two floors. Hard to tell for sure from here. We would have a separate entrance, and it looks like parking in the back. See if you can reach the man."

"You got it."

As Eduardo took his cell phone in hand and dialed the number, Sam moved from the carriage and went to the corner to check the side of the building. The workers did a beautiful job finishing the exterior. He noted that the molding on the glass windows were painted a bright red, which gave the building a third dimension. Sam then returned to Eduardo and Piccolo.

The door to the legal office opened, and a young man in his late twenties to early thirties came out. His name was Frank Fletcher, a young attorney, just setting up practice in New Orleans.

"Hello. Are you Mr. Sanchez?" Fletcher was directing his comment at Sam, who then glanced over at Eduardo. Sam never anticipated they would find themselves in an embarrassing situation. There was Eduardo, wearing his high top hat, along with his black frock coat with formal pleated tails that hung down to his ankles. Eduardo was being pulled along by a mule, while they were there to make a deal on a new office.

Sam had never thought when Eduardo made his phone call the man they wanted to deal with would be stepping out of this front office door. He had felt they might make an appointment and both arrive later, properly dressed for the occasion.

"No sir, I'm not," Sam answered. "My name is Sam Pennington. I represent Mr. Sanchez. That's Mr. Sanchez, over there."

Fletcher looked over at Sanchez, and Sanchez waved back.

"Mr. Sanchez is a bit of an eccentric," Sam said. "Are you from New Orleans?"

"No."

"Well then, in New Orleans we have many eccentrics. Have you ever heard of the Duck Lady?"

"No."

"Well there you go." Sam turned back to Eduardo, who was making his way down from the carriage.

"Alright, Mr. Sanchez." Sam said with enthusiasm, "We can see the office now."

The three men went inside and looked at both top floors. There was an old elevator in the back. It had been completely reconditioned and, while slow, it did the lifting well. Each of the two upper floors had some furniture, but they would need more. The rooms were large and well painted. Eduardo liked what he saw, and Sam was pleased also. Sam mentally figured what the price might be for both floors and he concluded it to be around three thousand dollars per month.

They started heading down the stairs, opting not to use the elevator. That would later be used to haul a massive amount of furniture into the offices.

"What kind of law do you people practice?" Sam asked.

"I do real estate law, two of my partners handle criminal. Our forth partner is a CPA, but he hopes to pass the bar in eight months."

"Where do you come from?"

"Texas. Houston."

"Well, we're glad to see Texas come to Louisiana." They hit the second floor, and Sam continued. "So what are you charging for the two floors?"

"We'll need two thousand five hundred for both. We've got parking for a total of eight cars in the back."

"That's a bit high for us. Mr. Sanchez represents a non-profit organization. He's been in business for six years, and now he's ready to prepare the organization to move some money to the right people. I was thinking of around two thousand might do the trick."

Fletcher was still apprehensive. He had never seen a deal to be closed so fast. "I have some questions for you to fill out in my office. Bank accounts, business dealings and so forth. Why don't you two come on in and we can…"

Sam interrupted as they hit the first floor and headed for the front door. "Mr. Sanchez, do you have a company check book?" Sam asked.

"Yes I do." Eduardo reached into his jacket pocket and pulled out a small plastic book of checks.

The three men moved out onto the street, and paused at the side of the carriage. Sam moved to Piccolo, reached into his coat pocket, and provided him with another Creamy Puff Doughnut, which he ate with great delight.

"Here's what we do," Sam said. "Mr. Sanchez, write out a check to this man for twelve thousand dollars. That will cover the first and last, and a security deposit, and then some months of rent included. You guys do the final figures."

Eduardo laid the checkbook down on the fender of the carriage and started to write a check.

"And give him a business card from the bank. Mr. Sanchez banks at Hibernia, just across Canal."

"Yes, we bank there too, Fletcher offered.

"That's good. And Mr. Sanchez, do you also have a card from the lady who handles accounts?"

Eduardo was becoming smug now. He knew well what was happening. He knew Sam was hustling Fletcher. It was only a matter of time before he offered to tell Fletcher he was a police detective.

"Yes, I have the check written, and here is the lady's card. Her name is Maria Sandoval."

"Yes, I know her, Fletcher added. "She also helps me with our account."

Sam quickly jumped in. "Well there you go. So you take this check, and call the bank, and get Ms. Sandoval on the line, and ask here if this check is good, and what the rating is regarding this account. She will tell you the check will clear immediately and the account is considered 100%. You of course know what that means?"

"Yes I do," Fletcher responded.

Eduardo climbed into the front of the carriage, Sam held back on the street.

"We'll have a lot of business to do, and we'll need some legal advice," Sam stated. "That may help you sell us to your partners. Here's my card. I'm a detective with the New Orleans Police Department. I operate out of Division 8, a block and a half from here, over on Royal. You and I are neighbors."

Sam climbed up into the carriage, and sat on the front seat near Eduardo. "So go talk to your partners, let's make a deal," Sam added. "Draw up some paperwork for us to sign. Then call Mr. Sanchez on his cell phone." Eduardo held his phone up high for Fletcher to see. "Or call me at the precinct," Sam gave him the thumbs up signal. "Let's ride, Mr. Sanchez."

Eduardo snapped the reigns on Piccolo's ass and they moved on up Bourbon.

Fletcher screamed at Sam, "What's the name of your company?"

"We're the Police Benevolent Association of America, Incorporated. Ask Mrs. Sandoval about it. She'll tell you what we do and where we get our money. Let's do some business."

It was the strangest meeting Frank Fletcher had ever had.

Sam was back in his office and started doing the things that cops do. They were always short-handed. With a bunch of detectives patrolling Bourbon Street, he and Wally had to fill in the paper work on other cases they never had a chance to handle. Wally handed Sam a stack of phone messages, at the top of the list was a call from the Internal Affairs.

"They want to know if you could drop by to see them at 11 o'clock tomorrow morning. They said it was just to review the file."

"Call them back. Find out which file they are planning to review. Tell them I wish to be prepared with the review of my file. Ask them what file I should bring. Tell them after I know what file they wish to review, I will first review said file, to make sure it is properly ready for review. Then tell them I'm out on assignment, and will call them back."

"And if they ask about 11 o'clock tomorrow?"

"Then tell them I will have to review tomorrow's assignment book. I'll call them back tomorrow morning."

"I think that will work just fine," Wally stated.

"Well, there you go."

At four o'clock, a hand delivered message came into Sam from Division 2 over on Rampart. It was from Mays. He and Mays had never corresponded by message before. It had always been on the secret phone hook up. Now it was different. He opened the envelope and read:

Meet me tonight at the jogging track at the Moon Walk. I'll be there from 10 to 10:30. I'll be wearing my sweat suit, you should do the same. If you can't make it, I'll call you at home starting at 11, then we'll get to another phone.

EAT THIS TRANSMISSION!

B. J. M.

Sam smiled at Bill's attempt at humor, but now Sam started to get serious. Mays was having problems with Internal Affairs. Now he had also just gotten a phone call from them.

"Wally," Sam called out.

"Yes."

"Cancel that last message to the IA. Call them and tell them eleven o'clock will be fine."

"You got it."

Sam tried the phone again, and still got no answer. "Gotta go Wally. See you later."

Sam walked five blocks to Hironee Jessup's house. It was located near Rampart, on Bienville, and knocked on the door. There was some movement inside, but then it got quiet. He knocked again, then called out through the door. "Ms. Jessup, this is Sam Pennington. I'm the cop that sent you home yesterday morning. This is not official business. I just wanted to know how you were doing."

At least a minute passed and the door slowly opened. The shutters remained latched. Sam could only get a glimpse of the figure that stood on the other side. Hironee wore no makeup, and looked as though she were ready to die. She was no longer the fast-talking woman who might challenge everything you asked her.

Hello," she said softly. "What you want?"

"I just wanted to know if you were okay?"

"You wanna have sex with me?"

"No. No sex."

"Okay then. I'll see you later." She started to close the door, then finally recognized Sam's face. "Oh yeah, you the cop. What you wanna do, beat on my body again?"

"Listen, if you need some help, if you want to get into a program, I can help. Just let me know."

"Oh yeah, you the do-good cop."

"Yeah, that's me. Here, take my card. If you ever need any help, just call this number. Okay?"

"Sure."

She looked like a wasted waif, a person who had had too much, and now the drugs and booze were taking their toll. Sam turned and walked away, and the door slowly closed.

At five minutes to seven, Sam walked into the Dixieland. There was a crowd standing on the street, and the place was almost full. Red and his boys were on the stage setting up for the first set. Red spotted Sam and waved him a hello. Sam smiled and waved back.

Sam found an empty stool at the bar, and ordered the usual from Leonard. Sam felt alone for the first time in many years. Perhaps he should set up a poker game for this Thursday; then again, perhaps not. There was a drum downbeat and Red Moon and his Dixieland boys broke out with their opening number, 'Do You Know What it Means to Miss New Orleans.'

Sam began tapping his foot with the music, and suddenly it all started again. It may have been the live Jazz, or the song they played, or the drink that Leonard served him. But whatever it was, by the end of that song, Sam was back to normal and loving every minute of it. Then Kelly came out.

Sam had never seen his girl look so beautiful. She still wore her black and red waitress outfit, and her hair was dressed in the same fashion. She had no special makeup on, and still had that same dynamite sweet smile. Whatever she changed did the trick for Sam.

As she climbed the stairs to the bandstand, Red made the introduction. "Ladies and Gentlemen, may I present our first lady of song, Miss Kelly Lee."

The crowd applauded with enthusiasm. Kelly took the microphone in hand and proceeded to knock them dead. Sam was amazed at what he saw. She was a pro, great voice, and the talent to sell the number. Then on her second and final go around, she turned and looked directly at Sam.

"'Won't you come home, Bill Bailey, won't you come home. I've been waiting all night long.'" It was like the night they went to her apartment. That was six days ago. A lot had happened in six short days.

Kelly continued with the song. "'I'll do the cooking honey, pay all the rent. I know I've done you wrong.'"

Sam's body felt like someone had hooked it up to a 220 power line. He sat mesmerized as she continued to work the crowed, but always looking at him directly in the eyes.

"'Remember that crazy evening I threw you out, with nothing but a fine tooth comb?'"

Sam started breathing heavily. He crosses and then re crossed his legs. He had not had this feeling for a woman since he was a kid.

"I know I'm to blame, it's a low down dirty shame, Bill Bailey, won't you please come home."

The crowd erupted with cheers, as Kelly left the stage and crossed through the room to Sam.

"Hi," she said.

"Hi," he answered. "Can you take a little break and come home with me?"

"Yes I can."

They left the Dixieland and moved swiftly up Bourbon. Their hunger for each other's body did not wane for a moment. As they entered the living room they both starting removing their clothing. Like teenagers, they scurried into the bedroom. Sam pulled the bed open with one violent toss of the top sheet, and Kelly fell back onto the center of the bed. There was no foreplay here, just the real thing.

Sam fell onto her, and Kelly reached her first orgasm the instant he penetrated her body. She had no recollection of how many orgasms she had, they all came together as a huge mass of total pleasure. Then it was over.

They lay side by side for over ten minutes, neither saying a word. Sam glanced at his watch. It was nine twenty. He moved from the bed to his side wall closet, took out his jogging clothes and started to dress.

"I gotta go meet a friend. Are you going back to the boat tonight?"

"Yes. I want to see the final color."

"Okay. Drive careful. Here's a key to the place, it also fits the gate out front. You're welcome here anytime you wish. *Mi casa es su casa*, if you get my drift. Over here I've emptied out another closet. Bring anything in you like. Stay as long as you want. Okay?"

"Okay Sam."

"And by the way, you did one hell of a song in there. I wouldn't mind your sitting on my chest and doing it again."

Sam left for the Moon Walk, and Kelly felt wonderful.

Chapter 14

THE EVENING OF DAY 7, CONTINUED.

IT WAS HERE on the Moon Walk that you got your first great view of the river. It was beautiful, and at night it was an amazing sight to see. A streetcar ran between where you stood and the river. It traveled from uptown to the end of the line at Esplanade Avenue. To your front was the mighty Mississippi and to the right, the two steel bridges that made up the Crescent City Connection, connecting New Orleans to the West Bank.

Sam was wearing his jogging clothes with white tennis shoes. He checked his watch, confirming it was just past ten. He walked down to the river. Sam didn't look for Bill Mays. Mays had already seen him, if he was there. There was no need to look around, that might draw attention to him. Just play it straight, just go jogging.

Sam moved across the streetcar tracks, and headed for the walking/jogging level. He could turn right and head uptown toward the Hilton Hotel, or turn left and go back down to Barracks street. He opted to go left. If Mays did not catch him, Sam would be heading for home, and they would make a later contact.

Sam reached the walkway, turned left and started a slow jog towards home. A moment later he heard a voice from behind him.

"Sam. Hey Sam, hold it up. It's me."

Sam came to a stop and turned around, spotting Mays coming up from behind him. Mays was also wearing jogging clothes that fit too tight around his middle, and he wore a sweat band. He looked like a middle-aged gentleman, wearing jogging clothes that might better be worn by a teenager.

Sam moved over to a bench at the side of the path, and sat down. Mays joined him, breathing heavily. They sat quietly for a moment. Mays was apprehensive, looking around. He then casually rested his head in his hand, subtly hiding his mouth as he spoke.

"I got some new news," Mays said. "I had my meeting with the cookie cutter, Roger Gentry. It's getting more complicated than I thought. He's the guy with Internal Affairs."

Sam looked over at Mays. He noted his hand covering his face. "What are you doing with your face?"

"You ever see a football game?" Mays asked.

"Yeah."

"You ever see the coach hold up his play book, to cover his mouth?"

"Yeah."

"Well why do you suppose he does that?" May's queried.

"So as not to give his play away to the opposition?" Sam looked around the area, and saw no one nearby. He casually brought his hand to his head, relaxed into a comfortable position, and covered his mouth. "And you think the opposition is trying to steal our play?" Sam questioned.

"You never know," Mays casually answered.

"Okay, go ahead," Sam said. He would play this scenario out, as Mays wished. He only hoped it wouldn't take that long.

Mays kept his hand over his mouth. "We talked for an hour and a half, nothing really, just bullshit stuff. Then he finally hit me with, 'I suggest you don't leave town until we have resolved this situation.'"

Sam quickly sat upright. No more hand to his mouth. "What's that mean? What's 'resolve this situation?'"

Mays looked carefully around. No one stood nearby. He clasped his arms in front and casually leaned back into the bench. "I asked him that. He kept tap dancing. He said, 'your pension could be in jeopardy if you leave town.'"

"He said that?"

"Yes."

"Or you lose your pension?"

"Yeah, in jeopardy, something like that."

Sam sat quietly for a moment, then he started to smile. Mays looked at Sam, and a smile also crossed his face.

"So you're not really bothered about losing your pension?" Sam asked.

Mays just looked at Sam, drew his body up straight, and smiled again.

"Did he put anything in writing?" Sam asked.

"No. I was thinking of sending him a fax, asking him to do that."

"Don't do that now. Leave it alone. If he had anything concrete to say, he would have put it in writing. Just leave it alone. When it comes time for you to leave town, just send him a note. Something like, 'Dear Cookie Cutter. My wife and I are leaving for a well-earned extended vacation. I will call and report in as soon as I return. Wish you were here.'" Mays cracked up.

"What's with your house?" Sam asked.

"We finished the deal today. I've already shipped about everything we own. My agent told me we could sign the final papers in five to six days, max."

"Then you're outta here."

"I don't want to leave you here alone. I don't like the idea."

"Don't worry about me. I'm fine," Sam said.

"The thing is, Roger kept bringing you up. I don't know why."

"Okay, tell me about Roger. What's he look like, where is his office?"

"He's average. Everything about him is average. He's in a big tall building on Poydras. He's got a small office, one door, no windows."

"A cookie cutter office?" Sam asked.

"That's it. A small desk, two chairs, and a picture of his average wife and average kids hanging on the wall. But I'll tell you, the rest of the building is fantastic."

"When we last talked on the phone, I mentioned a guy named Lupson Deland."

"What about him? Is he after you?" Mays questioned.

"No."

"Okay, so much for Lupson Deland. Who the hell would ever give a name like that to a kid?"

"He runs the show at the IA," Sam said.

"So what?" Mays responded.

"Okay, that's fine," Sam said nothing about his meeting tomorrow with the Office of Internal Affairs. He figured it would only cause Mays more potential grief.

"I took Eduardo to look at an office today." Sam said. "He liked it, and so did I. We can have the two top floors for two thousand a month. I told Eduardo you'd have to approve, before he signed the lease."

"You think we oughta get a place now?"

"I think we need a place sooner rather than later. We've held this position for ten years. We now have almost five million in the account. I think it's time to get ready to do the deal."

"Okay, I'm for that."

"Go tomorrow, take a look at the office, and see if you like it. Nothing will happen there until you've left town. We then sign the lease, and let the chips fall where they may."

"I feel like I'm leaving a real problem behind me."

"You mean me? You think I'm a problem?" Sam asked.

"No, it's me. I'm the problem."

"You're the problem? What the hell did you do? There's almost five million United States currency in the Hibernia Bank of New Orleans, of which every dollar was donated by people from a foreign county. Now what I want to do is open an office and move that money around. That money has been dormant for a long time. You agree with that?"

"Yes."

"And you know there is more to come?"

"Yes."

"A lot more?"

"Yes."

"Then let's get ready to move the money."

When Sam got to his apartment, Kelly was gone. The place seemed empty without her. Sam got his first shot of loneliness. He had never indulged in the feeling before, but when she was there, he had another presence in the room beside himself. If he was working in his den, she was just around the corner. If he was out late, she might be asleep, but she was there nonetheless. He opened a fresh bottle of single malt scotch and poured a drink. Then he went to his bedroom.

The room was dark when he walked in and fought to find the TV channel selector. She had placed it under his pillow. As the TV warmed up he turned on the bedside lamp and saw her note.

When she left she turned down his side of the bed, wrote a note, and left it there with a small chocolate she found in a bowl in the dining room. Sam sat on the bed and opened the note.

Dear Sam,
I'm heading back to the boat and I have your keys hanging around my neck

with some string I found in the kitchen. When I do visit, I'll give you proper advance notice, just to let you know I'm coming.

As I understand, it's Wil's plan to try to put the boat in the water this Saturday or Sunday. Please try to be there. If it sinks, we're going to have to play taps.

I love you, Good Cop,

Kelly

Sam placed the letter in his bedside table. All he wanted was to offer an easy way of getting together, but she wanted to let him know when she was coming. Women always have a way to complicate the issue. Sam would think more of that tomorrow. He sat down of the edge of the bed and removed his shoes and socks, and his mind refocused on Bill Mays and what they went through ten years ago.

Flashback

It was actually twelve years earlier and Sam was still working on the apartment house on Barracks Street with Shandor. He still lived at the single room over on Toulouse Street, and he had even found time to repair the bathtub drain.

But at age twenty-eight, Sam took some stock on his position in life. He loved being a cop. His folder held three major civic police commendations, one of which he received for bravery beyond the call of duty. It was nothing really; he just saved three lives from a burning house, over on Governor Nichols Street.

Sam was driving through the French Quarter. It was late one morning and he was about to go off duty. Sam was alone in a prowl car, when he saw smoke and flames coming from a well kept residence near the center of Governor Nichols Street. It was close to three a.m., and the street was deserted. In Sam's mind it was like the start of the big Chicago fire when Mrs. O'Reilly's cow kicked over a candle. It all happened that quickly. With old antique houses, built so close together, a fire in one could create a major disaster in many. Sam went into action. He got on his car phone and put out an emergency call. Emergency responded: "We're on the way!" Then Sam ran to the house and kicked the front door open.

The living room was in flames, walls and ceiling were ablaze. But with all the fire, smoke was not a problem. Air was sucking the smoke out through the top of the house, but the heat of the blaze caused Sam to jump back.

Sam screamed out, "Is anyone in here! Fire, fire!" But there was no answer. He took a deep breath and ran through the living room toward a back hallway.

As he moved through the room he felt fire licking at his back. He quickly thought of turning back, but as he was now in the middle of the room, he decided the best of all reasons, was to forge forward.

When he reached the hallway, smoke became his problem. It was thick, and black, and darkness quickly blocked his vision. His eyes started to water, he felt smoke in his lungs and he thought perhaps this was not a good idea.

Then he felt a door to his right. He reached the handle and pushed it open. For a brief moment the bedroom was dark, but when the door opened it sucked fresh air inside. The room quickly filled with a flash fire blaze!

A woman lay on the bed. Sam didn't know if she were alive or dead. He grabbed her by the arms and pulled her up, bent his knees and placed her over his right shoulder. He carried her body into the hallway, took another deep breath of smoke, and ran for the front door.

The street was still quiet, except Sam could hear the sound of a fire truck siren, approaching in the distance. He laid the lady down on the sidewalk and she quickly came to. She was a white woman, about thirty-five years old.

"My children! Where are my children?"

Sam was now alone on the street, with the house on fire, and a woman was screaming for her kids.

"Ma'am, I'll go back in and get your children," Sam said. "How many are there?"

"There are two babies in the back! Oh God, please help them!"

"Yes Ma'am, I'll get them." Sam headed back to the front door, took another deep breath and ran through the storming fire, toward the back of the house. It was no longer the heat of the flames that bothered him, nor the smoke, nor the pain of his scorched skin. It now became a job that he had to do.

He could now hear children crying in the back bedroom. He followed the sound to the end of the hall and opened to door. It was dark inside, smoke filled the room.

Sam coughed and sputtered. "Okay kids, where are you!"

He stumbled through the bedroom and found a three-year-old boy standing in his crib, screaming for help. Sam grabbed the boy in his left arm and turned back for the door. Then he heard another voice: a girl also started screaming. Sam could not see her, only hear where her voice came from. He reached out with his right hand, moving closer to the sound, whipping his arm back and forth before him. Then suddenly his arm met hers and the child grabbed onto his hand.

Sam grasped tight, not wanting to lose this one either. As it turned out, she was six years old, and a bit heaver than he had anticipated. If need be, he would drag her out by the wrist. But with his adrenalin flowing, he pulled her up to his right side, and when she grabbed her hands around his neck, he clasped her to his body. He turned and faced the fire of hell from the living room. It was one last run to fresh air. "Okay kids. Here we go. Hang on tight. I'm gonna count three and then you guys hold your breath."

The children grabbed around Sam's neck, and both placed there legs in locked position around his waist. They buried their heads into the protection of the side of his neck.

By now the living room was a wall of flames and Sam could no longer see the door. It was just a matter of running straight forward and hoping to God you didn't run into the wall.

"Okay kids, here we go," Sam shouted, "one, two, three, deep breath, here we go!"

With a kid hanging under each armpit, Sam charged through the flames like a lion chasing a wildebeest. His lungs were about to explode, his strength about to give out. With each step his legs felt heavier, his heart pounded faster, and he thought of God. He felt as if he had run a thousand miles, not knowing exactly where he was going. He pulled the two young bodies closer and closer, but there was no way of knowing if they were still alive or now dead. He simply had to charge ahead, into the valley of death, and so rode the six hundred. Sam had done the best he could, pushed as far as he could, and as he was about to fall, he hit fresh air.

He ran through the front door and onto the porch, standing there like a magnificent statue of truth, with two children of the world, hanging from his arms, for all to see. And somebody snapped a picture.

No one really knew who took the picture. There were some arguments as to who actually owned the camera. The photograph appeared on the front page, above the fold of the *Times Picayune*, with headlines that read, "N. O. Police Officer Saves 3 Lives In Fire."

If Sam had a publicity agent representing him, they would have arranged for the picture. There he was standing on the porch, holding the two kids in his arms, having just saved their lives. The legs of his trousers had been burnt off, his shirt was a mass of scorches, and his face was covered with soot.

The picture itself looked as though it had been manufactured by a movie company. Both of the kids had raised their little heads, and with arms outstretched, were reaching for their mother. Mom was rushing up to them from the right corner of the photo, wanting to take them from their hero into her bosom of love.

And in the center of it all was Sam. He was haloed by the light from the fire behind, an exhausted soldier, ready and well prepared to do his duty. He was looking up into the heavens, breathing the fresh air that God provided, and saying, "I gave it the best shot I could." It could have been the photograph of the Marines raising the American flag on Iwo Jima's Mt. Suribachi, on February 23, 1945, representing one of the most notable photographs of the war. It resulted in a massive statue on display in Washington D. C. signifying the honor and bravery of all men. But this was the picture of Sam Pennington, a small town cop, saving three lives on a street in New Orleans.

They wanted to take Sam to the local hospital, but he declined. Instead he took the night off, soaked in a hot tub, and placed some salve on his wounds. The next day he was ready to return to duty. But the news broke of his dynamic feat, and all hell broke loose.

As it turned out, the house was owned by an airline pilot, Rodger Jenson. He was on duty and had spent the night in Chicago. The house caught fire in a freak accident. A simple circuit breaker did not properly shut down, when the wires became overloaded.

The woman in the house was Mrs. Beth Jenson and her two children, Mary and John. Before she was married, her name was Beth Bean. As it turned out, her father was Judge Wilford Bean, who wound up making an honorary presentation to Sam in a public ceremony in front of City Hall. He once mentioned to Sam, "I wish I could adopt you as my first and only son." A nationally syndicated news service picked up the story. The story told of Sam's heroics, but it was the headline that caught the public's attention, "Judge Wants To Adopt A Cop." The Judge and Sam became very close friends.

Sam was given a two week medical leave and was asked by the Mayor of the city to join him in a series of luncheons concerning fire safety. Not being a fireman, Sam declined until said time as the Mayor's office demanded he participate. So much for politics. It took about two weeks for the front page of the *Picayune* to fade into oblivion. People quickly forget.

But Sam had a better idea. He was never a person who joined a group, but rather a guy who stood on his own. Living alone in a single room apartment did not do it for Sam. He wanted better. His current overhead was at the very basic need to sustain life. He always had money in his pocket, but the pay of a cop in this town was far from a satisfying amount to maintain the life style he wished to live in.

Sam wondered how other cops did it. Most of them were married, and some even had gone into debt to by a home. As frugal as he had been, Sam was living from pay check to pay check. But he was always working other jobs, getting double time for blocking the street when someone moved in or out, or working his butt off helping Shandor with the Barracks Apartment. He was now at a time in life when he decided to take stock. Sam felt it was time to associate him with people who not only liked him, but those who could also help him. He figured it would be better to be connected with those of importance, than to spend time in a bar with loser cops, who did nothing but complain about their life. They chose to become cops, to now complain about being one was self-destructive.

He set up a file in his one room apartment. It was a file of phone numbers of people he wanted to promote. The first file entry was of Judge Wilford Bean. His position with Sam was written in stone. Sam wrote:

"*Wilford Bean. Sitting judge. I believe he will be of great value to me. Must keep aligned with him.*" His next entry was of Eduardo Sanchez.

"*Eduardo Sanchez came to NO from Honduras, five years ago. He has a son named Pedro. His home town was demolished by a hurricane. He was president of a bank. Knows all about banking. Don't know where this may lead, but should keep in touch.*"

There were twenty four other notes in the file, each of them with potential importance. The final entry concerned, Captain Adam Loper.

"*Good guy. He's older, a black guy, about 64. Will retire in about three years. Heads the NARCO squad. We play a game or two of checkers after hours. He's good. Bought him a present of 12-year-old Glenlivet single-malt scotch. He loved it. Knows where all the bodies are buried. Good man to know.*"

It was two years later, a cold windy night in mid October. It was ten p.m., and Sam had just gone off duty. He was walking alone on Royal Street, and turned right onto Bienville. Normally Sam would have his partner Jack

Anderson with him, but on this night Jack was sick with the flu.

Sam strolled into the Shell Restaurant. The Shell was located on Bienville, a few doors down from Bourbon. This was the hot section of the Quarter. It was where it all started, where it always began. You stood on Bourbon in the second block from Canal Street, and things got immediately wild and crazy. From this corner, about ten blocks down on Bourbon, was the liveliest show anyone could find in America.

The Shell was a place where tourists came first. It was filled on most occasions, with an oyster bar that ran though the length of the first room and halfway into the next. Sam moved in and found a seat near the front door. A young kid came up and asked him, "What you want?"

"A dozen oysters," Sam answered.

"You got it," the kid said. He moved off to shuck the dozen.

Sam looked around the room. It was as busy as a place could be, a fun place. Sam had never been in the Shell. He had seen it before, promised himself he would go there, but in his ten years with the department, this was the first time.

The oysters arrived, plump and fat, on a large platter, with a bowl of crackers and wedges of lemon, and some salt and pepper and two loaded shot glasses full of horseradish and some ketchup and of course, the *piece de resistance*, tobasco sauce! Sam thought he had died and gone to heaven. He even bought a beer, to aid in the pleasure of washing down each magnificent mouthful.

Sam motioned for the kid to come back over. As he threw the final oyster into his mouth, he asked the kid to bring him another platter of a dozen.

"Yes sir," The boy said. "Let me ask you something? Are you a cop?"

Sam checked his uniform over, making sure he was properly displaying his badge, and still had his gun. "Yep," Sam said. "Why do you ask?"

"Well, we got a setup just for cops, in the back. Oysters go for one-half price, and beer is cheaper too."

"It's half price?"

"Beer and Oysters, half off of the original price."

"For the police?"

"That's it."

"So how come you didn't tell me that in the first place?"

"Wasn't sure you were NOPD."

"Okay, where do I go?"

"All the way back to the end of that second room. See that green curtain over by the right? That's it. Just walk on in and make yourself at home."

"Thank you." Sam rose and started to walk away. "And put this first order of oysters and beer on my new back room tab, at the half price sale."

The back room was definitely a cop hangout-type of place. The room was smaller than the first two, with three pool tables. The first two tables were busy with pool shooters, the third was covered with oysters and all the condiments. A waitress moved in and out with beer, just to keep service for everybody.

Sam originally only wanted another dozen oysters, but a dozen oysters leads to two more beers, and one pool game dissolves into three, and that's how the evening went. As the evening started to wane, Sam began to enjoy himself. He actually had a good time there. He enjoyed his friends: in particular, Sergeant Ralph O'Reilly. Sergeant O'Reilly was a short, heavy-set Irishman, in his mid-fifties. He handled the front desk on Rampart Street. This was also Sam's precinct. It was O'Reilly who originally aided Sam in getting onto the force.

When Sam first applied to join the police, he took the test at Rampart Street. After the test was completed, Sam waited to see how it all came out. He actually sat there for six and a half hours, waiting for the results. As O'Reilly left his office, he noted Sam sitting on a bench, and asked, "Hey kid, what you waiting for?"

Sam looked up and offered, "I just wanted to find out if I passed."

"So let me get this straight. You been sitting here for a half a day to see if you passed this fucking test?"

"Yes sir. It's important to me."

"Well shit, let's us go see if you passed."

They both walked back to O'Reilly's office and pulled out the test reports. Sam was listed with a passing grade.

"Well that's it. You passed. You are now a cop trainee."

Things got mellow in the back room at the Shell. Talk became looser, and things were said that didn't need to be repeated. There were five cops who gathered together at a back table, they were known as the NOLA 5, although nobody ever used that description in front of them.

The head guy was Mark Maher, a twenty-year cop with a chip on his shoulder. Sam shot a game of pool with Mark. Sam was good at pool. He had a knack for the game. He had somehow developed a way of lining up a shot, striking the cue ball just right, aiming it toward the proper spot, causing the ball that was finally hit, to cut into the selected pocket like magic.

As the game proceeded, Sam noted that Mark Maher would be interrupted from the game by several of the officers, who originally sat with him at a back table. While Sam was lining up for a shot, they would pull Sgt. Maher aside, and draw him to the back wall, and whisper in his ear. After a brief discussion, Mark would return to the table, and the other officer would leave the room through the back door.

After a few minutes, the officer would return from the alley, sit at the table, and then the entire process would happen again. Sam thought, "There's some business going on in this place; if not here, for sure in the back alley."

"Nice job kid," Mark said, as he reached into his pocket to pay off the five dollar bet. "You're not a hustler, are you?"

"No sir. That was the best game I ever shot. Check with me tomorrow. By then I'll be nothing more than red meat."

At around one fifteen, the party broke up. Sam asked the waitress how much he owed, and she declined to give him a bill.

"Hey, you're a cop," She said. "It's printed on your badge."

"Well, I ran a tab up front. I'll pay for that if I may."

"That's what we do here to keep our streets safe." She then hustled off to the kitchen, leaving Sam standing alone in the room. He finally realized just how cheap you could eat with a cop badge pinned to your shirt.

Sam entered the back men's room. He needed a quick whiz before heading home. But there was a man in the only stall, busily heaving his guts out. Sam moved up to the urinal, unzipped his fly, and gave the lizard a breath of fresh air. The lizard reciprocated by releasing his bladder of what seemed like two gallons of liquid.

The heaving sounds continued in the stall to his right, and after each heave, the man would chuckle.

"Hey in there, you okay buddy?" Sam called out.

"Is that you, Sam?" It was Ralph O'Reilly's voice.

"Yeah, it's me. You okay in there?"

"Oh yeah. I'm having a great time in here. I think I just threw up my left lung." O'Reilly then laughed, threw up, and laughed again. "If I was doing any better, I'd stick some beads up my ass and go to the party as a Mardi Gras float."

It was obvious to Sam that Ralph was drunk. Sam pulled the door to the stall open and peered inside. O'Reilly was on his knees, gripping the toilet, in a fashion that displayed deep affection.

"Com'on in kid, join the party. I think I'm going to fucking die."

"You want me to get you something from the kitchen?"

"Nah. It's okay. I'm about done."

O'Reilly tried to pull himself to a standing position. The will was there, but the body would not respond. "Aw, shit!" he screamed.

"Here, let me help you." Sam moved in and grabbed Ralph by the arm pits and pulled him onto his feet. He started suffering with pain in his left leg, and Sam felt he may not be able to get home.

"Where's your car?" Sam asked. "You got a car out back?"

"No, no car. I live in the Quarter. Three blocks over west and then a block and a half up. I can make it. No problem." He stretched his leg out, trying to get the blood flowing again. Slowly it started to come back. "There you go, I got it now. I'll be fine, thanks."

But Ralph O'Reilly would not be fine. Sam convinced O'Reilly to allow him to walk him home. They moved through the main room of the Shell and onto Bienville. Ralph would have to stop, and let his leg breathe for thirty seconds, and then move on.

"So what is with that leg?" Sam asked.

"Let me tell you about my leg. About three years ago I had a breathing problem. Couldn't move around much. My wife takes me to a doctor, and he tells me I need a triple bypass on my heart. So doctor does it. He took a vein from my left leg, and used that to splice out the shit in the veins leading to my heart. End of story? No way. My heart now works fine, but my fucking leg is killing me."

They continued to walk in silence, and then Sam started to prod. He had learned from experience how to talk to a drunk. The first thing you did was to lead the drunk into your subject. The simpler the question, the more information you might receive. Next, if there was a pregnant pause, you might throw in a line of agreement. It was important to agree with the subject. O'Reilly might later barely even remember speaking of this matter, so just agree with everything. Finally never challenge. O'Reilly might ramble, or fall asleep, but never challenge. You may wind up in a drunken brawl.

"So what was that back there at the Shell?" Sam asked. "Looked like the boys were into a big hot deal or something?"

"Come on, you know what was going on there?" O'Reilly said. "These boys call themselves the Nola 5. They're out there selling dope. It's no big deal. Just a few cops selling a little bit of happy powder in order to keep food on the table. No big deal.

"Hey, you're a cop, you know what I mean. Those guys back at the Shell, they got to work odd jobs, just to make the groceries. Cops in this town get lousy pay, and that's it. Three of those guys moonlight as bouncers at a local bar. Are you believing that? They make us do like bouncers, just to make ends meet!"

O'Reilly became silent and they walked on. Sam wanted more.

"You got that one right," Sam said. "You get a piece of the action?"

"Na, not me. I don't give a fuck what those boys do. It's not any'a my business." Then he was quiet again.

"Boy, you can say that again," Sam said.

"You bet," said O'Reilly. "And you know what else? You know who creates this prison problem? The politicians, that's who. Those greedy bastards did this thing."

"I can see that," Sam added.

"You know it. Now they've developed a bunch of people, hundreds, maybe a hundred thousand people, whose job it is to feed the cons, manufacture those orange jump suits, and keep them in jail. They got all these prisoners in jails across this country and for what. Huh? For what?"

Sam wanted to interject something else, but wasn't exactly sure where O'Reilly was going, so when Ralph O'Reilly looked at him for his reaction, Sam provided a thoughtful thinking expression. Fortunately, O'Reilly was on a roll and continued.

"I'll tell you what. Big fucking money, that's what! We spend more money jailing these people, feeding them, paying for all those guards to watch them, than the cops who arrest them. So it's the boys in the suits who have created a fucking cottage industry here. Now what about that?"

Finally Sam had a good response to add to the conversation. "Makes sense to me."

"You damn right it does. You ever hear about 'Just Say No?'"

"Yeah."

"That's the dumbest fucking slogan the government came out with, in the war against drugs. Well let me tell you, we are losing the war against drugs! And the worst of it all, the biggest bullshit of this whole mess is what the fuck do they do with all the money?"

"Good question," Sam answered.

Ralph quickly continued. "So we pick up this dude with ten grams of marijuana in his Mercedes Benz. The city takes possession of his car and they sell it. He winds up in jail and the guys who we pay to take care of the druggies are now making fifty thousand a year plus, just to incarcerate them. So what we got here is one fucking run around. They're giving the guy with the Mercedes free food and free Cable TV, and we, the cops, hafta pay for our food and basic TV. We're supposed to get a share of his Mercedes Benz, but that doesn't happen. Instead, the money goes to the bureaucrats. An all of this shit, winds up happening, over ten fucking grams of marijuana."

"So what happens then?" Sam asked.

"Well, shit happens then. The big head guys at cop head quarters finally get the message. If the cops don't get a raise, the cops will strike, or at the very least be very pissed off. So the bureaucrats at city hall all get together, having already taken the money from selling the Mercedes, along with twelve other luxury vehicles, and a big luxury boat, and four posh houses. They finally decide to give us, the cops, a twenty-five cent an hour raise. Hell, that doesn't even cover our cost of living increase."

They stopped at Ralph's place, a shotgun house on Burgundy. The lights were on inside, his wife was waiting.

"I gotta go in." O'Reilly patted Sam on the shoulder. "See ya."

"Hey Ralph, so what happens to all the money?"

Ralph turns from the front door. "Shit happens. I gotta go pee. 'Night Sam, and thanks for bringing my sorry ass home."

Sam slowly walked back to his apartment, giving great thought to the world and all of the challenges he faced. Actually it all boiled down to two choices. He could either forget about this evening at the Shell, tell whoever asked him about it that he knew nothing. Further he would tell them that he did walk Sgt. O'Reilly home, and O'Reilly talked a lot, which sounded like a drunken cop complaining about low pay for a man of his stature.

Or he could turn the entire lot into the Office of Internal Affairs, which would cause a massive disaster in everyone's life, including Sam. Some would call him a whistle blower, an officer of the law who became an open stain in the department.

But Sam didn't care about that. He hated dope with a passion. He didn't care about how many junkies were in jail or how much it cost to keep them there. That was the price we pay to keep a clean country, with laws to help people keep it straight. So Sam decided to become a whistle blower, and let the chips to fall where they may.

Finally Sam decided O'Reilly would not be his best witness, or ally. His best hand to play would be to infiltrate the ranks of the bad guys. Sam decided to return to the back room at The Shell.

Chapter 15

FLASHBACK, CONTINUED.

RALPH O'REILLY was not at The Shell when Sam arrived the next night just after ten p.m., but Mark Maher was there, handling business as usual. Then there was Steve Stewart, Jeff Rice, Angelo Barossa, and Henry Brown. Five white guys selling dope to an unwitting population. How sweet it was.

Sam's first initiative was to make a solid contact with the boys. He wanted to become one of them, a friend to be trusted. He shot seven games of eight ball on the first night, losing six of them. Three of those games were with Mark Maher, and that is where Sam saw to it that he lost all three.

Sam placed his pool cue in the rack, and turned to Mark. "Okay, that's it," Sam said. "I told you I'd be raw meat when this was over." Sam peeled fifteen bucks form his stash and laid it onto the table.

Maher picked it up and swiftly placed it into his shirt pocket. "You're doin' just fine," Maher said, with a cocky attitude. "I may spot you a ball or two the next time out."

Of the four men who were left, one stood out as possibly a decent fellow. His name was Jeff Rice, a cop who had been in service only a year longer than Sam. Jeff did not shoot pool, not good enough for the game, but Sam did find out what made Jeff tick.

Later that night, Sam walked through the unlocked men's room door, and a voice came from the closed stall.

"Hey, who's there?" Jeff called out.

"It's me, Sam Pennington."

"Oh, Sam, lock that door, will ya?"

Sam walked back to the door and twisted the lock into place.

"Thanks man," Jeff said. "I forgot to do that. I got a little toot I'm taking care of."

After a moment, Jeff came out of the stall, with a big smile on his face. He headed for the sink and splashed water on his face. "Whoa, that is some great shit," Jeff said. "You wanna try a snort?" It was obvious Jeff was not only selling the goods, but in the process of sampling as he went. "You wanna give it a try?" Jeff added. He reached into his shirt pocked and withdrew a folded piece of white paper.

It looked to Sam as though it were a BC headache powder, but soon realized it was a stick of cocaine. "No thanks, I'm trying to quit."

"You can't judge the goods until you tasted what you got." Jeff dropped a full stick onto the Formica sink top, took a single-edge razor blade from his shirt pocket, and started cutting and moving the white cocaine into snorting proportions. Sam decided it was now the time for men to place their bellies up to the bar. Jeff had now cut the cocaine into four equal lines. He then reached into his shirt pocket and withdrew two fresh cocktail straws, handing one to Sam.

"Okay, it's cocktail time." Jeff bent over the powdered lines and deftly prepared to snort the white stuff into his nose. He performed swiftly, like a pro. Jeff had just completed snorting some lines into his head while standing in the back stall, and now was about to do it again! He placed one end of the straw into his right nostril, and sucked back with his breath, moving the other end of the straw quickly down the line of cocaine, watching it disappear as he went. Then quickly switched the straw into his left nostril, and did the same thing in reverse, sniffing and moving the opposite end of the straw back up the second line.

Finally he threw his head back and said, "Whoa, is this great shit!" He stood there for an instant, enjoying the rush, experiencing the joy of a lifetime. He was breathing heavily, slowly coming down. Then he turned to Sam, and handed him a fresh straw.

"Here you go buddy," Jeff said. "Your turn to make history."

Sam took the straw and placed in up right nostril. He had just observed how to do it. Now, he had to make it appear as though he was a total pro. Not only did he do it faster, he made it look better. Quickly, he downed the first line, shifted to the left nostril and whipped back up to the top of the second line. Sam instantly felt the buzz of the drug entering his body. His blood started pulsing, and his breath became heavier. Once again he felt that severe pain in his head.

He recalled when he was about fourteen, and he and his pals had some airplane glue. They were inside the basement of his father's hardware store, and someone had an old brown bag. They were both older kids, age sixteen, and one of them convinced Sam to cop the tube of glue. They cut the tube with a Swiss Army knife and dropped it into the bag. Then they would quickly pass the bag around the group, each person sticking his nose into the open spot at the top, and sucking the acrid fumes deep into their lungs.

Sam took his whiff from the bag, and along with the feeling of dizziness, he also quickly developed a pulsating, stabbing headache. There was nothing about this experience that Sam found joyful. As a matter of fact he found it to be a pitifully ignorant attempt to have a moment of fun with a tube of glue that would eventually cause your brain to explode.

Now Sam, at age thirty-two, standing in a men's room on Bienville Street in New Orleans Louisiana, had repeated the same childish experience. The headache that stabbed him at first was now starting to ease. That feeling as the drug pumped through his blood vessels, was now starting to wane. Jeff was still enjoying his high, with a smile on his face that stated, "Hey look at me folks, am I having a good time or not?"

Sam rolled his head back and shouted: "Boy, is that great shit!"

Moments later Sam and Jeff left the men's room. Sam knew he had made a hit with Jeff. If a word was ever put out that Sam Pennington was a real great guy, he was certain that Jeff would be the guy to deliver that word. He also noticed that Ralph O'Reilly had arrived, sitting at his usual table in the corner. Sam crossed in and sat across from him. He had a feeling that Ralph was hiding something. Even worse, his face was pasty white. It appeared as though Ralph was little better off than a dead man walking.

"How's it going Ralph?" Sam asked.

"Hey Sam, fine, just fine."

As they exchanged formalities, Sam noted that Ralph avoided looking directly at him. He most assuredly had something to say, but didn't know exactly how to bring it up.

"Can I buy you a drink?" Sam asked.

"Yeah, sure, thanks. Whisky, with a water back."

Sam called the waitress over and placed the order, along with a beer for himself. Then they both sat silent until the drinks were served. O'Reilly took a sip of whisky, then turned and looked at Sam. It had been a series of awkward moments, then Ralph O'Reilly found the guts to speak out.

"Listen, I gotta tell you something."

"Sure, go."

"Well, I said a lotta shit last night."

"No problem. A lotta shit doesn't bother me."

"Well, I may have mentioned what the boys do here."

Sam feigned not to know what Ralph was talking about. He pulled his chair closer, and leaned in. He now looked at Ralph directly in the eyes, but said nothing. As soon as their eyes met, Ralph looked away.

"Look, I don't know how it was put, but it goes something like this." Ralph said. "I was rambling last night, that's all. Just shooting my mouth off." Ralph turned back and directed his gaze at Sam. "You got it?"

"Rambling, shooting your mouth off. I got it."

"An I don't even recall much of what I said."

"Gotcha. I understand. No problem," Sam said. He looked at Ralph and smiled, even winked his eye.

"Well I'm glad to hear that," Ralph said, as he picked up his drink and took a long swallow. "Any of this ever gets out and we could all spend a long time in jail."

Now the words were said, openly and clearly. Ralph O'Reilly was worrying about going to prison.

"What, for a little bit of happy powder?" Sam asked. "Don't worry about it Ralph, to each his own."

Ralph was a happy man again. The color seemed to start to return to his face.

Sam returned to the Shell every night for over a week, each time he would steal his way in closer into the workings of the NOLA 5. Each night he managed to lose more money on eight ball. By the end of the week, he was almost broke. He wrote a check to Mark Maher for twenty dollars, and asked him to hold off depositing it until payday following Tuesday, as he was running a little short of cash.

Mark was as dry as always, never giving an inch. He never did spot him a ball on any game. That was just how it was. This time, Mark Maher developed a soft side.

"That's okay kid, don't worry about it," Mark said. "Tuesday will be fine." Then after giving it some more thought, he invited Sam to join him at the back of the building. They both stepped into the alley, Mark lit a smoke and Sam declined. "No thanks, gave it up."

Mark leaned back against the wall and took a few puffs; Sam looked around. He had, on occasion, glanced at the outside from the back door. There was a two-story car garage that lined the opposite side of the restaurant. Other than that, it appeared to be no more that, any other alley anywhere in the city.

"Listen," Mark Maher said. "I don't want you to take anything I say out of order."

"No sir, not me."

It was now late, almost two-thirty and Sam noticed Mark had consumed his share of various adult alcoholic beverages. Ralph O'Reilly had stepped into an alcoholic transgression a little over a week ago, now it seemed as though Officer Mark Maher might be ready to fall into the same trap.

"You married?" Maher asked.

"Nah, gave it up for Lent."

For the first time Sam saw Maher chuckle. "What's so funny?" Sam asked.

"Nothing, I just got rid a mine for the same reason."

They both chuckled together. Then Maher got to the point. "I understand from one of my boys, you and he had a hit on some coke in the bathroom."

Sam looked quickly at Maher, who took his last drag on his smoke, and tossed the butt into the alley. He was looking straight ahead, not at Sam.

"What do you mean by that?" Sam asked.

"You're not going to tell me that you and Jeff Rice didn't snort some shit in the shitter are you?"

Sam took a deep breath. "No sir, we did not."

"You want me to bring Jeff out here and see what he says?"

"No, that won't be necessary. We just did it once. We just tried it out, that's all. No big deal."

With a big smile on his face, Maher placed his arm around Sam's shoulder. "Come with me a minute. I'm not your enemy, pal, I'm one of your friends."

They walked across the alley and into the garage. It was empty with the exception of a few civilian cars, along with three police vehicles positioned near the doorway. Mark Maher pulled Sam with him, and they walked to Maher's car parked in the front position. He pulled the keys from his pocket, opened the trunk, and pulled the edge of the carpet back, revealing a stash of small white folded paper envelopes, containing what Sam believed was cocaine.

Maher pulled one stack of the small envelopes from the trunk, and held it up to the light from the alley. The stack contained twenty five units of the drug, and Maher pulled out five individual packets. He tossed the remainder back into his trunk and placed the five units into Sam's shirt pocket.

"Here you go pal. Go have a party, on me."

"Hey, thanks," Sam said.

"I knew you were getting a little short, so go get it on. It's okay. You cheer me up."

"Well I mean...really...thanks."

Maher slammed his trunk shut, placed his arm back over Sam's shoulder, and they both headed back across the alley.

"Don't worry about it. No problem," Maher said.

"How much does this stuff cost anyway?"

"Each one is a stick. I gave you five. If you cut it nice an' thin, you can get about eight lines in each stick. We just sell them for chump change. We buy 'em from the source at one buck and sell them for five bucks each."

When Sam was with Jeff, he recalled snorting two lines of cocaine which totaled a half of a stick. Jeff snorted the balance. Sam therefore concluded, Jeff was already a mainliner.

"We don't like addicts," Maher said. "Don't need the problem. Just simple guys out for a good time, that's all."

"I understand. No problem."

"You got it."

They got to the back door, and Maher removed his arm from Sam's shoulder. "Listen, I got an idea. How would you like to get in on this gig? The five of us make enough chump change to make a pretty good financial upgrade at the end of each month. You might wanna think about that."

"Yeah, I could handle that. I could do that."

"Tell you what. Come by tomorrow night. I like you. See if I can fit you in somewhere. You're a smart guy. Let's go in and have a nightcap."

If a police bust had taken place at that moment and with Sam walking around with five sticks of cocaine in his shirt pocket, there was no doubt in Sam's mind he would serve at least ten years in the slammer. That was not good enough for Sam. It was time to spill the beans to his superiors.

The following day was Saturday, normally his day off, but Sam had a job of blocking St. Ann Street while somebody moved in. After he was in position, Sam picked up his cell phone and called Adam Loper.

There were a lot of things about Adam Loper that Sam liked. As an African American police officer, he had come up through the ranks. He didn't care for the term African American, since he was born in Lake Charles, Louisiana, and preferred to be referred to as an American.

He received the promotion of Captain of the narcotics unit, as a result of his making several major arrests when he was a lieutenant, which resulted in a vast change of drug laws in the state. Sam was not in Loper's office, not under his jurisdiction, but he knew him to be a friend and a good checkers challenge. That is why Sam called Adam Loper.

"Hello." The voice was strong but quiet.

"Hello Sir, this is Sam Pennington."

"Hello Sam, nice to talk to you. What's going on?"

"Well sir, I have a problem. It has to do with the department. I need to speak to someone who can help me out."

"That sounds like right down my alley. Come on over, I'll give you lunch."

"I'm on a stake out right now, can't get off. And after that, I have to meet with some people. These people deal with drugs. They want to make a deal."

"Where are you?"

"I'm at the corner of St. Ann and Royal Streets."

"I'll be there in twenty minutes."

Adam Loper tapped at the passenger door of Sam's car, exactly eighteen minutes later. He wore a New York Yankees baseball cap and a brown and black jogging suit. This was the first time Sam had seen him in civilian clothing, no longer in his office playing checkers and winning all of his money. He seemed much younger now than Sam remembered before. He unlocked the door and Adam jumped inside. He handed Sam a wrapped Muffuletta sandwich.

"Here ya go. I already ate. Go on, do it to it."

Sam took the sandwich, unwrapped it, and started to munch. "This is great. Where did you get this?"

"I got it in the Quarter. Everything's great in the Quarter. You wanna talk about how great a Muffuletta is, or tell me about somebody dealing dope?"

Sam took pause. He quickly chewed and swallowed his third bite. Then he told Adam of his experience. He started with Ralph O'Reilly, told him of his involvement with the NOLA 5, then his experience with Officer Jeff Rice in the men's room at The Shell, and finally his meeting with Mark Mayer as he displayed his dope cachet in the back of his car.

"So what do you want to do now?" Adam asked.

"Well, I need some help. I go there tonight, we have a bunch of cops there on stake out. I go in and we make a deal, I signal somebody, and the cops come in and bust their asses."

"Okay, sounds good to me. What time do you want the cops there?"

"Well, they have to be standing around somewhere, ready to move in, and when I signal, they go!"

"Let me ask you something. Have you thought this thing out?"

Sam thought for a moment. "To what degree?"

"Well, let's analyze it. You go in and do what you just said an you'll be called a whistle blower for the rest of your life. You want that?"

"If that's what I need to do, that's what I do."

"Okay, that's fine. But let's just think about the bust. What do we accomplish there? What do we get out of that? All we get is five chicken-shit dopers, selling sticks of cocaine on the street, at five bucks a pack. Is that what we want?"

"Well, that's a start."

"Instead of thinking that way, let's see how we can finish this thing. Think of it as you and me playing checkers. You lose every time I play you, right?

"Most of the time. Sometimes I win a few."

"When you get lucky."

"Okay, I agree."

"And do you ever figure why you lose so many?"

"No, but I guess you'll tell me."

"When you play checkers you have to think ahead. You think one, two, even three moves ahead. You try to suck your opponent into a situation where you can demolish him. If he jumps your man, you can jump two men back. That's how you win. Think ahead."

"Okay," Sam said. He was listening carefully now, not learning how to play checkers, but how Adam Loper thought.

"I'll tell you what I want out of this game. I want to know where these boys are buying their dope. Without that dope, these boys are not chicken shit cops, they're nothing but chicken shit."

Sam nodded. "I understand."

"What do you want out of this deal? What's more important to you than these five dopers? What does Sam Pennington want out of this situation?"

"I want to make more money. I'd like to be promoted. I've been here for ten years and it's time to get into the upper ranks."

"You want to be a Detective?"

"Yeah, that would be good."

"Okay, you got it. I'll check around and see if there's a Detective position available. If not, I'll cause one to be created. One month from now you will be the biggest dick in this town. Now back to the chase. You go to your meeting tonight. Find out what's going on. Report back to me. We then analyze, and decide on our next move. Nobody will ever hear about you. You will not be in my file. You will never blow any whistle. Got it?"

"Yes sir."

"An' you have no more time to spend on any street watching some assholes moving furniture in and out of this town. Got it?"

"Yes sir."

"You got anything else to tell me?"

Sam reached into his left shirt pocket and withdrew five sticks of cocaine. He then handed it to Adam. As Sam did this, one of the cocaine sticks had opened slightly, and a small amount of the powder had fallen into his shirt pocket. As he pulled the sticks out, some residual dust fell onto his shirt and trousers. Sam brushed it off. "This is what I was given by Mark Maher last night. It was a gift, because I was broke."

Adam took the five packets and opened one. He looked around, searching to see if anyone was watching. He then licked the tip of his finger, and placed it into the white powder. Once the white stuff stuck there, he drew it to his face, and rubbed the substance onto his upper gum line, just in behind his upper lip. Then he closed his mouth and moved his lip back and forth, so as to provide a sensation of the substance in his mouth."

"Boy, that's good coke!" Adam announced. "What made Maher think you were into this shit?"

"When I was in the bathroom with Jeff Rice, he cut some lines up. He offered me some and I took it. I figured that was my best way to convince him I was straight. I believe he bought it. I think that was why Maher grabbed onto me."

Adam sealed the open paper back up, and stuffed the five sticks into his shirt pocket. "Smart move. We'll play checkers again someday. I think you'll do better. After you're done with this gig, go home and write me a letter. I want the names of every person involved in this matter. I also want all of your time spent checking this thing out and all additional expenses you have incurred. Whatever you spent in cash out of pocket, along with the time, will be reimbursed from my office. Got it?"

"Yes."

"You're a good cop; don't change that. Keep this file current. I want a note in my mailbox every few days. An don't put your name on that letter. Sign it as Agent 33. I'll know who it's from. Go to the precinct and stuff it in my mail box. After your meeting tonight I want to hear from you. Call me any time of the day or night. See you around." At that, Adam Loper left the car and walked on down St. Ann Street.

Sam arrived at The Shell at nine o'clock, and found the main room busy as usual, but the back room was very quiet. Ralph O'Reilly wasn't there, nor was Jeff Rice or Angelo Barossa or Henry Brown. Only Mark Maher and Steve Van Zant were shooting pool.

"Hey guy, how ya doin'?" Mark said.

"Doin' fine," Sam said. "Got an extra gig today. I'm here to pay my bill and give you another chance."

"My kinda guy," Mark said, as he snapped the eight ball into the side pocket for the win. Angelo paid Mark off and headed for the men's room.

"Set 'em up, let's go." Sam offered.

"Nah, let's sit down, have a beer. Got some bad news to tell ya." Mark moved into a booth at the back end of the room, Sam followed, feeling a bit suspicious.

"Here's the deal," Mark said, as he slid his ass across the leather. "We gotta shut down for about a week. Goods are no longer available. At best I can take care of only a couple of our best customers, and that's it."

"Hey, no problem." Sam slid in on the end. "We'll get this going again later."

"I'm serious about this. I had you all set up. I got a place in Algiers, like I said. I made a nice deal with a bar there, owned by a neat lady. She's ready to rock and roll. She's ready to hang tough till we get this straightened out. No big deal."

"That's fine with me," Sam said.

"Okay then, how about a beer?" Mark picked up a half-full pitcher of

Abita Amber, while Sam grabbed a glass from the side table.

"So what's the hold up?" Sam asked.

"We're supposed to get a delivery every week. This time something happened. So because of that, next Thursday we get a double order at half the price." Mark poured the beer and raised his glass in toast. "Here's to double the money."

They clicked glasses and sloshed it down.

When Sam returned home he called Adam Loper and advised him of the situation. "You're doing fine, son. Just keep those cards and letters coming," Adam said. Sam next prepared a file for Agent 33, showing all of his charges and expenses. Then he walked over to the Rampart Street Police Station, and placed it in Lopers mail box.

The following Tuesday, Sam received a check covering his salary and expenses. He didn't know how it happened, but Loper did it. On Wednesday of that week the office became extremely busy. The FBI was present, some wearing suits and ties, and a few in windbreakers with the logo, FBI, printed on the back. They were all over the place, on the upper floors, in and out of offices.

When Sam prepared to leave from work that Thursday night, he was handed a note from his dispatcher. It read, "*See Me.*"

Sam walked into the office of Sgt. Shad Willmont. Sgt. Shad was an African American cop, who was one of the three dispatchers in the busiest police office in the Parish. He was a big man, stood six feet four, most assuredly not a person to take issue with. There was a line of four cops to speak to Sgt. Willmont. Sam waited patiently.

"Next," Shad announced, with great authority.

"Yes, Sergeant – Sam Pennington. You asked to see me."

"Pennington." Sgt. Willmont took a clip board from the wall and thumbed through a large stack of papers. "Pennington, Pennington, here it is. You Sam Pennington?"

"Yes sir I am."

Shad read from his file. "You are temporarily removed from your present duties, and are placed on a special sting force, tomorrow night. You make contact with Detective William Joseph Mays. His phone number is on this sheet. Should you fail to make contact with Mays, call me back at the number on this sheet."

Sam got to a phone and called the number for Detective William Mays.

"Hello, this is Mays."

"Hello, this is Officer Sam Pennington."

"Hey there, Sam. I just got a call from my office to reach you."

"Well, I beat you to it."

"Listen, we got to talk. Where are you?"

"I'm still at Division 2."

"Walk down Rampart heading south. There's a place across the street called Lucy's Bar and Grill. I can be there in ten minutes."

"Okay. I'm in uniform."

"That makes you a stand-out. I'll find you,"

Lucy's was not crowded; too early for the off duty crowd. Sam took a small table in the back and waited for Bill Mays to arrive. When he did arrive, being that Sam was the only uniformed cop in the place, Mays made a beeline for his table.

Sam stood up and held his hand out for a greeting. Mays was ten years his senior, about fifteen pounds over weight and had a warm and friendly smile. They clasped hands and sat down at the table.

"Nice to meet you, Sam. What do you want to drink? I'm buying."

"Just coffee, thanks."

"Well I've had a real bad day and I'll have a double scotch."

A waitress came up to the table. "Okay boys, what may I offer you today? You want a menu, or are you representing the Alcohol, Tobacco and Fire Arms in order to see that the merchandise from the bar is being properly dispensed?"

"Molly is the house comedian." Bill said.

Mays ordered a double Johnny Walker Black, neat, with a water back, and Sam ordered coffee. Drinking while in uniform, was a 'no no' with the NOPD.

The two men became fast friends, sharing their past history with the force. Mays was to retire in ten years, Sam in twenty. Mays remembered the photo on the front page of the *Times Picayune* newspaper, showing Sam standing in front of the fire, holding the two kids.

"I loved that picture, it said it all," Mays said.

"Thanks. I gave it my all."

Then the conversation got down to the nitty gritty.

"We have to be at the Port of New Orleans at two o'clock tomorrow. A ship will come in and dock at around six o'clock. We meet with an FBI agent, Lloyd Pierce. I'm only telling you what I know about this. This was given to me on a need-to-know basis. Anyway, Agent Pierce takes us out to a boat, where we have control of what happens out in the river. The boat is anchored near the docks. This is a prime position for us to observe all that happens."

"So what happens?" Sam asked.

"Don't know."

"Did you ask Lloyd?"

"You must understand Lloyd. Lloyd only gives the information on a need-to-know basis. He will not answer any question you may have that you don't need to know. This is what these guys do. They talk and you listen, and then you do what they say. That's it."

The waitress returned with the order, placed in on the table, and left.

"You got a car?" Mays asked.

"No, but I got use of a cop car."

"No, no, no cop vehicles allowed. Listen to the deal. We come in wearing fishing gear. You fish?"

"No."

"Well, I've seen these guys fishing on TV sometimes, when I'm surfing around looking for a show. They wear baseball hats, an old jacket, Levi's and white sneakers."

"Okay, I got that."

"That's good. I'll pick you up around one-fifteen. We gotta take our own food and drink. I got a plastic cooler. When I go out on these things my wife packs half the refrigerator. So I invite you to lunch and dinner, compliments of me and my lady."

The deal was done and Sam walked home to his single apartment on Toulouse Street. Once there, he dressed in his work clothes, strapped his tool belt around his waist and made his way up toward Barracks Street and Shandor's apartment house. Sam was not the type of guy to allow grass to grow under his feet.

Sam worked late that night, and on returning home he stopped at the St. Ann Market and purchased a whole Muffaletta sandwich and a six pack of Cokes. At one fifteen the following afternoon, Mays picked him up at his apartment, and they drove to landing twelve of the Port of New Orleans. No one was there. Sam got out of the car with his Muffaletta sandwich and six-pack of Cokes, and Mays with his huge plastic camping picnic cooler.

Mays had a tough time trying to carry all he would eat.

"We go down there, to that building at the river," Mays said. "That's were we find Lloyd."

When they walked into the warehouse, there were what seemed to be a hundred men milling about. The count was actually eighty-eight. This was, in fact, the biggest operation either of them had ever seen before. There was FBI all over the place. Cops and sheriffs. The place was a madhouse.

"Do you think we have enough guys here to accomplish this sting operation?" Sam said, a bit sarcastically.

"Beats the hell outta me," Mays answered. "Wait here. I'll go try to find Lloyd."

As Sam waited, he picked up other bits of information. Two guys behind him were talking about the choppers that were held in an area that would take only minutes to arrive, and another who spoke of freeway congestion that might develop should arrests be created. All in all, it sounded like a massive operation that required a great deal of thought and planning.

"Hello Sam," Lloyd said, holding out his hand. Sam was startled by the voice coming up from behind. "I'm Lloyd Pierce, FBI."

"Sam Pennington. Nice to meet you."

Sam noted Lloyd was also dressed in simple fishing clothing. Sam wanted to ask Lloyd who his costume designer had been, but he decided this was not the time to make bad jokes. Mays was also there, becoming more involved with the magic of this situation than he could have imagined.

"Boy, you really got a lot of people involved here," Mays said.

"That's right," Lloyd responded. "Let's get you two in place. We have to get both of you on board in our time slot, so please grab your stuff and follow me out."

Mays reached down and picked up his lunch, leaving Sam with his Muffaletta and Cokes. An assistant of Lloyd's came up from behind, carrying two large cardboard boxes. Lloyd never introduced the assistant, nor mentioned the boxes.

They were now out onto the pier, and the sight was outstanding. There were ships up and down river, docked at the pier, loading and unloading goods. They finally made it to the edge of the Mississippi, and loaded everything into a four man dinghy. Lloyd's assistant placed the cardboard cartons into the dinghy and walked back to the warehouse as the three men climbed aboard the dinghy.

"Grab the oars and we row out to that boat over there," Lloyd stated.

Sam looked for an oar, Mays did likewise. Both men found an oar, but neither of them had the expertise to properly fit them onto the boat. Instead they both put the oars into the water, and started paddling it away from the pier, as Lloyd sat like Washington crossing the Delaware.

With Lloyd's direction, they finally reached an old shrimp boat that was advertised for sale. The sign hung on its side, and gave the phone number of the owner. Its name was the *Miss Lee*, and Sam judged it to be about seventy-five feet long.

Everyone pulled the stuff from the dinghy and all hauled everything aboard. They next made their way into the pilot's cabin. The door had been left open, with the keys lying on the console.

This was only one of many tasks that Lloyd Piece had to accomplish on this day. He reached into his two jacket pockets and withdrew two radio telephones.

"Okay guys, here we go. I now hand you each a telephone. It is on now. You hit this button to start it and it will ring. A voice will ask you your number, and you reply, 'Zero-eight.' Zero means you are in a boat on the river, eight is your position. Got it?" Both Sam and Mays nodded in the affirmative. "That's good. Now open up these boxes."

Sam and Mays peeled the boxes open, revealing two matching Remington Automatic Rifles, each with a sniper scope. There were extra clips available for both rifles, and they appeared to be ready for a wild game hunt in the outback.

"So what's with the scopes?" Sam asked

"Not a clue," Lloyd answered. "Look, I'll make this very easy for you. There will be no shooting going on tonight. We have everything wired. But if it happens, do not fire at the dock. You could hit one of our boys. Whoever put these scopes on was not advised of the need. That's how shit happens. Your assignment is to avoid the shit and do the job.

"At around six o'clock this evening, a ship will pull in and be docked at the first birth position. They will start to unload. Sometime tonight, they will take off a bunch of large pipes. These are big round things, sewer pipes, made out of a baked clay material, about four feet across and twelve feet long. Whatever you see or hear, you report it on the radio phone. That's it. That's all there is to it. I'll leave you with my flashlight, it gets dark out here."

"May I ask you one more question?" Sam asked.

"Sure," Lloyd responded.

"So it's the sewer pipes you guys have an interest in?"

"That's right."

Sam turned to Mays. "Okay, Mays, it's a pipe that's four feet around and twelve feet long. When we see one we hit the button on the phone and say, we see the pipe, an' that's it."

"That's it," Lloyd said.

"No, that's not it," Sam said. "There's more. You guys aren't interested in a bunch of sewer pipes. You are interested in what's in the sewer pipe, right?"

Lloyd was about Sam's age, possibly a few years younger. He quickly glanced at his watch. "I've told you all you need to know."

"Really?" Sam said. "So what do we do with these rifles you've set us up with, shoot ducks? Duck is out of season now, don't you know that?"

"Okay," Lloyd said. "That's enough."

"No, it's not enough," said Sam. "I want to know everything you know. Is this a dope bust? Are you boys looking for dope packed in those sewer pipes or what?"

By now, Lloyd felt his body was being pushed tight against the wall. He decided to shove back.

"You must have heard that by now," Lloyd commanded. "Common!"

"No way, pal, I want the straight facts. Is there dope packed in those pipes?"

"Yes!" Lloyd answered, with a mean hiss from his mouth. "And don't you know that?"

"Yeah, I know it. I just wanted you to say it! Now, who are the bad guys on the dock? And how many of them are there, and what ammunition power will they be bringing?"

Lloyd had about reached his final position. Once again he glanced at his watch. It was now almost three o'clock and Lloyd had others to move out into position, on other harbor vessels.

"Who's on the dock is our business!" Lloyd shouted out.

"Listen Lloyd, I'll also make this easy. You've got a buncha boys out there. What the hell are you expecting, a battalion of dope dealers, ready to kill anybody who steps in their way? I want to know who's expected on the dock! This isn't going to become another FBI-Waco, Texas-Davidian blow out? Remember that one? You may not be old enough to recall. The FBI came in with the strength of Attila the Hun, and you boys blew up everybody, including women and children. Not going to happen here, Lloyd. You got that?"

Lloyd thought this would be easy, but it turned out not to be. "Okay, there's one hundred million dollars of dope, being brought into this port tonight. That's one hundred million dollars of wholsale value. The dope is packed in the sewer pipes, with large plastic caps on each end. When they come off, they will bring in sixteen wheelers to pick the dope up and haul them to wherever the dope is to be delivered.

"We have people up on the I-10 to follow them, choppers in the air to aid them. There will be some dope dealers arriving at the dock. They will be here to gather up their purchase of goods. We anticipate no more than about twelve. We figure that once they get the idea, and we move in, they'll give it up. Okay?"

Sam and Mays looked on in amazement.

"One hundred million dollars of wholesale value in drugs?" Mays said.

"That's right," Lloyd offered. "It's a major bust. If I knew exactly what was going on, I'd be in charge of this operation."

"Okay, we now understand," Sam said. "Thanks for the information."

Lloyd left on the dinghy, and Sam and Mays sat in the pilot house. They both wondered what they had gotten into. Neither said a word.

By five o'clock the sun had started to set. Sam and Mays had eaten their lunch. Mays had two chicken sandwiches, and reserved his two ham and cheese sandwiches for dinner. Of course there was a bowl of potato salad and another bowl of cole slaw. Mays ate half the potato salad and only three bites of the slaw. *It's no wonder,* Sam thought, *why he's fifteen pounds overweight.*

"Wanna take a look around the boat?" Mays offered.

"Sure thing."

The *Miss Lee* had been fitted out to handle deep-sea fishing, along with some shrimp boating, whichever became more profitable. They wound there way down into the bowels of the boat, where the caught fish would be stored. It was a large area, complete with an ice machine, and large bins to hold the fish in place. The smell was enough to gag a maggot, and on catching one sniff, Mays headed back to the pilot house.

"Where's the engine?" Sam asked.

"Got to be forward, below," Mays said. He moved around and found a trap door in the floor. "Here we go, this is it."

He reached down and grabbed a finger hook built into the door, and pulled it up, revealing the dark space below.

"Where's the flashlight?" Mays asked.

Sam had it at hand, turned it on and flashed it down and into the cavernous hole. The first thing the flashlight revealed was the engine. There were two large marine engines, easily capable of driving a boat of this size around the world. The light was now on its spot beam. With a switch, Sam turned it to flood to reveal a broader area.

What they next saw was a stack of green army duffel bags, stacked on both sides of the engine. Sam quickly moved the light around the engine room, revealing other duffels, stacked all around the lower area. They were against the right and left bulkhead, and covered almost the entire open area, as if someone had placed them there to store...something.

"What the hell's he got down here?" Sam asked.

"Beats me," Mays said.

"Hold the light, I'll go look," Sam added.

"No, I'll go. I can use the exercise."

Mays put one foot on the ladder and headed down below. Sam tried to position his light to give Mays a proper view, but Mays would get into the way from time to time, causing Sam to move from side to side.

Mays grabbed one of the bags from the left side of the engine room, and dragged it back across to the opening of the trap door. In doing so, he heard a tear take place, perhaps at the bottom of the bag, and then something fell out.

"Oops! Made a boo boo," Mays said.

"What is it? What did you do?"

"I think I tore the bottom of the bag."

"What did you do?"

"I tore the fucking bottom of the bag open, that's what I did. I hit a nail or something. That's what I did. Can you please phase the light over here so I can see what fell out."

"Okay, okay, here I go."

Sam moved to the opposite side of the opening, and pin pointed the light at what fell from the bag. It was a stack of papers, small in size, and held together with a rubber band.

"That's it. There it is. Right there." Sam called out.

May's hand reached in and retrieved the paper. "Okay, I got it. There's a few more that fell out too. Here they are. Let me see."

Then things got awfully quiet from below.
"What you got there? Sam asked. What is it?"
"It looks like wads of one hundred dollar bills," Mays answered.
"Oh," Sam said.
There was a pause for about a minute, as Mays continued to look at the money. Sam kept the light still as he looked on, but said nothing.
"Yeah, that's it," Mays proclaimed. "Each one a stack of a hundred dollar bills. That's what we got down here."
"Would you care to toss one up to me?"
"You got it."
Mays tossed one wad of bills up through the hole and Sam caught it on the fly. He held the bills in one hand, and they stretched out over his open palm.
Sam first flicked through the bills. They were used, one-hundred-dollar American currency with an engraving of Benjamin Franklin on the front and no consecutive bank note numbers. He next counted the bills, and it came out to be a total of five thousand dollars.
"What do you get up there?"
"Five thousand."
"Okay. I will now count out what's in this bag."
Sam watched him pour the entire contents of the duffel bag onto the deck. Then he watched him as he placed each bundle back inside, counting as he went. When Mays finished he called up to Sam. "I've got a half a million dollars in this bag."
Everything grew very quiet. Both Sam and Mays just gave thought to the situation. Mays then climbed up the ladder and neither man said a thing. They were thinking of what they had found, and how they could best deal with the situation. Mays walked out to get some fresh air. After some time had passed, Sam moved outside and stood by Mays.
"I think we should we call on the radio and tell them what we found," Mays said.
"Better we don't advertise this over the radio," Sam replied.
"Okay, I'll tell Lloyd about it when we get off."
"Makes sense to me." Sam's brain was racing. "I wonder how much is down there?" he asked.
"Got to be a bunch," Mays responded.
"We should know. Don't you think we should know?"

"Yeah. When we turn it in we should have at least a general accounting of what we're talking about."

A call came in on the radio phone. "This is unit one to all units. We have been advised of a delay of ship arrival due to traffic on the river. We now anticipate a one hour delay."

"Well, there you go," Sam said. "I've got an extra hour to go down and count some bags."

In the next hour and ten minutes, Sam hustled the duffels back and forth, and when he came back to the top deck, announced he had found one hundred and four bags. He had actually made a sample of only three others, but his final conclusion was if the rest are full of cash, they totaled fifty-two million dollars!

"You sure of that?" Mays asked.

"No, I'm not sure. You wanna go back down and check them again?"

"Fifty two million. I can't believe that."

Then the sound of a large boat, closing in on their position drew their attention. It was the *Maria Isabella*, a cargo ship licensed from Spain. It slowly made its way to the dock and anchored there, in a position to discharge its cargo.

Sam grabbed a rifle and with his Swiss Army Knife, removed the scope from the barrel. He peered through the scope, and got a clear view of the dock.

"Here you go," Sam announced to Mays. "This will help you see things better."

Mays took the scope, while Sam removed the other from the second rifle.

It was now just past midnight and Sam and Mays sat there and did nothing but watch and speculate. They looked at the dock, watched the *Maria Isabella* offload their goods and silently speculated about the fact that they were sitting on fifty two million dollars.

The large cranes were moving in and out, unloading various sections of cargo onto the dock and into the many trucks that were there to take it away. They watched the movement until two o'clock, when it finally happened.

A crane pulled a large load of what appeared to be a large stack of round sewer pipes, about four feet around and twelve feet long, from the hull of the boat. Each section of piping was grouped in twelve and they were encased with a slatted wood material and bound with bailing wire.

While this unloading took place, several 14-wheelers pulled onto the dock in perfect position to receive their goods. It was like a well orchestrated square dance, with everybody knowing exactly when to twist and turn. Sam and Mays continued to watch with great anticipation. Then all hell broke loose.

It happened from the area of the dock. Somebody screamed, "Okay, hands up, this is the FBI." Immediately after that, a massive amount of gun shots started to explode on the dock. A single bullet pierced through the window glass of the *Miss Lee*, zipped its way through the cabin and crashed into the back bulkhead. Sam grabbed Mays by the neck and hauled his body to the deck.

"They're shooting at us!" Sam screamed.

As Sam pulled him down, a second bullet pierced the window glass just in front of Mays. As he hit the deck, pieces of glass fell onto his face and hair. Sam noticed none of this, but Mays was most assuredly aware.

Mays quickly huddled into a protective fetal position, while Sam got on the radio.

"This is Zero-8, can you hear me?" No one responded.

When Sam left the key on the telephone open, the shooting from the dock echoed through the phone like a hi-fidelity recording. It sounded to Sam as though this was the worst bombing catastrophe that had taken place since the Viet Nam war.

Sam crawled out onto the outside deck. There he believed he could get a good view of the action. He slid forward on his stomach to the bow of the boat and when he peered over to the dock, could see nothing but smoke.

The *rat-a-tat-tat* of automatic gunfire continued at will. Who was shooting at whom, and who was killing who, could not be determined. Sam pressed his head to the deck and waited for it to end. He could hear the sound of a chopper from overhead, and a large boat motor coming in from his left. He looked to his left and saw a Coast Guard Patrol Boat, with all hands aboard, armed and ready to shoot. But shoot they did not, as they were also too blinded by the smoke.

Then the quiet came. The radiophone started conversation once again. Zero-4 called in, asking "what's going on," followed by Zero-3, and then Zero-5. Finally Station 1 came on the line, signifying that all was under control. Sam stood up and moved back into the pilot house.

Mays had also gotten up into a standing position. He peered out into the night, looking for a sign of life. What he saw were two bullet holes in the window of the boat. Slowly the smoke started to clear. They could see five ambulances had pulled in, with men picking up the dead and wounded. Police cars and vans were all over the place, officers trying to figure out just what happened. Mays was busily attempting to get his heart started.

"I thought Lloyd said there would no gunfire," Sam said.

More smoke had cleared, and they could see criminals wearing hand cuffs being shoved into the back of police cars, and others being slipped into body bags and placed in the Coroner's vehicle. The scene looked like Somalia on a national holiday.

"You know you saved my life," Mays said. He was looking directly forward, at the bullet hole that Sam had pulled him from, just before it exploded into a mass of broken glass.

Sam looked at the same bullet hole. He didn't want to get all syrupy here. "No, not true," Sam said. "When I pulled you down, you grabbed my arm and took me with you to the deck. That bullet was meant for me. You're the one who saved my life."

"That's right," Mays said. "I did it. That was my plan. Well, I'll never forget what happened. And you can take that to the bank."

It took forty five minutes for the FBI to get a shuttle boat out to pick Sam and Mays from the *Miss Lee*. They were transported to the far right of the dock. They had waited in a mob while all boats on the Mississippi were discharged of their people. Then Agent Miller appeared from the remaining smoke. He was an older man with an attitude and he announced with a commanding voice:

"I'm Agent Miller. You people are now released from special duty. The FBI wishes to thank you for your cooperation in this operation. Please deposit all FBI arms, radio phones, and other miscellaneous material to the guards at the gate. You may now move ahead to the parking area."

"Excuse me. Could we find Agent Lloyd Pierce? He's the agent who gave us this stuff?" Mays asked. "I also need to speak with him regarding another matter."

"That will be impossible," Miller replied. "Agents are now involved in clearing the crime scene. No one may enter that area of the dock. On behalf of the FBI, I once again thank you for your support." Miller then turned and left.

Sam and Mays drove out of the exit, heading for the I-10, and were met by a massive traffic jam. It took them almost a half an hour to reach the I-10, and another twenty minutes to pass the blocking condition.

FBI, Police and sheriffs were out en masse, stopping traffic and making arrests on both sides of the freeway. As they passed one area, Sam saw a man he recognized. It was his old pool-shooting buddy from The Shell, Mark Maher. Mark stood alone at the side of the highway, looking lonely and distraught. Mark's hands were cuffed behind his back, as a Sheriff's Deputy came up to him, placed a hand on his shoulder, and moved him to an open van.

So much for Mark Maher, Sam thought.

It was almost four o'clock when Mays pulled up in front of Sam's apartment. They had not spoken a word since they left the scene of the incident, and Mays felt a need to say something. "My Watch Commander goes on duty at ten. That's when I call in and report the money."

"Okay, sounds good to me."

"Okay then," Mays said. "Thanks for a good job out there, and thanks for saving my ass. I'll never forget that."

Sam left the car, then turned back to face Mays. "Look, we're cops. You watch my back and I'll watch yours. So let's not make a big deal out of this. Okay?"

"You got a deal," Mays answered. He threw the car in low gear and started to move away. As he drove off he lowered his window and hollered back at Sam. "But I will never, ever, forget that!"

Sam climbed into his shower and washed the scum of this night from his body. After the shower he poured a Glenlivet 12-year-old, pure single-malt Scotch whisky. He dressed himself in a pair of Levis and an old work shirt, opened the front door and sat on the steps of his apartment. The street was empty a cool breeze was coming in from the north.

As he sat there, enjoying his drink, he thought of the wise words of Adam Loper. "When you play checkers, you have to think ahead. You think one, two, even three moves ahead. You try to suck your opponent into a situation where you can demolish him. If he jumps your man, you can jump him back two men. That's how you win. Think ahead."

Chapter 16

FLASHBACK, CONTINUED.

SAM SAT ON the steps until five fifteen Saturday morning. The sky in the East was just developing an orange glow. An old red Ford truck came by, with a guy in the back, tossing newspapers out. He spotted Sam and made a perfect pass, which Sam caught over his shoulder, in excellent wide receiver fashion.

Sam moved into his apartment and quickly thumbed through the articles. There was nothing there regarding the drug bust. Sam knew the paper was put to bed by ten o'clock the previous night, and six hours later they would be delivered to homes across the New Orleans area. But he wanted to make sure.

His TV was tuned to Channel 3 and his radio was tuned to station WWL/640 AM. There was no news on either. Then at seven-thirty, he heard the first report from the radio. The show he was listening to was a general talk show format, and then the stock music played over the conversation and another voice interrupted.

"We interrupt this broadcast with breaking news."

The reporter told about what had taken place, all of which Sam knew, but the reporter never spoke about who was actually on the dock. It never mentioned who was killed or who survived. By eight-thirty he could only get a rehash of the same information. He shut down the radio and concentrated on TV.

The three networks were standing at the gate of the pier, with cameras at the ready. However the only information they had gotten from the FBI, or the local police, was sketchy to say the least. TV crews were still not allowed to move onto the dock itself. Sam decided to call Mays.

"You looking at the news?" Sam asked.

"Yeah, I got it on. Nothing."

"You going in today? This is Saturday, you know."

"Yeah, I work today. I got a computer there. I'll see what's on it."

"You alone now? Can you talk freely?"

"Yeah, she went to the store. They got some specials on stuff that I like."

"Let me ask you a question. Did you ever give one thought to stealing that money?"

"No way," Mays quickly jumped in. "I've got enough. I'm a happy camper."

"Stop the spin," Sam asked.

"What's that mean?"

"I mean you're spinning words to fit your situation. That's what that means. Suppose there was no way anybody could ever catch you. Would you steal the money?"

"The thought did cross my mind."

"Mine too. Now we get to the hard stuff. We were released from the dock. Why didn't we report this money to the men in charge of the bust?"

"Oh hell, that's easy. By the time we got our shit together, and got off the boat, they wouldn't let us talk to Lloyd, so I decided to just call my Watch Commander at ten the following morning."

"You're spinning again. The fact is, what you did was to leave fifty two million dollars in an old shrimp boat with no one in attendance, and then plan to make a phone call to your Watch Commander some eight hours later."

"Hey, what are you saying here?" Mays questioned with some indignity.

"What I'm saying is, if you now call the Watch Commander, your ass will be grass!"

"Oh shit, I'm going to jail."

"Your spin just ended," Sam stated.

"I fucking knew this would happen."

"Don't worry about that. I'll be in the cell right next to you."

"Aw shit!"

"Listen to me. Relax. Think this through. The only way we can stay clear of this is to never admit to seeing that money."

"Well, I sure as hell was down there. So were you. We left fingerprints all over the place."

"Somebody will wind up with this money, be it the drug cartel, the police, the FBI, or the owner of the damn boat. Whoever lays claim to that cash won't give a rat's ass what two cops did down in that hull. They'll have the fifty two million bucks."

"So what you want to do is ignore we ever saw the money?"

"That's right."

"We just lie about it and we're off the hook?"

"Correct."

"Okay then that's what we do."

"So now who do we worry about?"

"I don't know, who?"

"You and me, that's who. Are you worried about me?"

"Yes," Bill said.

"And I'm worried about you," Sam replied.

"Well that's good."

"So there you go."

Once he was convinced that at least for now he was not going to jail, Bill Mays started to change directions. "Okay, so we never admit to taking a look at the money."

"That's right."

"Okay, so maybe we should explore other possibilities."

"Okay. What's on your mind?"

"Suppose I want to buy the boat?"

Sam took a pause. His mind started reeling. "That presents a load of additional possibilities, not to have even yet been anticipated."

"You got that one right," Bill Mays said, with a slight chuckle. "But you and I never saw the cash."

"That's right."

Mays thought again. "I gotta go in to the office. Give this some thought."

It was understood, as a matter of importance, that Sam and Mays were both thinking on the same page, but neither wanted to discuss it openly with each other. Phones could be tapped, and live conversations might somehow be recorded. Each had decided to play the cards close to the vest, and to speak to each other only when they knew they were in a protected environment.

It was ten o'clock, Saturday morning, when Sam arrived at the headquarters, and found things were still in a state of confusion. The FBI was still on the premises, with agents wrapping up their files. Sam walked upstairs to Mays' busy office. He saw him there working on his computer. Sam stood out in a hallway, watching him through a side window as Mays struggled with the files. Then in frustration, Mays rose from his desk, seeking a cup of coffee.

As he crossed to the coffee machine, Mays noticed Sam. He paused for a second then moved on, shaking his head no. Sam got the message. No information.

This was the end of the week for Sam. He was off today and tomorrow, Sunday. No one controlled his movements on this day, and his presence at the precinct went basically unnoticed. There was still a question. Was the money still on the boat? He decided he would drive down to the pier and check that out.

At ten thirty, Sam drove his cop car down the I-10. He noted the last of the TV crews were leaving the dock, driving in the opposite direction. When he arrived at the parking area it was now almost empty. The dock was busy as usual, but the *Maria Isabella* was no longer there.

Sam walked down to the scene of the crime. He stood on the exact area where carnage had taken place. When he looked out onto the river, he saw the *Miss Lee*, with her "For Sale" sign, still displayed on the bow, looking like an old trollop, waiting for a new owner. Sam placed his hand in his pocket and withdrew his Swiss Army knife. He studied it for a moment, and then figured he would find it on the *Miss Lee*.

The dinghy that had taken them to the boat last night was now placed back into its docking position. Sam got into the small boat, and with one oar in hand, slowly maneuvered it over to the *Miss Lee*. Once there, he pulled himself up to the top deck and looked around. It wasn't Sam's purpose to study the beautiful geography of the Mississippi but to see if anyone on the shore was watching him.

He held a cop flashlight in his hand so that he might search for his knife, even in broad daylight. One never knows where a Swiss Army knife might fall in times like this. He searched his way into the pilot's cabin, then over to the trap door leading down to the engine room. Once there his eyes drifted back to the dock. He saw the two bullet holes left in the windshield from the night before. He further saw that no one was watching.

Sam bent down and grabbed the finger latch from the trap door and pulled it up, revealing the engine room below. He turned on his flashlight and peered down into the area. Everything was as it was the night before.

Sam actually started counting the duffel bags as they sat where he had placed them the night before.

He closed the trap door, and looked around again. Still no one was watching. He bent over and feigned finding his Swiss Army knife lying on a torn brown couch cushion. Using his Swiss Army Knife, he cut a strip of cloth from the cushion and upon closing the door to the pilot house, managed to trap the piece of the cloth between the door and the jam. It was a kid's trick, so they would know if anyone had entered the room.

Sam was satisfied. The other side door, along with the back door, had both been secured from the inside. Only this door could be opened from the outside and, when opened, the cloth would fall out. This situation was not about what Sam and Mays had found here the night before. This was not about the fifty-two million dollars in unmarked U. S. one hundred dollar bills. It was all about Sam finding his sixteen-dollar Swiss Army knife.

While out on the top deck, Sam got into a semi-crouched position with his head level to the piece of brown piece of cloth he had closed into the door. Then he looked around at the skyline, searching for a spot where he could see the boat and the hanging piece of cloth. The only spot he found was a Mexican restaurant called El Torero. It was located at least a quarter of a mile behind the dock.

Sam drove from the dock, and up a small road toward the I-10. There, on the right hand side, was the El Torero. It was a small Mexican food place, one where dock workers would join for an after-work beer and some tacos. Sam got out of his car, put his binoculars around his neck and entered the restaurant.

The *El Torero* was run by a guy named Harris. He was a young man, playing the dice game of Horse with three of his regular drinkers. It was now three o'clock, and the place was almost empty except for Harris and his regulars. But Harris always had the best of the situation. They would bet a dollar on each game and Harris would always win more than he lost. It was like shooting pool with Mark Maher. You give what you need to, and then win just enough to stay in business.

Harris was a slithering fellow, Sam's type of guy. He never remembered you from one day to the next, never knew your name, and could care less what you did for a living. This was, without a doubt, a place where you could get lost in a heartbeat.

Sam ordered a Mexican beer, Dos Equis, from Harris and moved on out to the front porch. It was built of wood, with four tables surrounded by chairs, and each with a large, red and white Martini & Rossi umbrella. The umbrellas were the only thing in the place that looked clean.

Sam pulled a chair over to the railing, and sat down. In front of him was the Mississippi and the entire canal system. Dead center was the *Miss Lee*. Sam removed his binoculars from the case and drew them to his eyes. He saw the boat and zoomed in closer to what he had prepared. The boat itself almost filled his area of vision and there he was able to see the brown piece of cloth, subtly placed between the door and the jam.

Sam poured the last of his beer into glass and then he gave some serious thought to his situation. The fact was, neither he nor Bill Mays were thieves. If he could get control of that money, and it could then be used to benefit the city, that would be a good thing.

Then he thought about the cops. He recalled the conversation he had with Ralph O'Reilly. He thought of those cops who don't make enough money to pay the food bills, and had to do outside part time work, to make ends meet. A germ of an idea crept into Sam's mind. *Suppose we had a company, right here in New Orleans, that offered a bonus of a thousand dollars to be paid for every cop involved in a drug bust*, Sam thought. *That would really put a crimp in drug sales.*

Sam gulped his beer down and left.

Eduardo drove a mule carriage for tourists around the Quarter. He was a nice guy, with knowledge of banking that fascinated Sam. Eduardo arrived at Sam's apartment around eleven fifteen. Sam continued to develop his idea, but he wasn't sure how Eduardo might take it. He poured two shots of tequila into two tumblers and offered Eduardo a toast.

"Here's to you, pal."

They threw the shots down and Eduardo smacked his lips. "Boy, that is great stuff."

"Let me try a hypothetical question on you," Sam asked.

"Okay. I can handle that one."

"Let's suppose I had, at my disposal, a bunch of money. And let's say it's dirty money."

"You mean as though it's not legal money?"

Sam looked at Eduardo for a long moment. He had known this man for close to five years, and now was about to find out what he really knew.

"Right," Sam added. "Let's say its illegal money."

"So how much you talkin' about, dis illegal moneys?"

"Well let's say in the millions."

"Whoa, that's big money."

"Okay, stay with me here. Now suppose I wanted to move this money to another country, let's say your country, Honduras. How would we go about doing that?"

"What you wanna do that for?"

"Well, maybe we could somehow get it into a bank there, and then have them issue a check back to us."

"Oh, I got it. What you wanna do is to get the bank to wash the dirty money and make it clean, so when you get it back, you're okay. Right?"

That was exactly what Sam was thinking about, but Eduardo just made it clear. "Yeah, something like that," Sam said.

Eduardo gave deep thought to the hypothetical situation. With his second tequila in hand, he rose from the couch and headed for the front door, peering out at the street beyond. He sipped at his drink and gave monumental preponderance concerning the possibilities. Then he turned back into the room.

"Okay, here's what you have to do." Suddenly Eduardo's broken English became less broken. "Let's say I mail a million dollars to one of my relatives in Honduras. When he gets it he changes the envelope I sent him, and he deposits it into the bank under my name. After the money clears the bank, he sends a check to me."

Sam nods at the suggestion.

"No," Eduardo continued. "A million dollars is too much, too big. Let's make that one hundred thousand dollars."

"How about just a thousand dollars," Sam interrupted. "Nobody would easily spot that."

"That's true, but it will take a while."

"So what if we get more people involved?"

"You have a risk factor there. You must know everybody you are dealing with. Each of them must be advised of the risk and each must take their chances for the money they make."

"What money?" Sam asked.

"You don't expect a person to wash your money for nothing? Do you? You must be willing to pay for what you get. What you need here is a complex organization that will do exactly what must be done. Otherwise it can become one big mess. I don't wish to play with any more hypothetical questions. Tell me what's going down, and I'll try to help."

"Well, I'm thinking of starting a new company, an operation that would help people." Sam stood up and walked to the bathroom. "I gotta take a leak." When he closed the door, Eduardo rose and started on the attack.

"You know what you need, Sam? You need a friend. Someone you can trust. Tell me what you want and I'll try to help you."

He had walked to the bathroom door, and listened carefully for the response from within. Nothing was forthcoming. Only quiet.

"May I remind you of what it was like for me and my son to come here? After the hurricane, we left Honduras with nothing. I lost my wife and everything I owned. You found me and my boy sleeping on the streets. You took us in. You took me and my boy Pedro in, and you gave us shelter. You helped me to make Pedro into a man. I owe you for that and my life. So if you're ever looking for someone to trust, trust me. I've already traveled to hell and back. How much more can I give to you off of my brown ass?"

The toilet flushed and the door opened. Sam stood there, facing Eduardo.

"Okay," Sam said. "Start from the top, one more time. Let's think it out."

They both sat down and Eduardo gave it the "big think."

"First you need a lawyer," Eduardo said. "Somebody to form a corporation. What's the name of your new company?"

"I was thinking of something like, the Police Benevolent Society."

"Of America," Eduardo added.

"That's it, The Police Benevolent Society of America, a non-profit organization."

"That sounds important."

"It could be. What we do is we give money to every cop in New Orleans. We pay every cop who makes a drug bust. We give him a bonus. Let's say one hundred bucks for a marijuana bust, and five hundred for heroin or cocaine, and a thousand for a major bust."

"That could mean a lot of money."

"That's just a thought. Nobody has decided exactly how much will be spent, but we will be prepared to hand out millions."

"Okay. So you get a lawyer to form a corporation. Then we take one thousand dollars, and open an account at our bank here. Next I go to Honduras. First thing I do there is to open a second bank account for the Police Benevolent Society of America. I will make a deposit of fifty thousand dollars, which I will bring with me in cash. This I will claim is my money to be used as seed money to start the corporate account.

"The big man in Honduras is Louis Rey. My brother Emilio sends me a box of old newspapers every month. Mr. Rey heads the Banco Pacifica. They now have over sixty banks in my country. Six years ago, when I was there, there were only fifteen banks, all of them small potatoes, nothing much. But now, Mr. Rey has built them up. Now he's got power.

"Then I arrange to meet with Louis Rey. Mr. Rey is a wealthy man. He will be happy that we have placed fifty thousand dollars in his bank. Mr. Rey is also involved in other activities. If I was to tell him that the Police Benevolent Society of America might be willing to donate fifty thousand dollars to one of his 'pet' activities, I believe he might become a very good friend of mine.

"I tell you what. I read that Mr. Rey is trying to build onto a hospital. He wants to put up a wing for cancer research, in honor of his wife who died of that disease. So I tell him I would be interested in aiding him to build his wing. I suggest we could call it the Louis Rey Cancer Research Center. How do you think that would make him feel?"

Sam was feeling strange. He was sitting in his one room apartment on Toulouse Street, sipping tequila, talking to a man who drove a mule and carriage for tourists in the French Quarter, and discussing spending fifty thousand dollars for a guy named Louis Rey to open a Cancer Research Center in Honduras.

"I think he would feel very good," Sam answered.

"Next, I will find as many close relatives as possible and get them to go along with us. I tell them they each receive, in the mail from us, eleven hundred dollars per week. Out of that they keep one hundred. I will tell you, one hundred dollars a week is like five hundred in America. That's a big deal.

"They open the envelope, take out one hundred for themselves, and place one thousand dollars for deposit to the bank, in another envelope. These are bank envelopes that I get from Mr. Rey after we have lunch. When Mr. Rey starts to get a thousand dollars donated from, let's say ten people a week, I'm sure of becoming a very good friend of his. Okay, what you think?"

"Sounds interesting."

"So now I telephone you. I say, send the money. I say send it every week. I give you the names and addresses of my people. We may find a way to break the amount of deposits up. One guy puts up eight hundred and twenty dollars and the next guy puts up over a thousand. We reverse all of that each week. Nothing we do fits the usual mold. That makes us hard to get caught.

"Now I check on all of my people. I make sure they do the right thing. I make sure they destroy the envelope you mailed to them from America. They burn it. It is gone. Now we cannot be caught with our chicken trapped in a pot."

"Our mitts in the grits," Sam added.

"That too. When I am sure Louis Rey has his first ten thousand dollar deposit, and he is impressed with me and my activities, and he knows I will now issue him his first check for his cancer clinic, and I am now considered to be his most special friend, I come back to New Orleans. I bring my corporate checkbook back with me, the one from the Banco Pacifica. Now, after about a month, I write one check, for let's say, ten thousand dollars. This amount to be moved from Honduras to our bank in New Orleans. When the New Orleans bank starts to see that, they gonna love me again! That's it. That's banking! That's how we bankers do our thing!"

Sam called Bill Mays at the precinct and told him to meet him at the El Torero in a half an hour. He arrived at the El Torero just before three. As he walked through the almost empty bar, he ordered two tequilas from Harris the bartender. When he got outside on the balcony, he checked on the *Miss Lee*. She was as beautiful as ever, with her piece of brown cloth still tucked neatly into her door jamb. Shortly after, Mays arrived. They sat down at a table.

"I met with a banker today," Sam said. "We have structured a way by which we can move this money to another country and send it back here, with no association to us whatsoever."

"What do you mean no association? Suppose somebody came by last night and took that money off? Then I just spent a bunch a money for a bucket of bolts."

Sam passed Mays his binoculars. "Here you go. Take a look at the boat."

Mays took the binoculars and fixed them to his eyes. "Okay, I see it."

"Now do you see that bit of brown cloth hanging out between the door and the jamb?"

"Yeah, I see that."

"Well, I went out there this morning and I did that."

"You went back there today?"

"Yes I did."

"An' you put that cloth in the doorway?"

"Yes I did. And nobody saw me. Nobody."

"An did you look to see if the money was still there?"

"Yes I did, and it's still there. And we still have no association with the money. If we need to, we could buy this boat and never admit to ever seeing the money."

"And what if tonight, somebody comes along and causes that cloth to fall down from the door jamb."

"Then we lose it all. No harm, no foul."

"I've been fascinated about that much money," Mays said. "I don't need it, can't use it. But wouldn't it be just great to make use of it?"

Sam looked over at Mays. He was like a kid with a new toy. He kept staring through the binoculars, thinking of what might happen.

"Yeah," Sam said. "It would be just great."

"I called the owner today," Mays offered. "I wanted to find out what he knew about the money."

"And what did you say?"

Mays put the binoculars down, and rubbed his eyes. "I asked what he wanted for the boat. He told me one hundred twenty five thousand. I told him that was too much. He said 'make me an offer.' I told him I would have my agent call him back. An' he said good-bye."

Sam saw a young girl coming out onto the porch. She stepped out from the darkness of the "cavern" that she worked in and was immediately blinded by the sunlight. She wore a red pleated short cocktail dress, one of those outfits that loose women wore who danced and sang in old-fashioned western bars, those women who never saw daylight. Her legs were encased in black net hose with an enlarged hole just to the right of her ass. Her face was pasty looking with a heavy coating of pancake makeup. Her hair was piled high on her head and her skin looked as though it would burn if she got a second more of sunlight.

"Here ya go, boys," She said, as she placed the two drinks onto the table. "It's sure bright out here. Need some sunglasses for this job. Normally we don't handle this area." She now shielded her face with the bar tab. "Anything else for you guys?"

"Yeah." Sam said, "Two more tequilas."

"Okay," she said gruffly as she hobbled back to the bar on red shoes that obviously pinched her toes.

"I thought you said the place works well?" Mays asked.

"Well, you have to train the staff." Sam remarked.

"So you finished talking with the boat guy, and that was it?"

"That was it."

"He never mentioned what was in the engine room?"

"Never brought it up. I don't think he ever went down there. He said it had been up for sale for nine months, and I should make an offer."

"Did you talk to your wife about this?"

"You mean about the boat? Yeah. I told her I saw a boat that I wanted to buy. I told her about you. She said, 'that's okay honey.'"

"What's her name?"

"Barbara. She likes me. She likes me a lot. It's an amazing thing when a guy finds a girl and she absolutely loves his socks off. She's got money. I'm not a millionaire; I'm more of a thousandaire. She got a nice bank roll when her father died."

"I'm sorry to hear about that, I mean about her father."

Mays looked at Sam for a moment, then he changed the subject. He took a batch of printed computer paper from his jacket pocket. "Here's what I got from the computer. Most of this stuff will be in tomorrow's newspaper."

Sam took the papers in hand and read some.

"BIG DRUG BUST. FBI and local police have squelched the largest drug bust this city had ever encountered. One hundred million in street value dollars of heroin and cocaine have been apprehended by FBI, along with local authorities."

There was an article by Martin Willis, who dealt with the names of the people involved in this massive drug bust. There were photographs of those responsible for the shipment. Sam read on.

"Two men, both brothers, members of the Gambia Family; the oldest was Ernest Gambia. Ernest Gambia was killed on the dock by gunshots to the chest and stomach. His youngest brother, Leon, died at Charity Hospital ten hours later due to gun shots to the head."

The article went on to explain how the Gambia Family had ruled the New Jersey area for twenty-five years. The Gambia Family had murdered, robbed, sold dope and were involved in prostitution.

"That's raw information from our people," Mays said. "The rest comes from the *Times*. It'll be in tomorrow's paper."

"So what do you think?" Sam asked.

"I think the good guys killed all the bad guys." Then a wry smile crossed his face.

As Sam and Bill Mays left the El Torero, Channel 3 was playing at the bar. It was a Special Breaking News report. "This may be one of the largest drug raids in the New Orleans area," The reporter announced. "More, when we return."

Sam and Bill Mays walked though the room, and out the front door.

At five-thirty that afternoon, Sam drove his cop car down to visit with Judge Wilford Bean. The judge was now in his mid-seventies. Having passed his judicial retirement age of seventy, he was still a sitting Judge and was now doing ad hoc work for the court.

Sam drove to his car to Lafitte and moved into the gated residence. His property line made it easily accessible for a large shrimp boat to be pulled free from the bayou waters. Back in the thirties, this property had been a major dry dock for shrimp boats that needed service. In the early seventies, when Judge Bean bought the place, it had been subdivided into two parcels. The Judge still owned one of the original large rigs used to haul a boat of seventy-five feet in length from the bayou into the docking area. In past years, Judge Bean only used this rig to help out a neighbor with his small thirty- to forty-foot boat, but Sam had something else in mind.

The Judge had a housekeeper whose name was Norma Rolland. Judge Bean had been married four times before, but this time it was not about marriage, it was just for someone who could keep the house clean, cook the meals and have sex. At least, that's how the Judge figured it.

Norma Rolland was a hard working lady. She had been the Judge's clerk for fifteen years and had suffered through the final three of his four marriages. When the Judge divorced his last wife, it all but coincided with Norma's first divorce from her first husband, who was an alcoholic and an abuser. As the two of them sat alone in his chambers one evening, the Judge asked if she might care to come and live with him. She quickly answered yes. That started a long and perfect love affair.

Norma was a natural beauty. She wore little or no makeup and could have been a movie star. She had golden hair and chiseled features that reminded some of the old-time movie actress, Greta Garbo.

Sam met with the Judge in his living room. Norma had prepared some iced tea. "I'll tell you the whole truth. It's a bizarre story." Sam went through the facts of life. He told them everything. He mentioned about his partner Bill Mays, where Bill and himself found the money and the shoot-out at the dock. He mentioned the fact that no one claimed the money. He told them that this money was apparently lost in the confusion of things that happened on that night, even possibly the death of the two mobsters involved in shipping the dope in the first place.

Sam went on to tell them of his return to the boat, seeing the money was still in place and putting a brown rag over the door to the cabin. He then told them of his meeting with his partner, when he told Sam of his wife's ability to purchase the boat because of a windfall from the death of her father some years ago.

Then as Sam continued to move on to the telling the situation he had discussed with Eduardo, he started to sweat. He quickly realized he had lost his audience. Both the Judge and Norma sat there watching him, never asking a question. It was as though he was speaking too fast – or perhaps it was the tequila. Sam decided then that tequila would never again be his drink of choice.

"So I talked to this banker I know from Honduras and he advised me as to how we could mail the money in to some of his relatives, and they would deposit it in the bank there to wash the money and when we get it back here, we put it in our bank and then we have the money to use."

While his audience sat with stone expressions, Sam took a long drink of his iced tea. He next used a cocktail napkin to wipe more sweat from his face. He knew it was over. He knew he was toast. He wanted nothing more than to end his diatribe and go home. He also knew there was no way a man like Judge Bean would even consider involving his prestigious career in such a bizarre situation.

"So when we have enough money back here in the States, we plan to develop a situation whereby we will award cops who make drug busts, with a bonus. Then we got the money to deal with. It's in large heavy Army duffel type bags. There's a hundred four of them, and we figure somewhere around fifty-two million dollars, an we need to get them off the boat, an put them somewhere, an count the money, an then store it someplace, an when we find out where to mail it, we need to put it in an envelope and mail it. Then we wait and see if it all works. It may take a couple a years, or more, for it all to come together. This thing started only yesterday! A lot has happened since then, and I'm just trying to figure the best I can to make it all work. And that's it."

Sam took another long drink, not wanting to even peer into the eyes of his audience. He simply looked about the room, waiting for the other shoe to drop. Judge Bean leaned forward in his arm chair.

"Well, I'll tell you one thing. There's no way I'm going to get involved in one of those 'funny money' things."

He pulled himself up from the chair and headed for the bedroom. Sam took a deep breath. He was glad it was over. No more pipe dreams. No more anticipating what might or might not happen. No more concern about the authorities. No buying the boat, or any worry whatsoever about anyone else but himself.

"Well, thank you for the iced tea," Sam said. "I think I'll get back to town now."

"So that's it?" Norma said. "Is that all there is?"

"Yes ma'am. I'm glad it's over."

"Evidently that big dream of yours wasn't worth the effort."

"I'm just glad it's over."

"Good God almighty. This is not over, it's just starting! You want to put your boat into dry dock? You've got the phone number. Call me and I'll have crew here to handle it within twelve hours. Then you take the rest of it one step at a time. Your mind moves very quickly. We're a bit older. We have to think things out. Make yourself a real drink over at the bar. I'll be back in a bit."

Norma left the room. Sam sat there, feeling like he had cookie crumbs all over his shirt. He moved to the bar in the corner of the room and poured a tall scotch. He then walked out to the front porch, sat in a lounge chair and stared at the setting sun. Norma was right. All he wanted to do was to pull a boat out of the water into dry dock. The rest of it was one step at a time.

Fifteen minutes later, Norma stepped outside and sat on the steps. "Okay, we have a deal. There is only one single restriction. Don't ever mention where you got the money. We'll do whatever needs to be done. Just don't mention where you got the money. If you want to bring it in here and open it up and count it out, no problem. If you need someone to make an accounting, write envelopes, take it to the post office. No problem. Just don't mention where you got the money!"

Sam stood up and walked down the stairs. When he turned back to look at Norma, he could see through the screen door the Judge standing in the living room. The last piece of his puzzle had now been solved, and now it was his turn to make it all happen. Sam was watching the Judge as he spoke to Norma.

"Thank you. I understand what you've said. I will never betray his confidence. I assure you we will make this work."

Sam drove to his one-room apartment. When he walked inside, there was an envelope on his floor. It was from his division HQ. It was from Adam Loper.

From: Captain Adam Loper
To: Officer Sam Pennington

Regarding: New Assignment.

Officer Pennington,
Please make contact with Detective Captain Carl Witherspoon at Division 8, of the Royal Street Precinct. This to be done sometime on Monday morning. Witherspoon has heard about you and wants to meet with you.
Regarding all other activities you were involved with concerning my department, they have all been concluded. Disregard all other activities concerning this matter.

Best wishes,
Loper

Over the next six months, things happened in rapid fire. The following Monday Sam had a meeting with Carl Witherspoon, who brought him into his office as trainee detective. He next called the owner of the *Miss Lee*, representing himself as the agent for the sale. He offered fifty thousand dollars and they finally agreed to seventy-five. Mays arranged for the transfer of money, and the sale was completed. Five days later they moved the boat to Lafitte.

They hired a licensed river pilot to pilot the boat to Lafitte, and the old engine barely managed to make it. There they were met by Norma, the Judge, and their crew of four. It took almost three hours of hard work to pull the boat from the bayou onto the dry dock. Sam and Bill Mays were there also, doing whatever good sailors do in these situations.

After that was completed, they covered the entire craft with large sheets of painter's drop cloth, tied it tight to the boat's railings and left it sitting there for the next six months. And no one was watching.

Sam next hired a cookie cutter attorney, one who could put a proper corporation together. Once that was established, he bought a ticket for Eduardo Sanchez with fifty thousand dollars in his pocket to visit Honduras.

Once there, Eduardo met with his family and found two brothers, four uncles, two aunts and six cousins, to join him in the establishment of the Police Benevolent Society of America.

Eduardo Sanchez next opened a bank account at Banco Pacifica. His initial deposit was for fifty thousand dollars of 'his' money. He next arranged a meeting with Louis Rey, who was the president of the banking organization that now operated just over sixty banks in Honduras.

Mr. Sanchez placed a call to New Orleans, Louisiana, advising them of the names and addresses of his selected relatives. Seven days later, each of those relatives received cash from the States, which they all deposited into the Banco Pacifica. With everything working well and with fourteen thousand new dollars having been deposited, Eduardo returned to New Orleans, having completed a successful job. A job well done.

Chapter 17

Day 8, continued

AT SIX-THIRTY Wednesday morning, March 8, Sam jumped into the shower and finished his bathroom duties. He wanted to call Kelly, but it was too early. She would probably be sleeping late. He was out onto Barracks at seven-fifteen, turned left onto Bourbon and walked down to the St. Ann Market. There he ordered coffee and beignets from Phil, who said nothing to him whatsoever, glanced through his *Times Picayune*, and after finishing his breakfast meal, walked on to the station.

Sam had a good feeling about this day. There were many problems lurking in the shadows, but Sam still felt good. He felt like a tiger, nothing could stop him. Tomorrow the New Orleans Jazz Fest would start. Something would always be starting in New Orleans. Tourists crowded the streets and Sam always offered them his greeting.

He arrived at his office at eight o'clock. Wally was already there with hot coffee at the ready. Sam sat at his desk and placed a call to Kelly. The cell phone number rang five times with no answer. As he was about to hang up he heard her voice. It was bright and cheery, one of eager anticipation, for what she had planned for the day.

"Hi Sam? How you doing?"

"Hey there. How'd you know it was me?"

"You're the only person who's got my cell phone number."

"Where were you?"

"I was taking a shower. I had to hustle to get the phone. It's good to hear your voice."

"Listen, I've got an easy day here. I gotta go to a meeting at two o'clock. After that I think I'll take the rest of the day off. Get down to see you, and see what's happening with the boat. You gonna be there?"

"The boys have already sanded the first base coat. When they put on the second, it dries in two hours. After that we put on the first finish cream white coat. It's in a matte finish. Then tomorrow we put the same cream color on, only this is in semi-gloss. I tell you Sam, it's going to be beautiful."

"I'm a believer. I'll see you around three this afternoon, maybe four. We'll have some dinner. I may even spend the night."

"That's great. I'll get some food. We'll barbeque."

"Bye babe."

"Good-bye, Sam."

Sam hung up the phone, sat back on his chair and took a sip of coffee. It was true, this was gonna be a great day!

The phone rang and Wally answered. "Hello, this is Detective White. How may I help you?" He listened but got no response. "Hello, may I be of some help?" Still there was no response.

Sam crossed over to Wally, reached out and took the phone. "This is Detective Pennington. May I help you?"

Sam could hear some conversation and laughter in the far distance, but no one was on the phone. Whoever had called had nothing to say. Sam was about to hang up when he heard faint female voice.

"This the do-good cop?"

For a moment, Sam was puzzled. Then he thought he recognized the voice. "Is that you, Hironee?"

"I think I'm gonna die here."

"Where are you?"

"My skin, I ain't in my skin. My head hurts so bad."

"Where are you? Are you at your house?"

"Yes."

"You hold on, I'm on my way."

Sam hung up the phone and ran for the door. "Get my car, Wally. Meet me at Bienville and Rampart, three houses in from Rampart on Bienville. Honk the horn twice and wait."

Without question, Wally was up and out. Once on the street, Sam ran to the left and Wally zagged to the right.

On a dead run, Sam turned right on Bienville, and made a mad dash toward Rampart. Four blocks later he ran up to Hironee's front door and knocked loudly. At first he heard laughter from inside, after his knocking, things got quiet. Then a black girl opened the door a crack. The chain lock was still in place.

"Yeah," She said, with a degree of sarcasm.

"I'm a friend of Hironee Jessup. She just called me. Is she here?"

"Yeah."

The door closed as she unlocked the chain, then the door opened wide.

"She down at the end 'a the hall."

Sam entered the room. There were five adults there: three women and two men. The room looked and smelled like the pits of hell. Sam had walked into a major drug party. There was a large mirror, sitting on a coffee table. It was covered with cocaine dust. Three single edged razor blades were also scattered over the face of the mirror. The coke itself was there in the small stick packets Sam had grown to know and appreciate.

On a side table was the heroin stash. Several candles that had been in use through the night were now just nubs, laying on the nearby floor. There were three teaspoons there also, each with a wad of cotton placed in the bowls. And of course there was the usual syringe and needles, three of them, parked at the ready should anyone wish to partake.

There was also booze. Whisky bottles and beer cans littered the area. Of course, there was the usual odor of marijuana, that sweet, sick, thick aroma that tells you there's nothing like lovin' from something from the oven.

"Where do I go?" Sam asked.

"She right down the hall there. Door at the end."

Sam made his way down the hall. He passed an open bedroom door, quickly noting there was more drug paraphernalia present there also. He arrived at the door at the end of the hall, and without hesitation, opened it.

It was the bathroom. He looked around and saw it was empty. He stepped into the room and closed the door behind him, moved forward, and then saw the totally nude body of Hironee, lying in the bottom of the dry tub, eyes closed. She still had her cordless phone in her hand, and when Sam reached down for the phone her eyes popped open.

"Hello there," Sam said softly. "What is it you took?"

Hironee had been drugged to the point of passing through this world into somewhere else. She was now seconds from a real bad coma, and minutes from meeting the real Grim Reaper.

"I don't know," she said. "They gave me something. I don't know."

Sam looked around the room, and saw a powder-blue bathrobe hanging on the back of the door. He grabbed the garment and then reached in to take Hironee by the arms.

"Okay. Here we go. We're going to stand up now."

"No, I can't stand no more. I'm sorry I called you. Let me here to die."

"Okay, here we go." He pulled her into a standing position. Then he placed the robe around her body."Well, there you go." Sam said. Hironee was cooperating, using her arms to balance herself. As he dressed her with a robe, Sam continued directing her moves. "Now we put the left arm in, then the right." She finally had both arms in position in the robe. "Now, put both hands around my neck."

She did that and Sam leaned back a few inches from her body, pulled the robe closed in the front, and securely tied the belt.

"Well, look at you now. Dressed up and ready to go. We got this one knocked, baby. Let's do it to it."

He reached his arms around her waist and pulled her from the tub, placing her bare feet on the floor. Then he walked her to the door. She stepped cautiously, with timid little steps. Sam opened the door and they were in the hallway.

"I ain't gonna make this," she said, her head tugging on his shoulder.

He was half-carrying her as they walked, her right hand was around his neck and over his shoulder and he was holding onto it with his right hand. His left hand was holding her at the waist.

"You're doing just fine. No problem here."

As they were about to reach the living room they heard two car horn honks.

"That's our car. We got about fifteen more steps and you are in the hospital. We got this one knocked."

They entered the living room. The party was still going on, but the action quieted down as soon as the group saw them.

The young girl who had opened the door for Sam, confronted them. "Where you guys goin'?"

"Going to get some more booze," Sam said.

They were about the reach the door when Sam heard a snap/cocking sound. Sam stopped walking and slowly turned back into the room. As he turned, he came face to face with a handgun, pointed directly at his head. It was a thirty-eight pistol, loaded for bear and ready to shoot.

The kid had to be between twenty and thirty. It was hard to tell. His hair was a mess, his face full of acne, his eyes blurred and his speech slurred. His T-shirt was printed with large block letters stating, "MISERY LOVES COMPANY."

Sam's arms were holding Hironee; his gun was in its holster on his right side. A move for his gun would surely result in a bullet to his head. It was one of the worst nightmares all cops must dream of. You're standing in plain daylight, kick a door in, and come face to face with a pitch dark room. You can't see the bad person, but he can most assuredly see you. You think of that often, avoid the situation at all cost, and when it actually happens, you want to bend over and kiss your ass goodbye.

"You gonna shoot that thing?" Sam asked, with a slight smile on his face. "You gonna shoot that thing, or are you just planning to clean it?" Then Sam's expression changed into a big smile.

The boy got Sam's sense of humor. He threw his head back and laughed out loud. As his laugh grew, he placed his gun to his side. Others in the party also started laughing. Sam was cracking up as he turned for the door. He leaned to his right, releasing his hold on Hironee with his left hand, and opened the door.

They stepped out into the street, Wally stood by the car. As she stepped down, Hironee passed out, literally fainted as she walked. Sam felt her falling, reached around, while at the same time bending over, and in one motion, picked her up in his arms like a rag doll. As Sam closed in on the car, Wally was there opening the rear door. Without stopping, Sam moved her into the rear seat. His only problem was that he had to fight his way through the brown llama carpeting which was in the process of being installed. The front area of the car was finished, but the rear hadn't yet received the pristine finished treatment.

Wally shut the rear door and ran around to the driver's side. As he jumped in behind the wheel he asked, "You want me to use the lights and siren?"

Sam had not told anyone in the house he was a cop, and he didn't wish to advertise that situation now. "No!" Sam screamed. "Just drive!"

After a few blocks Sam said, "Turn right at Dauphine Street and make it quick to Charity Emergency."

Wally made the move, and once on Dauphine Sam said, "Now! Hang the light and turn the siren on."

Wally finally got the idea. "No cops at the house. Now we turn the corner and then we become cops."

Wally turned right on Canal, placed the red light on the top of the car, and hit the siren button. Wally loved to drive with the portable red light placed on top of the car, and the sound of the siren whistling in his ears. It made him feel like the king of the road.

Sam reached for his phone, pulled it from his jacket pocket and hit the pound key and return. A familiar voice answered.

"Police central," Ethel said. She was the charming voice that Sam had talked to many times before, but never met.

"This is Sam Pennington. I need a Swat team at 1103 Bienville Street. Need it now. Got five druggies there, at least one of the men is armed and dangerous. Advise the narco squad. You got that?"

"I got it, sweetheart. Their vehicles are now rolling."

"Thank you, darlin', talk to you later." Sam hung up the phone.

Wally turned into the Emergency entrance of Charity Hospital. He turned the siren off, but left the red light on. Wally then jumped from the car.

"We need a gurney over here!" he shouted out.

Two attendance men moved out quickly, placed Hironee on the gurney, and ran her inside. Sam followed closely behind. Once inside, Sam told a young doctor what he believed she had taken, told him she was major witness in a crime, and further told him this lady must survive this incident in order to testify in court. He handed the doctor his card and Hironee was now an officially insured patient of the City of New Orleans.

Sam returned to the car, and jumped into the shotgun seat. Wally maneuvered out onto the street.

"Head back to Bienville," Sam said. "Let's finish this up."

They arrived on Rampart and Bienville and found the street blocked off with yellow tape. Five cop cars were present, along with a large black vehicle that supported the SWAT team.

Sam and Wally jumped from the car and headed for the house. A small crowd of civilians had gathered. Each of the five dopers had been cuffed and placed into individual cop vehicles, and other policemen were now taking out evidence from the house. The SWAT team, headed by a cop named Joe Fry, were at their truck. They wore all black fatigue style uniforms and were removing their 'swat' gear: bullet proof vests, metal helmets, and the like.

"Anybody get hurt?" Sam asked of Fry.

Fry looked up and recognized Sam. "Hey Sam, how you doing? No problem, just cleaning up the neighborhood."

At that moment, Sam heard the voice of Tom Phelps, a detective with the Narcotics Unit at Royal. He worked in an office down the hall from Sam that employed seventeen officers. Narcotics needed more men than Sam had for homicide.

"Hey there, Sam, you the guy who called this one in?"

"Yeah," Sam answered. Tom Phelps was a guy who always had a smile on his face. It was sort of a fake implanted grin that he wore like a medal of honor.

"Thanks a lot for helping us get these shit-heels off our streets."

"No problem."

"I understand you had a piece of shit point a gun at you?" Fry asked.

"That's right."

"This the gun?"

Tom Phelps pulled a plastic bag from his coat pocket, and held it up for Sam to see. Sam recognized it, same gun.

"That looks like it."

"Come over here with me for a minute."

Tom Phelps walked over to one of the squad cars and opened the rear door, revealing the boy who was in the house, the one who pointed the gun at Sam. Sam crossed in closer and peered inside. The boy was quiet now, not laughing.

"This the asshole who pointed the gun at you?" Phelps asked.

"That's him."

"Name's Gary. Doesn't have a last name, just Gary." As Tom talked, his smile got even broader. Tom enjoyed this. He enjoyed it a lot. "Let me tell you something, Sam. Gary's gun was loaded and the safety was not in place. Gary here could have put a bullet through your head in a second. Isn't that right, Gary?"

Gary looked away, out of the other window.

"The thing is, you people in homicide deal mainly with one person wanting to kill another. But we in narcotics deal with one person wanting to kill anybody, just for one more sack of dope. Isn't that right, Gary?"

Gary turned his head back and looked directly at Tom. Then he spat at Tom, the spittle hitting him directly in the face.

Tom didn't flinch for a second. He just remained there, frozen with intent and smiling like the face of evil.

"I guarantee you this, son, the day will come when you are sick and tired of jail, and you will want nothing more than to get out. An this little wad of spit will cost you at least ten more years in the can."

As Wally drove back to the office, Sam sat back in his seat and looked around. He first tried the window. It went up and down like magic.

"Car looks pretty good," Sam said. "Window works fine. Carpet looks real nice."

"Thanks," Wally answered. He was now waiting for Sam to make his signature comment about the finished carpet work on the rear compartment. But it didn't come. Wally parked in front of the precinct, as Sam needed the car for his two o'clock appointment at OIA.

They entered the office and Sam typed an e-mail to Tom Phelps. He typed his entire experience with Hironee, from start to finish, including his association with Gary, when he pointed a loaded pistol at him and almost blew his brains out. That was it. At one forty, Sam left the office for his two o'clock. As he left the room, he made his final comment on the condition of his car.

"I may not be back for the day." Sam said to Wally. "I've got some other stuff to take care of. Oh, and when you turn my car back in later today or tomorrow, you might want the carpet guys to check out the back seat. It might use a little more finish work there, if you know what I mean."

"You got it, Sam," Wally said.

Sam left the room. Wally smiled to himself. "He always gets the last word."

The building Sam drove to was one of the tallest on Poydras Street. Sam parked in the garage, which was professionally maintained. There, the management had placed live plants in the area, some decorator benches, and inside the glass doors leading from the garage to the elevators they constructed a large fish pond, with a fountain that sprayed out at the top. This was a definite signal that care had been taken to increase the beauty of the building.

He entered the first-class elevator and pushed the 26th floor. He was now riding in a thing of beauty. Sam had been in many 'rinky-dink' elevators in his lifetime, but this one was neither rinky nor dinky. It was special. Much larger than most, it was slick and fast. It wasn't an elevator, it was a beautifully walnut-paneled room with thick black carpet and cut glass sconces hanging from the walls.

When he exited onto the twenty-sixth hallway, the décor became even more majestic. The walls on either side were decorated with panels of ten-foot-high walnut, divided with smoked glass mirrors. The black carpet continued to flow through this area, creating a mood that presented a surge that meant business as well as a place built with serious money.

Sam was twelve minutes early. He went to the men's room, which opened a new thrill in his life. The place was even more imposing than the elevator. The decorations were impeccable, more walnut, more glass, more crystal, more everything. There were six marble stalls for the toilets. These were not standard stalls, the ones built with racks of plastic and aluminum framing. These were individual rooms, for the use of guests with integrity.

Each stall was built with a solid floor to ceiling door, and each one had a golden handle on the front. When you twisted the handle, the door opened into an area that was yours and yours alone.

Sam stepped into a toilet that was larger than any jail cell he had incarcerated many a felon into. The floor was laid with gold-veined off-white marble. The walls continued with the walnut and alternating smoked glass. What caught Sam's attention was that each stall had its own wash basin with a gold framed mirror hanging above.

Sam sat onto the enclosed toilet and looked around the room. He was alone in this massive *pissoir*, waiting to kill a few minutes from his clock, and wondering how in hell the Office of Internal Affairs managed to pay for this quality office space.

At exactly two o'clock, Sam opened the door to the main office and walked up to the secretarial desk.

"Hello. My name is Sam Pennington. I have an appointment with someone."

"May I ask what this is regarding?"

"Something," Sam answered. "I have this message from my assistant to be here at two o'clock, and that's about it."

"And who are you?"

Sam reached into his pocket for his badge and ID. "Sorry about that. Sam Pennington, Division 8, Royal Street."

"Won't you please take a seat and I'll see who is handling this case."

Sam sat down and thought about what was meant by "this case."

George Carey and David Kennedy had been on 'watch' in the Quarter, trying to find a serial killer that was about to kill number "four." They got a call to assist in a burglary in progress, located on South Tchoupitoulas

Street. They were now in the heart of the commercial section of the city. It had been proven in the book of world records that Tchoupitoulas was the most misspelled and mispronounced street in the world.

By the time they arrived to inspect the burglary, the burglar had been arrested and the crime was over. Shit happens when you're a cop. They turned back and drove up north on Tchoupitoulas and found a small sandwich stand, stopped and had a po' boy, then moved on.

They were five blocks south of Canal when they saw a car burning. It was located in the five hundred block of Tchoupitoulas. A fire truck moved to the opposite side of the street and stopped, totally blocking all traffic moving in either direction. Men jumped from the fire truck and headed for their job, extinguishing the fire. George and David were in no hurry. They casually sat there, waiting for whatever to happen – and happen it did. George was driving his silver-gray Skylark, and he looked out of his rear view mirror. It was just a habit, something all drivers do when they are parked while waiting for the fire department to put out a fire. Something caught his attention.

"David?" George said. "Take a look at the car behind us. Try to be subtle."

Using his most casual of approaches, David slowly looked toward the rear. Then he slowly looked back.

"I see him."

"You see who?"

"I see the guy we almost busted last Friday at the Cabaret, on Bourbon Street."

George was still looking into his rear view mirror. "His hair was bushier then, more curls."

"He was wearing a wig then," David said. "I think we got this bastard."

"Hold on. Let's think this thing out. He's trapped right there. I'm gonna go up to him, and ask to see his driver's. Then I'll come back to the car and we check it out."

On this day, Eddie Marshall had been to a market on South Peters. He had purchased food for a few days and was driving back to his building, which was located at 522 Tchoupitoulas. Turning left onto Tchoupitoulas, he fell in behind a silver-gray Skylark. Eddie drove for a few blocks and came to a stop. All cars had stopped, due to a car fire burning on the street ahead. At this moment, Eddie was only three doors away from his building. He became impatient. He looked around.

His car had just passed a small alley to his right. The alley ran East and West, and it "T-boned" into the major back alley which ran north and south, running parallel to Tchoupitoulas. If he could just back up a few feet, he could have turned into that small alley and parked his car behind his building. Now that was impossible, as another car had pulled up tight to Eddie. He was now trapped, and therefore had to wait.

Then he saw the driver's door of the Skylark open, and George Carey stepped out onto the street. Instantly Eddie recognized George! He remembered him from the situation at the Cabaret on Bourbon, five nights ago. His heart started pounding. As George drew closer to his car, Eddie started glancing around, seeking a route of escape.

George tapped lightly at Eddie's window. Eddie rolled it down and looked up.

"Yes?" Eddie said. "Can I help you."

George reached in his rear pocket and pulled forth his badge and ID. "I'm with the New Orleans Police. May I see your driver's license?"

"Sure thing," Eddie's mind was flooded with things that could have gone wrong. Five days ago he was wearing a curly wig, a pair of glasses and his face had a stubble beard. It was possible this cop might not make a connection. He pulled his driver's license from his shirt pocket and handed it to George.

"Thank you. I need to run a check on this. I'll be right back."

David had moved the rear view mirror toward the car behind, watching what was happening with George. George got back into the car.

"His name is Ed Marsh, licensed in Mississippi." George grabbed the radio hand unit. "This is Detective George Carey, Division 8 on Royal. Seeking info on a DL from Mississippi, number 589..."

"George, he's running!" David screamed as he jumped from the car while drawing his gun. George dropped the telephone mike and jumped out of the driver's side. He got a glimpse of Eddie as he disappeared running into the small alley. Drawing his gun, he followed David as they both quickly chased after their suspect.

As they both tuned into the alley, they could see Eddie running about fifteen seconds ahead of them.

"Stop, police!" David screamed out. Eddie was running as fast as possible. He glanced back over his shoulder. The two cops were struggling to keep up. Eddie rounded the corner, to his left, into the second larger alley. David and George ran another fifteen seconds and made the same turn. They saw the alley was empty. George stopped running while David ran further up the alley. Then he also stopped and looked around.

"Where'd he go!" David called out.

"He couldn't have made it all the way down to Julia Street."

"No way. He's got to be in one of these buildings."

"Stay here," George said. "Watch for him. I'll take care of the front. I'll get help."

Ten minutes later the receptionist came back out into the front office. "Mr. Pennington, right this way sir. Mr. Lupson will be handling your file."

Sam's 'case' had now turned into a 'file.'

"Is his first name Deland?" Sam asked.

"Yes sir it is."

They walked down the hall to Deland Lupson's office. Sam had met Deland once, at an award dinner. No cookie cutter lawyer was this guy. The problem for Sam was he had no idea what Deland Lupson might ask. He decided he would admit to anything – except the money.

When Sam entered the double doors at the end of the hallway, he saw one of the most beautiful office suites he had ever been in. There were large tinted windows through out the room. The office was on the North side of the building. You could look out and see a panorama of the city. At the far right, was the tall Hilton Hotel, with the magnificent Mississippi River flowing in the background. As your eyes moved on to the left, you could see the river boats, the *Robert E. Lee* paddle-wheeler and the ferry boat that ran over to Algiers. Past that was the St. Louis Cathedral, standing out like a majestic thing of beauty. Beyond that you could see the rest of the quarter, his apartment building and the path he walked every morning to St. Ann's Market. In the lower section of his view Sam saw the 8th precinct.

A door at the rear opened and Deland Lupson walked into the room. "Sam, how are you?"

Lupson was a 46-year-old company man. He had been the Director of the Office of Internal Affairs for twelve years. It was ten years earlier when Sam and Mays stole fifty-two million dollars that should have gone to the city. That was something else that Sam kept thinking about.

Lupson was a man without discriminating features. His sandy hair was combed straight back and wore Docker khaki slacks with a gray cardigan sweater over a pale blue polo shirt. He reminded Sam of Mr. Rogers, of that children's T. V. show. Of course, his shoes were brown penny loafers. And he smoked a pipe.

Sam rose from his seat. "Hello Deland. Nice to see you again."

They shook hands and Deland crossed over to a dual couch area. "Let's sit over here. It's more comfortable. Would you care for something to drink?"

"No thank you, I'm fine."

They sat at the more comfortable area, with the two couches facing each other, across a glass coffee table. They parried for a while. They talked about their jobs, life in general, and told a few old jokes. When it finally got down to the serious stuff, Lupson rose and moved behind his desk.

"I've got some notes over here," Lupson said. "Join me, won't you?"

Sam could read this act like an old vaudeville show. It was like the handbook of the CIA. *I'll sit here, you say that, we laugh, and when we get serious concerning the real thing you really want to talk about, we move to your desk, where you have kept a long list of notes.* Even Deland's dialogue was written by professionals. Sam rose from the couch and moved to a chair in front of Lupson's desk.

As soon as Lupson sat down behind his desk, he reached for his favorite pipe. He had a rack of six pipes there, but he preferred his standard 'woody,' to the three other pipes that were carved into buffalo heads.

This was a ritual Deland Lupson did, as his meetings moved from the sublime into the 'I'm gonna getcha' area. He emptied the bowl of the pipe with a pipe tool, then he filled it with a sweet smelling tobacco. After tamping it down with the same tool, he struck a long wooden match, and puffed on the pipe to light it.

Every move he made was a picture. He was fastidious. "The first thing I want to go through," *puff, puff,* "is your association with a police officer, a detective named William Joseph Mays," *puff, puff.* "Do you know William Joseph Mays?"

At this point in time, Sam felt he was being recorded. He had been there before, done that. He had sat in the courtroom with Donald Mosley, as he challenged the fact that he was going blind. Sam wanted to be careful. He also started to enjoy the sweet odor of his pipe tobacco.

"Yes I do," Sam said.

"Both you and Mays were involved in a case about ten years ago. Do you recall that?"

Sam now knew he was being recorded. The way Deland spoke, the phrasing of his questions, made it clear. *This bastard is trying to set me up,* Sam said to himself.

"Yes I do," Sam answered.

"You have a problem with Detective Mays?"

"Yes I do."

"And what might that be?"

"Personal. I have a personal problem with Detective Mays."

Lupson offered one of those buddy-buddy smiles. "Come on, Sam, you can tell me."

"Okay," Sam said. "It is a personal problem. It has nothing to do with police work. We both go to work every day and go home every night. And each day we do the best we can for the department. When it's all over, Bill Mays and I still have a problem. And it's personal."

"Well that's fine," Lupson said. "I can handle that."

"Thank you for your consideration," Sam said. He now sounded like a recording.

Deland Lupson had proven he did not like Sam Pennington. Sam was not a team player. Sam had quickly proven he hated Deland Lupson's guts. To Sam, it was a matter of *these guys are against our guys*. The Office of Internal Affairs against the cops. They would nitpick at every level, and in doing so would cause more of the bad guys to go free.

Deland Lupson was about to get into the real measure of his discussion, when his phone rang. "Excuse me for a moment," Deland said. "I have to take this call."

While Lupson took his call, Sam walked over and looked out of the window at the quarter. Sam could see the Dixieland from where he stood. He saw the spot where his partner was murdered on St. Joseph Street. At the same time, Sam could hear Deland had concern with some legal problem. That was what it was all about, legal problems. It all wound up with the difficulties between cops and lawyers. All a real cop wanted to do, was shoot the bastard who did the evil deed. All the lawyers wanted to do was protect the bastard's rights.

Lupson concluded his call. "Sorry about that, Sam. Let's get this thing finished up. I'm sure you have more important things to take care of."

Sam moved back to his chair. This was the point of decision. Sam had had all of the sweet talk he could handle. It was finally time to get serious. Lupson was not sorry about anything. Sam believed he was as phony as a three dollar bill.

"So who was it that got you and Bill Mays teamed up on that case in this first place?"

That was it, it was that simple. They were now down to the nitty gritty.

"That was Adam Loper, the head cop of the narcotics division on Rampart. He assigned me to the case. Then I met Mays later, and we did our thing."

"And who were you assigned to, with the FBI I mean?"

"It was a long time ago. I don't recall."

"Might it have been Agent Pierce?"

"That's it, Pierce."

"Agent Lloyd Pierce?"

"You seem to have it all written down right there," Sam said with a snide attitude. "Why don't you just show me what you've got and I'll tell you if it's right?"

"Let's just do this my way."

Sam braced himself. Would he ever ask what was on the *Miss Lee*? Might money ever be mentioned? Could fifty-two million dollars ever be brought up? Sam decided he didn't like the smell of Deland's pipe.

"It took us three months to finish our examination of the goods," Lupson said. "We were told we should receive one hundred million dollars of narcotics, and when our research was completed we only had fifty million."

"And it took you boys ten years to find that out?" Sam questioned. "Why is it I now need to sit here, ten years later, and talk to you about the fact that you couldn't find another fifty million dollars of lost dope? Do you think I'm stupid or what?! Let me tell you. I don't have your dope and I don't know where your dope is, nor do I know who took it. Not fifty million, nor one buck's worth. That's it, pal, end of story."

Deland Lupson's face started to turn red. He shuffled through his paper work, and found something else.

"Alright then. When you left the dock, were you not involved with an Agent Frank Miller?"

Sam started to relax. This was typical. Lupson was on a fishing expedition, and he thought Sam was the fish. Sam decided to play out the game.

"Let's see," Sam said. "Frank Miller. I don't remember a Frank Miller. As I recall, there was a Miller there, an agent. He asked that we leave the area. Told us to deposit our guns and stuff with the guard at the gate. My God, don't tell me you suspect agent Miller of being involved in pilfering fifty-million dollars of drugs, do you?"

Lipson was now seething. If Sam was to be Lupson's fish, Sam was playing himself like a shark. "I am not accusing anybody of anything."

"Then Frank Miller is not involved in drugs?"

"Knock that shit off. I'm conducting an investigation here."

"Investigation? Am I under investigation? I was told to be here, so you could check my file. Now all of a sudden I'm under investigation? I think I'd better get a lawyer."

Sam's pager started vibrating. He reached his belt and pulled it out to look at the number. It was 911.1.

"This is an emergency call from the head guy in my office. I'll have to call him right back."

"You can call a lawyer if you wish." Lupson said. "Actually I'd even prefer it."

Sam leaned forward, across the desk and displayed his phone to Lupson. He pointed to the read out phone number.

"See, here's the number. See there, it's printed out. See the 911.1. We use 911 between ourselves to say this is an emergency. The number one after that is my head man at the office. So what I need to do is call him back. Now!"

When Sam completed his call from George Carey, he quickly apologized to Deland Lupson and ran from the room. "I got a problem! Gotta go! Call you later!"

Lupson sat back into his chair and fumed. "Don't you worry, Detective," Lupson said out loud. "I'll be right here waiting for you."

Sam heard the words as he ran from the office. When Sam got to his car, he put the red light onto his roof, and headed for Tchoupitoulas with siren blazing. It took him only four and a half minutes to get there.

George explained the whole situation. He already had five police cars guarding the north and south streets. David had already run to each car, handing them the photo of the wanted man. They had concluded that this person was now hiding in one of the twelve buildings that bordered the back alley. For the moment, at least, things were secure.

"I got his driver's license," George said. "It's from Mississippi. We're running a state-wide check on it."

"That's good." Sam said. Then he walked back into the alley. Once there, he saw David. "Hey David, how's it go?" Sam asked.

"Real good Sam, real nice day."

"That's good. You check these back doors? Any of them unlocked?"

"Just two, that one on the right side over there, and another on Julia Street at the left end. You want us to go in and flush him out?"

"No, I don't think so. Just hang loose for a second."

"You got it Sam."

As Sam walked back down the alley toward Tchoupitoulas Street, he made a phone call to Ethel.

"Police central." Ethel said.

"Hello Ethel, this is Sam Pennington again."

"Hello sweetheart. What's happening?"

"I need another SWAT team at 522 Tchoupitoulas. Need it ASAP."

When Sam reached the front of the building he spotted Charlie Wong and George Carey, working over a five-year-old green Volvo. Charlie had two assistants with him, just to help him out.

"We got almost all the prints." Charlie said. "Most 'a them from the same guy."

"That's good, Charlie," Sam answered. "You guys done inside the car?"

"Yeah, we got that finished."

Sam slipped in behind the wheel of the car and looked around. He saw two large bags of groceries that they had pulled open on the passenger seat. Each item had been dusted with graphite, which was used take fingerprints. The glove compartment was also opened with its contents spewed onto the floor. Sam poured through the goodies and found nothing of importance.

As Sam slid out of the front seat he noticed a metal clip on the driver's sun-visor. Sam pulled the visor down, revealing a garage door opener with graphite dusted on it. Sam took the opener from the visor and left the car.

"Look at this, George," Sam said.

George moved in. "Looks like a garage door opener. We oughta take that and drive around the city, pushing it open all the way. When we see a door open, we go in and bust the bastard."

Sam smiled. He raised it in the air and pushed the button. The garage door at 522 Tchoupitoulas was activated, and the door started to open. Sam and George looked on in amazement.

"That was a good idea," George said. "Who came up with that idea anyway?"

Sam drew his gun and raced for the garage door. George raced in at Sam's left. The sun was setting in the West, just behind them. When Sam reached the door, he took two quick peeks inside. Sunlight poured into the ground floor, running about twenty feet inside. Beyond that it was black. Anyone could have taken a shot from anywhere in that dark cave. George pulled up, with gun in hand, standing directly in the opening.

"Get to the side, George!" Sam shouted. "You're backlit!"

George ran off to duck behind the side of the building. Sam dropped to one knee, and took another quick peek inside. It was a large room, but he could see nothing. He pulled back and hit the garage door device again, this time closing the door. When it was closed, both Sam and George relaxed.

"Thank you for that," George said. "I wasn't thinking."

"That's okay. When you chased the guy into the alley, did you see a gun?"

"No. No gun."

Sam stepped back, so he might get a better view of the top of the building. It was three stories high, with the building at the left being six stories, and the building at the right being nine.

"I've got the SWAT team on the way," Sam said. "They'll smoke him out. If he gets on that roof, the only thing he can do is give it up or jump. Either way we got our guy."

Chapter 18

Day 8, continued.

IT TOOK ONLY eighteen minutes for the SWAT team to arrive at the location. By now the area had been cleared of everybody and everything. Even the vehicle that had been extinguished by the Fire Department had been towed away. People on the opposite side of 522 Tchoupitoulas had been pulled back from both sides, to a distance of one hundred feet in each direction. Those people in stores that fronted the area had been ordered to shut down and leave the building.

The big black SWAT truck arrived and was driven by Joe Fry. Joe was the same cop Sam had seen that morning at Hironee's house. The back door of the truck opened and five of the SWAT team's finest jumped out and prepared for the attack. They all started to decorate their bodies with bullet proof vests, helmets, rifles, pistols, radios, knives, mace and whatever else they could think of that might give them the edge over their enemy.

Sam walked over to the truck, as Joe climbed from behind the wheel. His second in command was Andy Jackson, a big African-American man who climbed out of the shotgun seat. Andy took nothing from nobody.

"How you doing, Sam?" Joe asked.

"Fine Joe, just fine. And you?" Sam said.

"Couldn't be better. This is the second time today we heard from you, right?"

"Yep. Second time."

Joe started putting on his bullet proof vest. "You may have set a city record, two in one day," Joe said.

"Maybe so," Sam said. That was enough small talk. "Time to get busy."

"Well okay then," Joe said. "What ya got? This guy have a gun?"

"We figure he's murdered at least three women. We figure he's got a gun."

"Well, you know what I figure? Better be safe than sorry."

When Joe Fry was on the scene, the entire process turned over to him. Joe was responsible for, first of all, protecting his men. They were highly trained individuals; ready to go to battle, but Joe was the final decision maker.

Joe's second order of business was to secure the area. No one did that better. Once he understood the situation, they would crash into the room, screaming like wild animals, causing as much confusion as possible from within, and rend the perpetrator or perpetrators immobile. That's what Joe Fry did for a living.

Sam walked Joe over to the now closed garage door. He had drawn on a piece of paper what he saw when the garage was open.

"Here's the door opener." Sam held it out to Joe, who took it. Joe pushed the button and to door started up. After moving a few feet, he pushed the button again and the door stopped. The next push of the button and it closed again. It was the standard operation for most of the garage door openers in the world.

Andy Jackson, along with five men, gathered around Joe. Andy handed Joe a 'bullhorn,' a handheld loud speaker. Joe stepped back and took a look around. He didn't like what he saw. He put the speaker to his mouth.

"Alright y'all, listen up," he shouted. "I want everybody off of this street. Move back on both sides to each intersection. This is not a TV show. Nobody gets to watch!"

As police moved the crowd back and out of the way on Tchoupitoulas, Joe walked back to Sam.

"Okay, show me the map," Joe asked. Sam showed him the sketch he had drawn.

The building ran the distance from 522 Tchoupitoulas, to the back alley, about five hundred feet. When the garage door was open, and Sam was looking inside, on the left was a two hundred foot wall which ran from the front into the middle of the building. It also ran from floor to ceiling, which was about twenty four feet high. In front of that wall, were three large freight elevators.

On the right wall there were some work tables and a large old passenger elevator, built around the late thirties. It was built with iron and heavy decorative wire and a wood planked floor. You could see from outside, the passengers that were inside. You could see in until it passed through the ceiling, leading onto the second floor.

Finally there were two automobiles there. They were both parked near the back wall and it was too dark for Sam to see them well enough to give Joe a proper description.

George Carey and David Kennedy, along with Wally White, stood around Sam. George and David had seen this operation before. Wally had not.

Joe looked out at the street. The crowd was now moved back to the two opposite intersections of Tchoupitoulas. He turned back to Sam and handed him the garage door opener.

"Here ya go," Joe said. "I'll count to three and you hit the button. You raise the door about four feet high. Then hit the button again. It stops. We all roll inside. Once we're in you hit the button and close the door. If we're still alive when it's over, I'll invite you and your boys in."

Andy crossed in toward Joe. "We doin' the duck-slide-under?"

"You got it," Joe replied.

Andy turned to his men. "Okay everybody. Duck-slide."

The SWAT team quickly split up, four on the left of the garage door and three on the right. They were ready to go. Each man wore full combat gear, including a helmet with glass shield, tough enough to block a shot from a forty-five caliber pistol, shot at their head from three feet away. They all carried an Army AR14 rifle, fully loaded. Taped to the right side was a flashlight. Wherever they aimed the gun, they would be able to see exactly what they were shooting.

Wally watched as it unfolded. Things started to amplify. It was as if it were a bad dream, being conducted by a mad man.

Sam backed his people away from the door. Joe looked around, making sure everything was proper. "One, two, three."

On "three," Sam pushed the garage door button. When it hit about four feet, he pressed the button again, and the door stopped. The first to go in was Joe. Instantly he ran in, flopped down onto his back and his forward force caused him to slide and roll like a duck, under the door.

Andy was moving from the other side, a split second behind Joe, then a third, a fourth, a fifth, a sixth and a seventh. They were all inside within four seconds, and Sam closed the door.

They were all screaming from within! "Police, police, come out with your hands up!" Screaming and running footsteps were all they could hear. "Police, police! Come out with your hands up!" This was followed with, "Clear! Clear!" Sam realized they had started to clear some of the rooms. Then suddenly, it became quiet.

"What's going on?" Wally said.

"They're doing just fine," Sam stated.

They waited a full five minutes more. It was still quiet.

"I don't like this," Wally added.

David spoke. "I didn't hear any shots, did you?"

"No," George said. "No shots."

Then there was a tap at the garage door. "Okay Sam." Joe's voice could be heard from within the building. "Y'all can come in now."

Sam hit the garage door opener and the door rose up. Joe stood at the open door.

"Okay boys." Joe said. "We got the lights on down here. We have cleared the first floor, except for the trunks of these two cars. Your guy could be in one of those trunks. It's your decision, Sam. You want us to shoot it open, or what?"

Sam noted there were six members of the SWAT team, divided in half, standing with rifles at the ready and aiming at the trunk of each car. Sam turned to Wally.

"Who's the guy who does locks for us?"

"Yancy," Wally said. "Yancy's Safe, Locks and Keys."

"Call him."

Fifteen minutes later, Yancy pulled his truck into the garage. The sign painted on the side of his van was, "Yancy…Safe, Locks and Keys." Yancy was an old Swede, seventy-two years old and six feet two inches tall. He moved as though he were almost dead. His face had the map of the world etched on it, a face that said, *I have opened every car and safe designed by man for the last fifty years.* Joe crossed to him as he got out of his van.

"Yancy," Joe said. "We want you to open the trunks a these two cars."

Without saying a word Yancy, carrying his tool case, crossed to the first car, a five-year-old Ford Taurus. One of the other two men, aiming live ammunition at the trunk, was Andy Jackson.

As Yancy placed his tool box on the floor behind the Ford, he looked back at Andy. "You ain't gonna shoot my ass off, are ya?" Then he let out with a loud hardy laugh, if only to prove he was still alive. Yancy popped the trunk of each car, the Taurus and a Dodge Dart. No one was inside. Joe walked over to Sam and his group. "We're going to the second floor next. Here's what I suggest. This main floor is secure. I don't want a nut-ball, who murdered three women, coming in and surprising me from somewhere with a bullet in my head."

"Just tell me what you want?" Sam asked.

"I want this place to remain secure. I want the back door totally blocked off. Neither side opens. The front garage door is locked, by one lock, from either side. Something like that."

"Okay," Sam said. Joe walked over to his boys to discuss their next attack. Sam walked to Yancy. Wally moved with Sam, listening to every command.

"Yancy, we need some more work in here."

"You got it," Yancy said.

"Nobody gets in or out of the back door without a key."

"Gotcha."

"The only way in or out is the garage door. When we are in here, we want to lock ourselves in. When we leave, we want to take the same padlock and lock ourselves out. Nobody can get in or out without the key. And I want five duplicate keys."

"Gotcha."

Wally noted every word on his legal pad.

Once the SWAT team was ready, Joe led the boys onto the elevator. When they were on board, they all crouched down into a low position. Joe hit the second floor button. The elevator rose up to the second floor. Joe pushed the stop button, just as the top of the elevator cleared the second floor room. But the men inside the elevator, being in a crouched position, were concealed from anyone on the second floor, waiting to ambush them.

Sam could see the SWAT team clearly through the sides of the elevator itself. From his crouched position, Joe would quickly jump up into a standing position, glance around for a second, and withdraw to the crouch. The second time he did this, his look around the room was a little longer. The third time it was a constant search of the area. Joe saw that the room was empty.

With guns at the aim, all of the team rose and kept their eyes peeled. Joe pushed the number two, and the elevator rose to the second floor. When this happened, Sam lost view of the SWAT team. The wooden floor of the elevator, now completely blocked his view of the second floor.

Once again it was screaming and running. "Police! Police! Come out with your hands up!" And it went on and on through the search.

Yancy was still there. He had moved his truck to the front of the building, had it parked just in front of the garage door. He had removed his welding rig and was in the process of welding a brace onto existing metal brackets, to hold a padlock to the bottom of the door, inside and out.

Sam walked over to the spot, where the original builders had constructed three freight elevators. He looked up toward the third floor, and saw no elevators. Someone had removed them, possibly sold them for scrap.

"Anybody see a stairwell in here?" Sam asked.

George, David and Wally were standing across the room, listening to the noise from the SWAT team, as they continued their hustle and bustle on the second floor.

"No," answered George. "Joe never said a thing. We'll go check it out."

The three men walked into the other area of the building. Sam remained behind. He walked over and looked at a solid wall that was built, right next to the old freight elevators. There were old plans of furniture to be built, stapled to the wall. The area was covered with sawdust.

"They used to require a stairwell in buildings like this! It's a fire law!" Sam shouted out.

George could be heard yelling from the back of the building. "Yeah, this one was built in 1929. It's got a carved stone, outside on the top, dated 1929. That's when it was built. Maybe then they didn't require a stairwell. Looks like there are no stairs in here!"

Wally sounded in from another distance away. "I can check that out with the city records if you want!"

Then the SWAT team got quiet again. The elevator came down, carrying Joe, who slid the door open, as Sam and his team moved toward him.

"Okay boys, we're finished with two. Now we go the three and the roof."

"Wally, stick down here with Yancy," Sam said. "When he's done, come on up and find us."

"You got it."

Joe, Sam, George and David, got into the elevator and went up to floor two.

It was different from the first floor, with a twelve-foot high ceiling. This time Sam and his boys did not even bother watching the SWAT team, as they went up to the third floor. They had been there, done that. While Joe and his boys tramped and screamed above them, Sam, George and David, looked around to see what they could find.

Sam saw a door that was ajar, just past what seemed to be a reception office. He walked to the door and pulled it open wide. The door was constructed of heavy metal and had a four inch square glass plate, eye-high, positioned in the middle. Sam walked into the large closet. It was built of pine wood shelving, with paneling on all three back side walls. It originally held a variety of office supplies, now most was gone. Only trash remained.

Sam got a call on his radio from the third floor.

"Okay Sam," Joe's voice pounded over the radio. "We got a problem up here. I'm sending the elevator down to you. Bring your boys and come on up. We'll talk about it."

When Sam and his boys arrived on the third floor, he was amazed at the place that Ed Marsh had constructed. It was beautiful. This may have been the spot where the spider invited the fly to come up for a drink.

"This asshole built himself a real palace of pleasure up here," Joe announced. "The thing is we can only get to the first half of this floor. It's up to you, Sam. You're the guy in charge. Either we shoot the shit out of this place and open it up, or you find us a trap door."

Sam walked into the bedroom area and looked around. From his position he could see the blood red kitchen, the fine furniture, and the lavish decorations that were so beautifully positioned there. Then he studied the walls that led to the back of the apartment. Every eight feet, there was a decorative perpendicular strip of molding, running from floor to ceiling.

Sam knew construction. His father had taught him well. He studied the back wall of the room, figured it was built with eight by twelve lengths of dry wall. The perpendicular strips of molding, placed every eight feet, were there to conceal the dry wall seams. Or, he figured, they were placed there to conceal an opening.

Joe and his boys stood back, took a break in the action. They had all removed their helmets, waiting patently for the next command. George and David were quiet also, watching what Sam was up to.

Sam walked down the full distance of the back wall, tapping lightly at the surface with his doubled fist. As he moved and punched, he found the surface to be firm. It was built with a framework, probably two by fours, all of which were in proper alignment, and spacing. Sam stepped back and took an overview of the situation.

The wall was decorated with many pieces of art. There was a large painting on the left side of the room, another group of smaller painting in the center. Then there were two silver vases, separated by about eight feet, which contained artificial flowers. But these were placed behind a tall Chinese table.

What finally caught Sam's attention was an antique wooden shelf, about two and a half feet wide, placed on the wall where no furniture might block. It held a white porcelain swan with wings spread, preparing for flight.

Sam moved to the swan, reached out and touched the antique shelf. It was tight to the wall. He then reached up and touched the swan. It had been glued to the shelf. That was it. Sam found his opening. It was a hidden "push-pull" latch lock he once sold at Pennington's Hardware in Atlantic City. Sam gripped the shelf and pushed it forward. He heard the drop of the latch. Then he pulled it back and the door swung open.

Sam got a glimpse of the huge second room. His heart dropped for a moment; he had expected someone to be there. He jumped back and to the right, hiding behind the wall. He then quickly glanced back at Joe and his SWAT team. They were instantly putting their helmets back on, and when ready, charged through the door, hollering and screaming, like a pack of wolves seeking a hot free dinner.

Sam next looked at George and David. They were on the floor, with guns drawn. Once the SWAT boys were inside, George and David got to their feet, and brushed themselves off.

"Nice move boys," Sam said.

"Thanks," George responded.

The SWAT team finished with their screaming and hollering, and moved up the backstairs onto the roof. Sam and his boys moved cautiously through the back apartment, with guns drawn. When they reached the stairs, Joe hollered down. "Okay Sam. Building's all clear."

Everyone was out on the rooftop. The building at 522 Tchoupitoulas had been cleared, and Eddie Marshall had not been found. They had all felt the pressure of the search, and they might have to do it all again. But for now it was a moment to kick back and relax.

It was a large flat roof, with cement four foot high abutments, built around the entire building. There was a ten foot high structure in the middle of the building, there to house the heavy cables and machinery, used to move those three freight elevators up and down. Sam sat on the flat right corner of the abutment, boarding the back alley, allowing some sun to shine on his face. George and David sat on the opposite side, smoking. Joe and his boys had removed their helmets and bullet proof vests. Sam's phone rang. It was Wally.

"Hey Sam," Wally said. "Yancy is done and leaving. I got the five keys."

"Let the SWAT team out when they get there. Is Charlie Wong still out front?" Sam asked.

"No sir. They took a late lunch."

"Call him. Tell him come back. Tell him we got a real mess on the third floor, more prints to do. Next release the street out front. Traffic and pedestrians may move at will. Hold a car covering the back alley, and another to cover the front. All they need to do is to look for our big tall fat boy. And make sure they're street smart, no ticket writers."

"You got it," Sam hung up his phone, as Joe came over to offer a goodbye.

"Nice job boss," Joe said. "We now leave you with this shit to clean up."

"Thanks Joe," Sam turned and looked at the rest of the team. "You guys did a good job. I appreciate it. Wally's waiting downstairs for you, to let you out."

All of the thanks having been said, the SWAT team headed to the front elevator. Sam walked over to George and David.

"Did you get any lunch?" George asked.

"No," Sam answered.

"We could use something else to eat," David added.

"You already had lunch?" Sam said.

Then David mentioned, "Sure, but that was almost three hours ago."

As they walked out through the upper third floor, they were amazed at the amount of trash that was there. They could see the bed that Eddie had slept on, the papers and photographs that covered the walls.

"Stay out of this area." Sam ordered. "We wait for Charlie and his boys to run the place for prints."

They found Eddie Marsh to be a filthy man. As they passed through the large room, they saw five years of how Ed Marsh truly lived. As beautiful as his display was in the living room, this back area was designed from the pits of hell. Forget the fact that he had murdered three prostitutes; he was a person who lived and slept like the worst white trash that anyone could imagine.

Wally stood alone on the first floor. Sam and his group were the last to arrive, all others had left. Wally handed out the keys to the garage door, to each member of the staff. As they all walked to the front door of the garage opening, Sam kept thinking of something that bothered him.

Wally knelt down to unlock the garage door, Sam said, "Hold on Wally, I got a little problem here."

Wally looked back at Sam. He stood up as Sam headed back to the elevator.

"You want us to come with you?" Wally asked.

"Not necessary. I'll get it."

As Sam walked back to the elevator, Wally, George and David, simply shrugged their shoulders and followed.

When they landed at the second floor, Sam made a 'beeline' for the storage closet he had seen before.

"The thing that bothered me was this heavy thick metal door," Sam said. "Then I noticed the same type of door is upstairs leading out to the roof. So I figured this must be a fire door."

"Okay," George volunteered. "So what?"

"So who puts in a fire door to protect a storage closet?"

Sam moved into the closet, pulled the string hanging from a light bulb in the center of the room and the light went on. He turned around and above him, he saw a large heavy professional door closer, but this one had been deactivated. The bar which caused the door to hydraulically close was now detached and hung down beside the wall.

Sam turned back into the closet. Wally was close behind. George and David stood just outside the open door. No one was suspicious, it was just that Sam was a bit curious.

Sam walked over to the right side of the closet. He pounded lightly on the wall and found it to be secure. This wall panel was obviously anchored into cement. As he pounded his way to his left, on the back wall, the same sound happened. Then he reached the wall to his left. This wall was placed in the direction of the west side of the building, the one that faced Tchoupitoulas. When his fist hit that wall, what Sam heard was a dull sound.

George, David and Wally reacted. It sounded to everyone that this was a fake wall. Sam studied it for a moment. He then noticed there was a shelf built onto it. It was about four feet from the floor. *This was cheap construction,* Sam thought .

Sam got a tight grip on the shelf, and pushed it forward, away from him. Then he heard the drop of the "push-pull" drop latch. The door popped open, about one forth an inch.

Sam took a step back. He reached up and pulled the string on the naked light bulb, hanging in the center of the closet. The closet went dark. No one said a word. They stood for a moment, allowing time for their eyes to get used to the darkness.

'Okay boys," Sam spoke softly. "David, you and Wally step back out of the closet." They complied. "George, get over into the far corner. Stay back tight." George did as directed. Then Sam moved back and stood to the right of the door. He had everybody positioned in a safe as place as possible. Sam reached out with his left hand, grabbed the shelf, and pulled it inward. The door opened slightly, Sam could barely see through the small crack. He aimed his gun at the door and pushed it slowly open wide. It revealed a staircase, leading from the second floor down to the first. No one was there. Cautiously Sam moved out onto the top landing.

There was a small window that faced Tchoupitoulas, which allowed some light to come in. The stairs were constructed of poured cement. They had ten steps down, then a landing, and you went left, turned completely around and walked on down, ten more steps. Then you were at the bottom of the staircase. There you turned to the right and moved forward, which apparently let you out onto the first floor.

Then Sam noticed there was a light switch, located on the wall, to his right. He reached over and threw the switch on. The area lit up with a few of the florescent lights that were still working. Of most interest to Sam was that dark area below him. Now there was one fluorescent light, flickering on and off. But Sam could see what was below. What he could not see, was that area just beyond the final landing.

Sam thought he heard something below moving around. It might have been a rustle of papers, or even the sound of a rat. Then it got quiet.

"Police!" Sam shouted out. "Come out with your hands up!"

With his gun drawn, George had moved out onto the second floor landing. He decided it would be best for him to move down a few steps, staying close to the wall. As he did this, David moved into where George stood before, at the top of the second floor landing.

Wally finally moved from the closet and stood just behind Sam.

"Police!" Sam shouted again. "Come out with your hands up!"

Then things became very quiet. Sam had started to wonder if he had even heard a sound coming from below him. He thought it may have been his imagination. Everyone stayed quiet for at least one minute. They heard no movement from below. They started to relax. Sam was about to move down to the bottom level when it happened!

Eddie appeared with a scream from hell. Eddie and Sam's eyes locked one to another. Eddie fired one round from his thirty eight police special, directly at Sam. Sam started leaning back, just before the shot went off. The bullet barely missed his face, crashing into the cement wall behind him.

Then there came an even louder scream from Eddie, along with three more shots at Sam's position, and four more towards George. Both Sam and George sat down on the back of the steps, and squeezed their bodies tightly against the wall. The three shots at Sam hit the cement wall just above him, causing debris and dust to fall from the wall. When the four shots were directed at George, his situation became more difficult. Three of those shots hit the front edge of the cement steps, causing pieces of chipped raw cement to fly through the air, some of them hitting George in the face.

Wally and David hit the cement floor. More bullets flew above their heads. The upper part of the stairs were now covered with small pieces of cement, along with the dust.

Wally had crawled back, trying to breathe and starting to cough. Sam could hear Eddie screaming for the third time, and then he heard loud running footsteps, followed by a heavy crash.

Sam leaned over and looked back down into the well below. The place was filled with dust and smoke. He heard another scream from Eddie, followed by yet another heavy crash, this one splitting something open.

Eddie's body crashed through the false wall he had built on the first floor. This was the spot where Sam stood about an hour before. This was the wall where Eddie had used some old plans of furniture to be built. While Sam earlier stood there on the first floor, looking for the freight elevators, the two men were no more than five feet apart. Eddie turned and ran to the back door, hoping to find an escape.

Meanwhile Sam was coughing and spitting. The place was so covered with dust and debris, you could no longer see a hand in front of your face. "Is everyone okay?" Sam asked.

"Okay," Wally answered. Followed by an "Okay," from David.

"George. You alright?" Sam asked.

"I don't know," came the answer. "I'm picking pieces of cement out of my ass."

Sam reached out and grabbed the rail, pulling himself to a standing position. He could hear from below where the sound was coming from. He heard some pounding in the back of the ground floor. Eddie was trying to exit the back door! Evidently, Yancy had done a good job. Then there were more running footsteps and then fiddling with the garage door.

Sam slowly started to make his way down the steps. The area had started to clear a little now. He could see a few feet ahead. As Sam walked down the steps he could see George, sitting there cleaning spatters of blood from his face, with his handkerchief.

"Hey George," Sam said. "You need more rest time, or shall we just move on down the stairs and kill this motherfucking bastard?"

"Okay." George said. "I'm ready when you are."

As the two men walked down the stairs to the ground floor, they could hear Ed, now trying to open the garage door. Once again, Yancy had done his job.

David and Wally were following close behind Sam and George, who had almost reached the bottom of the stairs.

"Everybody hold right here," Sam ordered. Then he heard the sound of the elevator. Since Ed found he couldn't get out, he must have decided he would go up. They had left the elevator on the second floor. Ed had pushed the button calling for it to return to the first.

Sam cautiously walked to the final landing. He now could clearly see where Ed had been hiding all along. He saw bottles of water, some of them empty. A few were filled with urine. Ed was nowhere in sight. Sam inched his way forward, and finally spotted him, standing at the elevator door, as it made its way down to the first floor. Sam raised his gun, pointing at Ed.

"Police!" Sam screamed. "Stop or I'll shoot!"

In an instant, Ed wheeled around, and with gun in hand, took three quick shots at Sam, who dove for cover as the first shot was fired. Unfortunately, his cover was behind the fake dry wall that Eddie had built there. The first bullet went through the wall six feet high, the second at four feet and the third two feet. The third bullet creased the back of Sam's jacket.

Sam lay there, breathing heavily. This truly was a rotten business. Then Sam heard the elevator stop, and he heard the door slide open and then close. Then the motor started again.

Sam rolled over onto his side, and peeked out through the door. He could see Eddie was in the elevator, and halfway up toward the second floor.

Eddie was only twenty five feet away from Sam, just across the garage floor. Sam took careful aim and fired a single shot. It hit Ed in the center of his stomach!

Sam used a forty-five automatic pistol. This was the type of gun one might use to kill a buffalo. But Ed took this shot well. He winced in pain, looked back at Sam and fired three more rounds, as he passed into the second floor and disappeared from view. The three wild bullets flew around Sam like a fourth of July fireworks show. Eddie was shooting, not aiming.

"Let's go, boys!" Sam screamed. "Our turn!"

Sam jumped up and ran for the elevator. George was second, with David and Wally close behind. When Sam got to the elevator shaft, he pushed his gun through the wire grate, and fired six quick shots at the bottom of the elevator itself. Sam's forty-five bullets crashed through the oak wood floor planks and careened around the elevator.

Inside the elevator, bullets were bouncing around like crazy. Four of them accidentally found their target and two did not. But Ed Marsh, AKA Eddie Marshall, could have cared less. Pain was his pleasure.

The first shot bounced off of the back metal wall, and hit Ed in his back, piercing his left lung. The second hit the right wall, and then struck Ed in his left side, slicing through his right hip. The third was a direct hit, catching him in his buttocks, and ending up in his kidney. The fourth struck him in his left leg. Then Wally, David and George joined in force, and started shooting as well. Eddie was being struck in the body with bullets from all sides.

The elevator reached the third floor, and Eddy was now bleeding profusely. He limped as quickly as possible through the living room and headed for the back stairs.

Sam and his group were patiently waiting on the first floor for the elevator to return. Sam looked around at his group. They were covered with the grime and the dirt from hell. George was pocked with cement slivers on his face.

"Okay?" Sam asked. "You boys, you ready to go in and finish the deal?"

Everyone was tired, but all nodded. When the elevator finally arrived they all climbed inside. Then they saw the blood. It was Eddie's blood. They had no idea what damage they had created by shooting at the wooden floor of the elevator, but now they knew Eddie had been mortally wounded.

"Wally, get an ambulance here," Sam said. "David, call Joe with the SWAT team, tell them to stand by again." As the elevator passed by the second floor, both Wally and David started to dial on their cell phones. Then a radio call came in from a cop located in the back alley.

"Hello, Sam Pennington. Come in please."

"This is Pennington. Who's this?"

"This is Officer James Bouding. We're down in the back alley. We got your guy in our crosshairs, standing on the roof. He looks like a jumper."

"Don't shoot! I want him alive! We're on the way!"

They jumped from the elevator on the third floor and ran to the roof. Sam was the first to get there. He paused to look outside, saw nothing, and then moved out slowly. Sam was cautious. He had his .45 caliber at the ready. His radio sounded.

"Detective Pennington, this is Officer Bouding again."

"Yes Bouding. Go ahead."

"Your guy is now standing on the right rear corner of the roof. He's up on the railing. He looks like he's drunk or something."

"Thank you, Bouding." Sam cut his phone off. As they reached the door Sam said, "Okay boys, we're here now. Stand by." Sam inched his way around the stairwell wall and caught sight of Eddie. He was standing in the same spot where Sam had taken some sun, about a half hour before.

The term "Dead Man Walking," applies to prisoners who were walked to their execution. Eddie was a "Dead Man Standing." His gun was still in his hand, but he had difficulty in raising it, to take a shot. He had lost a lot of blood. His breathing was labored, and he appeared to be a hundred years old.

Sam showed himself from behind the stairwell wall. Ed saw him too. He looked at Sam straight in the eyes.

"Listen to me, Eddie," Sam said. "I've got an ambulance on the way for you. We'll take you to the hospital. They will fix you up. So drop the gun, and give it up."

Eddie thought about his life. He thought of the moment he had become tired and bored with the killing of women.

FLASHBACK

FIVE YEARS EARLIER.

When he murdered the first whore, it filled him with intense excitement. His first ten deaths completely satisfied his thrill of fatality. Killing a whore truly made his day. But after that, things became drudgery. The forty-five minute ride to Slidell became tiresome, the burying of the corpses became tedious, the digging of a newly-planned grave was a back-breaking job. After he had killed twenty ladies of the night, Eddie started thinking of a change.

He now thought of Ralph Barkley, the killer he read about when he was twelve years old. Barkley had murdered eighteen women and made a poignant suggestion to all. "Make it simple, don't change 'modus operandi' and you will never be caught." But Eddie didn't listen to Ralph Barkley's advice. Instead, he allowed himself to become bored with the job. And that was Eddie's fatal downfall.

When he buried his twenty-sixth victim, Eddie left the killing field in Slidell for good. It was now time to play head-trips with the police. His first victim of the new order was Penelope Andrews.

As he had done with the other women, he already established a routine with Penelope. She would come to his lavish apartment and enjoy his food and drink. She was a loner from Pittsburg, Pennsylvania, a runaway with no pimp to care for her and nobody to really be bothered. This was one of Eddie's prized subjects.

For the one hundred dollars he paid to Penelope, he got a few hours of entertainment. He would ask that she undress and accomplish a few various obscene acts. Mind you, he would not ask that she touch him, nor he to touch her. This was just a matter of two adults having fun, with nobody touching anybody. But he did not kill her on this night. He had not yet properly prepared her final resting place.

The following day he found the spot. He was looking at cars on a used car lot, on Airline Drive in New Orleans. The lot was full of used cars, and used car salesmen. No one paid much attention to Eddie.

There was a black car, parked near the side street. He asked the salesman to open the trunk, so he could look inside. As Eddie looked into the trunk, the salesman walked over and started a conversation with one of his associates. Eddie closed the trunk down, but gently, so the latch didn't catch.

Eddie had a date that night with Penelope. While she was involved in displaying one of her obscene acts, Eddie took his aluminum little league baseball bat and pummeled her brain into mush.

Then he had designed his master plan. This was a message for the cops.

He knew they would want to know who did this, and he wanted them to know also. He wanted to confuse them with his genius.

He used a pair of rubber gloves, every time he touched anything that came in contact with the murdered girl, or anything that might be used in accomplishing the crime. He wrote a note, he believed the authorities would find. It was written on a small piece of note pad, stating, "*Do not go here. She's mine.*" Then below he wrote the number "*1.*"

Mind you, Eddie had already murdered twenty-six women. He had dug their graves and buried them in his killing field graveyard in Slidell. But this was the first murder he committed just for the cops. Now he had to place the note into her body – and what better spot to place his note but into the whore's vagina. It was so perfect.

He rolled the note into a small package, and stuffed it into a condom. The condom would protect it from the moisture of her body. He pushed it inside with his index finger. Eddie always wore his plastic disposable gloves on these occasions. When he withdrew his finger, the condom had stuck to his glove. He tried again, this time twisting his finger around, trying to remove condom from his gloved hand. But when he pulled his finger out, the condom once again appeared.

He looked around his room and tried to find something that would easily introduce his package into her body without sticking to the subject matter. When he went to the drugstore to purchase a package of condoms, he also had need for a fly swatter. He found one. It was a standard fly swatter with a blue plastic handle. The handle itself was five inches long, and had a twisted wire from the handle to the actual swatter, that measured another ten inches. Eddie bought this to aid him in riding those nasty, biting, southern mosquitoes. Now this would do the trick.

He inserted the handle into her body first. Then he pushed the handle forward, catching the condom, and pushing forward, for another seven and a half inches. Then he slowly retrieved the handle. It was perfect. The condom stayed in place and his flyswatter was withdrawn, unscathed.

He put her naked body into one of those black body bags. He then placed the bagged body into his white Volvo station wagon and drove to the car lot on Veterans. He had alternate plans, should this one fail, but fail it did not. The trunk to the black car still hung slightly open. He moved the black body bag from his Volvo to the trunk of the black car. Nobody was watching.

He unzipped the bag and unceremoniously, dumped the naked girl into the trunk. He then snapped the trunk shut, threw the black body bag into the back of his car, and drove home. A perfect deal, and wasn't Ralph Barkley wrong about this one?

Over the next few days, Eddie read the newspapers, and monitored all TV and Radio news reports. Then for three weeks, there was no mention of Penelope Andrews. After three weeks, they had most assuredly found her body, but evidently it was not newsworthy.

His second murder was Darleen. Eddie never knew her last name. Since no one had noticed Penelope Andrews, he decided to place his written message closer to the front of her vagina. He used the handle of the fly swatter once again, this time only pushing it as far as the handle reached, five inches. *There would be no way,* he thought, *for the cops to miss this note.*

Eddie had driven down the lonely road, past the El Toro Restaurant, over the last month. He had checked the location on three occations. He found the window of opportunity on this night, to be between two and four in the morning, because no one was ever there.

Eddie pulled his Volvo Station Wagon past the dock, to where the food lockers were located. It was two forty-five in the morning. He carried his bolt cutter, which he used to pop the padlock, on the first door he came to. When he opened the door, cold air blew out, into the hot summer night.

Eddie enjoyed the cold air. The cubical he was in was about the size of the bed of a sixteen wheel trailer. There was an aisle down the middle with meat hanging or stockpiled on either side. The storage area was almost full, but Eddie found a spot to store his meat, close to the back door.

He removed the naked body of Darleen from the black body bag, and placed her at the front of the locker, with her back against the side wall. He closed the door and placed the broken lock back into place. Then he got into his Volvo and drove off into the night.

Two weeks later, after checking all the papers, listening to all the news that was available, there was nothing said about Darleen. And still, nothing was said about Penelope Andrews either.

What bothered Big Eddie was that cops were stupid. He had murdered twenty-six young women in the past five years, and during that time only four had been in the newspaper. Four dead people out of twenty six! And of those four mentioned, all were named as missing persons. And they were mentioned in the news only once! It was the ignorance of the police that led Eddie to become more brazen. At that moment, Eddie was thinking about killing Beth Hayden, a girl who came from Blanco, Texas.

On a cold rainy night, Eddie coaxed her to his apartment, but Beth had requirements. She would get naked and have sex with Eddie, performing in the missionary position. That was it. There would be no kissing on the lips. No oral sex. No anal sex. For one hundred bucks, you could get your rocks off using the standard *missionary position!* At that point in time, Eddie grabbed his aluminum baseball bat and bashed her brains out. And that was it for Beth Hayden.

DAY 8, CONTINUED.

Sam Pennington peered around the corner of the "You hear me, Ed? Drop the gun!" It was the sound of Sam's voice that caused Ed to drift back into reality.

Ed still stood on the four foot wall that surrounded the building, but he was getting weaker by the moment.

"Come on, Ed," Sam said. "Do the right thing. Give it up and save your life. The ambulance is almost here. Call it quits and drop the gun. Let us take you downstairs and put you in the ambulance. What do you say?"

"I'll tell you what I've done, pal." Eddie said, with a staggering and shaky voice. "I've executed women who needed to die, that's what I've done. You couldn't do it. The courts couldn't do it. But I did it. I got rid of the trash of this city. An when they write a book about me, they'll realize just what I did." Eddie looked up at the sky, and with a soft smile on his face, rocked back onto his heels, and fell back onto the alley below.

The sound his body made when it hit the pavement was something between a splat and a thud. Sam ran to the ledge and looked down. With his gun still in his hand, Eddie had landed flat on his back. His eyes were still open, with a dead stare. Sam had a feeling he was still looking up at him. He would never forget that stare.

Charlie Wong and his two assistants were busily taking care of the fingerprints of the day, and starting to take blood samples from the kitchen floor and walls. The place was a shamble. Charlie Wong was working alone in Eddie's bedroom. He had almost completed the printing of the place, when Charlie also found a map. Eddie had placed it on the back wall. It was a section of a road map, just north of New Orleans, the town of Slidell. Charlie walked to the door and called for Sam. "Sam. You wanna come in here and take a look at something?"

When Sam arrived, he saw the map. He also saw Eddie's diary. The hand written statement at the top of the map said: "My Killing Field Graveyard." Then below, numbers were written, one through twenty-six. His diary told them exactly who was buried in what spot. Eddie wasn't lying. He had worked very hard.

Sam's first call was to Ronald Demeraux, the Chief of Police of Slidell, advising him they would soon be there to inspect the site.

Sam drove his car, alone. Wally followed, with George and David behind him. The sun was just starting to set and the sky had a magnificent cloud formation, with beautiful red and orange colors, against a sky of bright blue, all of which would soon grow dark.

They arrived at Eddie's killing field. Chief Ronald Demeraux was already there, along with at least half the police force of Slidell, two fire engines, and a city truck full of lighting equipment. In addition there was an Entergy truck, with an executive from the lighting company. And there was Yancy. Yancy's Safes, Locks and Keys. Yancy had obviously contracted with as many local parish police as possible. Yancy was a rich man.

They all got out and walked the three hundred yards to the gate. Firemen were taking shovels from their trucks, preparing to go to work. Yancy had just "popped" the lock, as Sam and his crew arrived. No one spoke. There were thirty-six men there, ready to accomplish whatever needed being done.

Sam led the way up the small hill, toward the downgrade on the other side. One had the feeling that no one wanted to see what they were about to see, but they all knew it was there. Sam stopped at the top of the hill, and looked down into the small valley below. Five officers brought heavy battery operated lights. They turned the lights on and shined them into the area of question.

For five years Ed Marsh had been here. Nobody saw him. He had dug twenty-six graves. There were three rows, starting with ten in the back area, then ten in the second area, and finally six more. The shovel he used was lying beside a tree. There was a pick there also, to aid him when the ground got too hard.

Sam walked alone, down the slight hill, over to the actual grave area. When some firemen started to follow, Chief Ronald Demereaux held his hand up. They immediately stopped and waited. As bad as this looked, it was worse for Sam.

Sam walked to the graves. In the five years since Ed started this, the back row of graves were now almost concealed with grass. Then to the front of

Sam, just before his feet, were the newest graves. Here you could see the fresher sod, lying against the older grass. Sam looked back at the people standing at the ridge. "Okay, we start here at this one, and move back."

When they opened the first grave, a stench erupted that would kill a skunk. It was a hot summer night, with not even a slight breeze present. The humidity was at seventy-eight percent. It was one of those nights you wanted to look for a cool air conditioned bar, with soft music and a frozen daiquiri.

Ten minutes later the coroner arrived, along with his crew. They had some jars of camphor with them, which they applied to the upper lip of whoever need it. It did little good. By the time the workers had uncovered the first seven bodies, the smell of rotten flesh had taken over the area.

Sam was sitting on a boulder, about ten feet away from where they were digging. He saw one man gag as his shovel hit another body. Sam decided it was time to go. There were better things to do than this. Sam walked over to Chief Demereaux.

"May I assume your people will be calling my people to see who's responsible for this?" Sam asked.

Chief Demereaux was holding a handkerchief to his nose and mouth. All he could do was shake his head yes.

"Thank you Chief. I appreciate all you've done. I bid you goodnight." Sam walked back up the hill to his car. He would drive to his office, then his apartment, or to any place but this place.

Chapter 19

DAY 8, CONTINUED.

IT WAS LATE Wednesday night, March 8th, as Sam drove from the killing field in Slidell. He thought of Kelly. The job he was doing had caused him to completely desert her. Being a cop, being a soldier, being a whatever, you almost never got a chance to pay your dues to the lady you loved, and Sam dearly loved Kelly. He had missed her dinner that night, something she had prepared with her very own hands. And she was helping him out with his boat, painting and scraping. If there was someone who commanded attention from him, it was Kelly Lee Jones. He placed a call to her on his cellular.

"Hello," she said.

"Hi. This is Sam."

"Hello Sam. I just heard about you on the news, five and six o'clock, with a special at eight thirty. You captured one of the bad guys."

"Yeah, we got him," Sam said. "Sorry I missed dinner. I'll make it up to you tomorrow."

"Oh, don't worry about that. I change my mind on the meal. Instead, I got some beef to make beef curry, but the whole thing messed up. I should have put flour in, but put baking soda instead. Thank God you weren't here."

"Sounds good to me."

"Yeah, sure. Are you okay?"

"I'm fine. Got to go in with Wally and make a report. Take us about an hour. Then I gotta get some sleep."

"Sleep well Sam. I'll be thinking of you."
"And I'll be thinking of you. Goodnight, baby."

It was now ten thirty. Wally was on the computer, typing voluminous notes from his massive photographic memory, related to the day's activities. He entered who said what and the time it was said, and who said what to who and when and where. Everyone who did anything of importance was named, the exact time they did it was listed, and Sam watched in amazement as the story unfolded. The phone rang. Sam crossed back to his desk and picked it up. "Detective Pennington."

"Mays here."

"Hello Bill. Nice to hear a friendly voice."

"I saw the news. You okay?"

"Yeah, I'm fine." Sam looked over at Wally. He was concentrating on what he was typing, didn't hear a word they said. "What's with you?"

"Well I'll tell you, it goes like this. I just got my house kicked apart by five officers of the narcotics squad from the Rampart Division, that's what. They came in about three hours ago, showed me a search warrant, a court order that they had the right to search an' seize, and they blew through my place like shit out of a tin horn."

Sam took a big breath. Things were now getting difficult. If he could just get Mays out of town, it might be easier. Sam walked out into the hallway. It was quiet out there; he didn't want to bother Wally.

"How do you stand now?" Sam asked.

"How do I stand? I'm standing in shit! You gotta see that place. I had over fifty boxes packed and ready to go to storage. They opened every one, dumped the stuff out, and pawed through it like animals.

"My wife is in the bar with me now, sitting at a table over by the window. I brought her here just to get her out of the house. Normally, if I insist, she has one beer. Now she's on her third whisky sour." Mays looked over at his wife. She was a lovely middle-aged woman who just ordered another whisky sour.

"Change that to four whiskies," Bill answered. "Now you want the capper? About twelve years ago I bought a load of three-quarter-inch plywood. Hired two guys to come in and lay a solid floor in my attic. It took them three days to finish the job. So tonight, these guys want to see my attic. Mind you, they're still looking for dope. Huge tubs and vats and barrels and truck loads of fucking dope! So they climb up into my attic and do a search."

"I got it Bill, they made a mess."

"Made a mess? Are you kidding? There was nothing up there. It was clean. I had taken everything down and out. They came up to the attic with hammers and two crow bars and ripped up the total floor, every single piece of wood. Then you know what? They next came up and tore out all the pink fiberglass shit."

"I know. They made a mess," Sam interjected one more time.

"No! You don't get the final *coup de gras*. These bastards were in my roof, and one of them tripped, and put his foot through into my living room. I got a fucking hole in my living room ceiling about three feet wide. An you know what else I found out? This shit came from the fucking Office of Internal Affairs, that's what!

"Okay, relax. I need you to stay cool."

"Tell you the truth Sam, I'll be glad when glad when I get to go to you-know-where."

"Did you go look at the office?" Sam asked.

Bill Mays quickly changed his attitude. "Oh yeah, and the place looks great. Good spot. Eduardo pleaded his poor mouth routine and got the price down to fifteen hundred dollars a month. We shook hands on the deal, and sign the papers tomorrow. Move right in."

"I'm going to offer a suggestion," Sam said. "You may not like it, but give it some thought."

"Okay. I'm ready," Mays volunteered.

"I want you to get out of this town, now. I have a gut feeling about this. You've been worried about me? Well I'm becoming seriously concerned about you."

"Come on. What the hell can they do with me?"

"Let me tell you, this whole plan deals with you. Once you are in *home base*, we have natural security. I need you to get there now."

"Are you talking about Honduras?"

"Yes. But I'd rather you don't mention that name on this phone."

"Oh God help me. Please dear God."

"God won't do you any good right now. Just listen to me."

"Of course I will. I always listen to you. My wife thinks I'm crazy because she bought a boat. She's never seen the fucking boat. A year later and I give her her money back plus interest. Where's the boat, she asked? My God, did I have to talk my way out of that one. So come on. Let's go again. Whatcha got for me this time?"

"I got a deal for you. Leave that bar right now. Take your wife. Get into a cab and take a trip to Metairie. You know of the Pelican Suites Hotel?"

"Yeah, I know it. It's a big deal fucking posh spot."

"Okay, take a cab there. Just walk away from your house and your problems. Ignore them. They never happened. Ask for Renaldo. He's on duty now. Just tell Renaldo you were sent there by Sam Pennington. Don't offer any other information. No name, no sign in. He'll give you a room, or even a top floor suite if it's available. After you get the key, leave a message for me with the room number. Then just go upstairs and relax. Order some food. Get a bottle of booze. Buy whatever you need. Get some tooth brushes. Get a razor. Get whatever pleases you. It's all comp. I'll be there in about an hour. Okay?"

"What have you done there? You own a hotel now?"

"Are you going to do as I ask?"

Mays agreed and Sam walked back into the office. Wally was just putting the finishing touches on his file report, a tired kid that had been involved with one bad day. "Okay Sam, here it comes. Read it and weep." Sam was tired too. He took the final pages from Wally and perused them quickly.

"Good stuff," Sam said. "This works for me."

"That's fine," Wally said. "Hey Sam, do you mind If I sleep on the couch here tonight? There's a crash of gun shots ringing through my brain. I don't wanna drive home tonight. Is that okay?"

Wally had always been the first one there and the last to leave. Sam had never considered Wally as part of the family, always left outside looking in. Now it was time for a change.

"You know what, Wally, I have not been properly taking care of you. Tonight we go the Pelican Suites Hotel in Metairie. Take your car. Follow me."

As Sam shut down the office, Wally waited at the door.

"May I make an observation?" Wally asked.

"Sure, shoot."

"I gotta tell you, I thought you were amazing out there today. You got more action going than most can do in a week, or longer."

"Well thank you Wally, nice of you to say."

But Wally was not finished. He had more in his gut that he needed to expel. "A guy almost shot at you at that house this morning, and then you got shot at again on the lower stairwell, and more gun shots at the top of the roof, and you handled everything like a pro."

"What are you looking for, tomorrow off? Come on, let's go. I'll get you a good room."

Sam and Wally arrived at the Pelican Suites Hotel, checked their cars in with the parking staff, and walked to the desk. It was a beautiful place; Wally was impressed. Sam asked for Renaldo. Neither Renaldo nor Sam had ever met before. Renaldo came out from the back room. He was either a fair Castilian Spaniard or a Basque. He was a man of fifty, distinguished and soft spoken. Renaldo dealt with business in a business-like fashion.

"My name is Sam Pennington," Sam flashed his badge. "I'll need a room for this man for tonight."

Renaldo opened a drawer, took out a key, and handed it to Wally. "Yes sir. Will there be anything else?"

"I sent two people over here earlier. Did they leave a message for me?"

Renaldo turned to the message board, flashed through the file and withdrew a piece of paper, handing it to Sam.

When they got into the elevator, Wally showed Sam his key number; it was 1222. Sam looked at the note. Mays was in 1224, just across the hall.

They got to the twelfth floor and entered 1222. Wally saw a massive, well-appointed living room, which led to a magnificent bedroom and bath. Wally was in seventh heaven. Sam had already seen the best toilet in town when he visited the washroom at the Office of Internal Investigation, and now he couldn't be bothered.

"This is beautiful," Wally said. "I can't get over this."

"Yeah, well. They got twenty-four hour service here. Get some food, get a drink, get some shaving stuff, whatever you want. It's all on comp. I'll see you in the office at twelve noon."

Sam walked to the front door and moved into the hall. "See you, kid. Have a good night." He closed the door behind him and walked across the hall to 1224 and knocked on the door. Bill Mays opened the door, standing there in his underwear.

"Hey Sam, come on in." Mays was smiling. This was the best night he had spent since they found the money, ten years ago. Sam moved into the room, Mays closed and locked the door.

"I got some stuff for you," Mays said.

Sam walked over to the beautifully carved coffee table. There he found a fifth of Jack Daniels Whiskey along with another fifth of Glenlivet Scotch.

"Boy, you really know how to take care of a guest," Sam said.

Bill's wife had passed out in the bedroom. She was done for the night. Sam and Mays sat down, had a drink, and discussed a plan.

Forty-five minutes later, Sam and Mays (who had dressed again) left Mays' room, and crossed to room 1222. Sam knocked on the door. After a moment Wally's voice could be heard. "Yes?"

"It's me, Wally, Sam."

Wally opened the door, also in his underwear. Sam and Mays walked into the room, Sam closing the door behind.

"You live here?" Mays asked Wally.

Wally did not have an answer to that question. Sam took charge.

"The deal is off," Sam said to Wally. "I now make a new deal. Get dressed. We go back to the office and type a formal letter to Mr. Mays' boss. Take us about an hour. Then you take Mr. Mays to his office on Rampart. He goes in and deposits the letter in his boss's mail box. Then you both come back here and get all the fun and happiness started again. And Wally, in return for your extra effort, I will give you two days off. That means tomorrow and Friday. That's a total four-day weekend.

Wally studied both Sam and Mays with great intent. He was a young man with finely developed intuitions, a person who was aware of the meaning of honor and honesty.

"Are you aware," Wally asked, "that they have HBO and Showtime here?"

The three of them drove back to Sam's office and wrote the letter.

> TO: Al David, Director of Detectives, Rampart Division.
> FROM: William Jefferson Mays, Detective, Rampart Division.
> Dear Al,
> I'm sure by now you have heard the story of what happened to my home, but in case you somehow missed it, I now offer the condensed version.
> This evening, my house was attacked by narcotics officers from the Royal Street Division. What these people did to my house is inexcusable. They ripped through my home like crazed animals and left the place in a shambles. Should you or any of your minions wish to see what they did; I provide you with a key to my front door, so that you may inspect the damage.
> My wife is now in such a state of shock, I have taken her to the hospital, and she is now under a physician's care. As a result of this, I will not be able to return

to perform my final duties on the job.

I know this will not be a problem for you. You and I have both agreed that my back overtime pay, which I have not yet received, will more than cover the 'six days' that I am now required to miss.

I wish my pension to be delivered monthly to my attorney, David Springer. David will be in contact with you shortly. He will also have a Power of Attorney from me, so as to resolve whatever other problems you may have.

Warmest Regards,

W. J. Mays

As they walked to the office door, Sam gave both instructions. "After you drop this note off at Rampart, go back to the hotel. They have two swimming pools in there, one inside and one out. And they have an exercise area, and a massage parlor. You could get a facial. It's all on comp. Bill, I need a key to your house. I will get your passports and anything special you want for the trip. Make it simple. Keep it light."

Mays handed him the house key and told him where the passports were located.

"An my wife's got a small black get-away bag. On the shelf just above the passports."

"Okay, fine," Sam said. "You guys should get to know one another better. You could become good friends. So spend four days of fun in the sun. I'll handle the office. Goodnight."

Sam pushed them out of the office and slammed the door shut, returning to his desk. His first phone call was to Charity Hospital.

"Yes ma'am, this is Detective Pennington. I'm inquiring about a patient, a Ms. Hironee Jessup."

"One moment please." After a beat, she came back on the line. "Yes sir. I have you listed as the 'Person in Care.' Is that correct?"

"Yes ma'am. I get all the good news and the bad news."

"Ms. Jessup had a difficult day, but she has responded fairly well to a Valium drip. Her condition now is considered guarded. In twenty-four hours, doctors expect an improvement."

"Thank you very much."

Sam closed the office and drove his car to the parking garage. No one was there. He left his key on the rear right wheel and walked over to

Bourbon Street and into the Dixieland. Red Moon and his boys were on a break. It was close to midnight, a Wednesday, a notorious night for being quiet in the Quarter. Even Leonard was off for the evening. He asked the bartender for a double Glenlivet, but was told it was not in stock. He could see the bottle with his name on it, standing on a shelf.

Sam started this day feeling good. He felt like a tiger, nothing could stop him. But now he felt a little sorry for himself. Feeling sorry for one's self, had some merit. It allowed a person to go home and get drunk.

Without telling the bartender he was wrong, Sam thanked him for giving it his best try and left the bar. He next walked up Bourbon to Barracks and turned right. As he got close to his apartment he noticed a police van parked out front. There were also three cop cars on the street, parked nearby.

As Sam got closer to the apartment house, he noticed that a police officer was carrying a box of clothing down to the van. As the officer moved the box toward the van he noticed Sam. "Hey Sam, how ya doin'?"

"Hey there, Pete, working late?"

"Yeah, I guess so."

As Pete placed the box into the Van, Sam noticed his black shirts packed on the top. He next looked upwards to his apartment. All of the lights were on. Sam figured this one out in one short second. His apartment had been hit with a search warrant.

Sam started the slow climb to the third floor. He knew exactly what was happening and how it started. He was glad he had Bill Mays sequestered at the Pelican. He was delighted he had Wally there to watch over things. Now his goal was to stay absolutely calm.

He reached the top floor and walked into his apartment. Pete was walking up behind him, and another cop Sam didn't recognize was walking down, carrying yet another box of stuff.

Sam entered the living room area. The cops had already gone through this room. His kitchen was a disaster. Every cupboard was wide open. Stuff had been pulled from them, and spewed out onto the floor. The refrigerator was savaged, a number of items had been placed on the counter. Three boxes full of food stuff had also been placed on the floor.

Pete came back into the room, picked up one of the boxes from the floor and headed back for the front door. Sam glanced into the box. It contained baking material, flower and baking soda and the like.

"Hey Pete, you guys going to open a bakery, or are you looking for my stash of dope?"

Sam walked around the corner to his office. When he saw the room Sam realized he had been put out of business. This had been a working detective's home office, a place where he stored his material, using it for the job of catching bad guys. He had placed stick pins all around the room which held information and pictures that he needed to use. Now all of that was gone. His computer and printer were gone. His phone answering machine was gone. His books had been removed from the shelves, were opened and then strewn on the floor.

Every drawer in his desk had been pulled out and gone through. Every bit of paper, every business card, every hand written phone number, had been boxed and carted off.

"Sam?" The voice came from behind, Sam turned and looked. He saw Tom Phelps, the narcotics detective he had seen that morning at Hironee's house. Sam allowed a big broad smile to cross his face. This smile meant, *Okay mother fucker, you got me this time. Next time your ass belongs to me.* "Hey there Tom, how ya doin'?"

"Fine Sam. Look, I'm real sorry about this."

"Sorry about what? This is no problem. All in a day's work."

"I just want you to know this did not come from our office. We can't even put it back together. We're not even paid for that."

Sam smiled again, this one was even bigger than the first. "Don't you be concerned for even a second. So what if you and your boys have ruined my business? Who cares? Doesn't bother me."

A policeman came in from Sam's bedroom, paused at the door. "Sir?" He directed his attention to Tom. "We're almost done in the bedroom. We need to get into the attic."

"Ah. You need the pole to open the trap door," Sam said. Sam walked past Tom and headed for the bedroom. There he saw four officers of the law who had pulled his bed apart. The mattress and springs were laid against one wall. Sheets were pulled off and thrown into a corner. The closets were all open, clothing removed. Some of the clothes had been boxed up. In one of the boxes, Sam noticed his favorite black blazer.

Sam found the pole in his back closet, with which he went back to the hall and pulled open the trap door to his ceiling, which led to the attic. He turned on the light switch, and happily announced, "Okay boys. Go for it."

An hour later, Sam was lying down in his bedroom. He had pulled the bare mattress onto the floor, and tossed some pillows down for his head to rest. He had prepared an ice container from the bar and was lying down with a fifth of Glenlivet, watching an old war movie on HBO. Sam wished Wally was watching the same film. Tom Phelps walked to the door.

"We're done here Sam, got everything we need."

Sam hit the 'mute' button on his TV hand control. Still with a big smile on his face he said, "Hey, thanks Tom. You boys did a great job here."

"I'm just sorry we left such a mess. Like I said, they won't pay us to set it straight again."

"No problem, Tom. You did the right thing."

"We'll make a print-out of everything we have secured here for our investigation. I'll get it to your office tomorrow."

"I bet they pay you for that, don't they?"

Phelps looked at Sam. He caught the snide remark but ignored it. "I saw some TV news earlier tonight. Heard you had a problem. Got a serial killer, that right?"

"Yeah, It's no big deal. This guy killed twenty-nine women in the New Orleans area. It was a piece of cake. Not like what you boys go through, but what the hell."

Tom decided to end this conversation. It was only trouble down the road. "Okay Sam, see you again soon."

The smile slowly left Sam's face. He was now looking at Tom with a dead stare. With all of his bravado, Sam was now advising Tom of his real feeling. Sam held his glass up in a toast. "You got that one right." Sam then took a drink of his 12-year-old Glenlivet.

There was no doubt Tom took that toast as a *definite* threat.

It was now close to midnight. Sam Pennington wanted to see Kelly Lee Jones worse than anyone in the world. He ran to his garage at the front of the building, put the key in the ignition, and prayed God it would start. At the first turn of the key the engine jumped into action. Sam was right. This would be a great day.

There was very little traffic on the streets. Forty-eight minutes later, he turned onto Judge Bean's property, and got his first glimpse at the freshly painted boat. It looked like a goddess, just waiting to bite into the froth of the deep blue sea.

Day 9

Thursday Morning, Twelve Forty-Nine a.m.

Sam quickly climbed the ladder of the *Miss Lee*, stepped onto the top deck, and entered the pilot's cabin. He heard Kelly's voice coming up from the main quarters below.

"Who's there?" Her voice called out into the night.

Sam made a move toward the stairs that led into the salon. "Yeah, baby, it's me." He appeared at the top of the stairs. It was a moment of complete magic. The boat was in semi-darkness except for a full moon that lit the entire main salon, shining in from the west. As Sam walked down the steps from the pilot house, Kelly came up the steps from the cabin below.

They met in the middle of the room. She looked beautiful. She had been sleeping and was wearing a man's T-shirt, probably his. It covered her entire body, hung down just above her knees.

"I was just feeling a little lonely," he said.

"Well, I know how to fix lonely."

She wrapped her arms about his neck and planted a very serious kiss on his lips. It was the type of kiss that simply said, *I am ready for you, big fella, let's get it on.*

Sam started to run his hands over her body. She was probing her tongue into his mouth. His hands continued to move downward, feeling her back, then past her buttocks, ending as far as he could reach the top of her long legs. It was confirmed: she wore nothing but the T shirt.

As Kelly continued searching for his tonsils with her tongue, Sam ran his hands up the front of her body to her breasts. Sam had never been a major breast man. Mainly he was a leg-and-ass man. But now he was fascinated with what he felt through the T-shirt. He had felt them before, but now they became something special.

He cupped each breast in the palm of each hand. He felt the nipples harden. She pulled away from his mouth and laid her head backward. He decided it was time to unveil the treasure that was hidden under the cloth of mystery.

Sam reached his hands as low as possible behind her back, grabbed at the garment, and pulled it upward. As he did so, Kelly raised her arms into the air, providing him with total access to her body. In one motion, he whipped the garment over her head and tossed it to the floor, leaving her standing in front of him, totally naked.

In a second, Sam was back to the breasts. They were large but not too large, firm but just soft enough. And her nipples were now as hard as rock. He suckled at her left breast and with his right hand manipulated her left breast, gently moving the nipple between his index finger and thumb. Kelly was thinking she had died and gone to heaven and this was the only beginning.

Sam licked at the hard nipple of the breast for only a few seconds longer, then he stood up straight and removed his coat, his gun with shoulder holster, his shirt and tossed them to the floor. All the while, Kelly was back to the business of attacking his mouth with her tongue.

Finally Sam undid his belt and stuck both thumbs into the top of his underwear, taking everything down and out of the way. He next pulled her body close to his, and they both sank to the floor of the salon, with open mouth exchanges of deep throat pleasure.

She spread her legs wide, and guided his member into her body. And it was true, she knew how to fix lonely.

Kelly made some tuna sandwiches, and opened a bottle of fine wine. It was now two thirty in the morning. They looked at the boat. He saw the equipment Pedro had installed and Sam was impressed with it all. They went down to the bedroom, turned on the TV, and climbed into the sack. They cuddled. Then they made love again. It was slower than the first time, but had memories that would last forever.

As Kelly drifted off to sleep, Sam was still worried about tomorrow. He would have to get Mays and his wife out of town. That was his priority. He would take care of that first thing in the morning.

Chapter 20

Day 9, continued.

SAM AWOKE AT six thirty Thursday morning. He had only had five hours of sleep, but he felt amazingly invigorated. He dressed quickly. Kelly was sleeping softly. He leaned down and gave her a kiss on the lips.

She woke up without a start and gave him that sweet smile of hers. "Hello Sam. Where you going?"

"Got a busy day. Things to do and people to see."

She moved over to the center of the bed, allowing him room to come in. Sam rolled onto the top of the covers and kissed her again. Now she was awake and she eagerly took the kiss, as though it was the start of something exciting and new. Sam pulled away.

"Got to go baby. You stay here and finish your sleep. Keep your cell phone hot. I'll call you." He kissed her again and left the bed for the stairs. As he was half way up he heard her voice call out. "Sam?"

He paused and turned back into the room. She lay in the center of the bed, looking as though she was a lost waif, in a cover of down blankets. "I love you, Sam," She said.

"An' I love you too, baby."

It was now seven thirty Thursday morning, March 9. Sam drove his car onto David Street, in Algiers Point. The Mays house was at 712, and it was one and a half blocks from the Mississippi. It was a nice shotgun, well built, with a grand porch. From there you could see the water of the Ole Miss, the city of New Orleans, and to the left, the two beautiful bridges that spanned the river. It was a wonderful setting.

He parked his car two blocks down from Bill's house and walked past it, not glancing to the left or the right and moved on up toward the river. Sam was looking for cops. The street was just getting light, morning would soon appear in the East, but it was about an hour away.

As Sam walked toward the river, he paid no attention to the Mays house itself. He took short glances from the corner of his eyes, now and then, wanting to see if anyone was watching. The street ended at a cul-de-sac because of the river. He crossed over to the opposite side of the street.

As he walked back he went slower, casually checking each parked car. No cops. At the end of the block he quickly crossed the street again, walking up the five steps to 712 David. He used his key and let himself in.

Sam found the place looked almost as bad as his, except for the three foot hole in the living room ceiling. He moved quickly to the bedroom, found the plastic bag containing the two passports. He next searched for Barbara's 'Freedom' bag, her 'Get Away for a Day Bag.' Sam had never seen one, but Bill told him it was like a large briefcase, full of many plastic pockets, all containing everything a woman might or might not ever need. Sam rooted around and finally found the bag. He returned to the front door and peeked outside. No cops. He got into his car and drove to his apartment on Barracks.

Sam walked into his apartment and paid no attention to the mess he saw. He stripped his clothes off, took a quick shower and shave, and dressed in fresh clothes. He still had two black shirts, some dark grey slacks, and a brown suede jacket that the cops didn't bother with. They still had plastic covers over them from the cleaners. So much for the cops.

It was almost eight forty-five when he got to his office. He booted up Wally's computer, and searched for Adam Loper's address. Sam had to dig deep to find this one. It was ten years old and Loper retired later that year. He finally found it in a file of "Retirees:" *Loper, Adam, Rampart Division, 3248 Longview, Metairie LA, Apt. 201.*

Sam next looked up Donald Mosley. He found him in Wally's file regarding the Skanes case. 5422 Poydras Street. No room number was mentioned. Then he placed a call to Eduardo Sanchez.

"Hello?" The voice sounded as though it had been awakened from the sleep of the dead.

"Eduardo, this is Sam."

"Sam who?"

"Sam Pennington. One of your partners. I'm the tall one with the black hair."

"Oh. Hello, Sam."

"Listen to me. You and Bill Mays were going to the new office and sign a lease today. Right?"

"Yes. We were to go back at around one o'clock."

"You take care of that yourself. Got it?"

"Yeah, I can do that."

"Okay then. I'll see you later today."

Sam next walked three blocks down river, on Royal. Melissa Schwartz was now in her late fifties. Melissa was the premiere travel agent for New Orleans and all surrounding areas, including offices in Baton Rogue, Lake Charles, and Lafayette. The name of her company was very special to Sam. It had class, and feeling, and substance: "Melissa's French Quarter Travel Service." When Sam walked up to the building, she was just unlocking the front door.

"What you got for me, sweetheart?" Melissa asked. She then tossed Sam a kiss.

"Need a rush deal. Got an important rock star. I need a box of tickets, half-way around the world. An' I need them in a half an hour."

Melissa was a pro. Nothing bothered her. She threw her purse on a side table, flopped down onto her desk chair, picked up a pen and asked, "Starting where?"

"Here," Sam said back.

"How many?" she asked.

"Two."

"Going to?"

"Mexico City."

"Via LAX?"

"Yes."

"From there to?"

"Honduras." By now she had booted up her computer and had gained access to her booking file.

"Date?"

"First thing tomorrow."

"How about a flight on American at eleven?"

"Go for it."
"First class or coach?"
"He's a rock star, for crying out loud."
"Name?"
"Bill Mays."
"Stupid name for a rock star."

It was nine thirty, by the time Sam left Melissa's. She had not only booked all plane flights, but also hotel reservations for layovers.

The morning traffic was stiff. Sam made a call to George Carey's cell phone.

"George Carey here. How may I help you?"
"George, this is Sam. Where are you?"
"On the third floor on Tchoupitoulas. This Fat Boy definitely worked alone. And guess what? He wrote a journal."
"What's he say?"
"Not only does he name all of his hits, he also tells of all his failures. I'm just scanning through it. Here's one. 'I brought Marcy here last night. She would not come upstairs, didn't like the elevator. I told her I had booze upstairs, but no way. She offered to give me a blow job, right there, for twenty bucks. I said no way, and she walked off. I now will continue researching another girl, Stacy. More later.' I got over one hundred pages'a this shit here."
"That's good George, real good."
"Anyway, I'll make a copy of this and send it to Slidell."
"What did the Chief in Slidell think of that?" Sam asked.
"Who cares? It's his graveyard."
"I'll take care of that, I'll call him later today."
"You got it."
"Listen, when you get back to the office, I need you to baby-sit Witherspoon for me."
"No problem, he's sick with the flu. That's why he wasn't there yesterday. You own the store now. You the man!"
"That's good, George. Give me a 911 if you got a problem."
"You got it."

Sam arrived at the Pelican at ten fifteen. He left the car at the front and while waking inside, he noticed two bodies he recognized, sitting out by the pool.

Bill Mays and Wally White had now become friends. They were both sipping Bloody Marys, having just finished a breakfast of Eggs Benedict and champagne, served in the hotel's Escoffier Room.

Sam sat under an umbrella at the poolside, listening to Wally and Bill tell him of their fantastic evening and morning at the Pelican. Wally had the time of his life. He saw a great war movie on HBO but fell asleep halfway through the film. He would try to catch it again that night on HBO 2. Bill agreed that breakfast was fantastic and his wife was now at the beauty salon, undergoing a full body massage, facial, pedicure, and manicure. Later she would get her hair done.

Wally took a swim in the pool and Sam took advantage of the situation to speak privately to Bill.

"What's with your lawyer?" Sam asked.

"He was here twenty minutes ago. I signed the Power of Attorney, and the ball is now in his court."

Sam tossed him a large manila envelope he carried under his arm. "Don't open this out here. In there are your tickets. Your plane leaves at eleven o'clock tomorrow morning. You can stop over in Mexico City if you wish or a flight is also booked for Honduras. Full schedule is enclosed. There's also ten thousand dollars in there. Take what you need, do what you want."

Sam reached over to the table and picked up his wife's travel bag. "This belongs to Barbara. The two passports are inside. I took a look inside Barbra's get-away bag. Just between you and me, I've never seen so much shit packed into so many small compartments in my life."

Mays took the bag, and placed it on his table. "I know. It's an amazing thing."

Sam looked around the area, trying to spot Wally. He was out in the center of the pool, having fun with a beach ball and two kids.

Mays studied Sam. "You okay Sam? Something bothering you?"

"Don't you worry about me, I'm doing just fine."

"I'm supposed to be at the new office, at one o'clock, to sign the lease," Mays said.

"It's taken care of."

"What about my Captain, Al David? What's he got to say about my letter?"

"I'm sure by now he's read it." Sam said. "I'm sure he's tried to reach you. I'm sure he can't find you. And that's because?"

"I'm staying in a nice hotel, incognito."

"Right," Sam added. "Tomorrow morning at eight o'clock you take a cab to the airport."

"Wally could take us," Mays offered.

"Forget about Wally. Just do as I ask you. And I'll be here. You may not see me, but I'll be here. I want to see you on that plane and flying out. For now, you just stay out of harm's way."

"So who's gonna harm me?"

"Did you see that big hole in your living room ceiling?"

Sam next drove to Metairie, to see Adam Loper. He turned the radio on and got into the middle of a newscast. Someone was doing a live radiocast from the killing field in Slidell. He was talking to the mayor of Slidell, who was telling the reporter of what had happened here. No one knew exactly what they were talking about, who did what to whom, and how they had just found so many dead bodies buried here. Sam turned the radio off. He had already been there and done that. Besides, Sam was busy making his own news, news he hoped nobody would ever read about.

Adam lived in a three story apartment house, surrounded with shade trees. It was true middle-class American. Sam rang the bell at Apt. 201. After a moment, Mrs. Loper answered the door. She was a strikingly handsome woman, in her sixties. Every move she made, the clothes she wore, even her speech, showed nothing but class.

"Yes, may I help you?"

"Yes ma'am. My name is Sam Pennington." Sam showed his badge and ID.

"Hello Sam. It's very nice to finally meet you. Won't you please come in?"

Sam entered the apartment. It was well decorated, with a large classic glass menagerie, at one end of the room.

"Your husband and I worked together on Rampart Street, about ten years ago. I wanted to come and pay my respects."

"My name is Rose," she said. "Won't you come this way?"

She led him down a hallway to the back master bedroom, stood at the open doorway and paused, allowing Sam room to enter.

Adam Loper was sitting in a hospital bed, its back cranked up so he could be properly fed by the nurse, a white woman in her fifties. She held a bowl of cream of wheat in one hand and a spoon in the other, and she was feeding him one spoon at a time.

Adam Loper did not look like the person Sam last saw in his car on Royal Street some ten years ago. At that time he was a fast-talking, cocaine-tasting, decisive man of power and knowledge. Now he had literally turned into a vegetable. It was Alzheimer's that had done this to Adam. He had aged beyond belief. His gaunt eyes didn't recognize anything. His body was skin and bones. The nurse was trying to do her job, but feeding him was the job of the day.

"Here you go, sweetheart," she said, trying to cajole him. "Now swallow. Come on, let's swallow." As she spoke she took her left hand and placed it onto his throat. Then with her fingers, she massaged his throat downward, in order to try to excite his nerves into a swallowing effect.

"Okay, let's try again. Swallow. Swallow."

Sam looked back at Rose. She had placed her hand on her own throat, and was running her fingers downward, in a feigning attempt to cause her man to swallow. Sam caught her attention. She smiled at him.

"He sometimes forgets how to swallow his food," she said. "It seems like such a small thing, but sometimes he just forgets."

"Did Adam ever say anything about me?" Sam asked.

"Well, he once told me you did a job for him. Then he told me he got you a detective job over on the Royal Street Precinct, but that was all I remember. And over the years he mentioned you several more times, stating you were a very good cop."

"Thank you, ma'am. I'm sorry for what you must go through here." Sam leaned in and gave her a kiss on the cheek. He handed Rose his card. "If you need anything, anything at all, please call me."

By now it was twelve thirty, and Sam headed back to the city. There was no way in the world he could get any help from Adam Loper. Adam Loper could not even help himself. Not that Sam needed any help in the first place. He was simply attempting to ward off the evils of the night, should any come by to nip at his heels.

He got to 5422 Poydras Street at one fifteen, parked in the garage, and waited for the elevator. It was not as classy a building, as was the Office of Internal Affairs but it would do nicely in a pinch.

There, in the entrance hall, Sam found the directory listing, Mosley and Mosley – A Legal Corporation. On the second line it listed two names, Donald F. Mosley, and Donald F. Mosley, Jr., Attorneys at Law.

Sam took the elevator up to the second floor. It was an elevator not unlike the one you ride to the doctor's office. Fluorescent lights in the ceiling, an off-white plastic wall covering and a rubber wall to wall floor matt. This was nothing like the OIA.

Sam got off of the elevator onto the second floor. It was even more sterile than the rest of the building. The hall was clean, the carpet was not frayed, but it was…very medical. At the end of the hall he found two ten foot high, heavy wooden doors, with very posh hardware door handles. The wood itself was dark stained oak. It was as though these two doors belonged in another building. It was as though, behind these oak doors you would find the owner of the building. Sam pushed the door open and entered.

He had stepped into a palace like Dorothy dreamed of in the Wizard of Oz. It was utterly amazing. Sam quickly figured out what Mosley had done. He leased a suite of offices in a building with standard services. Then he proceeded to construct a magnificent office, displaying a contrast that would take your breath away.

The reception room was large, semi-round. A great marble table sat in the center, with fresh flowers, properly positioned for the proper decoration. Naturally the lighting was perfect, indirect lighting. All switches were located on dimmers. Sam felt he was in his apartment. Except for the receptionist, Sam was all alone. He was the only client in the room.

The receptionist sat at a marble topped desk, at the back center of the room. Sam crossed in and asked for Mr. Donald Mosley.

"Are you speaking of Mosley Senior or Mosley Junior?"

"I'll bet you must ask that question a lot?"

The receptionist, an African American woman of twenty-two, smiled at Sam. "I must tell you, I have been told by my boss to ask that question. I know the difference, but a lot of people who come in here can't make the connection. Junior is the son and senior is the daddy. You want the daddy, right?

Sam had subtly been put in his place. "Right," Sam said with a smile. "I would like to see the Daddy."

She made a call to someone in a back office and stated, "Detective Sam Pennington is here." After a brief pause, she hung up the phone and directed Sam to follow her.

Sam tracked behind her into a long hallway leading to two more huge double doors at the end.

"We're having a little celebration down here," she said, as they walked.

"What is that for?" Sam asked.

"We just won another one," she announced.

Sam entered Donald F. Mosley's office. Present was Mosley himself and his partners in the company, Donald Mosley Junior, who Sam had once referred to as Pin Head, along with three other middle-aged lawyers, all of whom were also African American. If Sam had been wearing an arctic ski suit, he would still have felt the chill in his body. Sam instantly realized he was not welcome there.

Sam quickly looked around the room. Directly in the center was Mosley's desk. It was a beautiful piece of furniture, Italian design. He had four large sculptures placed around the desktop he used for paper weights. He stuck papers and briefs under them, to hold them in place for when he needed them. This was the Mosley filing cabinet.

To the left was a much larger area. It was dressed out like an English pub, complete with bar, tables and chairs that seated up to twenty. There was also a dart board. Finally there was a large jeroboam of Dom Perignon champagne, resting in an ice-filled silver bucket sitting on a side table. Everyone in the room was drinking from cut-glass champagne flutes.

"Well hello, Sam Pennington," Mosely said in his most mellifluous voice. "I knew they would send someone over to offer congratulations. I just didn't know it would be you." The room had grown quiet. No one else spoke.

"I don't have an idea what you are talking about," Sam said.

"The Skanes trial," Mosley answered. "You mean you haven't heard what happened at the Skanes trial?"

Sam studied the room one more time. "I don't have a clue."

"Well that's a coincidence," Mosley said. "We have a hung jury. The judge proclaimed that two hours ago. We are now waiting to find out if the DA wants to go for a retrial. And if he does, so be it. My client has the money to fight this case until hell freezes over!" Everyone in the office raised their champagne glasses and drank with a cheer.

Sam smiled. "Well, congratulations on your success. You did a fine job and I applaud you."

"Well, thank you," Mosley said. "So why did you come here?"

Once again Sam looked around the room. He saw no reason not to tell it like it was. "I'm here seeking legal representation."

There were five African American men standing in that room who immediately stiffened up at the sounds of Sam's words.

Mosley looked at his partners. "Gentlemen, I need the use of this office for private reasons, if you will please excuse us."

The four men quickly left the room; Donald Junior trailed.

"Hold on a minute, Donald," Mosley said. "Sam, have you met my son?"

"Yes, we met," Donald jumped in. "We met quickly, briefly."

Sam walked over to the young man, holding his hand out. Donald Junior did not take it. Donald remembered the courthouse men's room; Sam saying to him, after using the toilet, "I don't wash."

As Sam crossed to the boy, he also recalled saying those words. He now wished he had not.

"Alright, Don," Mosley had quickly spotted some tension between the two. "Let me have my moment alone with Detective Pennington."

As Junior left the room, Mosley closed the doors. He then crossed around and sat at his desk.

"Alright Sam, sit down and spill your guts."

Sam sat down on an ornate French side chair. "I want you to represent me in a potential challenge against the Office of Internal Affairs."

Mosley studied Sam for a moment. "I charge one hundred fifty dollars an hour. For you, I'll do it for two hundred. In addition, I'll need a five thousand dollar retainer."

"That sounds good to me," Sam said.

A big smile crosses Mosley's face. "I'll have the paper work drawn up. What are you charged with?"

"I have no idea."

"No idea?" Mosley asked. "This is an easy case for me."

"At this moment, I have been charged with nothing."

"Well, you just call me when you get the charge, and I'll be there."

"You got a deal," Sam said with a smile on his face. After that Sam became deadly serious. "So tell me the truth, how many jurors voted Skanes Junior innocent?"

"Actually, it was only one," Mosley said, with a big smile on his face.

"And was that the black lady in the front row?" Sam asked. "The one with thick glasses?"

"I saw you looking at her, and she smiling back at you," Mosley said. "She liked you. She thought you were a nice guy. As a matter of fact, it was the sixty-eight year old white lady. She sat in the back left. She liked the way Skanes looked. Loved the light grey pullover sweater he wore. Loved his haircut, liked his style. Said he could never shoot anybody." Mosley then jumped into a major horse laugh. "I got you there, Sam. I know my jury. I know who's with me and who's against me."

"Next question. Did you ever ask Skanes if he shot my partner?"

"I never ask a client if he did the evil deed. That's not my job. I will defend him because he is innocent of all wrong doing until the prosecutor proves different."

"That's fine," Sam said. "Now you got what you want, so here's what I want. I want you, if it's ever necessary, to defend me in the same manner."

"I'll provide you with that," Mosley answered.

"I will increase my deposit from five thousand to ten thousand. It will also include another suspect, a Detective William Jefferson Mays."

"Where is this William Jefferson Mays?"

"I'll tell you that later."

"Where does a cop get that kind of money?" Mosley asked.

"I lead a frugal lifestyle."

"I doubt that," Mosley said.

"Well, let's try this. You never ask a defendant if he did the evil deed, but now you'll ask me how I can afford to pay my bill?"

"I apologize. I won't ask that again."

The two men shook hands. They had begun a friendship.

Sam next drove up Bourbon Street and parked his car near the new office. It was now two thirty. He ran up the stairs and found Eduardo, with tape measure in hand, measuring for the furniture he was going to buy.

"How's it go, Eduardo?"

"Hey Sam, how's it with you?"

"Fine. I'm possibly being charged with a felony dope charge."

As Eduardo stood up in shock and allowed his measuring tape to snap back into its case.

"Don't worry about it," Sam said. "I didn't do it, and I doubt if anything will come of it. I want you to write a check for ten thousand dollars to this man." Sam handed him a business card for Donald Mosley. "This is a deposit, just in case something bad happens. And this also covers Bill Mays. Don't even think about it, just do it."

"Okay. I'll do it right now."

"Messenger it over to Mosley's address. Make sure that happens."

"You got it," Eduardo said.

"So what are you doing here? Looks like you need help. You working alone?"

"Hey, I just signed the lease. Give me a break."

"Sorry about that. I'm under a bit a pressure. What's happening with the upstairs? You gonna move in there?"

"Sam, you wanna sit down and cool off a minute? You're moving too fast for me."

Sam took a deep breath. He walked into the front office area, and sat down in front of a large desk. The sun was shining directly into his eyes. He started this day at four thirty this morning and had not stopped to even eat. Eduardo followed him in and sat on the edge of the desk.

"Listen to me, Sam. This is going to work out just fine. At three o'clock I got two boys coming in to help me draw out a schematic of this entire space up here. Then we make up cardboard cutouts of all the furniture we need, an' put in onto position. Tomorrow morning, I'm gonna see three girls to work for us. I check them out. Later I see a woman who is an interior decorator. She's gonna tell me what she thinks we need to do. She's gonna tell me to hang something on that window, so the sun don't shine in you eyes. Then I got a meeting with those two attorneys and one accountant downstairs, and we start to talk about how we spend our money. Now, you wanna help me make up a plot for this office, or you got more important things to do?"

Sam smiled. "Eduardo, I trust you implicitly. Take your time. Do what you gotta do." He rose and walked to the stairs.

"*Hasta luego*, baby," Eduardo called after.

"You got that one right," Sam yelled back. As Sam walked on down the stairs he again called back up to Eduardo. "I got one more favor. Don't hire everybody you need. Leave room for a new one. You'll get her in about a month from now. Her name is Hironee Jessup. I'll fill you in on that later."

"Okay. You got it."

Sam stepped onto Bourbon Street and looked around. Jazz fest had begun. Tourists flooded the street and music could be heard in the air. Across the street a man wearing a red and white striped jacket was selling hot dogs from a decorative large plastic hot dog, about seven feet wide and three feet high, with the name "LUCKY DOG" painted across the front. It opened in the middle, and there he had his real hot dogs and all of the stuff required to make it taste great. Sam ordered one with chili and onions. As he walked back to his car a mule-drawn carriage passed him. He smiled at the people. It cheered him up, made him feel good again.

Sam next traveled to Charity Hospital and went to room 217. There he found Hironee Jessup, alert, recovering, still on her Valium drip.

"How you doin?"

"I'm better," Hironee answered. She was still shaky, but better.

"That's good. In a few days you start a program. Take you one month."

"I don't think I can do that."

"You can do that. An' when that's over, you got a job."

"What job?"

"Don't worry about what job. All you have to worry about is staying straight. Everything beyond that will take care of itself. I'll be watching you. I'll be in contact with you. All you have to do is stay straight." Sam pulled one of Eduardo's cards from his pocket. "Here's where you make contact to start the job. Be there, or be sorry."

Sam next drove his car to the enclosed parking lot on Royal. There he found Jimmy, the man in charge of repairs. He tossed him the keys, suggested he might finish the carpeting in the rear compartment, and walked on to his office. When he arrived there, he found George and David both on the phones, doing that busy detective thing. Sam got on the phone and called Kelly on her cell.

"Hello, this is Kelly. How may I help you?"

Sam wondered where she had gotten that verbiage from. Perhaps from George Carey. "Hey babe, what's going on?"

"Oh Sam, it's nice to hear your voice."

"So give me some good news."

"We're about finished with the last coat of paint on the boat. We had to hand-sand the entire outside, then when we sprayed it on, it came out to be just great. It's got to dry solid, one day, maybe two, then we put it back in the water."

"That sounds good. Listen baby, I can't make it down there tonight."

When Kelly spoke, she had deep depression in her voice. "Oh Sam."

"Not to worry. I'll bring dinner tomorrow night. Promise. How many people you got there now?"

"Well, there are five of us."

"Sounds good. I got ya covered. Be patient with me, baby. Trust me. I'll be there with the goods."

Sam concluded his call with Kelly and immediately placed a call to Bob Razzi of Central Market fame. It had been almost a week since he had last talked to Sam, and he wanted to know how Sunday's brunch finally worked out.

"Listen Bobby," Sam said. "This is the biggest deal I've ever done."

"Yeah, okay," Bob said, with a drip of sarcasm. "So who you gonna do now?"

"I'm not gonna do anybody. I want to have a party with you and your wife and me and the crew that's been working on the boat. This weekend we're gonna finally stick it back in the water."

"Well, congratulations."

"You remember where the boat is?"

"Sure do. Lafitte, right?"

"That's right. I want ten Maine lobsters; that's two more than we need, just in case someone drops by. Can you handle that?"

"All it costs is money."

"Don't worry, you're covered. And I need everything else with it, you know, corn on the cob and…"

"You got it, don't worry. What time you want us there?"

"Make it about seven."

"You got it."

Sam hung up the phone as George Carey crossed over to him. He handed Sam a report from 'Internal.' It was three and a half pages long, listing everything thing they took from his apartment in detail. Sam flipped through the pages.

"What happened to you?" George asked. "The cops came in and did that to you?"

Sam put the report in his left hand drawer. "No, It's fine," Sam said. "What have you got on for tomorrow?"

"Right now, were just marking time," George said. "The last homicide reported was last Wednesday, and that turned out to be a suicide."

"I just need someone with me tomorrow morning. Someone I can trust."

"You can't trust me," George stated. "I'm just a whore."

"That will be good enough," Sam said. "Pick me up in the morning, at the Royal Orleans, at seven thirty. Don't be late."

Night was falling as Sam left the office. The only call he didn't make was to Deland Lupson. He wanted to make sure he had delivered all the information he had to satisfy Mr. Lupson's small mind. That would wait until tomorrow, or at the latest Monday morning.

Sam was tired. He had never felt quite so weary. He walked up to the

Royal Orleans Hotel. Carl Witherspoon and Sam had used the Royal Orleans on many occasions. They would book a room for people they needed for investigation or court related situations. Carl also established the same deal with The Pelican Suites.

It was a five star hotel, which was one of the most beautiful landmarks in the French Quarter. Sam entered from Royal Street, and passed The Rib Room, the hotel's signature restaurant. He smelled the Baron of Beef, and saw the waiter cutting a nice slice for a customer. When he got to his room, he promised himself he would have a piece of the baron. Throughout the day, the only thing he had eaten was a Lucky Dog. Now he would take care of number one.

He walked up the massive staircase, to the second level. People gathered and talked. Running along the back wall was a large beautiful bar. Sam stopped there and ordered a glass of Glenlivet. The drink cost him five bucks. It was more than a double shot, served in heavy cut glass. It was a good deal.

With drink in hand, he walked through the bar area, and to the front desk, passing under one of the most magnificent chandeliers the Quarter had to offer. As he arrived there, he took out his badge with ID.

"Yes sir, may I help you?" The question came from a man Sam did not know. As a matter of fact, Sam did not know anybody in the place. He had been by the Royal Orleans a hundred times, but never once came inside. But tonight, would be his treat.

He presented his credentials to the man. "My name is Sam Pennington. I need a single room for the night, possibly two nights. Just a small single room.

"Yes sir. One moment please." The man left the desk, and luckily, Sam had his drink. He took a long sip, and it set the world right again. The man soon came back with his boss, Mr. Alberto Dove, an Argentinean who spoke some English. Not perfect, but he tried.

"Yes sir. How may we help you?"

"Okay, here's the thing," Sam said. "Maybe I shouldn't have showed your guy my badge. Maybe I should have just come in here off the street and asked for a room. Then there would have been no problem. But now it's become a problem. So what I want to do is start from scratch again. What I want is a small single room. And I want a prime rib dinner. May I please offer my credit card. I will pay for the room and the dinner. So how's that with you guys?"

"I can offer you a suite on the top floor," Alberto offered.

"May I please explain. I really don't like big rooms. You've heard of claustrophobia? I am an anti-claustrophobe. All I want is a one-bedroom place to lie down in and get a good dinner of prime rib and then, I'm gone. And I'll pay for the room, and the dinner."

Alberto thought of the situation. He wanted to do his job and properly represent the Royal Orleans Hotel.

"I can offer you the Presidential Suite," Alberto said. "It has a full kitchen and dining room, and three bedrooms, including the master bedroom, with a spa. The room of course will be with the compliments of the hotel."

It was obvious Sam had made a mistake in showing his badge. It was clear Alberto's English did not allow for the simple excuses from a tired cop. "That will be excellent," Sam said. "And I want to thank you for your help in this delicate matter."

Alberto called for a bellman to take Mr. Pennington to his room, even though Mr. Pennington had no luggage. They went to the twelfth floor and walked to the far end of the hall. When Sam entered the room, he didn't even turn the lights on, but he got a glimpse of a white grand piano in the living room, while the front door was open. The bellman tried to turn the lights on, but Sam blocked his entrance. He handed the bellman a five dollar tip, and closed the door.

Sam stumbled through the complex, and found a small guest bedroom with TV. He ordered dinner along with a razor, some shaving soap, tooth brush and some tooth paste. He thought of Kelly, wanted to call her. He decided to do that right after dinner. It was almost eight o'clock, and Sam had been up since four thirty that morning. He fell onto the bed to check out the mattress, and closed his eyes for just a second.

Chapter 21

Day 10

SAM WOKE UP quickly and sat up straight. He was fully clothed and the overhead light was still on. Sam had only fallen asleep for a moment, but he felt invigorated. He had to take a leak.

He jumped up and moved down the darkened hallway to the master bedroom. He walked inside and threw the light switch on. It was magnificent, a large room with a king-sized four poster bed and the all the fancy appointments one might expect. He walked on into the bathroom, threw on another light switch, and found himself in a thing of absolute beauty. At the right was a large glass enclosed shower with four shower heads, which were adjusted to every pertinent part of your body.

On the opposite wall was a large square Jacuzzi, complete with jets of water that exploded into a foamy delight. Sam was not impressed with this. It was the same tub he had in his apartment. There were two sink areas; both sinks were large golden clam shells, with beautiful high deco swan faucets. On the other side there was a toilet and a bidet. This room could be closed off, with shuttered doors, in case someone needed some special privacy. What Sam really liked was a commercial urinal attached to a corner wall, in the left back of the room. He walked over to the urinal and proceeded to drain the lizard.

Sam next walked into the living room, threw on the lights and looked around. It was also magnificently decorated. A white baby grand piano was the center piece of the room, in the opposite area, there was a 'ten seat' open bar. Sam didn't play the piano, so he headed for the bar.

He moved into the back bar area and found almost every brand of quality booze one might desire. Every bottle was a fifth, some closed and sealed and some opened, with pouring spigots at the top. They had gin and vodka and rum and whisky and scotch and brandy and tequila. In addition there were a variety of liqueurs, ranging from coffee to peach to whatever else you might imagine.

Sam studied the brand names. There was no mention of Glenlivet. But he saw a bottle of Glenfiddich, a single malt whisky. Sam decided to give it a try.

He took a tumbler from the back bar and filled it with ice from the under-counter ice machine and poured some Glenfiddich up to the rim. Sam took a long sip of the liquid. It tasted great. He thought of changing his brand.

His stomach started to growl and he thought of dinner. He had ordered it about a half hour before. Sam checked his watch. It was now five thirty-two. He read the watch again. It still said five thirty-two. He walked to the end of the bar and picked up the telephone, read the directions on the face, and pushed the number nine. A recorded voice came on. 'The time is five thirty three, and ten seconds.'

Sam was in a state of shock. He stood there for ten seconds, re-tracing his actions. "My God." Sam said out loud. "What have I done to myself? I'm now drinking whisky when I first get up in the morning."

Sam figured he had fallen dead asleep in the guest room the night before and had slept through the night for over eight hours. In two hours, George would be out front to pick him up. He now had to hustle. He picked up the phone and called room service.

"Hello, room service," the male voice answered.

"This is Sam Pennington, in the Presidential Suite."

"Yes Mr. Pennington. We tried to deliver your dinner last night, and even tried to reach you on the telephone."

"Yeah, I must have fallen asleep. I'll pay for the dinner."

"Oh no sir, that's fine. It's all complimentary."

Sam quickly decided not to fight the establishment any longer. "Okay. What I want now is an order of steak and eggs and some coffee in about a half an hour. And I also ordered some bathroom stuff."

"Yes sir. You should find that in a plastic bag, hanging on the door knob to your suite."

"That's fine. I'll leave the door open. Come on in and set up."

Sam swallowed the last of his Glenfiddich and found the plastic bag on the front door of his suite. He headed for the bathroom, got into the shower, wearing his socks and shorts, washing his underwear first, while they were still in position on his person. He next removed them and hung them out to dry, over the top of the shower. Sam proceeded to wash the scum of the day before from his body.

He had a refreshing shave, a fine cleaning of his teeth, and found two terry cloth bathrobes with the name Royal Orleans embroidered on the pockets hanging on the bathroom door. He put one on and grabbed some money from his trousers. He turned on the heater in the room to dry his underwear, and walked to the living room.

A waiter was already there, Ignacio. He was from Mexico, or Panama, or Cuba, or wherever. Sam knew his name, because of his name tag on his white jacket pocket, but he spoke no English. The only word he understood, or spoke, was yes.

Ignacio set up his breakfast at a small table near the east window. He also brought a *Times Picayune*, which he laid out onto the table.

"Good morning Ignacio," Sam said.

"Yes," He answered with a smile.

"You don't speak any English, right?"

"Yes."

Sam handed him a ten dollar bill. "Thank you for the service."

"Yes. Yes." Ignacio bowed and left the room.

Sam figured he would soon have to learn Spanish in order to properly communicate with the real world. He sat down and attacked his steak and eggs. It was delicious. He recalled his breakfasts at the Boardwalk. They were better, but this was a close second.

This was now early Friday morning. Sam and his boys caught Eddie last Wednesday evening. That night, when they drove to the killing field in Slidell, there was no media present. Sam and his boys were the only ones that knew of these mass murders.

On Thursday, the previous day, an article appeared in the Times, regarding a man who died, committing suicide on Tchoupitoulas Street. Now, on Friday, he opened the paper and saw the front page headlines.

SERIAL KILLER MURDERS TWENTY SIX WOMEN!

It read like the attack of 9/11. It held the power of Pearl Harbor. As the articles unfolded, it told a story of a man, Eddie Marshal, who murdered twenty-six women, and no one knew about it. It told of the graveyard in Slidell and of the problem of: "Which parish was responsible for the corpses?

These murders were committed in Orleans Parrish and then buried in Slidell. So who pays the cost?"

The first section of the newspaper contained sixteen pages of articles from nine different writers, most of them being pure speculation. Finally on the fifteenth page there was a mention of Sam, by veteran writer Margaret Miller. Her main article was a recap of all of the other writings. She concluded her writing with, "The Detective in charge of this operation was Sam Pennington, who was not available for an interview." Sam's cell phone started ringing.

Sam pulled it from the pocket of his robe, and looked at the face of the phone. It was a 911 call from Sandra Hemmingway, a lady who worked for Carl Witherspoon. He decided not to respond to the call.

At seven twenty-five that morning, Sam left the Royal Orleans hotel. George sat waiting in his car for Sam to arrive. Sam climbed into the shotgun seat.

"Morning Boss."

"Good morning George."

"Where to and what do we do?"

"Go to the Pelican Suite Hotel, park across the street. We observe what happens."

"You got it."

George parked in a fire zone, located just south of the Pelican, where they had a full view of the parking area. It was now five minutes to eight. Sam's phone rang again.

"You gonna get that?" George asked.

"No, not yet."

"Okay. That's fine. You wanna give me the whole gig then?"

"Alright. At around eight o'clock, a guy with his wife comes out of there and gets into a taxi. Keep them in sight to Louis Armstrong Airport. We park and follow them inside."

"Okay. I got it. You wanna tell me what's supposed to happen next?"

"If the guy is approached by the cops, I want you to go in, show your badge and ask, 'What's the charge on this man, and where he is being taken?'"

"Does that include his wife?"

"Yes."

"What time does his plane leave?"

"Eleven o'clock."

A yellow cab pulled up in front of the Pelican. Shortly there after, Bill Mays and his wife left the hotel and got into the cab.

"That guy looks like Bill Mays, works out of Rampart. Is that the guy we're following?"

Sam nodded his head yes. George now felt secure. He knew Sam and his tricks. He also knew Sam would never leave him high and dry. As the cab left for Louis Armstrong, he popped his car into low gear and headed off in hot pursuit.

It took the forty-five minutes to make the trip on I-10, to the airport turnoff. Traffic was difficult at that time of the morning. Sam had received seven more cell phone calls, none of which he responded to. George pulled up the ramp to "Departing Passengers." He parked in a no parking fire zone, showed the cop on the street his badge, and he and Sam walked into the terminal.

Bill Mays and his wife were standing in a long line of check-in passengers. Actually it was three long lines, twisting like a snake from beginning to end. Sam knew Mays' reservations had been taken care of by Melissa Schwartz, the travel agent. All Mays needed to do was to walk through security and check in at the plane gate.

George had split from Sam when they first entered the terminal. He took a position just outside the ropes that held the passengers in proper position. Sam took his cellular phone and called George. Sam could see George grabbing for his phone.

"George Carey here."

"George, this is Sam."

George looked around. He saw Sam standing ten yards behind him. "Yes?"

"Go up to Mays. Get his attention. Tell him to leave that line and walk through security. Tell him to go to the plane gate. They will take care of the rest."

"Got it."

Sam saw George put his phone back into his pocket. He then moved up to Mays and tapped him on the shoulder. George whispered Sam's instructions into Mays ear. Mays then looked around and spotted Sam. An expression of immediate relief crossed his face. With new vigor at hand, Mays moved his wife from the line and they headed for the plane boarding section. Only passengers could move through the boarding area. Those who wished to kiss their sweethearts goodbye would have to do that at this point.

There were five metal detectors in position to X-ray the carry-on luggage. The passengers would walk through the personal metal detector. Mays and his wife were held up for the second time with a long line.

Sam walked past the boarding passengers and was halted by cops on the other side. He displayed his badge and identification card and relinquished his forty-five automatic hand gun. He was then allowed to proceed, still carrying his thirty-two backup piece strapped to the calf of his right leg. Sam was still armed and dangerous. He moved about one hundred feet into the second section of the terminal, found a decorative ledge to lean against, stood and looked back.

Taking Sam's lead, George Carey also made the same move. He showed his badge and ID, gave up his gun, and moved in past Sam to a watching position at the opposite wall. Bill and Barbra Mays were slowly closing in on the first check point. Sam's phone rang. He finally decided to take the call.

"Sam Pennington here. How may I help you?"

"Oh Sam!" It was Sandra Hemmingway, the desperate voice of Carl Witherspoon's secretary.

"Yes Sandra. What can I do for you?"

"Oh Sam, Sam. All hell is breaking loose down here."

"Well just stay calm."

"I can't. Sick as he is, Carl is coming in. I've got the media here. Their asking how come we have twenty-six women murdered, for over five years, and homicide didn't know a thing about it?"

"I'll be there at eleven thirty."

"Oh thank you Sam. Carl has set up an interview with the three networks at one thirty. The *Times* will be there also. He wants me to tell you to..." She searched though her notes to find the right line. "...cool them off and buy us some time."

"Tell Carl I'll be there at eleven thirty."

Sam hung up his phone, and saw that Bill and his wife were moving through the inspection area. Bill had placed a small bag onto the x-ray machine. Everything went through without a problem. Even the ten thousand dollars Sam had given Mays did not register on the machine. As they moved though the inspection gauntlet, Barbra Mays looked up and caught her first sight of Sam.

She had known about Sam Pennington for ten years. Her husband had described him to a tee. She had put up money to buy a boat for her husband. When Bill had to sell the boat, she got her money back plus interest. But that was ten years ago. Now was now.

As Sam looked at Barbra, he saw a woman about fifty-five years of age. Her husband had kept Sam a secret for a decade. Barbra was a lady with a grand sense of humor, a person who could take a joke and still stand by her man. She still had no idea what was happening, or why it was taking place. She knew she was leaving town in a hurry.

As she and Bill walked past the security area, and headed for gate twenty eight, she glanced at Sam and gave him a flashing wink. Sam caught the wink and delivered back a soft smile. Mays trudged on ahead, unaware that a platonic romance had been born.

George moved in at the rear of Mays and his wife, following closely behind. Sam then walked a hundred feet behind George. Gate 28 was at the far end of the airport. There was a second check in station located there. George used his ID and badge to pass by the X-ray machine, while Sam still stood out in the concourse. It took another fifteen minutes for Bill and his wife to be passed through the X-ray. It was now ten fifteen. George took a chair at the back of the room. Barbra sat near the front desk, while Bill confirmed his seating arrangements, and all other flight plans. Sam still stood in the middle of the concourse, looking for evil cops. His phone rang.

"Sam here."

"Sam, this is Sandra."

"Yes Sandra."

"Carl just came in. He's feeling very weak. He's lying down on his couch. He wants to know when you will be here?"

"I'll be there at eleven thirty. That's one hour and fifteen minutes from now."

"Thank you Sam."

At ten fifteen it was boarding time. They called first class first, and when that was filled it was second class. At eleven two they pulled the plane away from the gate, and twelve minutes later Sam saw the plane take off. One problem taken care of.

Sam started walking back to the car, George fell in beside him.

"How'd we do?" George asked.

"Perfect. Now we gotta get back to the office by eleven thirty."

George looked at his watch. "I think I can handle that."

They gathered their side arms from the gate police and climbed into George's car. He placed the red light on the top, started the car, and sped ahead with the siren blazing. The speed limit on the road leading into and out of the airport was a painfully slow thirty five miles per hour. Adding an occasional horn honk, George pushed his car up to seventy-five.

He whipped onto the I-10, and holding into the left lane, he sped along at close to ninety. George drove like Moses parting the Red Sea. He hit the clover leaf, passed Xavier College, and the sky line came into view. It was one of the prettiest cities in the world. The Superdome stood out like a beacon. Sam's phone rang. He answered.

"Sam Pennington here."

"Sam, this is Sandra. When will you be here?"

Sam checked his watch. "Well, it's now eleven twenty-five. In about five minutes, I'll be standing in front of your desk. Is that okay with you?"

"Oh yes Sam, and thank you so much."

At exactly eleven thirty, George hit the brakes in front of the police station on Royal. "Okay Boss. Go for it."

"Nice job, George. Good driving."

Sam jumped from the car and ran inside, moved quickly through the busy lobby and walked through the hallway to Carl Witherspoon's office. His door was locked and Sam went one door down to Sandra Hemmingway's office. The door was open.

"His door's locked," Sam said. "Where is he?"

Sandra was busily working on some papers. She looked up and saw Sam. "Oh Sam, this has been a bad morning."

"Where is he?"

"He's asleep on his couch."

"Okay, fine. When he wakes up I'll be in my office. At one thirty I'll cover the press. After that, who knows."

Sam walked to his office and found David Kennedy surrounded by thirty-six boxes of material taken from 522 Tchoupitoulas Street. David sat at his computer and had now completed a list of six pages of material, that Eddie Marshall had gathered there.

Sam entered the office and looked around, seeing the disaster. "This looks like my apartment."

"Hey Sam, how ya doin?" David said.

"How are you doing?"

"I think I'm about half-way through with this inventory shit. I'm a cop, not a secretary."

"No problem. I'll get a typist in here right now. You make it work."

George entered the room. "There you go. George, you type. David's been on this all morning. I've gotta prepare for a news conference. By five o'clock we get done, and we're outta here. David, put the phone calls on 911. We can't handle one more call. We are tired and we need a break. That's it. Now get to work."

For the next hour and a half, Sam printed out a general statement to the Media. It reviewed everything that took place over the past nine days of the case. He hoped that would be enough.

He brought his statement into Sandra's office, asked her to make enough copies to satisfy all media who were present. He asked her to present it early, for all to be able to read the document. He then returned to his office.

David Kennedy and George Carey were working their brains out. They worked as fast as they could, having to decipher hundreds of notes from detectives and cops who didn't know how to spell or write clearly.

Sam got some coffee from Mr. Coffee. He walked to the window and looked out over the Mississippi. He felt secure in the fact that everything was now working out. Bill Mays and his wife were on their way to Los Angeles International. They would switch there to Mexicana Airlines, and head for Mexico City. Sam had a source, a cop who worked in the Los Angeles, Tom Bradley International Airport section. Sam would call him, at around five p.m. LA time and see if Bill and wife made a successful flight change.

He next called Bob Rizzo, just to make sure everything was going fine. Bob answered in the affirmative, and Sam called Kelly.

"Hello, this is Kelly."

"Hey babe, how you doin'?"

"Sam. How are you doin'?"

"I am fantastic."

"I'm glad to hear that."

"I've got to do a press conference at one thirty today. After that I'm outta here and on my way there. Bob Rizzo will get there around five this afternoon, loaded with fine food."

"Are you going to be on television?" she asked with childish innocence.

"I don't know."

"Well, this is a big story," she added.

"They're going to have the three major networks here. I don't know if it's live or canned. Turn it on at one thirty and look around. Anyway, I'll be there shortly after. How's the boat?"

"It goes in the water tomorrow morning."

"I wanna see that."

"It looks beautiful."

"I'll see you around three, maybe four. Bye baby. And I love ya."

"Bye Sam. Me too."

Sam hung up the phone. On his desk was a mass of evidence. On the top of one pile was the diary of Eddie Marshall. Sam looked through the pages.

On page one, Eddie wrote of the murder of his first victim in New Orleans:

"Name was Julie, rather pretty brunette lady. Small, like my mother. When I finally coaxed her into my apartment, she was amazed at what she saw. I Spent three weeks checking her out. She was from Chicago. We played some stupid sex games. Then I hit her in the head with my baseball bat.

Unlike my mother, she bled a lot. Put her body into black body bag and cleaned up the blood. Put her in the Volvo and drove to Slidell.

Turned off the I-10 highway, onto the property. Brought my bolt cutter with me and pick and shovel. I then cut through the rusty padlock.

I am in a state of euphoria. I have not done anything like this since I killed ma'am. It has been a long time since then. The same thrill came back to me. The perfect crime.

Dug a grave, about five feet deep. Hard digging. The hole was about two feet wide and four feet long. I got tired at the end and stopped there, five feet. Took the body out of the black bag and tossed it into the hole. Then put the dirt back in and packed it down.

Drove home...feeling great...I know I can do this again, and again, and again."

Sam rifled through the pages, and stopped near the end. Eddie described his last burial in Slidell. This was number twenty-six:

"Just got back from Slidell. Twenty six in the ground. I am tired of this shit. No more for me. I now quit those long rides on the freeway. I quit digging graves. I'll come up with a new idea. Need something that puts attention on me. I Need to see an article in the paper about a missing girl. I Want to read about a cop on the case That will add a thrill to the whole thing!"

Finally, Sam looked at the last page of entry. In the same manner, Eddie described the murder of Beth Hayden, and how he placed her in the dryer at the laundry. He then made his final note.

"I am sick and tired of dealing with stupid cops! These men are so painfully ignorant, they can't follow their nose to the crime scene. This time I get a girl in a dryer. The public will see her there. Now I will get some action. Now I will get the attention I deserve!"

Sam stood in his office, withdrew his black silk tie from his left hand jacket pocket, and tied it around his neck.
"How do I look?" Sam asked George and David.
"You look great." George said.
"Excellent." David added.
"Okay if we take a look?" George asked.
"Be my guest. Follow me onto the stage and I'll introduce you."
Realizing they would both be on television, both men started to check each other out.

The Media room was slightly smaller than the size of the one used at the White House, but as you saw it on television, it had the look of national importance. The background had a dark blue curtain, with the shield of the Crescent City of New Orleans placed neatly in the center. At one o'clock Sandra Hemmingway and one assistant brought the pages Sam had written into the conference room, placed one stapled section on every open chair, and handed the rest out. The room was now almost full. Technicians moved about, running cables, checking sound levels, and tweaking cameras.

At exactly one thirty, Sam, followed by George and David, walked onto the two step platform. Sam stepped to the batch of microphones, George and David stood behind. Carl Witherspoon moved into the room at the right side. Evidently, Sandra had awakened him. He was now functioning. Not well, but functioning.

"Good afternoon," Sam said. The room got quiet. Sam and his boys had just caught a serial killer who had murdered twenty-nine women. That figure may have set a record of deaths. That, in itself, caused this Media frenzy to take place.

"My name is Detective Sam Pennington, with the Burglary & Homicide Division of the New Orleans Police Department. Last Wednesday morning, nine days ago, a nineteen-year-old female was discovered dead in a French Quarter laundry. It was revealed that her name was Beth Hayden, of Blanco, Texas. Her family was notified and has identified the body. Other than the mention of Beth Hayden, no other victims of these crimes can be named until official notification of their families.

"One week later, last Wednesday, a man named Eddie Marshall was spotted by two detectives." Sam looked over his shoulder at George and David. He stepped back and brought them both to the front to stand with him, George on his right and David on his left.

"This is Detective George Carey on my right and Detective David Kennedy on my left. Also there was Detective Wally White, who is now on a rest and recuperation leave. Without their diligence in this operation, it might have continued with many more deaths.

"Eddie Marshal, AKA Ed Marsh, was cornered on the roof top of 522 Tchoupitoulas Street. Mr. Marshall committed suicide. At this point in time, Mr. Marshall is the prime suspect in this case.

"This is an ongoing investigation. We are now in the process of finding out if there were any other person or persons, involved with Mr. Marshall, concerning these murders. After Mr. Marshall's death, a search of his apartment revealed a map of twenty six burial places, located off of the I-10, in Slidell.

"The Homicide division is now withholding all other information concerning this case, until said time it has been proven whether Marshall had worked alone, or with others. Now I will take questions."

"Mr. Pennington," A voice called back from the darkness.

Sam shielded his eyes from the light, and pointed at the reporter from the crowd. "Yes, go ahead," Sam said.

"John Phillips," the reporter shouted out. "How is it possible that twenty-six women can be murdered over the past five years and your homicide division doesn't know anything about it? And now you have just changed the death figure from twenty-six to twenty-nine women." Then, with some anger and frustration, John Phillips added, "When will this stop?"

"Well John, this will stop when it stops. These women who were murdered were all or mostly transient women. No one, before we found the body of Beth Hayden, was suspected or charged with murder. We have found twenty-six women buried in Slidell and three women located in the New Orleans area. There may be more. We'll let you know."

A lady reporter from the times stood up. Sam pointed at her. "Yes,

Ma'am."

"Do you not now know where these women came from? And how long will it take for the identification of the bodies."

"Well, when you find a grave, and you open it up, and there you find a body, buried naked in the dirt, and it's been there for five years or longer, one must assume it will take some time to find out who that person is and where that person came from." Sam then pointed at a woman sitting in the first row. "Yes ma'am."

"Sally Shaw, Atlanta Herald. Detective Pennington, I have read your report with interest. I must admit, I find it to be strangely devoid of facts. It glosses over details that we are here to ferret out. Are the police of this city now trying to hide information from the press? So I ask you, were these women known prostitutes?"

Sam smiled. "Nice choice of words. Ferret comes to mind. When did a reporter become a ferret?" There was a slight chuckle through the audience.

Sam continued. "First of all, the New Orleans Police Department will not hide anything from you, or anybody else. We found the twenty-six women in their graves last Wednesday evening. The police finally got the bodies out of the ground at nine Thursday morning. They were delivered to our morgue here in five different shipments, starting at ten thirty yesterday morning and ending up at five thirty last night.

"Next, Doctor Arnold Feeney, our chief coroner, combined with aid from Slidell and four other parish police departments, started to open the body bags. They worked on this process until one o'clock this morning and started again at ten thirty this morning. It may take them a week, or longer, before they have developed identification of the subjects. And as I speak, they are sill in the morgue downstairs, continuing to arrange the bodies. Some of the early ones are nothing but bones that have to be arranged on the table, like a jigsaw puzzle. But we will continue to forge ahead.

"As to what these women did for a living, I have no idea. As soon as we find out the who, what, when, where and the why of it all, we'll get back to you. And thank y'all for coming, and have a nice weekend."

Sam quickly left the dais and saw Carl Witherspoon out of the corner of his eye. Sam walked to Carl, as he coughed into a wilted, stained, unsterilized hankie.

"Hello Carl. Looking fine."

"Oh yeah. Feeling a lot better. Come on into my office."

When they got there, Carl flopped back down onto the couch, as Sam headed for coffee. It was yesterday's, and cold. He decided to pass.

"You've done a hell of a job on this one, I'll tell you that."

"You mean that press conference?"

"No. Yes, you handled them just fine. Perfect. No, I was talking about how you finished the case, that Marshall guy."

"Eddie."

"Yeah, Eddie Marshall. What a prick. You got the bastard. Good work."

"Thanks."

"I think I'm cured of the flu. Now what I got is a bad fucking cold."

"Carl, you remember us talking a few month ago, about me taking a few months off?"

"Yeah."

"Well I'm feeling a little burnt-out. I'm feeling like I need the time now."

Carl started into a coughing fit. Sam's comment had dislodged a glob of mucus in his lungs that was impossible for him to bring up. He sat up and continued coughing. Sam moved to him and started pounding his back. After a moment Carl gained control. As he breathed, it wheezed. He wanted to cough again, but he was too tired.

"Why don't you go home now," Sam said. "Get back in bed. By Monday you'll be fine."

"Yeah, I think so."

"Okay then. See you Monday." Sam rose and headed for the door.

"How much time you want?" Carl asked.

Sam placed his hand on the door handle, turned and looked back at Carl. "Two, maybe three months."

Carl held his handkerchief up to his mouth. "Jesus, we are short-handed and over-budget. I don't know how we can do that."

Sam turned back into the room, took a few steps toward Carl. "I thought about that," Sam said. "Tell you the truth, I almost took a few bullets on that rooftop. I could have died up there. An' the thing is, this city would have still gone on, and this office would still be running, with or without me."

Carl jumped into another coughing fit. Sam ran over and again started pounding his back. Then Carl gave it his final and most powerful cough of all. The explosion of air from his lungs, along with the pounding on his back from Sam, caused the glob of mucus to break free. It quickly found its way to his mouth and he immediately expectorated it into his hankie.

"Oh my God, that was beautiful!" he exclaimed. "I can breathe again!"

"Go home Carl. Get to bed. I'll see you Monday."

Sam walked back to his office. George and David were back, still reading the list of items, still typing them out. Sam joined in and with two men looking and reading, and George Carey typing as fast as he could, the final box was sealed at five fifteen. That would mean it was three fifteen Los Angeles time. It would be another two hours before he could call his man at LAX, checking on Bill Mays' travel itinerary.

Sam walked over to his filing cabinet, and drew forth the bottle of Glenlivet Kelly had given him. He poured three drinks, and proposed a toast. "Here's to my two friends and closest associates. I love you both." Sam swallowed the scotch and walked to the door.

"I now leave you," Sam said. "I'm going to celebrate with the loveliest lady I know. I'm going to my car and drive off into the sunset. I bid you adieu." He turned and opened the door and had an afterthought. "And get the boys in property to come up and drag this shit outta here."

Sam felt good. He walked up Royal toward his parking area. It had been a good day, and an even better night was expected. Bill Mays was nearing the landing pattern at LAX. That was his last problem. A jazz band was playing in the bar just across the street. They sounded real good. Sam stopped and listened in. They were playing "Bill Bailey." As Sam moved on, he thought of Kelly.

Sam was a third of the block up Royal, before he would turn into the garage where his car was parked, when suddenly a man jumped into the street just ahead of him. Sam was about to react, starting to reach for his gun, but then he recognized the fellow. It was Detective Tom Phelps.

"Hey Sam. How ya doin?" Phelps had that same smile on his face. That saccharine smile that said, *you are an idiot and I am smarter than you.* The smile that said, *You people in Homicide deal with one person wanting to kill another, while we in Narcotics deal with one person wanting to kill anybody, just for one sack of dope.*

"I'm fine Tom, how are you?" Sam heard footsteps coming up behind him. He glanced back over his shoulder and saw four deputy sheriffs closing in. Sam slowly looked back at Tom Phelps.

"Sorry about this, Sam." Tom said. "Got a warrant for your arrest. Take him, boys."

The four deputies moved in quickly, taking Sam by both arms and pushing him to the patrol car.

"Take it easy, Sam," Tom said. "You know the routine."

Two of the deputies took Sam's arms and placed them on the top of the car. Sam felt his legs being kicked back, and suddenly he was splayed out like a cow waiting for the branding iron. He could feel his forty-five automatic gun being stripped from its holster, while four more hands worked down his body from head to toe. The hands at his right found his thirty-two caliber back-up pistol. Sam Pennington was no longer armed and dangerous.

From behind, one hand grabbed his right arm, pulled it behind his back and clamped a handcuff on his wrist. Next, someone else took his left arm, pulled it behind him and clamped the second cuff into place. Sam was now securely restrained.

They opened the back door to the cop vehicle, and while watching his head so as to not become bumped, they slid him into the back seat and closed the door. Sam sat quietly in the back seat. It was his first experience at being arrested.

He sat alone in the car and contemplated his options. His mind was rushing. He first analyzed his arrest. They didn't take him at his office, and why not? It was Friday night. If they could place him somewhere, and nobody saw it happen, they could keep him incognito until Monday morning. That was why Tom Phelps jumped out of the shadows, and four Deputy Sheriffs followed suit.

Sam was uncomfortable with his hands cuffed behind him. He squeezed himself around so that his back rested against his left arm. For the moment that felt better. Two Deputies climbed into the front seat and started the car. He could see the second car through the rear view mirror. Tom Phelps jumped into the shotgun seat, and they all drove off.

Sam wondered where they would take him. It would not be Division 2 on Rampart. Most likely it would be the City Lockup. This was a large prison complex, just off the I-10, on the outskirts of town.

It seemed logical that these cops did not want anyone to see what had happened to Sam. It was late Friday afternoon. They did not arrest him at his precinct. Instead they took him when he least expected, while walking to his car. Sam also believed it wouldn't matter which way he walked, or where he was headed. He was convinced there was a network of cops out there to nab him, in any number of intersections in the Quarter. They drove to Canal and took a right. Sam started to smile to himself. He was right.

They were heading to City Lockup.

It took the two cars fifteen minutes to drive into the back garage area of City Lockup. Sam thought, *No one ever comes into the side of the building, unless you've got a truckload.*

Sam knew this building well. He was employed at Division 2 for almost his first ten years in the cop business. During the last year and a half, he handled the movement of prisoners from Division 2, to City Lock up. He was also responsible for their booking, the taking of their pictures and their strip search. Once they were placed into their orange jump suits with the large "P" on their back, Sam would sign his papers and turn them over to the Deputy Sheriffs.

From their domain, the Deputy Sheriffs had total control of all who where locked up inside. From there, the Deputies would move the prisoners to the City Courthouse, and after completion of various court actions, would return them to City Lockup. After all of this was over, with bodies moving in all directions across town, they would have to be returned to Division 2, for either final release from jail, or to be processed out of there, possibly be sent to Angola Prison. Angola was the big daddy of all prisons. This was where druggies came to spend the next ten years of their lives. This was where murderers came to die.

Sam came into importance in this final move back to Division 2. He would have to drive his car, or the police van, back to City Lockup, to pick the prisoner or prisoners, and return them to Division 2 for process.

Basically, Sam thought of himself as a tour guide for the druggies and murders of the world. He would drive them from location to location, providing them with a lovely view of the city, and when their possessing was finished, take them back home. He was a limo driver, a taxi honcho. If this was what police business was all about, Sam was ready to quit the business.

The two Deputies got out of the front of the car, and walked back to have a conversation with Detective Tom Phelps. After a brief discussion, Tom moved off to his car, parked in the rear. Sam's door popped open and a deep voice said. "Okay pal, time to go to jail."

The voice came from Sgt. Rod Willmoth, a man of six feet two, weighing about two hundred thirty pounds, and could be described by most as a "redneck." He was a man about Sam's age, with dishwater blond hair. He had started balding, but had his head trimmed in a flat top.

They walked into the garage area, and headed for the freight elevator.

"Listen, nobody ever read me my rights, and I need to make a phone call." Sam said. Sgt. Rod reached out, grabbing Sam by the neck of his jacket and spun him around. Rod pushed Sam back up against the wall. His three partners only looked on, with similar redneck smiles on their faces.

"Are you a cop?" Sgt. Rod asked.

"Yes I am," Sam replied.

"Well, I don't need to read you your fucking rights. You already know your fucking rights."

"So I guess that makes a phone call out of the question?"

"You got that, little man. Now move it on and keep your mouth shut!"

They went up to the third floor, and walked down a string of hallways, winding up in the medical section of the building. Sam had also been here before. They entered a doctor's office. A wire clothing basket sat on a table at the left of the room. Someone had already prepared Sam with his "kit" for the night. It contained an orange jump suit, underwear and socks, and a pair of well used jogging shoes. There was also bedding for his bunk.

"Take everything out of your pockets, and place it on the table," ordered Rod.

Sam found eleven pockets on his person. He was amazed at how much they contained. At Sgt. Rod's direction, Sam placed his belongings into a large plastic "sealed" refrigerator bag. This included his cell phone, which Sam kept in his right coat pocket.

Rod was enjoying this. As a matter of fact, Rod was having a real good time. He had played football in college. He was a defensive tackle. He loved it when he could crash through the line, obliterate an offensive end, and smash his body into the quarterback, driving him into the ground. He loved the game. He enjoyed hearing the quarterback's body go *crunch*. He liked when he saw the quarterback's face looking back at him in shock. He wanted to punish him, to hurt him, to cause his career to end. But that was over. He was now a Deputy Sheriff, and there were laws preventing that type of action. So Rod relied on the modern facts of life. That being, the absolute power of the "hands-off" humiliation of the quarterback.

"Now, strip it down completely," The Rod commanded. "Put all your clothes into the basket, including shorts, shoes and socks."

This was it, Sam thought to himself. *They're going to treat me just like I did with Hironee Jessup, last Sunday night and Monday morning. An' I'll be very lucky if I ever see another phone again.*

Sam stripped it down to the bare bones. One of the deputies stuffed his clothes in the basket, while a second one opened a back door and called for the doctor.

Sam did not know anyone in this facility; he just remembered how things worked ten years earlier. He recalled: if you ever did get to a phone, your conversation would be monitored and recorded if necessary. They would gather information from prisoners over telephone monitoring and use that information wherever possible to gain the advantage.

Sam thought of whom he should call if he ever got the chance. Kelly was out of the question, as was Judge Bean. The last thing Sam needed was to have the Office of Internal Affairs run a check on the Judge Bean operation.

He next thought of his lawyer. Donald Mosley would have been fine, but he felt a cop would be better in this situation. George Carey would have been excellent, but he didn't remember his phone number. His number was written down in his pocket phone book, now located in the plastic refrigerator bag. Then there was Wally. He knew right where Wally was, at the Pelican Suite Hotel. He could reach him there anytime through the weekend. All he would say was, "I've been arrested. I'm being held at the City Lock Up. Get somebody down here with a Writ of Habeas Corpus to deliver the body. Good bye." Then the Doctor came into the room. His name was Dr. John Willard. He was a man of about fifty and had been working in this section for five years. He wasn't the least bit bothered by walking into a room with a naked man standing in front of him. Why should he? He was a doctor, and this was his job. And for that matter, why should Sam?

Sam quickly got used to his nakedness. At first he didn't know what to do with his arms and hands. He would clasp them in front of his body, try to look casual. But after being there for a few minutes, he started to let it all hang out.

Dr. Willard moved closer to Sam and announced, "I'm going to do a full body search." He started by running his fingers through Sam's hair, then asked him to open his mouth. He directed Sam to move his tongue up and down. The Doctor was obviously searching for contraband, drugs.

Dr. Willard then stepped back and took a good gaze at Sam's face.

"Hey. Aren't you the Detective I just saw on television about an hour ago?"

Sam smiled. "Yep."

"You're the guy who caught the guy who killed a bunch a women."

"Yep, I'm the guy."

"You know they are saying that you may have caught the guy who did more murders than anyone ever in the whole state of Louisiana."

"Yeah, there's talk about that."

"Even in the entire nation."

"There is that."

"Listen, could you give me your autograph for my wife? This would be a big thrill for her, the fact that I met you."

"Sure thing."

Deputy Sheriff Rod Willmoth's eyes rolled up into the top of his head. He glanced over at Pete, one of his assistants, showing him an incredulous look.

"Excuse me, Doctor," The Rod said. "We have a deadline with this prisoner. We need him in his cell in five minutes."

"Well excuse me!" Doctor John stated, loud and clear. "When you boys are in this room, I am in charge of this patient. With his permission, I could order a five bypass operation to his heart, and keep him in recuperation for at least ten days. So don't give me any of this five minute crap."

The Rod stiffened. He clenched his teeth. You could see the muscles of his jaw flex in an out, around his cheek bones.

Dr. John handed Sam a blank 4"-by-5" card they used for making filing additions on patients.

"Thank you," Sam said. "Should I make this to your wife?"

"That would be nice. Her name is Phyllis."

Sam signed the card. It read:

"To Phyllis,
With Love,
Sam Pennington"

Dr. John thanked Sam for the signature, pulled a rubber glove out of the box on the nearby shelf and pulled it onto his right hand. With his left had he withdrew some KY Jelly from the drawer of the table, placed some of the oily substance onto his gloved index finger, and asked Sam to turn around, spread his legs, and bend over with hands on the table. Sam did as directed. The inspection was slightly painful, but over in a few seconds.

"Okay," Dr. John announced. "This man is clear."

Sam straightened up, and asked, "How's my prostate?"

Dr. John was removing the plastic glove from his right hand. As he tossed it away into the trash, he said, "I wasn't checking that. I was searching for contraband. Dope." He reached back into the box of rubber gloves, pulled out a fresh one, and started putting it on his right hand.

"I'll go back in if you want? Won't take but a minute longer?"

"What the hell. I'm here. Won't cost me a thing. Let's do it to it."

Sam took the position once again, and Dr. John inserted his finger into Sam's body.

"It doesn't feel mushy," Dr. John said. "Feels very hard and solid."

The doctor pulled out, and as Sam stood up he handed him a wipe from a roll under the inspection table.

"Prostate is in fine condition. When did you get your last physical?"

"About a year ago."

"You're a young man. Should have one about every six months. Any problems with your kidneys, stomach, breathing? Any heart problems?"

"No, feeling real good."

The doctor placed a stethoscope into his ears and started to listen to Sam's heart. Then Sam did the breathe-in-breathe-out routine and looked over at Rod. The Rod had found a chair to sit on. Sam was having a good time. The Rod was not.

"I want to do a cardiogram on you, just to make sure there are no possible heart problems. You can put your shorts on. I'll send a nurse in to make the test. This will only take about an hour."

An hour later Sam, dressed in his orange jump suit, with the letter "P" printed on the back, and with hands cuffed behind him, was taken to his cell by his four favorite deputy sheriffs. Sam had just received the word from Dr. John that he was as healthy as a horse. They walked into the cell block marked as "MEDICAL PATIENTS ONLY."

The block held twelve cells, but no one was there. Sam was placed into the last cell on the left, his cuffs removed and the door slammed shut. It was Rod who turned the key into the lock. The three other deputies walked down the hallway and Sam crossed back to the bars.

"I just want to tell you guys, you've done a great job with me," Sam said. "You offered me great security and protected my first amendment rights: those being the right to free speech, to say nothing of the right of life, liberty, and justice for all. I'm not sure if that's all in the first amendment, but it works for me."

The Rod was still standing in front of Sam's cell.

"Is there anything I can do for you?" The Rod asked.

"Well, when's dinner?"

"Oh, I'm sorry. While you were playing games with Doctor Doolittle, you missed dinner. Breakfast is tomorrow at six o'clock."

Rod left the cell block, and all was quiet. Then a light was turned on, in a room just opposite him. A Deputy moved into the room and sat down. From his position the guard could see into every one of the twelve cells. Being alone did not bother Sam. Being grabbed and beaten and raped by a bunch of crazed thugs bothered him a lot.

He lay back on his bunk, happy that at least there was an independent cop to look out for his body. And he thought about Kelly.

Chapter 22

DAY 10, CONTINUED.

KELLY LEE JONES stood on the bow of the boat, scanning the skyline, searching for Sam. It was now about five p.m. Friday evening, and she was becoming concerned. He had told her he would be there around three, maybe four, but now it was closing in on five.

She saw Bob Rizzo's van pull onto the property. Bob and his wife were the salt of the earth and Bob was the sweetest man one could imagine. He was a good-looking Italian stallion, and Martha, his wife, was the pretty lady of the house that held the family together. Bob Rizzo parked the van near the boat, honked his horn and screamed out for all to hear, "Bobbie's here...let's eat!"

They were greeted by Pedro and Judge Bean, who helped them unpack the van. Kelly joined them as they came aboard. Kelly made drinks for all, while Bob Rizzo and his wife set up to cook on the top deck.

At six thirty, Wilford Bean was feeling quite mellow. He sat near the galley in a high-backed director's chair, sipping on a scotch and water, enjoying the bayou beyond. He knew the boat was about ready. They would put in the water tomorrow, start the new engine up, and take in out in the open sea, to give it a test. Then, in a week or two, Sam would want to take his trip.

Kelly came out from the galley, looked around at the road leading up to the property. "Come on Sam, where are you?" she said out loud.

"Where is that old boy?" Wil asked.

"He's running late."

"Just cop business. It's always cop business," Wilford Bean said.

Kelly smiled. "I know that. I've been told that before. I just worry about him, that's all."

Wil laughed out loud. She gave him a smile, and continued to look.

At seven o'clock, two new Deputies walked down the hallway to Sam's cell door. Sam was awake, on his partially made bunk. One of the deputies rattled his club across the face of the bars, the other screamed out, "Okay Pennington, time to rise and shine." Sam quickly sat up into an alert position. "Okay, I'm up, I'm up." Sam jumped to his feet.

The first deputy carried chains and cuffs for Sam's hands and feet. Sam knew this was not necessary, but it was all part of the show. It was intended to demean Sam as much as possible. He decided to be as calm, sweet, and cooperative as he could. He would ask for nothing, no phone call, no food, and as this harassment continued through the night, no sleep.

The second detective first cuffed him at the ankles. He would be able to make a thirteen inch step before the chain caught. This would be a short step, never a run. A chain was then placed around his waist, which acted like a belt, and his hands were then cuffed to the belt chain. He was allowed some hand movement also. Either hand would move up to his neck area, and then down almost to his knees. All of his movement was restricted, and he felt comfortable.

His guards walked him down the hallway. Sam wanted to cooperate. He developed a quick step, like a kid with short legs, trying to keep up with an adult. It was a long walk from his cell to the interrogation room.

They would turn left at the end of one hall, and move right at the end of another corridor. All the while, Sam was doing his very best to maintain a good fast stride. It reminded him of police boot camp, when his officers would challenge them to go for one more push up.

They finally stopped at a door marked, "Interrogation Room 4." Sam was breathing heavily; the two guards had not worked up a sweat. As one of them started to opened the door, Sam said, "Thanks guys, I appreciate that. That was a good work out."

When the door opened, Sam got a clear view of the room. He had never been here before, but it was almost a duplicate of the room where he had interrogated Hironee Jessup only five days earlier, in the jail on Royal Street. This room was small, with the usual two-way mirror hanging on the wall. In the center of the room was a table, one chair on one side, and two chairs on the other. Detective Tom Phelps sat on the side with two chairs.

"Hey Tom, how you doin?" Sam asked.

Tom was sitting there, going through a mass of paperwork. Sam quickly, "chain-walked" his way to the desk, and flopped down into the opposite chair.

"Is it necessary to have this prisoner cuffed in this manner?" Tom Phelps innocently asked, as though he had no idea what was going on.

One of the Sheriffs had a name tag on his shirt, "Newman." "Yes sir. It's in our directive. It's done for the protection of the prisoner and all other officers."

"It's okay, Tom," Sam said. "I feel very comfortable and secure wearing these chains. I have no problem whatsoever." The two deputies then left the room, leaving Sam and Tom alone.

"Okay," Tom said. "I'll give you the bad news first. When we went through you're apartment, we found an illegal controlled substance."

"And what was that?" Sam asked.

"I'll ask the questions. I will tell you of your problems and I'll advise you of where you stand. What I'm hoping for is to get your total cooperation in this matter."

"Well, you surely have that,.." Sam said.

"Okay then." Tom shuffled through his paperwork. He then pulled out one page from the file and read from same. "That illegal controlled substance was cocaine."

Tom looked up at Sam, and Sam looked back at Tom. Sam said nothing.

"Well?" Tom asked.

"Well what?" Sam asked

"Well, what do you say about that?" Tom asked.

"Did you ask a question?" Sam asked.

"I asked what was in your apartment, cocaine?"

"I'm sorry. I didn't understand that," Sam said. "I'm a little confused. You said 'please let me speak,' then you said you found cocaine in my apartment, but you never asked me how come you found cocaine in my apartment?"

"Alright then! I now ask you, how was cocaine found in your apartment?"

"Beats the hell out of me. Where did you find it?"

"Let me explain. You don't ask the questions. I ask the questions."

"I'm sorry," Sam said. "I apologize. You ask and I'll tell." Sam had figured he was being as helpful as possible, while Tom was screwing up the interrogation. "Do you mind if I get some water?" Sam asked. "I'm feeling a bit dehydrated."

"I'll get that for you," Tom offered.

Sam stood up and started to "chain-walk" his way to the cold water drinking fountain, located at the door. "I can get that," Sam said.

Tom started to realize exactly what Sam was doing. Sam knew the routine. He was aware that people were watching him through the two-way mirror. Sam had done this routine before. He knew what it was about and how it was done. It was stupid of them to play this game with Sam.

Sam pulled his arms up to gain control of the on and off button of the water fountain. He could only pull his right hand up to the button, but was unable to place his head down, far enough to cause the water to go into his mouth. He stuck his tongue out to lap at the water, but had to give that up.

Tom watched Sam with passive interest. He then glanced at the two-way mirror, shrugged his shoulders, and then back at Sam.

By placing his head down further, and lifting his left arm up, and pulling his right arm down, Sam was able to cause the chain connection in his arm control, to finally allow him to get his mouth closer to the water spigot, so that he could gain at least dribbles of water into his mouth. Sam drank eagerly. Like a rat on a treadmill, he lapped at the fluid of life until he was satisfied. Then he returned to his chair.

"So where were we?" Sam asked.

"We were discussing a controlled substance found in your apartment."

"That's right. I got it. And I asked where did you find that substance? And you said I ask the questions. Okay, what's next?"

Tom Phelps was now confused beyond belief. He decided to start at the beginning. His questions lasted for a half an hour. Phelps mentioned William Jefferson Mays and his relationship to Sam. Sam had already told it before in the filing of his report. Tom Phelps dug deep into Sam's activities on the night of the big drug bust. He asked who, what, when and where, and who said what to whom and regarding whatever. Tom even brought up the boat, the *Miss Lee*, but never made a connection with the boat and the missing dope, let alone any of the money.

Finally, having finished with that, Tom returned to questions regarding the fact they had found cocaine in Sam's apartment.

"Okay, I want to go back to the cocaine we found in your apartment," Tom said.

"Right, I got that."

"We can charge you right now. With the evidence we have found, I can guarantee you'll get a minimum of fifteen years in prison."

"Are you boys charging me with possession of drugs?"

"C'mon, Sam, this is you and me. We're beyond all of this bullshit."

"Okay, ask me what you want."

"I'll make it crystal clear. We are seeking fifty million dollars of heroine and cocaine."

"That's all this is?"

"That's all this is."

"I wish I could help you out there. I don't have it."

"Let me advise you. We are going back into your apartment house."

"That's not an apartment. That's a condominium. Everybody there owns their own condominium."

"Whatever. Anyway, having found a sufficient amount of dope in your condo, we now have suspicion that you have used this place to store the balance of the goods."

"You're kidding me, right?"

"Even as we speak, we have a team of men with dogs, sniffing out every nook and cranny in the place. That's your apartment and all the rest."

"You're kidding?"

"Nope. And we'll find it. Let me tell you, we know it's there. It's just a matter of time."

"So what did you do, move everyone out?"

"I ask the questions, you give the answers." Tom shuffled through his stack of paper work. "You know a guy named William Joseph Mays?"

"Yep. I know Billy Joe. You already know I know Billy Joe Mays. We have just discussed Billy Joe Mays. So why do you ask me if I know Billy Joe?"

"He was your partner ten years ago, on that major drug bust."

"Why do I feel like I'm being recorded right now?"

"Is that right? Bill Mays was your partner?"

"That's right."

"Tell me where William Joseph Mays is right now?"

"You mean you don't know where he is?"

"I asked you where he is right now?"

"Well, I know I'm in jail, an' I sure in hell don't know where he is."

"Don't fuck with me anymore, got it?" Tom Phelps said. Phelps was becoming agitated.

"No sir. I'm not trying to fuck with you. If you guys don't know where Bill

Mays is, how in hell do you suppose I should know? I'm in jail, for crying out loud. You guys want me to keep track of Bill Mays while I'm in jail? How in hell do you want me to do that? That's not my job. That's your job. I gotta tell you, I'm starting to wonder about where Bill Mays is myself. Did something happen to Bill Mays? Is that what it is?"

Sam jumped up from his chair, and took three short thirteen inch steps toward the mirror. Now he was talking directly to the mirror, and those located on the other side.

"I'll tell you one thing for sure. If you guys have done anything thing with Bill Mays, it's your doing. I've done nothing with Bill Mays, got it? But if you guys have done something with him, it's on your ass."

"This meeting is over!" Tom said. He pushed a button on the desk and stood up. The door quickly opened and Newman and his sidekick came into the room.

"Take him back to his cell," Tom commanded.

Sam smiled at his new buddies. "Hi there guys, nice to see you again." As they ushered him to the door, Sam twisted his head toward the mirror. "If you bastards did anything with Mays, and I find out, you better fucking kill me too!"

It was pitch black as Wil made his way back to the boat. He had gone to his house to make some phone calls, and tried to find someone who could help to get a location on Sam. It was now eight thirty. Bob was still holding dinner. Kelly was waiting as Wil climbed the ladder to the main deck.

"Anything?" she asked.

"No, nothing."

"Nothing?" Kelly asked. "I've called his home phone and his message machine is off. I tried his cell phone, and that message says the person you have called is not available."

"I've got some people checking it out." Judge Bean turned and called out to Bob Rizzo, who was relaxing over by the charcoal grill. "Okay Bob, toss those babies onto the grill. We're ready to eat." He then turned back to Kelly. "Stay calm. I'm on the case."

"What case? This is a case?"

"I misspoke. This is a situation."

"Now it's a situation?"

"Listen to me. I've called his precinct on Royal. They ran an emergency search of all local hospitals. No record of any accident. They gave me the number of the garage where he keeps his car. The car is still there. I told them I would check back. I asked them to keep an eye on the car. If Sam shows up there, they will ask him to call me here."

"He keeps his sports car in the garage at his apartment." Kelly said.

Will shook his head no. "Never drives it at night. Only takes it out on a weekend, when there's no rain and the NFL aren't playing. And that's just to charge the battery."

"So where's Sam?"

"I got the cell phone number of a guy in his office. Name's George Carey. He sounds like a sharp guy. He was in the office when Sam left. Sam told Carey 'I'm going to get my car and go see the loveliest lady I know.' That was about three this afternoon. Carey is going to check on Sam further. He'll call me back in an hour.

"Now listen to me. Sam's a little crazy. He loves that Dixieland music. He probably walked by a place, heard some jazz going on inside, walked in for a quick drink. He may have met a friend or two. Had another drink. You know Sam. I'm going to give Bob a hand. By the time the food is cooked, he'll be pulling in with another sad excuse. Don't you worry."

Wil left to aid Bob. Kelly waked to the railing and looked off toward the road, searching for approaching headlights. Either Will was lying, or he didn't know Sam as well as she did.

It was now eight-thirty. As Sam lay on his bunk, his mind continued to keep his brain on track. He could still see his attendant across the narrow hallway. The attendant provided Sam with some much needed protection.

There was a series of fluorescent lights hanging in the hallway. Lighting was very important to Sam. He hated fluorescent lights, spent many months decorating his apartment. In addition he spent two and a half more weeks, planning and charting where he would place incandescent lights. Then there was the wiring, and the fixtures, and the focusing, and measuring, and the balance of each unit. When it was finished it was a thing of beauty. Now his only light came from a series of fluorescent lights that hung in the hallway, and one of them was about to burn out. It flickered on and off, and had a constant high pitched buzz.

He further decided to stay awake, because the people in the interrogating room would be waiting for him to go asleep. He figured they would wait for that to happen, and after about forty-five minutes of complete slumber, they would wake him for yet another challenge. So Sam decided he would stay awake. He would stay awake the entire night. It didn't matter that he woke at five thirty-two this morning at the Royal Orleans Hotel. He knew he could beat these bastards.

He remembered when he was a kid, seventeen years old, at his father's hardware store. He recalled working one period for twenty-six hours straight, just to get the sale price marked on the goods to be sold. He could do that again, even now, and longer. He closed his eyes for a moment, and fell into a deep sleep.

Then there was the crashing sound of the club grating across the bars, and the voice of Sheriff Newman, who shouted, "Okay Pennington, time to rise and shine."

Sam jumped from his bunk quickly. He had a bright smile on his face. "Hey there guys. I'm ready to rock and roll."

Once again they chained him up from head to toe, and once again he quick-chain-jogged his way down the hallways to the interrogation room. When Newman opened the door of Interrogation Room 4, Sam saw a new face there.

"Hello Sam," the new face said. "My name is Roger Gentry. Come on in and take a seat. I think you and I can quickly resolve our little problem."

As Sam sat down, he remembered the name Roger Gentry. This was the guy Bill Mays had described as the "cookie cutter cop." He worked for the Office of Internal Affairs, and turned out to be a dead ringer for Bill Mays himself. Same size, same shape, same weight, but with one exception. Roger Gentry had a huge, bulbous nose. It looked like a W. C. Fields nose. Sam had to choke back his laughter as he looked at the nose.

"Here's the deal," Gentry said. "I may be able to get my people to agree to offer you something."

"May I ask you what time it is, and what day it is?" Sam asked.

"This is Friday," Gentry looked at his watch. "It's nine fifteen in the evening."

Sam's mind flashed quickly. Mays had left New Orleans at one o'clock. Nine o'clock would be his arrival time in Los Angeles. Bill Mays would switch to a Mexicana flight to Mexico City which left at ten o'clock. If all went well, and Bill Mays did his job, he and his wife would be out of the country by no later than ten o'clock, New Orleans time.

"Where's Tom?" Sam asked. "I thought Tom would be here."

"Tom's got the night off. I'm filling in for him."

"Okay, you were saying?"

"My people may offer you something?"

"Boy, that sounds good to me."

"Alright then. What I first need to do is to go through your previous testimony with Detective Phelps."

"Oh yeah, Tom. He's one of the good guys. I like Tom a lot."

"Well that's fine. What I want to do is go through your testimony and see if we can answer a few more questions. Is that okay with you?" Gentry pulled some paper work from his folder.

"Did Tom record my interview?"

"No, he made hand notes."

"He didn't make hand notes while we were talking. I never saw him making any hand notes."

"That's beside the point. All I want to do is to clarify some of the issues."

"Are we being recorded right now?" Sam asked.

"All I want is to offer you a deal. My people will agree to that deal if you will cooperate in setting some facts straight."

"Are we being recorded right now?"

"C'mon Sam, let's knock this shit off right now. You're a cop and I'm a cop. Were in the same business."

"Then you just tell me, are we being recorded right now?"

"We have a monitoring system that takes our conversations down, for the purpose of making changes, where the conversation becomes inaudible."

"And you as a cop, want me as a cop, to believe that shit. Is that right?"

"Jesus Christ," Gentry said with some desperation. "I am trying to help you. I am prepared to offer you a deal. How much more need I say?"

"The first thing you can say is, 'we are, or are not, being recorded right now.'"

Gentry was over his head. He was breathing heavily. "Yes, we are being recorded right now. You were recorded when you talked to Tom Phelps."

"Well, that's not right," Sam stated. "That's illegal."

"Oh please, let's not get into that jailhouse legal bit. Let's just solve this like two cops talking."

"That sounds good to me, except one of the cops is now recording me, and he wants to review the words that another cop had also recorded of me, and if he finds any discrepancies in what I said, said cop wants to use it against me. That's against the law!"

Roger Gentry wanted to change the subject. He reached into his folder and withdrew another piece of paper. "Here is a report on William Joseph Mays. You were asking where Mays was, but Tom Phelps did not have this information. This comes from another arm of the Office of Internal Affairs. The fact is, we have had Mr. Mays under surveillance for over two weeks and we know where his is right now.

Sam felt his heart skip a few beats. "Well that's good, real good."

"Yep. We followed him and his wife yesterday to Louis Armstrong Airport, and observed them boarding a flight to Florida."

Sam sat back into his chair. He took a quiet, deep breath. Roger read from his paperwork. "The Pacific Airlines plane departed at eight forty-five yesterday morning, and landed at Miami Airport at ten thirty. Mr. and Mrs. Mays were observed by our agents there, departing the plane and then taking a cab to the Sands Motel located on the south beach area."

"And why are you tailing Bill Mays?"

"We asked him to stay in town until we resolved this situation. We believe you and Mr. Mays were in collusion regarding the possession and sale of an illegal substance. Got it?"

"Do me a favor, will you? When you see Tom again, please apologize to him for me. I was wrong in saying what I said. I was out of line. The only problem I have is the recording. That shouldn't have happened."

"That's fine. I will do that. Okay, let's get back to the business at hand." Gentry put down the paper concerning the location of Bill Mays, and went back to the paper regarding Sam's meeting with Detective Tom Phelps.

"Tom asked you some questions while you and Mays were on the boat."

"I won't answer any questions regarding a conversation that took place in this room with Detective Tom Phelps," Sam said. "Got it?"

"This isn't going anywhere," Gentry stated.

"I know this is difficult for you. The thing is, when you record someone you must tell that person you are recording him. You seek his permission to do so. You then advise him that this recording may be used in a court of law against him. That's how it works. And if you don't do that, then you're just a stupid fuck. And Tom Phelps is also a stupid fuck. And as long as that recorder is recording, that's the last I have to say."

Sam stood up and minced his way across the floor to the two-way mirror.

"Alright Sam," Gentry said. "C'mon back here and sit down."

Sam paid no attention. He put his face right on the glass of the mirror, trying to look through it. Normally he would place his two hands on either side of his face, to block out the light from the room he was in. But now, with his hands cuffed to his belt chain, he could not raise them high enough to block the light.

Sam pushed his right eye as close to the glass as it could get. This caused the people who were watching, to scurry for cover. He could hear their little feet running away from their side of the mirror, desperately trying to keep their anonymity. Then a door opened, flooding the room with light. Sam saw the shadow of a man leaving the room, and he could also see five other faces standing against the back wall. Then the door closed.

Sam raised one arm as high as it would go and waived it. "Hi guys, how you doing in there? You got anything to eat in there?"

Then the door to Interrogation Room 4 burst open. Sam looked away from the mirror, and saw that it was Detective Tom Phelps. Detective Phelps was severely pissed off.

"Hey there, Tom." Sam said with a broad smile. "I thought you were gone for the evening."

"You're a real funny man, aren't you?" Tom said, with absolute hate in his voice. "You got a joke for every occasion, don't you?"

"Yeah, I'm referred to as the local stand-up comic."

"Deputies!" Tom screamed out. Newman and his assistant quickly entered the room. "Take this funny man back to his cell," Tom ordered.

"Hey Tom," Sam asked. "What's your problem? Are you angry with me for sticking my eye in your little window over there? C'mon Tom. You're not serious are you? I'm a cop. I've been a cop for twenty years. I've conducted at least five hundred investigations, in rooms just like this one, and I've sat behind the two-way mirror in rooms just like that one. So who the hell are you kidding. Not me, I'm a cop!

"And who are you kidding with these chains your boys hang all over my body, so they can shuffle me a half a mile from location to location. Is this stupid or what? What am I going to do, break out, beat somebody up?

"I've lied to criminals before, just to get a conviction. That's for pimps and whores. But I'm not a pimp or a whore. I'm a cop. I have over a hundred letters of commendations and civic awards in my personal file. So you wanna play kiddy games with me, that's fine. I can handle it."

Sam looked over at Deputy Newman. "Okay gentlemen, if you don't mind, please escort me to my cell."

Sam did his fast chain-walk, and moved down the hall, followed by his two attendants. Tom and Roger Gentry stood quietly in the center of the room, each giving thought as to what to do next.

It was now nine o'clock, Friday, March 10. Kelly didn't eat. She had lost her appetite. She sat on a stool over by the galley. The others were at a table in the center of the main deck. There was a look of gloom on everybody's face, with Sam having disappeared. They were hungry and ate the lobster, but not much else. The phone rang, Judge Bean picked it up. He listened to what he was being told and said, "Hold on a minute." He covered the mouth piece of the phone with his hand and looked over at Kelly. "Kelly, pick this up on the extension. It's George Carey. He may have found Sam."

Kelly jumped from her stool and ran to the galley. She grabbed the wall phone and said, "Hello."

"Hello Kelly, nice to meet you." George's voice was clear and soothing.

"Nice to meet you too, George. What about Sam?"

"This is not confirmed, this is just hearsay. I found a guy who was on Royal at around three o'clock today. He said he saw Sam picked up and placed into a New Orleans Sheriff's vehicle. Actually, my source said there were two sheriffs cars and four men; one was a guy in a dark business suit. They took off with Sam and headed down to Canal Street."

"Where did they take him?" she asked.

"My second source is a deputy. He handles the dispatch at City Jail. His computer tells him there is no booking on Sam Pennington. My source says he believes Sam is now at City Jail. He's checking further and will get back to me in an hour."

Kelly started to sob. "Thank you George, I'm very grateful."

"Listen, I'll call you back when I hear from this guy. And If I can do anything else for you, just let me know and I'll be there."

"I'm going back to town. I have a key to Sam's apartment. I want to see what I can find, if he left any notes, or something."

"When will you be there?"

"From here, about a quarter to ten."

"I'll meet you there, be standing out under the street lamp."

Kelly hung up the phone, and started to cry openly. They were mixed tears of concern and joy. She had now learned where Sam was, but was he okay? As she continued to sob uncontrollably, Bob Rizzo, his wife Martha, and Judge Bean, crowded into the galley to offer whatever consolation they could provide.

"What did he say?" Bob asked.

"They've got Sam," *sob sob, sniff,* "they think he's at the City Jail." *Sob, sniff, sniff, sob, sob.* "I'm just happy they found him alive." *Cry, cry, sniff, sob, sob.*

Martha Rizzo understood her tears. Martha also started to weep a little. Kelly and Martha were having a tearful release from tension that bordered on a playful high. The men who stood around watching this, simply didn't get it.

Kelly handed Judge Bean both her phone number on Toulouse Street, along with her cell phone number.

It took Kelly a half an hour to pack up to leave. As they helped her into her car, Bob Rizzo asked once again if he should at least follow her home. He had just a few more items to pack up.

"I'm fine now, Bob, you and Martha have been sweethearts. I'm sorry this happened tonight. Tomorrow I'll pick Sam up, and we'll all enjoy a fun story." Kelly got into her car and headed back to the city.

An hour later, Kelly pulled into a parking spot on Barracks Street, just a quarter of a block down from Sam's place. When she got out of the car and walked up to the apartment, she saw a man standing under a street light. It was now about ten-thirty at night. She was being cautious. Too many strange things were happening. She stopped walking and screamed out to the man up ahead. "George, is that you?"

"Yes," George called back.

If need be, Kelly was ready to run the few steps back to her car, start it up and drive off. "What is your last name?" she called out.

"Carey. George Carey. I'm the guy who works for Sam." He held up his police badge for her to see.

Kelly smiled and jogged to George. "I knew your last name, I just didn't know if it belonged to you." When she reached the street light, she stopped an offered her hand. George took it and there was an immediate bonding.

"Hello, George Carey."

"Hello there, Kelly Jones."

"Here's Sam's key. It opens both doors."

George took it and opened the downstairs gate. Kelly then walked ahead of him, and up the front stairs. As they climbed to the third floor, she asked him if he had ever been there before.

"No," George answered. "Sam doesn't talk much. I've picked him up here a few times, but I never came up stairs. He's kind of a private person."

When they got to Sam's front door, they saw it was secured with official yellow tape that had the printing on it stating, "POLICE LINE - DO NOT CROSS."

"What do we do now?" Kelly asked.

"Well I'm the police," George answered. He pulled the tape from the doorway, stuck the key in the lock, and entered the apartment.

There was a night light, plugged in to an electrical outlet, down near the floor. George paused at the open door, allowing Kelly to walk past him and into the room.

"Where's his light switch?" George asked.

"It's somewhere on this wall. Here it is." She pushed a button and the lights came on.

They both moved cautiously into the living room and found themselves in a state of shock.

"Oh my God, he's been robbed!" Kelly said.

George said nothing. He calmly walked through the rest of the apartment, checking the bedroom and bathroom, and saw the open ladder in the hallway leading to the attic. When he returned to the living room, he found Kelly seated at the dining room table. She was despondent. George slid down on a chair opposite her.

"Okay, what's your problem?" George asked.

"I am just not believing this," Kelly said.

"And what would that be?"

"Burglars! Some bastard came in here and did this!"

"Kelly, I think it was the cops who did this. Cops were looking for something, and they may have found it, or may not have."

"Found what?"

"Beats the hell out of me," George said.

"And what makes you think this was not a burglary?" Kelly asked.

"Burglars do not take pots and pans from a kitchen, and leave them on the floor. Burglars do not spend hours searching a place for detailed pieces of evidence. That's what cops do."

A security guard stepped into the room. His name was Judd. Judd was an old guy, somewhere between sixty-five to whatever. He wore a security guard's dark blue shirt with badge, and a shirt sleeve insignia. He also had on a baseball type guard's cap, dark blue, and the same insignia glued to the front it. Other than the shirt and cap, he looked like a person of the "homeless" persuasion. "What you guys doin' in here?"

George grabbed Kelly by they arm and pulled her toward the front door. "We just stepped in to see what happened. We're leaving now."

"Guess you didn't see that yellow tape outside. That tape says 'Police' on it."

"We saw some kids in here. The door was open."

As George moved Kelly to the front door, they walked passed Judd. They both caught the strong order of some brand of bathtub gin, emanating from the pores of his body.

"Well you better not come here again.' Judd said. "This badge I'm wearing means something, ya know."

They walked the three flights to the street and headed for Kelly's car. George's phone rang. He answered and spoke to someone for fifteen seconds, then hung up.

"Who was that?" Kelly asked.

"That's my inside man. He's the deputy at City Lock Up. He verified Sam was there."

Kelly heaved a sigh of relief. "Where are they located? I want to go there now and see him."

"You be wasting your time. Sam's not been booked, not been charged."

"How dare they do this to people? Who do these bastards think they are?"

"My dear, let me explain something to you. These bastards know exactly who they are. They are giving Sam the treatment. And it's the same treatment Sam has given to many other people."

"Aren't there laws against that?"

"Of course there are. And when we get caught they slap our wrist. But we win more than we lose. It's cop work, it's political. It's justice, for Christ's sake!"

"I don't understand."

"Okay, understand this. Sam was picked up around three in the afternoon. Now it's only eleven thirty-five. They can hold Sam for questioning for seventy-two hours. At that point they must either cut him loose, or book him and take him to court and charge him. And Sam already knows this. Sam is a pro."

"Alright, what do I do?"

"Go home and get some sleep. I'll call you the instant I learn the what, when and where. Here's my card, office, and home phone. I'll be at the office at ten tomorrow. Got some paperwork to do. Call me as soon as you wake up."

Day 11

It was Saturday morning. Sam had fallen asleep at one-thirty. At two o'clock he was awaked by three new guards at his cell door. These were the night crew, graveyard shift boys. It's never a good idea to have fun with graveyard shift boys. They have a limited sense of humor, if not none at all, and it could result in some pushing and shoving, if not poking and hitting with the baton. Sam silently named them the three stooges

He politely chain jogged his way down the hallways to Interrogation Room 4. When one of the stooges opened the door, it revealed a tired Roger Gentry, sitting at the small table. He had been cat-napping there, and woke up quickly.

"Hello Sam," Roger stated, and he made a broad yawn. "C'mon in and sit it down."

As Sam moved his way to the chair, he noticed an open box, containing a four by four one-quarter-inch Scotch magnetic tape, along with a brown manila envelope. Sam slid into his chair, glancing at the tape, and said nothing.

"Okay, where were we?" Roger said, trying to clear his brain.

Sam clearly spotted Roger's exhaustion. "You guys really keep long, late hours."

"Yeah. I got on this morning at seven o'clock. So at seven o'clock tonight I put in twelve hours, so now it's two-fifteen, so that's nineteen-plus hours."

"That's a shame," Sam said. "When do you get relieved?"

"They told me twelve o'clock. New guy was supposed to be here at twelve o'clock. Now it's after two. I gotta tell ya, Sam, I really don't understand this business."

"Me neither."

"First they tell you one thing then they do another."

"I know exactly what you mean."

"Then in a situation like this, you put in for a little overtime, and they say 'no way.'"

"I know, that's the worst."

Roger looked at Sam. He had now become fully awake. Roger realized he was a principal detective, with the Office of Internal Affairs, and Sam was a chained prisoner wearing an orange jumpsuit with a large P for Prisoner on his back. He further realized that his mention of long hours and bad pay to Sam was not a good idea.

"Okay Sam, here we go. I want to apologize to you for the recordings."

"Oh, that's okay."

"No, no. We were wrong there. We really wanted to use the tape just to catch anything that was said that was not clear."

"You mean not clear on the tape?"

"No, no. Not that it wasn't clear on the tape, but that it wasn't clear as it was spoken."

"I don't understand."

"Well, let's forget about all of that. Here's the tape we recorded, and here's the transcript of the recorded information. You can have it. Take it away."

"No, I don't need that. I don't lie, so I remember what I said. I'm just sorry I created a problem for you guys. The tape is yours. You can do with it as you wish."

"No. No problem. Here, take the tape and the transcript," Gentry offered.

Sam then quickly added. "You guys can go ahead and use this. I give you my permission."

Roger, the cookie cutter cop, was now being sucked in by a detective that knew more about this business than he did, and Roger Gentry knew it.

"Okay, that's fine." Roger Gentry leaned forward and pressed the talk button on the desk top speaker unit. "Alright, roll the recording."

A voice came back over the speaker. "We are now recording."

"This is Roger Gentry. I am a Detective with the Office of Internal Affairs. I am interviewing Mr. Sam Pennington, who is a suspect of drug trafficking. Mr. Pennington will you identify yourself?"

"Yes. My name is Sam Pennington. However, the first indication I had was just provided by you that I was a suspect of drug trafficking."

"I'm sure you know that by now," Gentry stated.

"I'm sure nobody had said a thing about it. And I have just been released a tape recorded by your people that will prove me right. This tape was recorded on this day by Detective Tom Phelps," Sam added.

"Alright then, that's fine. Now since you have released this recording to me, can I still have access to the transcript?"

"I told you it was yours, to do with as you wish."

Roger opened the envelope and withdrew the transcript. "Okay, here we go." Gentry shuffled through his papers. "You and Bill Mays were on the boat…"

"With one exception," Sam said.

"And what is that?" Gentry asked.

"Now that I have been advised that we are being recorded, I insist that my attorney be present."

Roger Gentry sat in complete silence. He stared at Sam as though he were an invading monster from outer space. Gentry was a heavy smoker, smoked Marlboro Regulars. He lit a fresh one up, took a few heavy puffs and said, "Sam, we're two cops, right?"

"That's true. One of us wants to charge me with drug trafficking, and I want my attorney to be here, to advise me of any improper questions."

Roger dropped his head to his chest. He reached over and pushed the speaker button. "Okay boys, you can stop the recorder." He then placed his fresh burning cigarette into the half-full ashtray.

"You don't need to do that," Sam said with a gentle tone. "I'm happy to speak to you about anything that was not previously recorded."

Sam was now changing his position. Gentry seized the opportunity to ask a different question. "Okay, there is a man living in your apartment, a guy named William Wild. Do you know a guy named William Wild?"

"Yes. But it's not an apartment. It's a condominium."

"Okay fine, a condominium." Gentry took a fresh Marlboro from its pack, and lit it up. He held this one between his fingers, not realizing his first one was only half smoked. Sam noticed this. Either Gentry was getting tired, or he was starting into a subject he was not comfortable with.

"How long have you known Mr. Wild?" Gentry asked.

"We go back about fifteen, maybe twenty years."

"That's when you first joined the force?"

"That's right. Willie Wild was a musician's musician. And he still is. He's around eighty-five now, but he still plays his horn, three sets a night, at the Jazz Hall over on St. Phillip Street."

"We had an interview with Mr. Wild. He has testified, and I quote him, 'I been buying his crack for the past eight years. Sam Pennington has always sold me his crack. He always approaches me and I buy it.' What have you to say about that?"

Sam smiled. He knew Wild Willy well. He knew Wild Willy would never say that. "Let me tell you about William Wild. He was born on December 25th, 1925. He was called the Jesus Baby. He learned to play the trumpet. He became quite proficient in that instrument. Over the years he developed a reputation of being one of the leading trumpet players to ever blow the horn.

"New Orleans gave him the name, 'Wild' Willie Wild. In the forties and fifties, he was one the most noted Dixie Land Jazz players in the city. Then in 1963, his only son died of an overdose of heroin. His son's death devastated him. He started drinking, went on the skids.

"I had been a cop for about five years. I ran into William Wild sitting on a bench in Jackson Square. I recognized him, remembered his picture on two of the albums I owned. I took him in, and we became friends. I helped him get straight. I got 'Wild' Willie Wild off booze, not drugs.

"The fact of the matter was, and is, Willie Wild hates drugs. He never touched one of them. He hates narcotics with a passion."

Sam stood up and walked to the center of the room. He glanced at the two-way mirror and then back at Gentry. "So now you and your boys have come up with a new idea. You now tell me that 'Wild' Willie Wild admitted he bought dope from me? All I can tell you is that you have made a bad mistake," Sam said. "And I'll tell you something else. If you boys take me to court and charge me, 'Wild' Willie Wild will be there to testify on my behalf. So you better be there to make your story right. Otherwise, you and your boys will be hanging out like dead meat."

Roger Gentry smiled. Sam had seen that smile before. It was a fake smile. He recalled that same smile from his Thursday night poker games. It was the smile that said, "I've got you beat," and then that same guy, with that same smile, wound up sucking his own swamp water.

Roger became very tired. He was even becoming bored with his monkey-puke style of questioning, and at three thirty in the morning, the two attendants brought Sam back to his cell. He flopped back onto his bunk, and closed his eyes. His mind started to wander. He thought over what he had just said to Roger Gentry, but was unable to recall exactly what started his own tirade, or for that matter, what even brought Willie Wild into the conversation. It would only get worse in the next twenty-four hours. As his sleep deprived mind continued to sputter, Sam decided he would best remain quiet.

Chapter 23

Day 11, continued.

IT WAS NOW eight o'clock Saturday morning. Everybody who needed to be there was there. Judge Wilford Bean was in charge of the operation. The *Miss Lee* was about to be moved into the bayou. It would slide in first at the stern and as soon as the boat made contact with the water, Pedro, who was in the pilot's cabin, would start the engine. Roberto was standing on the front deck, making hand signals to Judge Wil, directing his movement on the cable system that slowly eased the boat's way back into the channel.

Judge Bean had also hired a tugboat to be present, hovering near the dock, just in the case of an emergency. It was a medium-sized local tug, with a 'catch' front, made of heavy rope, prepared to push the *Miss Lee* back to land, should a problem take place.

In the pilot house of the *Miss Lee*, Pedro stood with his hands on the wheel, waiting to feel the bayou take hold of her rudder. At Roberto's direction from the front deck, Pedro could hear him directing Judge Bean to continue to move the boat backward. The stern of the boat was painted with its name, *Miss Lee*, and below that, *New Orleans, Louisiana*.

The stern of the boat finally made contact with the water. It seemed for a moment the boat would sink! Water flowed up and over the top aft deck. Roberto quickly shouted out to Judge Bean. "Hold on. Stop it!"

Judge Bean hit the stop switch of his massive winch. The tug boat was prepared to move forward, to give *Miss Lee* a shove back up onto the land. Then, *Miss Lee* finally broke from her land-based housing, and popped up free and floated onto the water.

Pedro could see Roberto on the front top deck. Roberto gave him a 'thumbs up.' Pedro smiled back and turned the ignition key on. There was a grinding sound emitting from the engine room below. The engine was chugging. It had been built to start. She was prepared to start. Pedro twisted the key one more time and the engine exploded into life.

At first, black smoke swelled from stern of the boat. As Pedro continued to work the throttle, the smoke turned into a blue haze. Pedro popped into reverse gear, and slowly backed *Miss Lee* into the bayou.

Once he had completely floated the boat, Pedro shut down the engines. Roberto quickly moved to the stern, leaned over and grabbed hold of the cable that was attached to Judge Bean's winch. He found the connection and pulled the heavy unit from its hookup, dropping the cable into the bayou.

Roberto next ran into the pilot's cabin. "How we doin'?"

"We're floating," Pedro answered.

"Floating? That's good," Roberto said. "I'm going down below and check the bilge pump."

Pedro started the engine once again. This time it came to life instantly.

Judge Bean was at the dock, winding up his winch cable. The boat looked good in the water. There was something about her. She no longer looked like an old beat-up shrimp boat, the *Miss Lee* showed the beauty of a fine-lined pleasure vessel.

Pedro slowly eased the boat down river, toward the mouth of the Gulf of Mexico. He had to be gentle. They would break the engine in at half throttle, for at least one hundred hours. After that, they would change to a lighter oil, push the throttle open, and see what she had.

Roberto returned to the pilot cabin. "The hull is as dry as a bone. We did a good job done there." Pedro smiled.

It took them almost two hours, and finally Pedro cleared the Mississippi River and entered the Gulf of Mexico. It was now ten o'clock and the water was smooth as glass. The boys would circle the boat for about two hours, and then return back to Judge Bean's place. It had been a perfect shakedown cruise. All were totally delighted.

It was now ten o'clock, Saturday morning. Kelly waited in line at the Hibernia Bank for the doors to open. This was the same bank she had told Sam could only be seen from Bourbon Street. When the doors opened, she proceeded to the first teller available and purchased six cashier bank checks, each in the amount of five thousand dollars. With interest and small deposits of her money from the Dixieland, she left seven hundred in the account to hold the account open.

Day 12

At ten o'clock the following Sunday morning, Sam was once again taken from his prison bunk. He had now been pulled from his bed at thirty minute intervals, since his arrest on Friday evening at around five-thirty p.m.

"What time is it anyway?" Sam asked.

One of the guards answered, "Ten o'clock."

"What day is it?"

The second guard moved forward to Sam, with Sam's manacles in hand. "Let's go, Sam. Let's hook you up."

"No, I'm serious. What day is it?" It appeared as though Sam had become mentally confused.

"This is Sunday morning, ten o'clock. They want to see you back at interrogation. Let's go. Let's hook up."

Sam quickly took a position, with his back turned to the deputy, hands clasped at the front of his waist, feet spread about a foot apart. Sam had now been without constant sleep for fifty-two hours. He started the day before when he awoke with about eight hours of sleep at the Royal Orleans Hotel. Then he and George Carey followed Bill Mays and his wife to the airport. They saw them off on a trip to California. Then Sam handled a press conference at the Royal Street Precinct. Following that, Sam was arrested. He was arrested on Friday evening at about three o'clock. Now it was Sunday morning at ten a.m.. In his mind, that calculated to be fifty-two hours with no constant sleep.

The guards walked him back down the two long hallways and they entered Investigation Room 4. A new man was there. He introduced himself as Agent Paul Winfield.

Paul was a decent-looking young man. Sam guessed he was about twenty-eight. Sam also figured he was a weekend trainee lawyer, doing the best he could to crack the case. Sam was placed in the chair at the desk and the two sheriff's guards left the room.

Paul didn't look at Sam while Sam stared intently at him. Sam had decided to be nice to young Paul, who spent a few more moments going through the voluminous pages of information that had now been gathered regarding the theft of fifty-million dollars of cocaine.

Sam watched him as he worked. Then slowly he let his head drop down, eased his body forward, and flopped his head onto the desk.

Paul Winnfield looked up from his paperwork, saw Sam was now apparently sleeping on the front edge of his desk. At first his hand moved out to touch Sam's shoulder, but Paul pulled his hand away before touching. Touching a sleeping suspect might cause a problem. Paul then turned around and looked into the two-way mirror. With shoulders shrugged, he silently asked: "What should I do?"

A moment later the door opened. The lead guard entered the room. He crossed over and looked down at Sam, then up at Paul Winfield.

"You gotta wake him up. You gotta keep him awake," The guard said.

"Okay, wake up!" Paul said loudly.

The guard placed his hand on Sam's shoulder. "Okay Sam," the guard said. "Let's go. On your toes."

Sam quickly opened his eyes and looked about the room. "Hello there. What time is it?"

"It's ten-twenty a.m., Sunday morning."

Sam was close to collapsing. He had originally figured it could be seventy-two hours before they either had to book him or release him. He also figured he could handle the problem of sleep deprivation for that period of time. As it turned out, the mind was willing but the body was not.

"So how many hours has that been since we started this?" Sam asked.

"I don't know. We don't keep a record," The guard said.

"Well somebody's got to know. Don't you have a switchboard? Call the girl and ask her; how long has this shit been going on?" At this point in time, things got very confusing for Sam.

Then Roger Gentry came into the room. He motioned for Paul Winfield to leave. It was a quick point at Paul, with his index finger, followed with his thumb pointing to the door. Winfield got the message and made a quick exit.

"Take him back to his cell," Gentry said. "Let him sleep for an hour. Then wake him and bring him back. I'll take it from there."

Sam half-walked, and mostly stumbled his way back to his cell. He was allowed to start into a heavy sleep for one hour. When he was brought back to Interrogation Room 4, it was Roger Gentry he faced. It was the same old stuff, the same old questions, the same old answers. Sam believed he was doing quite well, but in his afterthoughts, he would question his performance. When all was said and done, he knew full well the question of "money" was never asked and never mentioned.

It was now seven p.m., Sunday evening. Sam was now in his sixty-third hour of sleep deprivation. Sam had been run through nine more hours of constant interrogations. His mind and body started to short circuit. Normally he would quickly jump up with a smile on his face, and proclaim, "Hello boys, let's get it on." But now things had changed. Sam didn't know where he was. His hands were shaking. He was breathing heavily. He was involved in total mental breakdown.

Two guards entered his cell, one carried his manacle's. Another guard said, "Okay Sam, let's get going." But Sam was not having any of this.

"Get away from me!" Sam screamed. "Keep away from me!" he hollered again.

The two guards stepped back for a moment. One of them blew a whistle. It was loud and piercing. Sam didn't know what was going on, or where he was. He raised his hands to his ears and squeezed tight, trying to block the screeching sound.

Three more guards ran into the cell. On seeing the first guard, Sam doubled his fist and threw a right hook into the side of his head. The remaining guards quickly wrestled Sam to floor. One of them placed his boot on the side of his face, forcing him to the cement floor of the cell.

As the guard exerted more pressure on the side of his face, Sam's head was forced even tighter onto the cement floor. Sam felt the pain which grew stronger by the second. The left side of his head was now pinned tightly to the floor. The sole of the guard's boot was on the right side of his head, pushing down harder and harder, for Sam's total resignation.

As Sam struggled, the pressure on his head increased. He felt his mouth being forced open by the pressure from the heel of the boot. As he struggled, he noted that the raised heel of the boot was now being forced down onto his jaw. His jaw was about to crack.

Sam could see the man wearing the boot. He was a large man, looked like a professional football line backer. Sam later learned it was Sgt. Dave Rivers. They made eye contact. Deputy Dave's look was one of, "Okay mother fucker, give me one more reason to stamp your head through this floor!"

Sam finally gave up the battle. He allowed his body to totally relax. The boot on his head stayed firm. Then Sam heard a loud pop, somewhere in his head. Perhaps that pop he heard was his jaw.

The men were buzzing over Sam like bees in a pollen frenzy. Two of them quickly cuffed his hands behind his back, and two others secured his ankles. Then, on a signal from Deputy Dave, the boot was removed from Sam's face, and Deputy Dave quickly grabbed a hand full of orange cloth from the back of Sam's jump suit. The five guards picked him up like a hog-tied individual and headed for the hallway.

At first Sam wanted to check out his jaw. They were carrying him with his face down. All he could see were their feet, walking forward, and the floor. He opened his jaw slowly. It popped. He opened in again, and this time there was no pop. Whatever happened, his jaw popped back into place. Then, the pain of the chains controlling his body got Sam's attention.

"Okay guys!" Sam shouted out. "I can walk now! Put me down! I'll walk for you!"

The guards didn't listen. Sam had misbehaved. They would show him what it was like to misbehave. Someone jerked at the chains on his wrists, and another pulled on his ankles. Sam winced in pain. They reached the end of the first hallway, turned and moved to the second hall.

Sam started to weep uncontrollably. His nose started running his mouth was full of mucus. He coughed and spit it out, and the tears kept flowing.

"Oh Jesus," Sam said. "Please, just let me walk. I'll walk fine. Please, just let me do it."

The guards said nothing. They just walked on to Interrogation Room 4. Once there, the lead guard opened the door, and they all carried Sam inside. They unceremoniously plopped his body onto the floor. Sam lay very still.

A man walked over to him. Sam could see his legs. He wore brown penny loafers and khaki trousers. Then he heard him speak and Sam recognized the voice. He was with the main man from the Office of Internal Affairs, Deland Lupson.

"Okay, he'll be fine," Lipson said. "You can un-cuff him and sit him in the chair."

Someone unlocked the cuffs on his wrists, another sat him in the chair and Sam looked around the room. Lupson was still wearing his Mr. Rogers cardigan sweater. His pipe was still smoldering in the ashtray on the table. He looked down at Sam and realized Sam belonged to him. Tears were uncontrollably streaming down Sam's face. Sam tried to gain control, wiping his eyes with his hands, but to no avail.

"I'm sorry," Sam said through his sobs. "This is just pitiful."

"It's alright, Sam," Lupson said. "You boys can go now. I don't think we'll have a problem here." The five guards left the room.

"I'll tell you anything you want to know," Sam said. "I'm just so tired, that's all."

Lupson placed his hand onto Sam's shoulder. "It's all right, Sam. You'll feel better when you get all of this off your mind." Deland Lupson next moved behind the table, glanced at the two-way mirror, and presented a revolving motion with his finger. This meant, "Roll the tape."

Lupson next slid into his chair and clearly stated, so that the recorder could pick up his voice, "The time is now seven twenty-six, Sunday evening. My name is Deland Lupson, and I am with Detective Sam Pennington. Mr. Pennington, do I have your permission to record this interview?"

As Lupson took his pipe from the ashtray, Sam, still weeping uncontrollably, said: "Oh hell yes. Let's put this in the record. I'm about to give you the confession of a lifetime."

"Very good. You understand we are seeking information regarding some fifty million dollars of a lost controlled substance. Please continue."

"Okay, okay. But if I'm gonna spill my guts here, I wanna get something from you first."

"And what would that be?"

"I wanna know where you guys found cocaine in my condo?"

The two men stared at one another. Sam took a fresh Kleenex from the box and blew a heavy wad of snot from his nasal cavity. Lupson looked away for a moment, wishing not to see the finish. Sam threw the heavy wad into the trash can. It landed there with a resounding thunk.

"It's been driving me crazy," Sam said. "I gotta know. Where in hell did you guys find cocaine in my condo?"

"Okay, I'll tell you. We found a small cardboard box up in your attic. In the box were two police uniforms, your old police uniforms. In one of the shirt pockets, I believe it was the right pocket, there was some residual dust. There was also some dust on the front of the shirt, and also some was found on the trousers. We had that tested, and it came up positive."

Sam thought for a moment. Then he started to laugh. "That's it? This is what it's all about? You found cocaine in my old shirt pocket? That's all you got?"

"We have much more than that."

"Well, I'll give you much more than just that! I'll give you the whole truth and nothing but the truth! One night, about ten years ago, I came into a place in the Quarter, on Bienville, the Shell Bar and Grill, to get some dinner. Somehow, and I don't remember exactly how, but I wound up in the back pool room. There were five cops there. When they were finally arrested they were known as the NOLA Five. You know about them, don't you?"

Deland silently puffed at his pipe. He said nothing. He wanted Sam to continue spilling his guts.

"Okay," Sam said. "Okay fine. That was before your time. So I get involved with the cops, five of them. They were selling the dope out of the back of the Shell Bar. One night, I walk into the men's room, and find this guy named Jeff Rice. Jeff asked me to lock the door, then he took a stick of cocaine out of his pocket, opened it up, and spread it out on the counter. He took a razor blade and chopped it into four lines. Then he took a straw and snorted two lines. Then he offered me another straw and said: 'Here's for you. Go for it.'

"So I stood there an figured out what to do. This guy was a professional, a real dope-snorting pro. So what do I do? He handed me a fresh straw, so I poked it in my nose and sniffed two lines. I did it just like he did it. And when I finished, I thought I was going to die. But I proved something to them. I proved I could snort shit. Then a few nights later, the head guy, a guy named Mark Maher came up to me. He was a Sergeant. We shot pool. He won. Anyway, he takes me out to his car, out into the garage. He opens the trunk of his car, and there he's got a whole supply of the stuff. He takes five sticks of cocaine and puts them into my pocket. And he says, 'Here ya go pal. Have a party on me.'

"So the next day, I'm in my car on St. Ann Street, holding the traffic while somebody moved their apartment in or out, and I called Capt. Adam Loper. He's one a the good guys. So he meets me in my car. I told him the whole story. I show him the five sticks of dope. When I pull it from my pocket some dust falls out all over the front of my shirt. I wiped it off. Adam took the five sticks from me and stuck his finger in his mouth to get it wet, dipped his finger into the stuff, and placed the dope on his upper gum line. Then he said: 'This is good shit.'

Sam had stopped crying. He had lifted the weight of the world from his shoulders and now felt like a human being once again.

"So Adam made me Agent 33," Sam added. "I was directed to stick with the NOLA 5, and find out who they bought their dope from. That's it. That's all there is. So do with me whatever you want."

Deland Lupson's pipe went out. He placed it back onto the ashtray and leaned back into his chair. "All right Sam, let's knock off all the bullshit. I'm not really interested in your silly little dope games. We both know what I want."

"And what might that be?"

"I want fifty million dollars in drugs, laid right here on this table."

Sam took another Kleenex and blew his nose. It wasn't as bad as the last one but still a challenge for anyone to see.

"Tell you the truth, Deland, I still don't know a thing about fifty million dollars in drugs. That's the God's truth. I wish I could help you, but I can't."

Deland Lupson's face spoke volumes. His lips started turning a dark shade of blue. "I'll make you a deal." Lupson said, in a tight rasping voice. "You plea bargain a deal with us, and I will see to it you serve no jail time."

"No jail time?"

"That's right."

"But I don't have it. I haven't seen fifty million dollars of cocaine in my life. The only thing I ever saw was five sticks of cocaine the night Mark Maher stuck those five sticks into my shirt pocket. And I also snorted a half a stick that Jeff Rice cut up with a razor blade. You got me for that. You got me for sniffing two lines. I admit it. That's all I did!"

Deland Lupson now crowded in for the kill. He rose from his chair and started pacing around the room. "Suppose I were to tell you we have testimony form a known drug dealer who is willing to testify in court, that he purchased, for a period of eight years before this drug bust happened, large quantities of cocaine and heroin from you."

Sam looked at Lupson in amazement. "I would tell you you've been talking to a lying sack of shit."

Lupson smiled. "I don't think so. Suppose I were to tell you this man has already served ten years of a fifteen year sentence. And this man is very upset, for serving ten long years, just to protect you from incarceration."

"I would still have to tell you that you are still talking to a lying sack of shit."

Lupson now chuckled. "And suppose I were to tell you, this man had provided us with names and places of people you have introduced him too, who will also testify against you in a court of law."

"I would then tell you, that those people who he claims I introduced him too, are also lying sacks of shit."

"And if I told you his name was Mark Maher, what would you say to that?"

"Then I would say to you, you got bad advice from a guy who served ten years of a fifteen-year sentence, because he wants to get our of jail five years early. And Mark Maher is a lying sack of shit!"

Deland Lupson pushed the button on the desk and said, "Turn the recorder off and send the guards back in."

Within two seconds, the five guards came back into the room.

"Take this defendant downstairs and book him," Lupson commanded.

Sam and his gang of prison guards took the elevator to the second floor, and arrived in a section of rooms marked Photograph and Fingerprints. He stood in front of the camera, while the photographer shot one front view and a left and right side view. The guards then moved him to the next room, where Sam met Cecilia Moore. Cecilia was an African American woman, five feet six inches tall, and weighed at least three hundred pounds. She was in charge of fingerprints.

"Ya'll gotta take the cuffs off a his hands," Cecilia said.

The head guard, Sergeant Dave Rivers, stepped in and unlocked the cuffs. When Cecilia moved in to manufacture Sam's prints, she noted the severe damage to his wrists. There were deep cuts on the inside of both wrists, and covered with dried blood.

She spoke softly into Sam's ear. "What you done to you arms?"

"I tripped and fell down some stairs," Sam answered.

"What are you, some sort a suicide?"

"No ma'am, I just fell, that's all."

"Well, you fell like a spinnin' suicide, that's all I can say."

"When I fell I was wearing the cuffs. I did this to myself."

"Okay, if you say so." Cecilia looked up at Deputy Dave. "I gonna get a nurse in here to take care a this mess. I can't do no prints on this boy over this mess. How can you boys bring a prisoner in here lookin' like dis?"

A few minutes later, a female nurse came in, cleaned the area and then spread some Neosporin Plus Antibiotic ointment over the wounds. She then applied a gauze dressing around each wrist to keep them clean. The nurse left and Cecilia proceeded to manufacture two strips of prints for each hand, and then turned Sam over to the Sheriff.

"Okay boys, he's all yours. You think the five'a you big fellas can take this one boy back to his bunk, without allowin' him to fall down any more steps?

Deputy Dave stepped forward with cuffs in hand, heading for Sam to secure him for the trip back to the cell.

"I know ya'll ain't gonna put them cuffs back on this boy like that. I believe since ya'lls is…five big men…like ya'lls is…ya'll has the ability to move this boy back to his cell, without cuffin' him up. An' if ya'll feel ya'll need to use them cuffs, I will personally be checkin' in on his well-bein'. So this boy betteah be fuckin healthy when he get's theah. Ya'all got that?"

There was something about Sam. He always managed to find some good luck when bad luck had all but done him in. Dating back to his days in Atlantic City, when every person he came in contact with was always someone to pick his pocket or throw him out of town. But always at the end of the day, there would be someone like Cecilia who would step forward to help him out.

"Okay boys," Deputy Dave said. "Let's just walk him outta here."

As they started to lead Sam out of the room, the phone rang. Dave took the call. After getting instruction from upstairs, he hung up the phone and announced: "We have to take the pictures again."

Sam was taken into the men's room. Deputy Dave laid a can of shaving soap and a razor on the shelf top.

"Here ya go," Dave said. "Clean up your face an we shoot the pictures again."

Sam walked up to the sink and took a good look at his face. The plastic mirror he had in his cell was less than perfect. It was not only plastic and dirty, it had visible discrepancies. The light in his cell came from behind, from the hallway. When Sam looked into that mirror, he appeared to be an outer space creature, who looked dark and slightly out of focus. But now, for the first time in two and a half days, he was looking at the real thing. His face was covered with a growth of dark beard stubble, and his eyes looked like two burnt holes in a blanket. His hair was even scragglier.

Sam placed shaving soap on his face and worked the razor over the stubble. When he finished he looked like a clean-shaven bowery bum. Deputy Dave loaned him his pocket comb. When Sam was finished he offered the comb back to Dave. Dave suggested he keep it.

Sam wore an orange one-piece jumpsuit, with a big P on the back. Without removing the whole suit, he squirmed out of the top section, and let it fall around his waist. Sheriff Dave then put him back into his black shirt and his brown houndstooth jacket. Apparently they wanted Sam to appear, in these new photographs, as though he had just been arrested.

They walked back to the photography section and took three more photos. Sam did the best he could. As the photographer snapped each shot, Sam even manufactured a slight smile. But his eyes made him look like a captured enemy prisoner.

They re-dressed Sam in his orange jumpsuit and moved him back into the elevator and up to his fourth floor cell. As they removed his leg chains, Deputy Dave moved over to Sam.

"You won't be bothered any more tonight. Tonight you get a full sleep," Dave said. Then he and the four other guards left.

Sam lay back onto his bunk and closed his eyes. His ordeal was over, at least for the moment. For the past sixty-five hours, he had only been allowed periodic moments of sleep. As his body faded into never never land, he thought of Kelly.

Day 13

At six Monday morning, Sam was awakened to a new day. He had slept a full eight refreshing hours. He quickly became alert to his situation, but his body felt logy. The guards slipped him a tray of food through the service port in the jail door, and Sam ate it with delight. The eggs were cold and the bacon was greasy. Sam loved every bite.

An hour later, he and eighteen other prisoners, all wearing the usual orange jump suits, boarded the yellow Sheriff's bus and headed for the courthouse.

They reached the I-10 and were met by a throng of traffic heading for work in the city. Sam sat on the left side by a window. He glanced out to his left and spotted a young boy in the front passenger seat. Their eyes met. Sam smiled at the boy who was about ten years old. Probably his mom or dad was dropping him off for school. Sam smiled and waved at the boy.

The boy reacted with alarm. He leaned away from Sam and said something to the driver. At first, Sam could not see who was driving. His dad leaned down and looked up through the windshield, spotting Sam. His glance at Sam showed nothing but contempt. It said, 'How dare you drive common criminals on the same street as me, and allow my son to see them!' He then pulled forward and changed lanes.

Sam slumped down into his seat, so as not to be seen by others. As they drove on, Sam glanced at his bandaged wrists. It did look as though he had tried to commit suicide. He removed the bandages and placed them in his side pocket. Sam decided this was going to be a tough day.

It was eight thirty when Sam and the other prisoners arrived at the courthouse. They were ushered into the back service elevator, and up to the fourth floor. This was the same floor where Judge Marshall Williams held his court. It was a little over a week before when Sam was testifying regarding the Skanes, Jr. case concerning the murder of his partner, Jack Arnold. Now Sam was only twenty feet away from Judge Williams' court, in another courtroom, regarding another crime that he was not guilty of committing. Sam smiled to himself. *Wouldn't it be interesting if the cops had gotten the charge right?*

They all sat quietly until eight fifteen, then two young lawyers from the city came into lock up. The first lawyer, a young man named Phil Mitchell, made a general statement. "Alright gentlemen, pay attention. I am Phil Mitchell. This is Mr. Al Davidson, and we are both lawyers. As none of you have an attorney, we are prepared to defend you at no charge for the filing of your plea in the matter that you are charged. We have forty-five minutes before court begins. So let's do it to it."

Davidson and Mitchell moved through the room, talking to each prisoner and making notes. Finally it was Davidson who came up to Sam, and sat down on the bench beside him.

"Hi there, I'm Al Davidson. You are Sam Pennington?" Al Davidson was scanning through Sam's file.

"Yes I am."

"Alright sir. You are being charged with…"

"Not guilty," Sam said, interrupting.

"Well, I want to list what the charges are."

"It doesn't matter. Whatever you have listed there, I'm not guilty."

"Okay, that's fine. I'll be right there with you when we file the plea."

Kelly Lee was there, waiting in the outer hallway. There were about forty-five others waiting to get in. It was not the nineteen prisoners who were there to plead their charge, but a newsworthy murder case that would follow, which was the main issue here. At eight forty-five the doors to the courtroom opened and Kelly walked into the room. Kelly looked nice. She was dressed to a T. She was wearing a newly purchased black outfit: black ankle-length skirt with black boots, black blouse with a black shawl, and a black knit hat. All of this black highlighted her beautiful face that God would have died for. She sat in the rear of the courtroom and waited for the procedure to begin.

At ten minutes past nine, the nineteen prisoners were led in. At first glance, Kelly could not identify Sam. She wondered if he was even there. Finally the Judge came into the room. All stood as he was introduced. He was Judge Maxwell Freeman, a man about fifty years of age. He was a soft-spoken man, one who obviously possessed great intelligence. Five of the prisoners were drug dealers, with thirteen more charged with the use of a controlled substance. That left Sam charged with a more complicated issue.

Judge Freeman started running through his list of charges. Everyone he called on pleaded not guilty by either Al Davidson or Phil Mitchell. Their bail ranged from a minimum of five hundred dollars to as high as ten thousand. Trial date started on June twelfth, and moved on up into the days of the month. This was March thirteenth. Due to the overloaded schedule, the calendar of the bench was delayed three months.

Sam sat quietly in his seat. He analyzed this. It appeared as though he could get his vacation without bothering a soul. Sam kept glancing around at the audience, trying to spot someone he knew. He may have spotted a lady wearing a black outfit, but with a quick glace around at all of those people, he still spotted no one he recognized.

Judge Freeman ran through his calendar quickly, and finally came to the final name on the list, Sam Pennington. Judge Freeman looked up and spotted the man in front of him. He recognized him. "Mr. Pennington, are you an officer with the New Orleans Police department?" Judge Freeman asked.

"Yes sir," Sam said. "I'm a detective Division 8, the Royal Street office."

"Did I not see you at a news conference last Friday afternoon, concerning your capturing of a serial killer?"

"Well sir, I didn't really catch this person. It was actually two men in the department who made the connection."

A man stood up, a few chairs to the left of Sam. "Your honor, if I may?"

"And who are you?" Judge Freeman asked.

"My name is Clark Fisher. I represent the Office of Internal Affairs, with the New Orleans Police Department."

"Proceed."

"I believe I have new information that might greatly aid in providing a proper disposition in this matter."

"Well, that's very good. From what I've read over the last two days, your people have incarcerated Mr. Pennington."

"No sir, not incarcerated, rather 'held' for questioning."

"Okay, that sounds better. What can you provide me in making a proper disposition in the matter?"

"Your Honor, this situation is regarding an ongoing investigation. I believe your file clearly shows that this man possessed an illegal substance. And we have also proved this man has sold this substance over eight years to at least one other person. We are presently engaged in finding the location of a large stash of this illegal substance, and when found, will result in proper and legal determination of this case.

"I therefore suggest to the court that Mr. Pennington is a flight risk, and further ask that he remain in prison until we have completed our investigation."

"And how long will that take?" the judge asked.

"Well sir, it's ongoing."

"So what you want me to do is to put this man in jail for as long as you and your people are 'ongoing' with their investigation, is that right?"

"Yes sir. We believe that..."

"Hold on just a moment," the judge asked. "I think I can simplify this issue. As I read your complaint, you have provided only two items that break the law. One, that the defendant was in possession of an illegal substance, and two, sold this substance to another person, who will later be available in this court, to testify of those transactions. Is that correct?"

"Well, sir we have two witness against the defendant, but we believe that..."

"Hold on." Judge Freeman glanced through his paper work one more time. "The second item has to deal with hearsay. That being that this defendant has sold this substance to an individual or individuals for over eight years. That remains hearsay, until said time as your witness testifies to same in this court. So that ends that for now. Let's just deal with the illegal substance. What did you find, where did you find it, and how much was there of this substance?"

Clark Fisher was rapidly moving between a rock and a hard place. He knew full well his charges did not hold water. He was addressing his opinion on what the Office of Internal Affairs told him to do. And he didn't believe a minute of it.

"We were not able to account for the exact amount of the substance," Fisher said. "There was only residual amounts of the substance in the defendant's possession."

"How much residual amount of the substance was their present?" the judge asked.

"I don't have that available at this moment."

"Okay then. Let us recap. All we have of a positive charge against this defendant, is that you found him holding a residual amount of said illegal substance in his possession. Is that correct?"

"Yes sir. But what we believe is…"

"Hold on. What you believe is what you believe. What you can prove will be stated by you when this case is heard in this court. I now give you the following information.

"This man has been with the New Orleans Police Department for twenty years. He has numerous commendations in his file of record. Mr. Pennington had, last Thursday evening, been involved with the capture of a serial killer, who had murdered twenty-nine women in the New Orleans area. The fact of the matter is Mr. Pennington is now given the stature of a national hero. He has received newspaper headlines ranging from the *Los Angeles Times* to the *New York Times*, not to mention the *New Orleans Times Picayune*."

Judge Freeman looked over at Sam, who stood before him in silence. "Are you aware of this, Mr. Pennington?" The judge asked.

"No sir."

'So you haven't read a newspaper?"

"No sir. Not for three days."

"Have you made a phone call?"

"No sir."

"You haven't talked to an attorney?"

"No sir. Well, I just spoke to Al here. Al Davidson. He represents my plea."

"I've heard enough. This case will be heard in this court on May fifteenth. I will now set bail at the maximum I can levy for a person charged with holding one ounce or less of a controlled substance. Bail is set for five thousand dollars." The judge banged his gavel onto his desk. "This court is adjourned for fifteen minutes."

As Sam was marched with eighteen other prisoners into the holding room, he glanced back into the court room to see if anyone had come there that he would recognize, but saw no one. Sam had been kept incognito for almost thee days, so who did he think might know of his situation anyway? When he got back to the jail, he could now demand his rights, at least the use of a telephone. He would take care of business as usual.

In the court room, Kelly made her way to the front desk. She had made several attempts to wave at Sam, but he never saw her. She reached the front desk and a lady sat there with a phone strapped to her ear.

"Yes ma'am. How may I help you?" The lady asked.

"I want to pay the bail for Sam Pennington, five thousand dollars." She reached into her purse and withdrew the envelope from the Bank of Hibernia. She pulled one of the five thousand dollar bank checks from the envelope and laid it on her desktop.

"Ma'am, we don't do no banking here. You got to go downstairs to the first floor, room 101."

Kelly took the elevator to the first floor, and moved down the room 101. When she walked inside she found the large room was covered with lines of people. It was like visiting the Driver's License Bureau. There had to be at least thirty people in various lines in front of her. Each of those people had a need to get questions answered. It was a lesson for Kelly on the bureaucratic well-being of America.

It was now lunch time when Deputy Dave put Sam back into his cell. Sam asked if he could make a phone call.

"I gotta get the word from the guys upstairs," Dave said.

"Okay. That's fine." Sam had answered his own question.

"When I got home this morning, I saw your picture on the front page of the Picayune. You did some special stuff there."

"Yeah, special stuff."

"As soon as they let me know, I'll get you a phone."

"That'll be fine, Dave."

Dave left the cell. He had more respect for his prisoner than he had before. Sam was tired. He laid onto his bunk and thought of his future. He would call Eduardo, and get five thousand dollars into the process of freeing him. As he faded off to sleep he thought of Kelly. He wanted to make sure she was on board. He wanted her to be with him.

Chapter 24

DAY 13, CONTINUED.

IT WAS TWO-THIRTY when Sam was awakened. Deputy Dave was standing above him, shaking his body.

"It's okay, Sam. Let's go boy. You been bailed out."

Sam pulled himself from his bunk, rubbing his eyes, searching for some quick reality. "Okay. I'm with you. Here we go."

"You been bailed out, man. I'm takin' you downstairs to property. We get your things together an you're outta here."

"I've been bailed? Who bailed me?"

"Beats me."

Sam quickly looked around the cell to see what stuff he had left. After a quick examination he saw he had no stuff left. They took the elevator downstairs to the property room.

Once there, Sam sifted through his stuff. Everything he came in with, he received, including his badge and his gun. Well, his cell phone was no longer there, but he could care less. He dressed in an alcove and walked out like a normal person.

"Okay Dave, thanks a lot for your help."

"Thanks Sam. You were the best prisoner I ever dealt with."

Sam Pennington walked out into the sunlight. At first, his eyes had to get used to the brightness, then he spotted Kelly. She was standing beside her little blue convertible sports car. She wore the same black outfit she had on in the courtroom. The instant she saw Sam, she started to move towards him. After three steps, the move turned into a dead run. Finally she jumped into his arms and kissed him solidly on the lips.

"Oh God, Sam, I'm so glad to see you again."

"You look marvelous, baby. I'm glad to see you too."

"What happened Sam? What did they do to you?"

Sam took her by the arm and headed across the parking lot. "Is that your car over there?"

"Yes, the blue one."

He started to walk faster. "Let's go."

When they got to the car, Sam asked, "What is it?"

"I think it's a Hillman, or something."

"You drive," Sam said.

They drove to the Mississippi River, to a spot that only Sam knew. They were about a quarter of a mile north of the French Quarter. There was a small opening, surrounded by storage buildings on the right, and a small walking area to the left. Sam walked Kelly down to the river. When they arrived at the riverfront, Sam took her to a rock built for two. As they sat there, they felt the breeze of the Mississippi.

It was a lovely sight. The paddlewheel boat, the *Robert E. Lee* was just making its turn for home base. It was their lunch cruise, seventy-five customers on board. As the boat passed in front of them, Sam and Kelly could hear the sound of the "on board" Dixieland Band, stomping out the classic, "When The Saints Go Marching In."

"This is a beautiful spot," Kelly said.

"Yeah, I even own this rock."

She smiled and nuzzled her face onto his shoulder.

"How's the boat?" Sam asked.

"Oh, it's beautiful. I spoke to the Judge Saturday afternoon. He said the boys took it out to the Gulf, and she worked perfectly. Do you want to talk to the Judge? He can fill in the details. Here, I have my cell phone." She started to rummage through her purse.

"No. We don't make any phone calls here. People can track that down."

"Alright," she said.

"Where did you get the bail money?"

"I won it at a casino when I first came here."

"You never cease to amaze me."

"I've still got twenty-five thousand dollars left."

"Now I'm amazed even more."

"You want it?" Here, I'll give it to you." She started to reach into her purse for her stash of cash. Sam reached over and softly took her hands.

"Listen baby, I don't want your cash. All I want is you. This police situation will soon be resolved. That's all you need to know. For now, you've just got to trust me. Blind trust."

"But why did they put you in jail?"

"That has nothing to do with you. If I get involved in a major court action, I don't want you to get involved. Trust me on that one."

"Alright Sam, I trust you." Tears started to well up in her eyes.

Sam reached into his pocket for a hankie. "You don't need to cry. This will be a grand adventure for everybody." He handed her the hankie. She took it and blew her nose, then handed it back.

"Now here's what we do. I've got to get outta town. I want to leave at dawn tomorrow morning."

She started sniffing again, then light sobs. Sam handed the hankie back.

"Go to your place. Pack a bag of clothes. Pay your landlord in advance for three months' rent."

"I'm going with you, then?"

"Well sure, if you want to."

"I would love to do that with you."

"Listen, I've given a lot of thought to this, you and me. I don't have any family. They are all either dead or they ran off. In twenty years on the force, you are the only person I've met that I would like to share the rest of my life with."

"Oh Sam!"

"The thing is, I'm still a cop. I got ten more years on the force. Then, if you want to, we'll get married. The thing is, as long as I'm a cop, and I'm still being shot at, I don't want my wife sitting at my funeral, and walking away with the American flag under her arm. She started to sob, hard uncontrollable sobs. She placed her arms around his neck and he wrapped his around her body. As her sobbing continued, he looked across the Mississippi.

Sam wasn't good at this. He knew it. He didn't really know how to explain his feelings. He decided to give it one last try. "So I guess until then, I'd like you to be my steady."

"Oh Sam." She placed her hands on his face and pulled him to her, placing a deep kiss on his lips. "I will be your steady." Then she kissed him again.

He took the hankie, that was now almost completely wet and dried most of her tears.

"Alright, after you get your stuff from your place, drive directly to the boat. Meet with everybody. Include the Judge in this. Tell them we leave tomorrow at dawn, have the boat fully packed. All the food and booze we need, including our special stuff, the Judge will understand what our special stuff is.

"I'll be there around seven tonight. We'll make our final check. I'll bring a bag of lobsters and batch of CDs, with enough movies and music to make the natives very happy. Now you drive me to my place. I'll try to start my car, if it's still there.

"We'll be back in town in three months. Then I'll finish business. I don't want you to know anything about this side of me. If it ever comes to pass that you must testify against me, you will have nothing but the truth to say. You say 'So help me God, I don't know a thing about it.' You still want to make this trip with me?"

"I would love to do that with you."

"Well baby, I'm your ticket. Let's sail."

They got back into her car and drove to his apartment on Barracks. There was activity there. The large banana tree that was in his patio, in the front garden, had already been pulled up. It was now resting in the street, awaiting the trash pickup. This was accomplished by a small tractor rig with a front scoop. The entire yard had been all but demolished, and the tractor had dug down even deeper, in an attempt to locate fifty thousand dollars of cocaine.

Sam left Kelly's car, and opened his garage door. His 1979 vintage Alfa Romeo Spyder was covered with dirt. The cops had already been there. They had removed portions of the ceiling, seeking contraband. As the workers pulled the wood down, pounds of dirt and silt fell to the bottom, covering his car, with a thick film of filth.

With his hand, Sam swept the dirt from his tonneau cover, unzipped it, and jumped in behind the wheel. He had last driven it Sunday, when he first took Kelly to meet Judge Bean. When he turned the key, the Spyder jumped into life. Sam looked back at Kelly. He smiled and gave her a thumbs up. She smiled at him, put her blue sports car into low drive, waved goodbye, and raced into the distance.

Sam backed out onto Barracks Street. He was feeling good. His house was being torn apart, but that would soon be resolved, which might wind up being a major cost to the city.

He first drove to Circuit City on Veteran Highway, in Metairie. Over the years he had purchased many items here, including his big screen TV. There he saw Andy Crocket, an old friend. Andy and Sam made a deal for the best laptop computer they sold. Andy would have the boys in the back, load it with all of the programs Sam might need, along with programs he didn't care to ever see.

"I'm putting in a casino game," Andy said. "It's got everything in it, including poker. If you get bored, give it a shot."

In addition Andy had a telephone hook up for his ship-to-shore connection. In this manner, Sam would be able to send E-mail messages, anywhere in the world. In addition, Sam also bought a new cell phone. This one was radio-operated, allowing him more distance per call to his closest database. Sam paid for it all with a Visa card. He next drove to the French Quarter. He had hoped to find William Wild there.

At 726 St. Peter Street, there was an old two-story brown building. It looked as though it was deserted, a blighted building that time and care had forgotten. The brown front had developed a patina. There were splashes of green and splotches of red there. The six had fallen off of the 726 address marker. They would probably want to fix that, but then again, maybe not.

This was the Preservation Jazz, located in the heart of the French Quarter, half-way between Bourbon and Royal. The building was dedicated to the preservation of jazz. Not modern jazz, but Dixieland Jazz. Each night, the old timers of the music business, would gather there and blow and sing some of the most fantastic music one could ever expect to hear.

Right next door was Poppy's Grill. That was where Sam expected to find 'Wild' William Wild. It was Monday night. On Monday, they served red beans and rice. Red beans and rice with a pork chop on Monday night was a Louisiana tradition. On this day they served a free order of red beans and rice to any musician playing a set at the Preservation Jazz. That was where William would be.

Sam found a parking space near the St. Louis Cathedral. This cathedral was the oldest minor basilica in the United States that still offered daily services. As he walked across the square, Sam recalled the time he first met William Wild, eight years before.

Flashback

Nine years later

It was the Christmas season, December 22, a cold day. A freeze was expected that night. Sam was wearing his cop uniform, walking through the square, and he saw a small group of musicians had gathered at the side where the benches were located. There was a crowd around; they had a following. All were enjoying an old blues standard, "You Know What It Means To Miss New Orleans." Sam decided to stop and listen for a moment. After a few tunes, he decided to move on. As he started to head for Royal Street, he noticed an African American man sitting on the church steps, also listening to the music. As Sam started to pass him, he recognized the man. It was 'Wild' William Wild.

William – he never liked to be called Willie – had at one time been a musical star of the New Orleans world of jazz. By now he was in his early eighties, but when it all began he had worked with Louis Armstrong, Jack Teagarden, and Lionel Hampton. At one point in time, he even owned a share in a club on Bourbon Street.

But in the late seventies, things started to fall apart for William Wild. His wife died and he started drinking. He disappeared from the music scene, and now Sam found him sitting on the steps of the St. Louis Cathedral. William, by now, was a broken person.

"Excuse me," Sam asked. "Aren't you William Wild?"

"You got me, officer. I'm moving on." William started to pull himself up.

"No, no. That's okay. You can sit here, it's legal."

"Thank you, officer," William slid back down onto his step. "I appreciate that sir. Just gonna rest here a minute."

It was obvious to Sam that William was homeless. He was still five feet seven inches tall and still weighed in at one hundred twenty-five pounds. There was a gaunt quality about him, one that said, if nobody will help this man, he will surely die.

Sam said, "Listen, Mr. Wild, I have to go to the station to check out. I've also been working on an apartment house over on Barracks. There are open rooms there. If you like, I could come back here and take you there. Give you a spot to relax. Get a warm night's sleep."

William looked at Sam for a long moment. He studied his face. It wasn't what he said or how he said it. It was the meaning of his emotion. "I appreciate your offer. I will sit here on this step until hell freezes over in the hopes that you return."

Sam checked out at the Rampart Street Station and walked back to the St. Louis Cathedral. The cold was unusual and biting. The freeze was closing in as predicted on television news. The streets were now all but deserted, but Sam kept chunking along. When he rounded the corner at St, Louis Cathedral, nobody was there. The square was deserted. Deserted, with the exception of one half-frozen man huddled in a corner of the Cathedral steps. It was 'Wild' William Wild.

After some effort Sam got William walking. They went over to Royal and up towards Barracks. Sam and William stopped at a local market. Sam purchased a half of a Muffaletta, and a fifth of red table wine. Then they walked on to the apartment.

Sam had the key to Shandor's unit on the first floor. It had only been three days since Shandor had disappeared with his black girlfriend, and two nights ago that Sam had his tryst with Shandor's wife, Svetlana. It was a little messy, but good enough. The bed was in the front room, and a small color television set was near by.

Sam turned the heat on and the place quickly warmed up. William sat down on the bed. Sam poured two glasses of wine, one of which he handed to William along with a slice of Muffaletta.

By nine o'clock, William was warm, full, and mellow. As he drifted off to sleep, he promised Sam he'd vacate the premises first thing tomorrow. Sam said he could stay until the cold snap ended.

In the few days that followed, Sam learned that William had never collected Social Security. He was entitled but never thought of it. Sam brought the papers home, and they both filled them out. William's first check was one thousand, three hundred twenty seven dollars. And that was for every month for the rest of his life.

It's crazy what happens to some people. One minute you can find them in an alley freezing to death, and the next moment, after you've offered a little love, seasoned with some encouragement, amazing things can happen. William immediately stopped drinking hard liquor. He started concentrating on a fifth of wine a day. Sam got him a deal to pay three hundred a month for a single apartment in the back.

Then one day, William decided to walk down to the old Preservation

Jazz. He had played there some years ago, before his wife died. When she passed, William gave up all hope. But now hope was back. He said hello to all his buddies, and was invited to join in on one set. One of the boys offered him an extra trumpet. William put the horn to his lips and blew a perfect series of notes. Playing a horn is like walking and chewing gum. Once you know how it's done, you never forget.

Day 11, continued

Sam walked onto St. Peter Street which was getting busy now as tourists started moving in. It was close to party time. He crossed over to Poppy's Grill and walked inside. There was a long counter to the right, and a series of fifteen tables on the left. The room was half full, but William was not in sight.

"Have you seen William Wild here today?" Sam asked the guy cleaning the tables.

"Yeah, he's here. That's his table over there. He went to the toilet. He'll be right back."

Sam sat at the table and waited. The bathroom door opened and out walked Wild William Wild. He was still five feet seven inches tall, and had a slight gimp on his right leg. He was half blind in one eye and now wore an eye patch over that condition. His hearing was badly impaired, totally deaf in his left ear, and half shot in the right.

The problem with his ears was that William played the most powerful horn one could imagine. At five feet seven and a hundred and twenty-five pounds, he manufactured the loudest trumpet one had ever heard. After over sixty years of playing this horn, it was no wonder his ears suffered.

On seeing Sam, a big smile crossed his face. "Hey there my man, what's happening?" He sat down at the table.

"Nothing much, how are you?"

"I'm fine. Been looking for you."

"What about?"

"Had some police come into my place, asked some questions, wanted to know about you."

William was easy. If anyone had a subject they wanted to discuss, just sit there for five minutes and William would bring it up.

"What did they want to know?"

"I don't have any idea. Swear to God. They didn't make a damn bit of sense to me."

"So what did you talk about?"

The water moved in and set a plate of red beans and rice down in front of William.

"Ah ha," William said with glee. "This is the food of love." He took a bottle of Worcestershire sauce and pumped it twelve times into the bean dish, then he added ten dashes of Tabasco. Add some pepper and salt, and it was time to dig in. After the first fantastic bite, he said: "Hey, you want some? I'm buying."

"No thanks, already ate."

"Okay then. You missing a real good dish."

"So what was your conversation about – with the cops, that is?"

"Well, we rambled on and on, about nothing important, then this guy asked me If I had ever bought any crap from you? I thought that was a strange thing to ask me, so I sorta joined in, and I said, I been buying your crap for over eight years. I was kinda hoping to get a laugh. but they didn't laugh."

"They asked you if you had ever bought *crack* from me, right?"

"That's right. An' I said I been buying your *crap* for years."

Sam started to smile. He made his speech very clear. "They were asking you about crack. That's crack cocaine. You understand that, right?"

William became visibly agitated. "I know about that. That's the stuff that killed my son. That and heroin. I don't want anything to do with that stuff. You're not selling that, are you?"

"No, I'm not."

"Well, good for you then. Hey, you wanna come over and watch a set tonight? I'll get you a seat."

"I wish I could, but I got to move on. I just wanted to say hello."

"Well, you already said hello. When you eat some red beans and rice you can say goodbye." William looked around for the chef. Spotting him he called out, "Hey Charlie! Another order of beans and rice for my friend."

Sam next drove to Tower Video and Music. He went inside and purchased every current DVD they had, and included a dozen of his old favorites. In the music section he bought whatever looked good that may sound good. Then he was off to P & J's Seafood on Rampart.

P & J's had a contract with five local restaurants in the city to supply them with lobsters. They imported them from Maine. It was getting late, now about four thirty. Sam bought the balance of their stock, twelve fat chicken lobsters and two dozen soft shelled crabs, and a gallon of oysters.

Throughout the day, Sam drove with one eye on the road and the other on his rear view mirror. He wanted to make sure he was not being followed. Now as he drove over the bridge that crossed the Mississippi, he took special care. After they left tomorrow morning, he would write an E-Mail to Eduardo Sanchez, Carl Witherspoon, and his attorney Donald Mosley. But for now, he definitely did not want to be followed.

Once on the East shore, he turned off at the first off ramp. Then on the surface street, he doubled back. He pulled into a parking lot at a Home Depot, sat and watched the cars moving in and out, then headed back to the highway. No one followed.

Twenty-five minutes later, he was on the road to Judge Bean's house. He could see the boat tethered down at the dock. No one was around. He drove on, and parked a half of a mile down the road. He waited there for fully five minutes, and nobody followed. Then he turned around, and drove back onto the property.

Sam parked his car near the boat, beside Kelly's. Sam got out of the car, and took a good look at the *Miss Lee*. The crew had done a magnificent job. She was beautiful. Then Pedro walked out from the pilot's cabin. Sam looked up at him. Pedro stood there like the captain of the vessel.

"How's it go?" Sam asked.

"She is beautiful."

"Ready to sail?"

"Whenever you say, boss."

Then Roberto came into view. He had been on the other side of the boat. "Hey boss, you want help with stuff in the car?" Roberto asked.

Sam popped the trunk open, revealing some of his purchases. The remainder sat in the front seat. "Get the lobsters in the tank first."

"You got it, boss."

Then Kelly came out on deck. She looked like the duchess of the castle, a thing of grace and beauty.

"We are about ready to travel," she called down.

"I can see that. I'm going to go talk with the Judge. See you in awhile."

She threw him a kiss as he walked across the yard to the house.

Judge Bean and Norma were sitting on the porch, he on the swing and she in a lounge chair. Sam walked in, and said with a smile, "Good evening, everybody."

"Ah, Sam," Judge Bean said. "Where the heck have you been?"

"I've been tied up."

"That's what I hear. Are you okay now?"

"Yes sir. Everything is fine. We'll be going as soon as we can get ready. I'll be leaving one full bag here, so you can keep making the payments. When I get there, I'll send you a card. One of those, 'having a great time, wish you were here' types. When you get that card, you can stop all payments. We'll handle the rest from there."

"Good sailing, my boy," The Judge said. "We wish you the very best."

"I can't begin to tell both of you how much I appreciate what you've done."

"Forget that," The Judge said. "You just take care of yourself. Take care of the crew."

"Will Kelly also be going?" Norma added.

"Yes."

"God bless you both." Norma walked over to Sam, gave him a big kiss on the cheek and a tight hug.

"I'm sure I don't need to tell you this, but you guys are as close to family as you can get."

"I know that," Judge Bean said. "An' we'll be sitting right here, ready to do it all again."

Sam saluted the Judge and left the porch.

Dusk turned into pitch black darkness. It was now six-forty p.m. Sam and his two shipmates went down to the cement storage locker, near the back dock. He unlocked the door and each started carrying one bag at a time back to the boat. Each bag contained fifty thousand dollars, and they were heavy. By the time they had made thirty trips, which was ten trips each, Sam took a breather while the two boys moved the bags down into the engine room.

Sam walked down the stairs and into the master suite. Kelly was waiting for him. They hugged and kissed.

"You feel okay?" she asked.

"Yeah, just a little tense."

She moved around behind him and massaged his shoulders.

"That feels great," Sam said.

"What are you so tense about?"

"As soon as we get out onto the Gulf, I'll be ready to party."

"Is there anything I can do?"

"Just stay as pretty as you are."

It took two more hours to finish transferring the bags to the engine room. It was now eleven p.m. Then they went through the supply list. Everything Sam requested was there. Pablo even showed Sam the gun cabinet, located at the rear of the wheel house. He opened the door, revealing three semi automatic Army AR 15s, each loaded with twenty rounds of banana clips and enough auxiliary ammunition to either start a war or end one, whichever came first. There were also two 12 gage shotguns, and three 45mm handguns. Sam felt comfortable traveling to a strange, foreign country in unknown waters, carrying millions of dollars in contraband, knowing that all was safe.

The three of them sat down on the back deck and each had a beer. They had a long trip ahead of them, possibly three to four weeks. That included estimated gas and food stops along the way.

"You guys did real good," Sam said.

Both Pedro and Roberto signaled their appreciation by raising their beers in a toast. It was now close to one in the morning.

"So, you ready to go boss?" Roberto asked.

Sam looked at the two young men. He could easily feel their eagerness to get started. "Yeah, I guess we start out at dawn."

"What's wrong with starting out right now?" Pedro offered.

"Well, it's dark out there," Sam said.

"C'mon, you're not afraid of the dark, are you boss?" Roberto asked.

"We got big running lights in the front," Pedro stated. "We take it easy, move out nice and smooth."

Finally it was Roberto who added the final comment. "Then we hit the Gulf around dawn, and we make a right turn and head for the big time."

"So I guess you guys want to get started right now?" Sam said.

The boys both sat and smiled at Sam. He flashed over everything in his mind, and knew they were prepared to travel. Sam got up from his chair and looked around the boat. It had taken them about eight and a half years to get this boat together. It took two years just to strip the old hull down to the hard wood. Then there had been rain storms and floods during the construction time. They had waited eight months for two new engines to be delivered. Now it was all ready. Now it was the time of challenge.

"Okay boys, start her up," Sam ordered.

Pedro moved into the pilot's cabin and started the engine. It roared to life like a beast of prey. Roberto was on the foredeck, pulling the containing rope free, while Sam did the same at the aft deck. The boat started to float free.

Kelly came up onto the upper deck. Sam walked over to her.

"Are we going now?" she asked.

"Yep, we're gong to do it."

Pedro put the boat into reverse and backed out into the bayou. Then when he got into position, he turned the wheel, shifted direction to the south, popped the engine into first gear and headed for the Gulf.

Sam and Kelly were still on the top deck, watching as they pulled away from the Judge's house. Then they came a-running: the Judge holding onto Norma's hand. They had heard the boat start up, and wanted to be a part of the finish. They stood on the bank and waved goodbye. Kelly started to cry. As they turned at the first corner of the bayou, Sam saw Judge Bean pulling up the rope from the dock and securing it. Then they passed out of view.

When Sam and Kelly walked into the pilot's cabin, Roberto had already turned on the flood lights. Pedro could see at least fifty to sixty feet ahead. That was all he needed.

"We're going to be just fine here," Pedro assured them." It's going to be about four hours of this at this minimum speed before we reach the Gulf." Kelly was infatuated with the running of the boat, and Pedro enjoyed explaining it all. Sam went down to the parlor and opened his new laptop computer. Following his instructions from Circuit City, he quickly established a telephone connection. Then, using the E-Mail, he wrote a note for Carl Witherspoon.

Dear Carl,

I am taking my three months' vacation. I realize this will be an inconvenience, but I truly hope this will not be a major problem for you.

I am heading for the Bahamas to relax in the sun and get my battery charged. My suggestion would be to have George Carey run the office until I get back. George is a good man. They are all good men, but George has the background to handle the job.

If you need somebody else to cover my job, or should you decide to replace me, that's up to you. When I check in late in May, and there is no position for me, I will understand.

I hope you're over the flu. You have been a true friend and have helped me through some bad situations. I will never forget that.

With love,
Sam

Sam's second letter was to Donald Mosley. It gave a history of Sam's situation, with the major attention on the disservice of the Office of Internal Affairs along with the man in charge, Deland Lupson. Sam told of everything, including his association with the NOLA 5, his dealings with Adam Loper, his association with William Jefferson Mays, and the destruction of his condo by the evil Deland Lupson..

Finally, he told of his discussion with Deland Lupson while he was in jail. A discussion regarding Mark Maher.

Lupson told me that Mark Maher had given him the names of people and places that would be willing to testify against me in a court of law. Lupson implied to me that all of this took place some eight years earlier, that I knew Mark Maher at that time, that I was instrumental in arranging a connection for Mark to get into the dope business.

Sam then advised Mosley where he may be contacted, by hard mail only. Sam's final E-Mail was a short one, sent to Eduardo Sanchez.

Dear Eduardo,
Leaving today for a vacation. Call you when I get back.

With love,
Sam

As they traveled south, they always stayed in sight of land. After two weeks, they hit Cancun, Mexico. There was a major resort there, with American tourists looking for a good time. They docked the *Miss Lee* and took a five day holiday. After a period of fun in the sun and Sam's purchase of two dozen Pacific lobsters, they hit the sea again. Their Maine lobsters were now totally depleted.

A few days later a letter was addressed to Sam Pennington, at Sam's direction, from Donald Mosley. It was addressed to care of William Jefferson Mays at 1428 Megapolla Street, Calligero, Hondouras. The envelope read,

"Please hold for Mr. Pennington's arrival." Sam would not get this letter for at least another week and a half.

Donald F. Mosley, Esq.

*5422 Poydras Street
Ste. 400
New Orleans
Louisiana, 70116
Phone 555-3961
FAX 555 3944*

Dear Sam,

I am pleased to advise you that your situation with the New Orleans Police Department is all but resolved. I list as follows:

Through the Freedom of Information Act, I secured a file copy of a hidden report from the office of Adam Loper, who was the person in charge of Narcotics Division on Rampart Street. On October 9th, ten years ago, Mr. Loper noted the following:

"I met Agent 33 on St. Ann and Royal Streets. He told me of illegal activity at the Shell Bar and Grill. I asked him to continue surveillance. Send a financial statement to me, regarding your expenses."

I later made contact with Adam Loper's wife. We had lunch together. A nice upright woman. I was able to later cajole her into giving me Mr. Loper's diary. Loper is still alive, but his Alzheimer's condition is progressing rapidly. In his diary I found the following:

"I made a deposit of five sticks of cocaine from Agent 33 into our vault. I wrote a check to Agent 33, for $248.53, to cover expenses at The Shell Bar and Grill."

I next reviewed your checking account of ten years hence, specifically October 18, 1993. My review shows that you took a check, signed by Adam Loper, in the amount of $248.53, and deposited same in your checking account. May I say you also noted on the back of the check, "To cover expenses at the Shell Bar and Grill."

Armed with these pieces of information, there was no doubt in my mind you were Agent 33, and had worked undercover to secure information concerning the NOLA 5, a group of five policeman who were in the process of dealing drugs.

I met with the court this morning, Judge Maxwell Freeman. Also present was your old boss, Carl Witherspoon, along with the Assistant District Attorney Jerry Weinstein. It took Judge Freeman only ten minutes to study the documents, and stated:

"There is no doubt in my mind, Detective Pennington has been improperly arrested for dealing in narcotics. This police officer has been unfairly and improperly charged.

"I therefore am dismissing all charges against Officer Sam Pennington. This case is closed. I further instruct you to satisfy Mr. Pennington with regard to any and all matters concerning this case, to his and his attorney's satisfaction."

The problems created by Judge Freeman's decision are far-reaching. This is going to cost the Big Easy a few bucks. I just received a phone call from Carl Witherspoon.

"Tell Sam he's got his job back. Tell him I never once suspected him of doing what they charged him with. Tell him he can come back any time he wants. Tell him I'll promote him to Chief of the Division of Burglary & Homicide."

And by the way, your pal, that Deland fellow, who runs the Office of Internal Affairs? Well they are very upset with him. He should not have done what he did. Talk about a rush to judgment. They now have Mr. Deland Lupson on his way to court, to provide an explanation of what happened.

Sgt. Maher's problem was having served ten years in jail and believing you were the one to blow the whistle on him, which caused him to now take any necessary action to get out of prison. When Deland Lupson came upon the scene, Maher decided to tell whatever lies he could to get out of the slammer.

I can imagine the hatred Mark Maher held in his heart for you every night when they shut the lights down. Ten years of "lights out!" He was a perfect prisoner, always in the right position, saying the right thing, doing whatever was necessary. Then, after ten years, he came before the parole board.

They met on March first, this year. Two men and one woman. They turned him down! That was it! Maher came to understand: being a dope dealer is one thing, but being a dope dealer as well as a cop is something else.

So what happens next is Deland Lupson somehow finds out about this guy. He meets with him on Sunday, March 5th. And Mr. Lupson listens for five hours as Mark Maher spews his guts out. Maher told Deland ten years of lies. Lies he laid in his bed and manufactured about you. Lies full of hate and misery. He told of knowing you eight years earlier. He told of you getting him started in the drug business.

I now have a file containing Maher's testimony. I'll send it to you if you want to read it. But here's the big finish!

On Monday, March 6th, Deland Lupson makes a deal with a local judge to have the last five years of Mark Maher's jail penalty reverted to 'Time Served.' That means Mark Maher is a free man. He leaves the jail and heads back to New Orleans. Deland Lupson is with him. These guys are by now real good pals.

Deland checks him into a class hotel. The Pelican Suite. Deland has him on the top floor, with enough room to handle a basketball game. Then on Tuesday, March 7th, Deland sends a car to pick up Mark Maher. But Mark Maher has checked out! Mark Maher has "flown the coop." Ha ha ha.

On Wednesday March 8th, the district attorney held a meeting with Deland. He asked what the hell was going on here? I'm sure Deland explained how he was used and abused by the lies told to him by Mark Maher. So Deland Lupson has now become the victim of this tragedy.

Let me know when you read this. Make contact with me, and then and I'll fill in the holes.

Warmest Regards,

Donald F. Mosely

Donald F. Mosely

THE *MISS LEE* had been docked in the bay of Cancun, Mexico. After four days of a restful vacation and stores replaced with great food and drink, they made their way south toward the Caribbean Sea, heading onward to Honduras.

Sam had shared "the slings and arrows of outrageous fortune," but now the world was good again.

As the *Miss Lee* continued on a Southerly direction, Kelly's sweet voice could be heard as she sang her favorite song.

"Won't you come home Bill Bailey, won't you come home?
I've been waiting all night long…"

Printed in the United States
24478LVS00006B/48